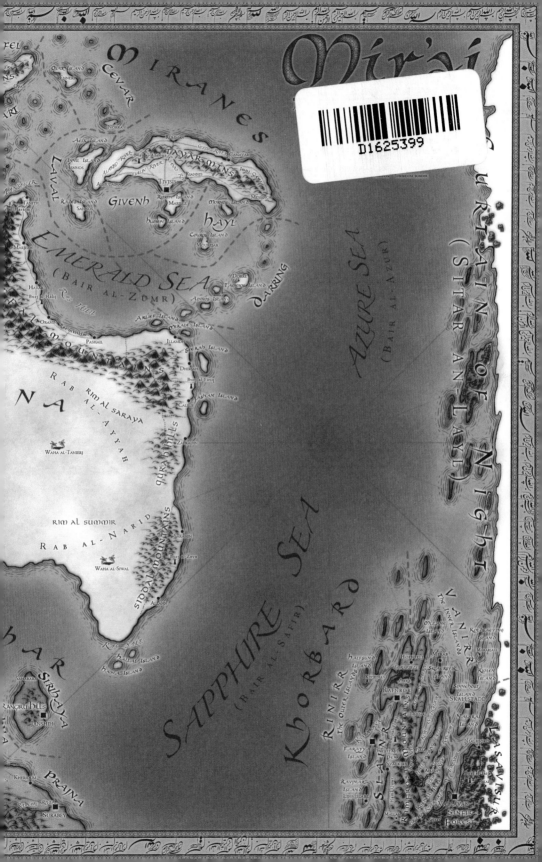

IN THE SHADOW OF SWORDS

VAL GUNN

Errant Press

An Errant Press Release

IN THE SHADOW OF SWORDS

This book is a work of fiction. Names, characters, places, and incidents either are the product of the author's imagination or are used fictitiously, and any resemblance to actual persons, living or dead, business establishments, events, or locales is entirely coincidental. The author and publisher does not have any control over and does not assume any responsibility for third-party websites or their content.

Book Design by *Joshua Vizzacco*
Cartography by *Chris Gonzlez*
Cover Illustration by *Samir Malik*

This book has been typeset in Gentium, a relative newcomer to the game and was chosen despite the fact that it is available free of charge. The serif typeface was designed by Victor Gaultney for a dual purpose—both to fulfill academic requirements and to meet a global need. The design is intended to be highly readable, reasonably compact, and visually attractive. Think of it as 'lotion for the eyes'.

Cataloging-in-Publication Data is on file with the Library of Congress.

ISBN - 13: 978-0-615-23269-0

ISBN - 10: 0-615-23269-8

PRINTED IN ICELAND

0 9 8 7 6 5 4 3 2 1

Errant Press hardcover / First Edition / February 2011

www.errantpress.com

Introduction

IN THE SHADOW OF SWORDS is the first book in the tales of Ciris Sarn. This is not the Lord of the Rings. Growing up, our house was filled with many books from authors my dad liked to read; Eric Ambler, Graham Greene and Robert Ludlum—to name just a few. Of course I found my way into the realms of fantasy and fell in love with J.R.R. Tolkien's epic prose. But I was also enamored with the sword and sorcery of Robert Howard and the English translations of One Thousand and One Nights. This book blends elements of fictional espionage, dark fantasy and historical thriller together and pours them into an exotic locale full of intrigue and danger. Mir'aj is a place steeped in the Arabian Nights tradition; a wonderfully fresh setting for me. I am just dipping my toes into the water of this world—hopefully much more of it is still left to come. I'm not an expert on the historical cultures this story takes creative license with, and the responsibility for any error is my own.

Acknowledgements

AT LAST. It has been a seemingly endless journey, and I hope your enduring patience will be rewarded. This book could not have been finished without the incredible support of my family and friends. My appreciation goes to all of you who looked at the manuscript at some point along the way and offered suggestions. I still have a long way to go, but hopefully I can get better at this craft. I am ever grateful to Sasha Miller for first mentoring me and never accepting less than my best. Also to James Carmack for his insight and wonderful workshops—your guidance allowed me to take the story in another direction and make it something much more original. I would like to give credit to Jesus F. Gonzalez for his work in helping me to make the plot flow at a breakneck pace and literally jump off the pages; Don Peters-for stepping into the game late and providing a big assist; Eric Uhland who is a master wordsmith. Further, I am indebted to Alan K. Lipton, Josepha Sherman, and Judith Tarr for each of their contributions. I would be remiss in not mentioning Samir Malik for the wonderful cover art; Chris Gonzalez in creating an amazing map of the world; and Joshua Vizzacco who designed the book for Errant Press. A job well done. To my beta readers—Bob Nagga, Phil Telford, and Laura Haglund—your feedback was much appreciated. Thanks to my peers at Absolute Write and SFF World who read parts of my book and shared their knowledge and expertise. In addition, to everyone else who crossed my path and offered to help me in some way—I am beholden to your kind hearts. This dream would not have become a reality without the support of my wife. I save the last of my profound thanks for her, who has been with me through all the ups and downs. *Sorry this one took so long.*

Mir'aj

IN THE YEAR OF ALA'I 793 SC

SCALE IN FARSANGS

0   25   50   75   100

■ MAJOR CITY   ⚓ JUNGLE
● CITY   🌴 OASIS
● MAJOR TOWN   – – – NATION BORDER
🌲 FOREST   ········· SHEIKDOM BORDER

MIRANES

CEVAR

OLAR ISLAND
ESNEER

NORRA

RUMJIAN

AZIX ISLAND
INVIL ISLAND
HENNOS

ALBERO RIVER
BURJ AL-ANSOUF
TAVAR MINSTIR
SETIR RIVER
CANAVAR

IBRI RIVER

LALIN RIVER

ALMUDADNA
RIANNES

TIVISIS

ANSOUR

ASTANITH
IL HARAJIM

LAVAL

RADOS ISLAND
SANNES

GIVENH

REPKIN ISLAND
MARILLE

hAyL

OIORNOS ISLAND

MESSION

MARJEEH

HULMIN ISLAND

COLEROS ISLAND
MOUBEJAR

HAVAR
BURJ AL-HALIJ

EMERALD SEA
(BAIR AL-ZUMR)

RES HUIL

ORANIN
BURJ IM AL-HAFI

DOBRE
T'ADRIOS ISLAND

ARLIEF ISLAND

ANNOS ISLAND

DARRING

PASHAIL

MERALE ISLAND

SUB-OGUNNA

MOUNTAINS

ILLAMEH

STERAB ISLAND

DHIRJAH
BURJ AL-FURIQ

RAB AL-SARAYA
RAB AL-AYYAH

RIM AL-SARAYA

CALILIE

LASHAN ISLAND

NA

WAHA AL-TANIERJ

ZAFRADIN

SURAB HILLS

RIM AL SUMMIR

RAB AL-NARID

SARAHN

SINNUDRA
MOUNTAINS

BURJ AL-ZAYA

WAHA AL-SIWAL

ALLAPH

AZURE SEA

(BAIR AL-AZUR)

GURFAIN OF NIGHT (SITAR AL-LAIL)

SAPPHIRE SEA

(BAIR AL-SAFIR)

KHORBARO

RAS VALE

HALLAL ISLAND
HAWA ISLAND

SAHARARA
SRIHAYA

NGRUI HILLS

JANSHIH

KHERIDUM

PRAJNA

KHAR

RADHAR RIVER
SURABEY

VANIR
THE INNER ISLANDS

KOLSKEGVING
ISLAND

MERAB

MARARJALL

KLOLEN
ISLAND

SNAEKSVIK

SINNEHOST
ISLAND

SKALLSTADD

ALSKA
ISLAND

NIALHJORD

RI-NIRR
THE OUTER ISLANDS

HALFSUND
ISLAND

KIVIKOLLS

HOFNFJELL
ISLAND

RAFNROR

INISJARL

KONNY
ISLAND

FJALL

AS-ABU TAIJI ISL.

FARSY
ISLAND

NETTEFJALL
PEAK

SVALKIRE

HAMI QOPT

BURJ AL-TAIJI
SEAFY

RAVJNAR
ISLAND

LINNISLARF

AELFAS

MALLAM

VALLAVAN
SINIR
FOREST
GIAD

for my Dad

Prologue

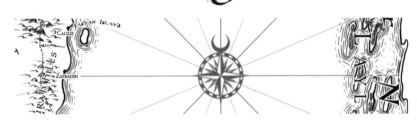

THERE WILL BE BLOOD

24.3.791 SC

1

HE WAS *almost* there.

Hiril Altaïr's heart pounded furiously as he raced across the square. A drum hammered in his head, until he felt as if it would explode from the pressure. Every breath shot agonizing pain down his sides.

Not now.

Not yet.

Sweat trickled into his eyes, blurring his vision. Still he ran. Each step thundered against the great expanse of stone, echoing, waking foreboding in his mind. Altaïr scanned the buildings for a familiar sign. Light flickered and caught his attention.

At last.

He spied a long standard of burgundy with gilded edges, swaying seductively in the wind. Blazoned in the center was a *Qurnaj* calligram of the word *Eliës*, rendered in the shape of a falcon.

Sanctuary.

But would they harbor him? Could anyone be trusted with the knowledge he held?

Nearing exhaustion, he stumbled and nearly fell just three paces short of the entrance to the Eliës embassy. The twin doors that faced the square were closed. Altaïr paused, panting, and dashed sweat from his eyes. This deadly game was finally at its end. Just three steps. Once he was across the threshold, he would be safe.

For how long, though?

The Eliësans would give him sanctuary. They were fiercely independent from the Sultanate of Qatana and the Rassan Majalis of Miranes'. Altaïr carried with him the proof—and could show them even more. He would make them believers, and they would have to protect him.

Altaïr was still half stunned by the revelations he had uncovered. Everything he'd been taught to believe was a lie. It had cost his friend's life and the lives of four others.

How many others had already been killed?

He staggered up the remaining three steps. Just as he reached for the door handle, a faint whisper behind him broke the silence. Before he could react, something grabbed his shoulder with hideous strength and spun him around. Lifting him into the air as though he were a child's toy, the unseen attacker slammed Altaïr into one of the embassy's stone pillars, shattering bones, and then tossed him effortlessly back down the stairs. For a moment, Altaïr faced a wall of darkness as he landed on the ground, screaming in agony. The darkness receded briefly as he fought to stay conscious. Altaïr's blurred vision found his attacker—a tall, menacing figure cloaked entirely in black, stretching a hand out toward him.

Ciris Sarn. *Kingslayer.*

A wave of dark scarabs flowed from Sarn's fingertips, sweeping down on their prey. They flew to embrace Altaïr, shrouding him in a pulsing, inky mass. The creatures tightened around him and punctured his flesh, plunging Altaïr into unbearable pain.

The doors to the embassy promised sanctuary, but for Altaïr it was too late. He gave one last great strain against the merciless onslaught, to no avail. The spellbound creatures stripped away his skin, ripping apart muscle and sinew as he flailed helplessly— and hopelessly—to escape.

Altaïr looked up into the cold black eyes of the assassin. The hooded form of Sarn gazed back at him with no trace of mercy or remorse, his face lined in angles, sharp and unforgiving.

The pain swelled as time slowed, seemingly endless, and Altaïr knew that the sight of the assassin would be his last.

It ended with the sharp, swift movement of a thin blade whispering through the air. Cruel steel pierced Altaïr's eye and drove deep into his skull. His head wrenched back in a silent scream as a crimson curtain fell, then faded into eternal darkness.

His last thought was of his wife.
Marin.

2

THERE WAS only one thing left to do.

The scarabs had done their work. Now that Hiril Altaïr lay dead before him, Sarn reached into the folds of his clothing and removed four thin, leather-bound books and laid them next to the body. Dassai wanted these books, but Sarn was not concerned with his avarice.

For now, he had his own matters to attend to.

ثب خل ا ف ش كت ة ي ف خ ة

He spoke the arcane words as he sprinkled a pinch of ebon dust from a small glass vial. The disk-shaped granules covered the body and sent out a clear message.

An assassin's mark.

A bright flash lit Sarn's eyes as he gazed at a shimmering mirror of blue-metallic liquid outlining dark blood and shards of bone—the last remains of Hiril Altaïr. It continued to expand before engulfing the ruined body in a pool of cobalt.

Soon the alchemy began to subside. The mark was invisible to all others save for one man.

Sarn rose. He had fulfilled his duty. He was jinn-bound to the Sultan and thereby his lackeys, men such as Dassai. He had been compelled to kill Altaïr, but he did not care about the books. Let Dassai retrieve them himself.

Pealing across the city, the bells of many *masjids* tolled sonorously.

Istanna had ended.

Across the great square, Sarn disappeared into a small passageway, a shade lost in deeper shadow. The silence lasted for only a brief moment, until a flock of sable-winged gulls gathered, squabbling greedily over their newfound feast.

The doors to the embassy remained closed.

3

I AM a coward.

This thought plagued the mind of Nabeel Khoury as he watched the man die.

He did nothing.

Said nothing.

He watched it happen and wept.

As the *Rais* of Havar, Khoury had known the man who would be killed. He also knew the assassin's identity. Sarn had killed before in Havar, and Khoury had let it happen then, too. Still, he felt unclean, his conscience tainted by the evil done.

Yet he did not stop it.

Because I am a coward.

Khoury was under orders from Emir Malek himself, delivered to him by Fajeer Dassai. You did not cross either man if you wanted to live. Havar was a valued sheikdom of Qatana, and the Sultan's reach was long. Malek and Dassai played politics as they pleased, and there was very little the sheikh's chief administrator could do about it.

Hiril Altaïr was to die—and Nabeel Khoury had made sure it happened.

Khoury felt shame as he witnessed the execution, watching from a safe perch high above as Sarn marked the mutilated form that had once been a man. He knew his life would be irrevocably changed after this—and it would not be for the better.

You are a coward.

Yes, he thought again. *No one came to Altaïr's defense, and I made sure of it.*

Khoury had met days earlier with an envoy of *Eliës*. There

would be a killing. It would take place in the square on the high holy day of *Istanna. Leave your mind free of guilt,* he'd told the envoy. It was of no concern. *Just be sure that you do not open your doors to this man or hinder the assassin in any way, and there will be no trouble.*

Khoury said the words and left the bribe. Just as he had done with a dozen others.

He had met Altaïr twice before. The first time was years earlier, the second just a few days ago. Altaïr's reputation as a skilled *siri* preceded him—experienced, thorough, and loyal. *A good man,* thought Khoury—something he was not. Altaïr had come to Havar looking for answers. But Khoury was uncertain of the questions. He'd learned only a little, some from Altaïr, some from Dassai, who'd shown up two days later. And now Altaïr was dead.

Khoury fixed his eyes on Sarn. The assassin knelt beside Altaïr and laid something next to him, just outside the pool of blood that surrounded the dead man. Khoury could not tell what the object was, but Sarn's actions were strange and they'd caught his attention. Sarn stood and then was gone, leaving the square as quickly as he had entered it.

Was it a trap?

Did the assassin still lurk, just out of sight, looking to see if anyone would show? Dassai had mentioned nothing to him about Sarn leaving something.

Khoury wanted to know. He *needed* to know.

But caution and fear held him in place. Merely by interfering, he risked his own death. The royal family was never to be crossed, and apart from Sarn, Dassai might have been the most dangerous man Khoury had ever met. So Khoury waited, chewing his nails, and did nothing.

He was a coward.

He waited for several hours. Biding his time. The street remained deserted. It was late; there was no traffic. No one exited out of the building, either.

The ruined flesh and bones of Altaïr remained on the steps to the embassy, along with the object Sarn had laid down. The more Khoury studied it, the more he began to realize it was a book of some kind.

He looked up at the moons. Their positions told him it would be some time before the street below saw any life again.

Khoury looked again at the object that lay beside Altaïr's body. The urge to go outside and retrieve it was intense, but he resisted. The longer he stood at the window peering down, the stronger the urge became. Was he still a coward?

Only time would tell.

SILENCE.

Gone were the screams of unspeakable pain as wax-acid poured over feet and then legs, eating away tissue, muscle, and bone. Still, there were no pleas from Tariq Alyalah—nothing revealed out of desperation and terror.

The torture of the *sufi* had lasted for more than two hours. Each drop of candle wax sizzled as it seared skin and mingled with blood—a sickening sound that could be heard quite plainly once the wailing had ceased and the old man had finally died.

Fajeer Dassai looked over the corpse that leaned against the curved side of the room. The white distemper paint on the wall around the body, now charred black, had peeled away, and a thin layer of ash dusted the stone floor. Lifeless eyes stared out of Alyalah's emaciated face. Its mouth was agape. Shriveled, cracked lips receded to expose a scattering of brown and yellow tobacco-stained teeth. The *sufi's* blood-soaked *suriah* robe was torn away at the navel as though he had been bitten in half by a shark; there was nothing left of him below the waist.

The stench of melted flesh invaded Dassai's nose despite the clove-laced cotton stuffed into his nostrils. He blew out the last of the candles that had been used to torture the *sufi*, his face so close to the flame that it flared amid the gray, death-tinted shadows.

He had already worked his way through every room, from the top of the *misal'ayn* down the three hundred sixty-five steps to the crypt and *anbar* buried deep beneath the surface. This was the last room left. Soon enough he would locate Alyalah's private records. Somewhere within the walls or floor of this *mirsd* — this sacred chamber—rested a hidden cache of books that contained secrets so powerful they would change the beliefs of nearly everyone alive in Mir'aj.

Tariq Alyalah would have had Hiril Altaïr smuggle them out of Qatana, possibly turning them over to the Eliësans. Dassai had outwitted him, though, by sending Sarn out to murder Altaïr. The assassin would kill the *siri* before he could take possession.

It was imperative that Dassai possess these relics. This tower would not keep them secret from him much longer. Once found, these books would endow him with wealth and power to rival the mightiest of sultans.

The room was small and barren, with no windows or furnishings. Embedded in the floor was a mosaic of brown and tan square tiles laid out in an intricate circular pattern, progressing from large to small until it formed a ring, one foot in diameter, in the center of the *mirsd*. Within this ring was set a copper seal engraved with a burning sun. Light filtered down from a gap in the high domed ceiling, illuminating the pattern set in the floor.

It was here.

Dassai picked up a brushed brass candleholder, twenty-six inches long, fashioned like a spear. He rapped it hard against the floor, sending the stick of wax skidding across the tiles. Wedging the pointed end beneath the copper seal's edge, he worked it clockwise around the perimeter until it stopped against a hidden clasp. He pried until he had exposed the clasp, applied a quick, hard snap, and broke the barrier. Removing the disc revealed a shallow recess with just enough room to house several small books.

The cache, however, was empty.

Impossible!

Dassai screamed in rage, slamming his fists on the floor. He stared down at the empty hole, noticing that stone had been crudely chipped away from the bottom and filled with fresh dirt. Dassai dug his hand into the loose soil, searching until his fingers found the slender neck of a wine bottle. He pulled it out and wiped the grime from the green glass. Empty. He examined the smudged lettering.

It was his own fucking label.

Dassai seethed with rage. He should never have counted on Sarn. Hiril Altaïr was dead; there was no question about that. He'd received word himself only an hour before setting off to deal with Alyalah. But what he hadn't realized, until this very moment, was the possibility that the assassin had come here first. Dassai had wasted precious time waiting for Alyalah to return to the tower, obviously unaware that his abettor in the plot had been here only hours previous.

Did the assassin take them for himself?

The more he thought about it, the more enraged he became.

Sarn, he thought. *I will cut your head off and shit down your throat.*

Somewhere in Havar he *knew* the assassin was laughing.

Part One

NO WAY OUT

10.3.791 SC

1

"TOMORROW THEY'RE going to cut off your head, old man."

Sarn looked out into the night through the high narrow window of the old man's cell. Three moons hung in the dark sky; *Cilíin*, a milky crescent, shone brightest, illuminating a feeble, sickly figure draped in threadbare rags. The old man leaned against the wall, seated on a crude stool, the lone piece of furniture in the cramped cell. The intruder jarred him awake.

"It is all I have left to give," the old man said. "They have already taken my hands and feet."

He held out the stumps of his arms, sliding his leg stumps across a floor of sand and pebbles. He moved closer to the bars that separated them.

Sarn felt little remorse. The man was a criminal. Just after dawn, in the cold morning air, he would be taken out to the square and executed. That was the law.

"Did you bring the wine?" the old man asked.

"Yes," Sarn said. "Two bottles."

"Good. Very good."

Sarn retrieved a bottle from the folds of his black *juma* and uncorked it with the same lock-pick he had used to break in.

"Sorry, no glasses tonight," Sarn said, a barely perceptible smile lingering on his lips.

"Do not worry, my friend. I'm sure you will think of something."

Crouching down, Sarn passed the bottle between the bars and pressed it to the old man's lips.

Sarn let him get a small taste before pulling it back.

"Do you have it?" Sarn asked.

The old man nodded.

"Show me."

"Please. I promise. Give me another drink."

Sarn relented, allowing himself to play the game; he tipped the bottle again.

The old man sighed. "A strong red."

"Enough of the mirage. Now tell me," Sarn snapped, grasping the bars.

"You, too, are a fool, then. Did you not look into my eyes and take notice when you first saw me?"

Angered, Sarn nearly let the wine bottle slip from his fingers. "I did not have to come tonight," he said. "Remember that."

Lurching toward the iron bars, the old man rasped, "Look, damn you!"

Sarn had no choice but to continue the morbid charade. Steeling himself, he looked past the old man's haggard, bearded face, filthy hair, disheveled clothes, and sickly pallor. He tried to ignore the stench of piss and shit, putrid breath and brown, rotted teeth.

Sarn focused on the old man's eyes. One of them was false.

As recognition dawned in Sarn's eyes, the old man nodded and cackled. "I knew you would see the truth! Jehal did it for me! Burned it right out, he did!" He paused. Sarn waited. "There wasn't much pain. I'd endured so much already. He did a fine job with the marble, I'd say. They never even guessed it."

"How proud you must have felt," Sarn sneered, but his curiosity was piqued.

The old man squeezed his face between the bars. "Take it out! I'd do it myself, but you know I can't ..." He raised the scarred stump of his right arm.

"What the fuck for?"

"You know why," the old man replied. He looked hard at Sarn. "Don't feign ignorance with me; and don't insult me. Jehal hollowed out this glass orb. And that is where you will find it."

Sarn didn't hesitate. He pressed his thumb against the old man's eye socket, and with one quick motion, plucked the marble out. He dug the hidden object out of the hollow and palmed it.

"Now, give me back my eye," the old man said.

Sarn fitted the marble back into the old man's dank socket, fighting back a wave of revulsion.

He looked down at his prize: a small button with ridges carved in its surface, and five thin strands of what appeared to be hair woven in the buttonholes.

"Do not lose it," the old man warned. "I went to great pains to find this for you."

Knowing full well that it was the key to his freedom, Sarn carefully pocketed the object, then retrieved the second wine bottle from his *juma* and removed the cork. Sarn would let the old man drink his fill. That, at least, he deserved.

After some minutes, the old man's head nodded into oblivion, both bottles empty at his feet.

Sarn leaned in closer. "When morning comes and you pray to Ala'i for the last time," he whispered to the old man, "remember, father … God is great."

2

SARN WOKE with a start.

Something was wrong. He opened the shuttered window, and the sudden brilliance of the suns blinded him. After his vision cleared, Sarn observed his surroundings. Closely packed buildings of worn stucco and stone overlooked narrow streets that wended in all directions. A breeze carried the scent of honey, melon, and orange.

It was deceptively serene.

Sarn dressed and then stood for a moment at the foot of his bed, listening. He heard voices from below, faint but discernible. He had slept too long. Last night's encounter with Barrani had troubled him, but what he'd received nurtured a spark of hope in him. Dassai had lured the assassin into Havar by once again using Sarn's father as bait. It was clear with the death sentence that Dassai's patience with Sarn was at its end.

Yet this fateful meeting with Barrani had not proved fruitless.

Sarn reached into his pocket and fingered the talisman, calmed by his mere possession of it. Then he grabbed his gear and moved across the room. He listened at the door. Nothing. Sarn paused again for a few seconds before turning the handle and opening the door just wide enough to slip into the empty hallway. He left the key in the lock and descended the stairs.

He was in the coffeehouse of Azraf Lahteeb. The man was just one of many in the sheikdom whom Sarn knew well and kept close to him. Due in part to Sarn's efforts, Lahteeb had risen from a beggar-thief in the souks to a prospering business owner. He ran a number of busy coffeehouses, but also worked the black market and was a trafficker in women. Lahteeb would keep him safe. They shared mutual interest, though they did not trust each other.

When he reached the ground floor, Sarn stepped through a doorway and onto a wide veranda. Beneath the boundless blue of the sky was an even bluer sea. White cubes of houses cut a dazzling line between air and ocean. The high walls of arcaded terraces ran upward to the still higher domed mosques and cylindrical minarets of Havar. Beyond the south gate, olive-clad, vineyard-laden rolling hills shone green in the distance.

Sarn took a deep breath. How long would it be before he had to carry out more dark deeds for his paymasters? In the past, premonition had played its part—the unease he'd felt earlier would not prove unfounded.

He was in trouble.

A fountain bubbled in the corner, shaded by an almond tree. Sarn did not pray, but the ablution would clear his mind. He removed his shoes and washed his feet. When he was finished, he cupped his hands and splashed his face with the jasmine-scented water. He dried himself with one of towels that lay beside the fountain.

Running along the edge of the veranda was a low wall covered with flowering bougainvillea. From this vantage point, Sarn watched the activity of the port as the sound of midday bells rang, pealing out over the harbor. Crowds of people made their way from the quays and moorings to the north gate that led into the medina.

Sarn picked an orange from a low-hanging branch and bit into its sweet, blood-red pulp as he considered his options. He needed money. But to emerge now might prove dangerous. Sarn's exile had lasted nearly a year, and there were many people looking for him.

The most significant of those was Fajeer Dassai.

Two months earlier, Sarn had sent a message to Lahteeb, who was also a wine dealer, to have him look for prospective buyers of rare, highly desired wines that were exclusive to the cellars of the royal family. Illegal trading in wine was both risky and profitable, a chance Sarn was more than willing to take. However, weeks had gone by without word before he got an answer. Lahteeb had set up an afternoon meeting today with Sarn and a wine merchant named Aban Seif al-Din.

Lahteeb had wanted them to meet here, but Sarn refused. He never trusted anyone too far. He would take Lahteeb's money and hospitality, but caution still ruled. After some negotiation, they agreed to meet at the Najid shisha near the Badhel Souk; it would provide crowds for cover, and plenty of escape options.

Sarn decided against going back into the coffeehouse and slipped over the wall, dropping ten feet down to the street below.

Navigating his way to the souk, he scanned the faces returning from midday prayers. Most wore white *thobes*, some wore long *abayas* of bright-hued material similar to his own. His clothing, although designed to keep the wearer cool, felt stifling as he traversed the maze of narrow flagstone passages. A light wind drifted in from the sea but seemed to pass around him as though he were shielded by some unseen force, and gave him no relief from the heat.

The noise of the souk reached Sarn well before he entered it. The breeze was heavy with the scent of exotic spices, and the very air seemed to shimmer with color. Throngs of people dawdled at merchants' stalls to haggle and gossip. Peddlers called out, hoping to entice him with their wares.

But he took no interest; he maneuvered through the souk's labyrinthine byways until he reached the opposite end and spied a sign for Najid. The shisha-house rested on the corner of a wide street under the shade of green-leafed plane trees.

Sarn waited, hidden in the shadows. He watched as Aban Seif al-Din approached Najid. The man was alone, the street quiet at a time when it should have been much busier.

A cloud passed above, dimming the bright sunlight. Sarn watched the merchant closely. Another man, twenty feet behind, trailed al-Din. As the cloud cover deepened, a feeling of dread settled over Sarn.

Receding farther into the shadows, he scanned the street and the buildings. Last night's encounter had brought with it the foreboding of danger—and his instincts had never proved him wrong.

Sarn had to leave Havar immediately; he could not let himself be found.

Again.

3

TWELVE DAYS.

He'd avoided Fajeer Dassai for almost one full year now. A few more days and the curse would be lifted from him forever.

The curse had bound Sarn to the Sultan, and because of it, he'd become a slave-assassin, dispatching various enemies of the royal family—and anyone else who'd been foolhardy enough to cross the crown. At times, Sarn had despaired of being free of the curse—giving up hope of ever being able to live without the

suffocating hopelessness that came from playing the role of Dassai's puppet—his tool for killing. He'd escaped in the past but had
always been found quickly. This time, thanks to help from a friend
in Riyyal—Rimmar Fehls—he'd managed to stay on the run.

Just ... twelve ... more ... days... .

Sarn hissed. Defeat seemed the only option now. The button
and thread in his pocket were not enough to shatter the spell. He
needed an arcane word to use along with them. Without it, they
were not the keys to his freedom but the chains that bound him.
But he was out of time, and in this matter of fate there was no way
out. Somebody had recognized him again, and he would have to
return to Dassai.

But Sarn would not make it easy for him.

A company of assassins was hunting him. *But who?* mused Sarn.
The White Palm? Slen Thek? The Haradin? It could be any—or all—of
them. His own recklessness had led him to this predicament.

Sarn had nearly walked into the trap set for him at Najid. His
intuitive sense of danger saved him; and he'd spent a week on
the run—alternately hiding and then slipping out of one city and
into another.

Sarn crouched on a clay-tiled roof, surveying the city that
stretched out below him. As the twilight encroached on Oranin,
he felt that familiar pull in his stomach—a cold, elemental feeling. The curse was calling to him.

For more than twenty years he had done the bidding of
Raqqas Siwal, the Sultan of Qatana. Sarn had no choice. He was
jinn-bound. Yet the Sultan had rarely commanded Sarn himself.
That task was delegated to one of his sons, Malek aït-Siwal, and
one other.

Fajeer Dassai.

Sarn cursed again under his breath. With catlike stealth,
he leaped from his perch and landed on the empty terrace. He
paused for a moment before dropping down into an empty alleyway below.

He remained silent in the shadows. The narrow street was lit with oil lamps that flickered in the growing darkness, sending aromatic plumes of smoke into the air. He walked into a maze of deserted streets and passages that ran in all directions like the web of lies that had ensnared him. The second sun was beginning to set, its crimson orb sinking behind the tall buildings that loomed above him.

Daylight would soon abandon Oranin. Sarn had to make the most of it; there was no shelter for him in the night.

He was a marked man; enemies were endemic to the killing trade. Sarn ventured a quick scan of one of the city's main thoroughfares and then stepped back into the shadows of the alleyway. Years of practiced stealth and trained intuition took control of his actions, and he pinned himself against the cool stone wall.

The ever-present wind that channeled through Oranin's streets rose to a gale, as if it were intent on alerting his enemies. Suspicion rapidly turned into reality, and he knew that his gamble had cost him dearly. Yet seeing his father for the last time had given him half the prize he needed. Now he lacked only one thing.

A name.

Sarn took a deep breath and moved out of the shadows, keeping close to the walls as he slipped past several small intersections, his stride light and silent. He threaded his way through narrow streets and even tighter alleyways, moving toward the east gate of the city.

He knew from experience that one could wander the maze of Oranin for days on end. The city was a labyrinth of buildings, streets, and courtyards. Stark white structures coated in layers of gypsum plaster, they seemed to lean precariously forward like looming ghuls, creating narrow footpaths that wove throughout Oranin. Without local knowledge or a guide, it was almost impossible to tell each street apart.

Sarn paused once more as the streets darkened. He rested, crouching in an alleyway where there was no illumination from the windows above. Beneath his feet, the flagstones were rough but uniform. He listened, straining his acute hearing for any trace of sound. There were too many places for his pursuers to hide, too many safe houses where they might lurk.

A moment later Sarn was gone again, passing through an alleyway so small that he could reach out and touch the walls of the towering buildings on either side. Though it was only dusk, the street was lost in darkness. The city's old quarters were perfectly laid out for any man who wished to move from place to place and yet remain out of sight. Sarn had always found this reassuring but at the same time his gut told him that if he could hide here, then so could others.

Leaving the sanctuary of the dark, he crossed into a large square illuminated by soft starlight and the milky silver of a waning moon.

Suddenly, he pressed himself into the shadow of the nearest building, heart racing, skin prickling with anticipation. He pulled out a blade.

He was not alone

SARN HEARD the sound even before the arrow flew.

He threw himself flat and crawled toward an alcove. The arrow shattered against the wall directly above him, and tiny shards of wood, stone, and plaster peppered his legs. Sarn quickly considered his options.

From his temporary shelter, he could see the huge, rectangular courtyard, bordered on three sides by an arcade of arches. Doorways in the two opposing walls of the square—to his left and right—led into *zaouia* schools.

Centered opposite him was the entrance into the Grand Mosque of Sidi-Amorad, its towering minaret and fluted dome shrouded in night. Sarn slipped from the alcove and moved along the wall to his right, searching for another sanctuary from the unseen archer. He could sense the man's presence on the wall to the left of the mosque entrance. He could also sense two other assailants hidden in the corners. They were funneling him into Sidi-Amorad.

Sarn knew it would be empty. Evening prayers were over; the mass of worshippers that had been crowded into the square just one hour ago would all be gone.

A series of richly carved wooden doors extended almost the entire width of the mosque. All save two were closed; Sarn entered, keeping close to the walls. He wove through the columns and arches that led to the central nave.

The interior architecture was overwhelming. Each column and arch was beautifully wrought from alabaster and granite and inlaid with arabesque patterns of faience tiles. Sarn had seen few places of equal grandeur outside of Qatana.

He caught the glimpse of a red-robed figure retreating across the limestone floors, deeper into the mosque. Bait for a trap soon to be sprung with no way out. Sarn smiled. He was all in.

Sarn peered beyond the portico into the nave. On the east and west sides were the two sacred *mihrab* niches. Seven large bronze lamp clusters lined the domed ceiling of the prayer hall, each one shimmering with a multitude of glass lamps burning fragrant oil. Directly below, a circular *minbar* was built into the center of the nave. Numerous prayer rugs and carpets lay scattered about the floor. North, beyond the lamps in the nave, stood a tomb like a well-disciplined sentinel, shrouded in darkness.

He could just make out the silhouette of one assassin. But he could sense the presence of the others; he knew there were three killers in here with him.

Sarn drew back into the shadows.

Someone had given them payment. Sarn had little doubt that it was Dassai. He'd played this game before. Dassai fed on the violence, and it didn't matter whose blood was spilled.

Sarn pulled a small carved-stone box from a pocket above his belt. He opened it, revealing two scorpions, black and streaked with thin bands of white and yellow. He knew firsthand how dangerous they were.

Holding the scorpions by their tails, he whispered, البحث عن آخرين اليوم and flung them toward the nave.

He waited.

The air was heavy with the aroma of jasmine, burning frankincense, and the stench of sweat left behind by the departed worshippers.

Suddenly a horrific scream resonated through the vast interior of the mosque, shattering the stillness. Two red-robed figures shot from within the prayer niches, flailing their legs, trying to shake off the small but lethal creatures. They fell to the ground, kicking and slapping at their thighs and calves.

Their frantic cries continued; they frothed at the mouth, eyes glazed. Finally their screams and struggles abated. The scorpions emerged from the men's robes and skittered up their bodies and across their faces, crawling into their open mouths. Each man convulsed and then lay silent.

Now only one enemy still lived.

Twenty feet away a dark figure slipped from the shadows. Sarn gripped the hilt of his blade and braced himself.

The Slen Thek assassin drew his saif and advanced toward Sarn. "If you are looking for peace, you won't find it here. Dassai is tired of waiting for you."

"Is he?" Sarn knew from previous experience that Dassai found much pleasure in these tests.

The assailant struck with lightning speed.

Blade met blade with a clash of steel. The assassin followed through on his swing and Sarn leaped back, brandishing his weapon in a defensive move. The assassin's eyes narrowed, seeking an opening.

The assassin swung his sword again.

Sarn lashed out with his own, centering all his strength and concentration in the maneuver. Sword locked with sword.

The assassin stepped forward and lunged. Sarn ducked and brought his blade up, slicing deeply into his assailant's right thigh. The assassin let out an involuntary cry, and then jabbed with his saif again, narrowly missing Sarn's neck. Sarn stepped lightly aside and swung low, this time cutting into the back of his assailant's calves. The assassin stumbled.

Sidestepping his would-be executioner, Sarn brought his blade around in a quick downward motion, cleaving the man's head from his shoulders. Body and head separated and fell. Blood spurted from the severed neck, a cascade of scarlet painting the floor.

Sarn stood for some moments in the center of the nave, listening. Waiting. The *imams* had not noticed the brutal encounter.

Sarn edged his way back to the entrance. Peering out, he surveyed the square.

Deserted.

Sarn slipped out of the mosque and back into the empty streets.

This time, he wasn't followed.

SARN LISTENED.

As he prepared to leave, the faint calls of morning prayer drifted above the city, which had already sprung to life.

Prosperous Oranin had grown well past the established city walls to include hundreds of caravanserais grouped beyond each of the city's four gates. Among these, one of the largest, Isfahan Caravanserai, rested like a jewel beside *Ras'mal Hari*—the Cape Cities Road. Here, in this opulent but functional place, Sarn had passed a safe evening. Isfahan was a long rectangular *maidan* built of limestone blocks, remarkable for its size, with a broad exterior lined with a single continuous tier of portico, making it both accessible and well-protected.

The second sun was just beginning to rise; Sarn could already feel the growing heat of the day. It was doubtful he was still being followed. Still, because of the attack at the mosque, Sarn couldn't be certain.

As focused as Sarn was on leaving the caravanserai, he was distracted by thoughts of Jannat, his most recent seduction. One of Dassai's four wives, Jannat ran an extensive vineyard near the Haffal Mountains. Sarn had lived in secret with his very accommodating hostess for nearly a year, seducing and bedding her with pleasure, satisfying his needs with thinly-disguised contempt. Reflecting on the illicit relationship with Jannat, orchestrated for his own personal gain, Sarn realized with continued distain that the cost to her would be greater than she could have imagined.

Dassai would have to kill her.

Sarn smiled. Jannat was no longer the mistress of a vineyard, but instead a common whore, an intolerable disgrace in the eyes of her husband. She was of little concern or use now to Dassai or Sarn. Dassai had other wives to comfort him in his loss. Dassai also had pride, which he would not sacrifice at any cost. Sarn was the cause of his scorn and humiliation. Soon after, Dassai had arrested Barrani and put a price on Sarn's head. Dassai had as much derision for Sarn as he had for Jannat.

So be it, then.

Still reflecting on his satisfying indiscretion, as well as the price on his head, Sarn left his room and headed downstairs to the bar. As he passed the second-story landing, the morning light from the hallway window reflected dimly on the wall.

Sarn continued his descent to the lower floor of the caravanserai, pausing in the doorway as he peered into the dark bar. He canvassed every crevice, examining the shadows beyond the feeble glow of the jasmine-scented lamps.

He stepped inside, passing through the crowd of patrons. He found himself in the midst of a steady murmur of speculation about a deadly assassin, even as he walked by.

As Sarn's presence became known, a hush spread and the voices faded into silent stares. He pretended not to notice and made his way to the bar.

"Naveen," Sarn said, smiling as an attractive, dusky woman dressed in an *abaya*, her hair wrapped in a headscarf, approached the bar. Sarn leaned across and gave her a soft kiss on both cheeks, something that he would seldom have dared elsewhere.

"Coffee? Or are you here just to waste my time?" Naveen said with a faint smile. She was the proprietor of Isfahan and ran it with her sister, Layyena.

"Just one cup," Sarn answered, surveying the room, aware of eyes and ears focused solely on him. "I must go soon."

"Two *dirans*, unless you are going to pay me for the room as well." Naveen hadn't missed his mention of departure.

"Of course."

Like her sister, Naveen was no-nonsense and direct. She and Layyena were strong women. Without them and their network of caravanserais, Sarn would have been vulnerable last night after his altercation at the mosque. He might well have owed them his life.

As he sipped his coffee, Sarn spied the faces in the crowd—mostly locals, but he could see there were a few travelers. He watched the sisters go about their business. What an incredible asset to him they had already become. He could not afford to lose his connection with Isfahan and the two women who controlled it. Sarn's success depended upon his continued ability to manipulate them.

Layyena had not questioned him when he'd arrived late last night and asked for a single room at the top of the rear tower. He'd been in luck; one was available, and he was given a key. If any other assassins had followed him, they would have made their presence known. The fact that they hadn't—coupled with his observations of the patrons in the bar this morning—told him he was safe.

For now.

Traffic was already brisk on the Cape Cities Road outside Isfahan, which was crowded with caravans of horses and camels bearing men and dry goods. Street vendors were busy from the gates of Oranin all the way to the caravanserai, hawking their wares to passersby.

Time to go.

Without another word to the sisters, Sarn left behind his unfinished coffee and passed through the crowd, avoiding their questioning stares.

He slipped out of Isfahan and into the rain-scented morning.

6

NOT A WORD.

Three weeks, and nothing from Jannat. She employed a number of messengers, and he'd left enough of a trail if she felt the need to look for it.

Sarn had last seen her at the *riad*. She was leaving for Pashail, where Dassai wanted her in his bed. That never lasted, Jannat had told him. They would enjoy each other for a few days, then Dassai would get bored with her and the sea and go back to Riyyal. But after the traps laid for him, Sarn wasn't so sure Jannat was safe.

She might already be dead.

It was evening when Sarn left the Ras'mal Hari caravans, following a small road eastward, away from the coast. The heavy silence of the night matched his mood.

He was still being followed.

Most likely it was either one of Jannat's messengers or more spies working for Dassai. Sarn did wonder, however, whether Dassai had reached the end of his patience with Sarn's rebelliousness and replaced the spies with more assassins. Sarn developed a plan to deal with either, his hatred of Dassai and disgust for Jannat fueling his determination.

On the road he expected to encounter riders—mostly couriers ferrying information between the *misal'ayn* and Oranin. Few would challenge him directly, but there were rewards for relaying Sarn's whereabouts, as well as personal satisfaction. Sarn would study their riding styles, the better to spot those who paid too much attention to him as they passed.

It mattered little to him. There was a good chance Jannat was gone for good. If not, she wasn't clever enough to hire new messengers to hunt for him, and he knew most of those she employed.

Sarn stopped to give his horse a short reprieve, taking refuge at a *berkeh* surrounded by wild oats. There were better places farther along, but the horse was tired, and though the place was exposed, he could not afford to push his mount.

Sarn heard the two riders approach. With no time to seek cover, he held his ground, watching as they dismounted on the far side of the pond, conspicuous not only because of the timing— arriving shortly after him—but because of the superb condition of their horses. *Not couriers.* For Sarn, there was no such thing as being too cautious. He checked his weapons and his options.

The riders removed nothing from their saddles and packs, further arousing his suspicions—they were not planning to be here long.

"Six seconds," he whispered under his breath: the time it would take to reach the saddle, grab the reins, and wheel back onto the road.

"Ten seconds," he whispered again, for it would take that long to assault the two before they could respond.

He chose the first option, clicking softly to his horse. Her ears pricked and she turned immediately, knowing what was needed.

They'd been in this situation before.

Sarn ticked off the seconds in his mind as he jumped up,
slapped the reins on her flanks and disappeared into the night.

"Nine seconds," he whispered to her. "Not bad at all."

The riders followed, their purpose unclear, their employer
uncertain. But he was definitely the target. Was he to be robbed?
Killed? Followed?

None of these suited him. Sarn would either elude or slay
them. Nothing else was acceptable. Nothing would prevent him
from facing Dassai on his own terms.

The pursuers kept their distance. Not thieves or assassins,
then. These were trackers—paid to trail, not confront him. His
familiarity with the terrain and his riding skill soon separated
him from his pursuers.

Sarn mouthed thanks to them, as any small part of him that
had been willing to relax was gone. No man escapes his own
deeds, and his were darkest of all. He would always be hunted.
The two riders were just the beginning. There would be more
once he arrived at the *riad*.

Dawn broke as he drew near a stone spire that rose into the
pale morning sky. He gazed at the tower crowned with a massive
jewel, shimmering in the first moments of sunlight, windowless
save for slits ringing the uppermost level.

The *misal'ayn* was perched on a ridge in the foothills to the
west of the twin cities that comprised the sheikdoms of Oranin
and Havar. It provided a *sufi*—a mystic seer—with a commanding
view for at least a dozen farsangs in all directions. From the tower
he could see west to the Haffal Mountains, east to the sea, north
to Marjeeh and the sheikdom of Tanith, and south to Pashail and
distant lands beyond.

The ashen-hued obelisk of Burj al-Halij had long been in the
service of Qatana, one of many scattered throughout Mir'aj. It
was said to have been carved by stone-jinn ages ago. Sarn had
seen only nine such towers in all of his travels, though he'd heard
rumors of many more.

It was a majestic site; one less encumbered would pause to enjoy it.

Sarn did not stop.

And no one followed.

His path took him through deep valleys down to the sea, then up a steep, rocky path nearly washed out by recent storms, forcing him to dismount until the trail leveled out and became more stable. The track soon turned back eastward, wending through the foothills. Sarn stopped near a flowering acacia tree at the edge of a small stream. He pulled the saddle off his horse and let her roam in search of grass and water.

Sarn retrieved dried meat and hard bread from his pack and, leaning back against the tree, he let his thoughts wander on another path—the dark, dangerous road of his past that had brought him to this place. He thought of his father and his father's gift to him. Barrani was dead by now, but he'd given Sarn a glimmer of hope before the end. Skirting the edge of real emotion, Sarn allowed himself this moment of quiet reflection.

In time, Sarn lifted his pack, re-saddled his horse, and resumed his journey home.

He was ready.

7

SARN WAITED.

He'd stopped for a brief respite. Surrounding him were ancient vineyards, which were among the most highly regarded and most sought after in all of Qatana. Trellised vines of grapes draped the cloud-dappled hills. The wines produced here were excellent—dark and full-bodied reds as well as fruity whites with hints of citrus.

Am I doomed to forever relive the past? Sarn reflected, gazing out over the land. The scene reminded him of his childhood summers, when he'd toiled in his uncle's vineyards in Annafi: a distant memory faded almost beyond recall. Until now.

Where have the years gone? Sarn felt the impossible desire to reverse time to a point when he could have altered the course of his life. But he knew it could never be. There was no going back.

Sarn stood and listened. There was only the quiet breeze and a falcon's distant call. His horse had wandered farther than usual, the temptation of incense grass luring her astray. He was alone.

Sarn tired of waiting he called to his horse, who answered the signal with a ringing neigh. The horse cantered up, and he leapt into the saddle and galloped away. Sarn felt the rush of anticipation course through him, his pessimism sloughing off, replaced by a renewed vigor.

His fate still lay ahead.

Racing along well-worn paths that marked the final miles of his journey, Sarn could see the purple-blue silhouettes of the Haffal Mountains in the distance as dusk approached. The twilight failed to dampen his mood. Sarn knew that he would make it to the *riad* before noon tomorrow, where Dassai no doubt waited.

Neither killing nor his epithet—*Kingslayer*—bothered him. Having to kill at Dassai's orders—that was entirely different.

The talisman his father had given him was the key to his freedom. But to unlock it, he needed to confront the Sultan, and this would require the aid, willing or not, of the man who held his chains. Sarn relished the thought of breaking them, and afterward looking into Dassai's eyes as he slit the man's throat.

Sarn's thoughts focused on the coming confrontation. The yearlong affair with Jannat was an effective—and bloodless—weapon he'd relished using against Dassai. What better way to stab a man in the back than to bed his wife?

But it had not been enough. Dassai had been oblivious. So Sarn had arranged for him to find out; therefore he knew Dassai would be waiting for him at the *riad*.

Sorting it out in his mind, Sarn realized that some puzzles still remained. Shortly before he received the cryptic message to visit

Barrani in Havar, Jannat had disappeared. She simply left. Those she employed had not seen her depart, nor could they give him any information concerning her whereabouts.

Why? What was the cause? If she knew he'd betrayed her to Dassai, that would be reason enough to leave, to escape a certain and painful death. But he doubted her ability to recognize his true intentions.

He had no feeling one way or the other for Jannat's life or death. Yet her disappearance had been inexplicable.

Now he wasn't so sure.

SARN STARED in disbelief at the scene below him.

The flourishing landscape that he remembered was blackened, scorched, as if efreeti of the Rim al-Saraya had flown over the mountains with a demon-wind and burned the land in their wake.

Everything was gone.

Dry winds carried black streamers of smoke, streaking the horizon with long fingers of darkness.

His mount reared up as he pulled the reins tight and stared at what had once been his refuge—now razed to the ground.

This had not been part of the plan.

Sarn cursed, spurring his horse forward, hooves pounding the sun-baked earth.

As he descended the hill, he was met by the powerful, acrid odor of burning grapevines. Some grapes still clung to the vines, their once plump bodies now withered and bled dry.

Sarn slowed the horse to a trot, his eyes scanning what was left of the *riad*. The house showed no signs of life.

His nose detected a different scent on the wind. He knew it all too well.

The sweet, sickly stench of death.

Sarn slowly led his mount through the ruined gates of the estate, toward the burned-out *riad*. A grisly horror lay before him.

The reek of charred human flesh hung in the air. Vineyard workers had been cut down in the fields and left for the fire to consume. Most were scattered amid trellises and stone debris. Some had been hacked, some speared; arrows protruded from others' bodies. Others had been beheaded, or disemboweled.

Sarn jumped from his horse and approached the *qoos*, which still stood in the aftermath of the fire that had engulfed the house.

Some of the stone and brick from the *riad* had held firm against the flames. Most of it, however, lay in a pile of blackened rubble, still smoldering. The panes of lead-crystal windows were gone. Two lower walls and a tall chimney remained intact. But otherwise, everything was gone.

In the gloom of dust and ash that dimmed the light of the second sun, Sarn perceived movement within the ruins, a long shadow creeping across the smoldering wall.

It was Dassai.

9

"IT IS a shame that it had to come to this."

Fajeer Dassai stepped forward, facing Sarn. It was the same man Sarn had known for years; yet it wasn't. The fierce brown eyes still gleamed above the sharp nose. But his hair had retreated to the farthest reaches of his scalp, cut short and graying around small-lobed ears. Lines grooved his cheeks, intersecting the caverns that extended from the tip of his nose. Time had not been kind.

"Really, it is a shame," Dassai said calmly. "It pained me deeply to learn that my wife would consort with someone like you."

"I imagine it did."

Dassai smiled. "But I take some satisfaction in the discovery, despite your both taking such great pains to conceal the affair from me."

"You learned of it only because I wanted you to," Sarn said.

For the briefest fraction, Dassai's eyes widened in surprise before relaxing again. Few would have caught it, but Sarn was one of those who could.

He grinned.

When Sarn had entered the burned out building, he'd instinctively put his back against the *qoos*. It served him well now. Dassai pulled a slender, silvery-white rod from his robes and began tapping it against his left palm as he paced in front of Sarn.

Maneuver all you want, Sarn thought. *You can't get behind me.*

He made no move to counter Dassai. Sarn was better at the game than his opponent, and Dassai knew it. There would be no attack. Dassai would not take the gamble.

The source of the *riad*'s destruction was now apparent. The firestorm that had swept through the place had sprung from the mystical artifact in Dassai's hand.

Dassai stopped. "Interesting," he said. "You haven't asked about Jannat."

Sarn shrugged.

His opponent cocked his head to one side. "Have you no interest in her fate?"

"Not particularly."

"The whore got her wish. I sold her as a harem slave. Now she'll pleasure hordes of beggars until she's dead."

"I wouldn't underestimate her."

"How so? She'll never escape."

Don't be too sure.

"Probably not, but she will survive. The woman has talent." Sarn smiled wickedly. "But perhaps you never experienced that."

Dassai visibly struggled to contain his emotions. Sarn pressed the attack.

"So all this," Sarn asked, waving his hand. "This is your

revenge on her? Or me?"

"I did it because I could, Ciris," Dassai replied, lips curling in a twisted smile.

"Even if it costs you dearly," Sarn said, shaking his head. "That's not like you, Fajeer."

"What's hers is mine!" Dassai said. "You think you can come in here and help yourself to my possessions?"

"I did it because I could."

Dassai paused. "Predictable," he said contemptuously. "I am disappointed in you, Ciris."

"Why?"

"Did you honestly think you could just walk away? Surely you knew better. You cannot break this curse."

"I guess we will have to wait and see," Sarn said, glowering at Dassai.

"With all I have done, you should thank me for cleaning up after you."

"Give you thanks?"

"A man such as you must have gone mad, hiding in this place for a year, cowering like a rat."

"Well," Sarn said, drawing out the word slowly. "Your wife did make the time pass much more sweetly."

Dassai laughed. "Always quick with the tongue, just as you were as a child.

"But I'm not the only one looking for you. You're being hunted again. Had it not been I, others would have come to do the same."

"Perhaps. And the message to visit Barrani came from you?"

Dassai smiled.

"I thought as much," Sarn said, nodding. "His fate was sealed long ago, and not by you."

"No matter. Your father is dead. Did you like my other gifts?"

"The quality of your assassins is lacking," Sarn said. "You should have spent more."

"Don't mistake my actions," Dassai said, waving off Sarn's reply. "They accomplished what I wanted them to do: like dogs driving prey toward the hunters. It was all meant to lead you here."

"I would have come anyway."

"And if I had wanted you dead, you would be."

"Many others have said that, and yet I still stand."

"Don't mistake me," Dassai said. "You are skilled in your craft. You've been a useful tool."

"Fuck you," Sarn said, stung.

Dassai smiled. "Easy, my friend. You usually have more restraint. I'm afraid you may have forgotten that it was my instruction which has served you so well."

Yes, it has, Sarn thought. *And soon my skills will be used against you.* Sooner or later, he would get vengeance.

Sarn spied Dassai's minions creeping out of the lingering smoke, winding through the blackened debris, ready to intervene.

But he was unconcerned. Dassai wanted him here for a reason, and Sarn did not think it was to cut him down. No, Dassai had something else in mind.

"Your men need work," he said, nodding toward the minions.

"I see your confidence does not waver," Dassai said.

"I see no reason that it should."

Dassai's servants stepped from the shadows. There were twelve in all, well-armed, with crossbows at the ready. Taking Dassai now would mean sacrificing himself.

Is it worth it?

No. That time would come.

"You know I can have you killed," Dassai said.

"You said that before. Same answer—perhaps. But if that is your choice today, it will be the last one you ever make."

"But where you were once just a thorn in my side, you have given me the justification to dispose of you."

It was true. The crime of dishonoring a man's name was grave. Jannat would soon pay the price, if she had not already. Those around her had as well, because they had been aware of the disgrace. The crime for adultery extended to all involved in the act. Sarn felt a rush of adrenaline.

"If that is your desire, so be it," he said. "Honor is hard; death comes easy."

"Calm yourself. I still have need of you," Dassai said.

"Do you?" Sarn said warily.

"As I said before, I allow you to live because I still have some use for your … ah … particular set of skills."

"Oh? Sarn asked, intrigued in spite of himself.

"You will return to Havar and find a man named Hiril Altaïr. And there you will murder him."

Sarn knew the man's name—a very capable *siri. But why would Dassai want this man dead?*

Dassai continued, "Mark him when you are finished. I need to know it was you who made the kill. Then leave for Riyyal. The Sultan has called for you."

"What use does the Sultan have for me?"

"That is not for you to know," Dassai answered.

It was clear to Sarn that Dassai didn't know, either.

Sarn looked at Dassai, then at his men who had come to surround him. "Not much of a choice then?"

"You never had one," Dassai said. "Every time you run, you are lying to yourself. There are only two things that you do, that give you any worth: you kill to survive, and you survive to kill. Never forget that."

"I must try to keep that in mind," Sarn responded. "Someday soon I will revel in spilling your blood."

"You have your duty."

"So be it," Sarn said, brushing past Dassai and through his men.

They will all die, Sarn decided. It would start with Altaïr—but it would end with Dassai.

"Pity this place had to burn." Dassai called out as Sarn mounted his horse. "But what is it they say? 'Nothing in life is without loss.'"

Nothing indeed. There was little more to hold Sarn here, but then again, there never really had been. Sarn gave it one last glance before spurring his horse and galloping away.

He did not look back again.

70

AT LAST.

Dassai's mind raced as he watched the horse and rider grow smaller, fading into the landscape like a wisp of smoke in the wind.

His plan was set into motion, and Ciris Sarn would serve as the centerpiece in this game of deception. The attention surrounding the assassin would afford him all the time he needed.

He reveled in the thought. Sarn would deliver him the seeds of power, while orchestrating his own destruction.

It was perfect.

A cruel smile lit Dassai's face.

Part Two

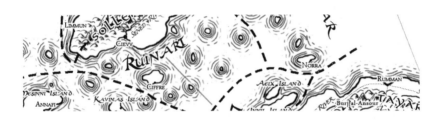

CRUEL FORTUNES

22.3.792 SC

7

MARIN ALTAÏR scanned the horizon.

The wind picked up and whitecaps began to form as the ship cleared the Ruinart headlands and sailed into the open water of a powerfully running sea. She had no reason to look back at the shadows of the Soller Mountains or the towers of Cievv, a city that could never be her home. This was a moment for savoring freedom. She wanted to feel free. But instead, she felt empty—a traveler merely passing through her own life.

Rising gusts tugged strands of hair from her scarlet hood, blowing them across her eyes like the fine gold bars of a cage. She brushed them aside with a warrior's grace. She sniffled at the ocean air. Her eyes were wide and bright with emotion. The sailors, squinting against the wind and bright water, cast her sidelong glances as they went about their business, but otherwise left her alone.

Marin's destination was no secret. She had secured passage to Messinor in the kingdom of Hayl. Those of the Illam faith would have recognized the silver cinerary urn that lay beneath the bunk in her cabin below. They would understand this young woman's pilgrimage beyond Messinor and into the foothills of the Tayar Mountains. They would know, from the expression on her bold, angular face, that her year of mourning was nearing its end—and that she planned to be at *Sey'r an-Shal*, the Falls to Heaven, on the anniversary of someone's death.

She had no idea where life would take her after she discharged this sad duty. Right now she had far too much time to reflect upon how life had brought her to the deck of this ship, sailing westward with her husband's ashes.

Marin Altaïr knew it would be a long voyage.

2

A CANOPY of gray mist hung low in the afternoon sky.

The suns had waned, lost in the shadow of approaching nightfall and rain. Winds wailed beyond an outcropping in the distance, and thunder rolled over a far away part of the island, but all else was silent. Marin, draped in a green cloak, glided silently over the uneven stones of a disused road, an ancient thoroughfare bordered by walls of eucalyptus.

A damp breeze blew steadily; strips of bark hanging from the tree trunks waved and fluttered, and strands of Marin's hair escaped the cloak's hood. The careful movements and slow sweep of her gaze marked her as a hunter. Who else would be out here? She couldn't guess how far she was from her prey, but she knew she was closing in.

As she passed the line of trees, a light rain moved in, hissing among the leaves. It wouldn't make travel any easier. The light under the trees grew darker at the edges of the road, and soon enough she would be creeping through shadows. Marin shivered and looked over her shoulder again at the horizon. The late-season storm showed a solid front, with no sky peeking through.

But Marin was the last person to give up a chase, especially when she sensed that she'd almost run her prey to ground. The rain pelted her. She pulled her wet cloak tighter and continued, firm, cautious, sweeping the landscape with her gaze.

At one time, the road to Sannós had been well traveled. Now it lay abandoned, unpatrolled and dangerous. Few of the people who inhabited the untamed island of Aeíx dared to come this way anymore. Instead, they were leaving their homes and sailing for Inníl or Rades, letting ruffians and crueler things menace the island at will. In the woods—and even along the coast now—half-human ravagers sacked and plundered the once peaceful towns. These days, the crumbling road to Sannós saw only a few hunting parties, men and women clustered together in fear of being attacked by the things they sought to kill.

Marin left the road soon after it had passed through the belt of euca-lyptus, but kept it within sight as it led her over knolls of dense scrub down into weed-choked fields. The thing she pursued had left the road here for some reason, and she followed its faint track through the mud and tangled ground cover.

Ruined stone walls lined this stretch of road, even more crumbling and overgrown than the cobblestones, mottled with countless years of lichen and moss. The straight lines and level roadbed reminded her of a canal cut through the fields by ancient engineers. But no one farmed here now. No one followed this road. Times were different, and the land looked tired and unwelcoming.

The rain fell in hard, steady sheets.

Marin pulled her cloak tighter. The green fabric was frayed with wear and splotched with dark stains, but it gave her some protection from the dismal weather. She'd been through worse. The cloak was a familiar reminder, one that kept her pushing westward toward the van-ishing suns.

In her right hand she held a small bow of ash. A quiver of arrows was slung over her shoulder within easy reach. From her belt hung a light sword that could be in her left hand at a moment's notice.

The thunder grew louder as the heart of the storm drew nearer. Marin listened to the fading echo as it bounced off the dark forest wall just ahead of her. Another sound caught her ear, slowly rising. She paused and looked back, wondering why it had taken them so long to catch up with her. Just like the storm's low, ominous rumble, her pursu-ers also drew steadily nearer.

She crept back through the brambles toward the road, dropping into a crouch behind some downed trees and the wall's tumbled stones. She drew her sword, gathered her cloak around her, and steadied her breathing. The hard splattering of rain against stone and decaying wood gradually transformed into the thudding of horses' hooves.

They were coming.

3

MARIN WAITED.

As the horses approached her hiding place, she could make out riders in green cloaks. Wind tugged at those cloaks, revealing the glint of worn chain mail. Their mounts were fine and tall, each standing over seventeen hands, and still running strong after miles of rough road. The group's leader cantered easily just ahead of the others. In the fading daylight, Marin saw an emblem on his horse's caparison: a staggered cross, the sign of the Four Banners.

Marin rose and swept back her hood, calling out, "Tread softly into unknown lands, Torre Lavvann." Her voice was low, but it carried over the clatter of the horses' hooves.

The lead rider pulled hard on the reins. His coal-black steed shied and almost reared. Strands of silvery hair poked from beneath Lavvann's helmet of tarnished steel as he regained control of his horse and stopped just across the barrier from her. Marin noticed his sword half drawn, and then sliding back into its scabbard as he recognized her. The corner of his mouth twisted upward in mild amusement as their eyes met.

"Wise words that you rarely heed." Lavvann's tone balanced respect and mockery. His sword hand rested on the hilt and his other hand gripped the reins as his horse circled in the center of the road. "You left your horse at Darós. It's well to tread softly, Marin Hanani, but that was foolish."

"There was little time," she said. "Had I waited to alert the company, the kayal would have been lost in the woods." A smile played across her lips. "But I see you found my message."

"Reckless. To go out alone and give chase to a kayal is a fool's errand." Lavvann said. "You can be far too careless. One day it will cost you, Marin. That in itself would be a grave loss. And what if it cost the lives of others? Perhaps others in this company?"

The rebuke from her captain was sharp, but it came with an undertone of affection and respect. He knew her skills, and he was genuinely concerned. Marin bowed her head at his words, but she would not submit completely. This was her chase, and she would not fail.

Her company had been on a routine patrol of Aeíx when it received a message from Prince Laman Piríst, whose son Maeros had been missing for eight days. Panic had gripped the royal house.

For years the people of this island had suffered at the hands of the kayal, and now the dark things were no longer just a farmer's problem. The powerful and fortunate had felt the kayal's evil touch. Maeros had been taken.

Finding him alive was a mission of the Four Banners, especially in a place where the laws were weak, and Lavvann's company had a solemn duty to see it through.

But there would be no happy ending.

Five days later, the prince's son had been found dead—butchered in a stable outside the village of Darós. He had been nailed to the rafters by his wrists and ankles, and sliced open from throat to groin, entrails splayed on the floor below him in a macabre web. His fingers had been hacked off just above the knuckles, his feet removed at the arch. Signs of a struggle indicated that Maeros had been mutilated while still alive. The stable too had been defiled, with evil runes and cursed images scrawled on the walls and dirt floor. Whatever the killer's reasons for this insane carnage, the murder was a message: no one was safe.

The kayal were horrible creatures, demonic fiends that escaped through the veil of the unseen world to prey on the living in the mortal realm of Mir'aj. Were they spawn of the Jnoun? Or demons from another dark abyss? Marin did not know. But she knew the kayal were capable of unspeakably wicked deeds.

Piríst's heralds called upon Marin's company for help because the very name of the Four Banners evoked dread in the hearts of most ene-mies—most natural enemies, that is. The kayal had no regard for flags or nations, although their killing of Maeros suggested an understanding of political motives. And while the Prince must have known there was little chance of catching any kayal before they fled back into the darkness, all he could do was appeal to an alliance known for solving the unsolvable.

Beyond the stable where the Prince's son had been slain, there was only a scattering of clues. And Marin, sometimes frustrated by Lavvann's caution and the routine of managing a company of riders, impulsively took up the chase alone. Convinced she would succeed on her own—or force her company to follow her strategy—she set out just after dawn the next day. She left her horse in another stable at Darós, one that had not seen any butchery, and continued westward on foot. She knew her comrades would come after her.

It had been a long trek. The suns were invisible in the gray sky, and the passing hours seemed endless. Damp wind and spits of drizzle soaked and chilled Marin as she made her way across rough, wild country. But, as she told herself again and again, she had seen worse.

She would never stop hunting.

"WE ARE wasting time," Marin said.

She measured Lavvann's reaction to her words and saw he was no longer amused.

Still, despite his silence, she stood strong, her tone quiet but firm. "Yes, I was wrong. But let me make it right by finding our ghost, if our voices have not already spooked the thing."

She glanced toward the dark openings in the wall of trees just ahead. "This kayal is alone and very near. We should make haste or we'll lose it in the dark," she said, looking up at Lavvann's face.

Behind her captain she noticed six of her fellow riders scanning the landscape. She knew what they were thinking. Weathered hills, wild woods, and cold streams at nightfall added up to a place of extreme danger. Here the conditions favored the kayal.

"We will follow your lead, Marin," Lavvann said at last. "We have little choice in the matter."

Marin moved onto the road. At a signal from their captain, the riders closed in and flanked her. She knelt to study the crumbling stones and sprouting weeds beneath her feet—all that remained of the ancient road. Hunched over on her knees, studying the ground while her companions peered into the shadows, she smiled discreetly at having forced Lavvann's hand.

She shook her head, unable to find anything of use to their mission. She rose, pushed past the horses, and hopped over the low wall of rough-hewn rock into the field that bordered the trees. Here she found some hope: faint claw marks gouged into the soil, and a flake of that ashy dander which the kayal often left behind. Though it was only the smallest of traces, Marin knew the thing had recently passed here.

Their prey was still nearby.

Lavvann raised two fingers to his eyes, a signal commanding two riders to join him. Both nodded and guided their horses closer.

"Speak your thoughts, and make them quick," said Lavvann.

"It is too risky if we continue from here," murmured the first rider. "We have encroached on territory beyond our control. I fear an ambush."

"It will be pitch black very soon, and night favors the kayal," said the second. "If they are out in force, then their powers will be greater than our strength."

Marin glanced back at Lavvann to observe his reaction. Slowly he shook his head at the others. "Valid complaints. I too fear an assault in the dark. Still, I doubt that they are out in numbers. We shall not let the Prince's killer slip through our fingers as we close in on it. Marin has done good work." Turning to her, Lavvann said, "The matter is settled, for now. Lead on, but be wary. I sense a trap."

At his signal the riders fanned out once more.

"Stay alert," Lavvann whispered to Marin.

She moved forward with a grin of triumph, away from the company of riders toward the shadowy tree line.

The steady rain soaked the hard, rough ground, and Marin had to search long and hard in the gloom for another sign of the kayal. She noticed a few more claw scrapes where the kayal had pivoted and crossed to the other side of the road. But there the tracks were once again lost in the ground cover. She turned back toward Lavvann and motioned him forward.

"It has run into woods here," she said, pointing to the dense stand of bay trees to the north.

"I will take the company to the far edge and wait there." Lavvann's hand swept in a broad curve. "You will flush it out into the open. We will decide then whether to kill the thing or spare it."

Marin wondered why her captain would consider sparing the life of something so nefarious, but she nodded silently as Lavvann signaled to the riders. The rain had stopped falling, and here under the forest canopy, she could hear only muffled snorting as the horses cleared water from their nostrils.

She moved away quickly, slipping into the darkness.

MARIN RAN.

Her long strides covered the ground quickly and silently, but she remained cautious as she moved across the damp mulch of the forest floor. She held her breath as she listened to the stillness, and swept her gaze steadily, watching for the slightest movement in the shadows. The bay trees were closer and thicker than the eucalyptus had been, and it was dryer here. Steam rose from her cloak as her body's heat warmed it. The kayal's footprints and dander would be impossible to find here without striking a light, so Marin had to rely on other tracking skills.

The ground sloped gradually downward. She ducked beneath a fallen bough that she sensed rather than saw, and the soft crunch of dry leaves beneath it echoed far too loudly in the still air. The ground then leveled into a stretch of mud that sucked at her boots before it began another gentle upward slope.

Moving from tree to tree, she crept along, bow in hand. Each step surely brought her closer to the kayal. And—was that it? Just ahead she glimpsed a black figure moving in the same direction—away from her— but not as quickly as she.

Making no sound, she closed on the figure, drawing an arrow from her quiver and nocking it to the bowstring by touch.

Marin was only ten paces behind the fleeing kayal. She braced herself against a tree, feeling behind her to make sure its wide, solid trunk would be adequate cover if she needed to fall back. She raised her bow, drew back the string and took aim. Yes, it was still there, pausing as it sniffed the air.

Marin doubted one arrow would kill the dark thing. Although she wanted it dead, she would force it to run, not turn to fight. Lavvann's company beyond the trees should be in position by now.

Her fingers tightened as she steadied her aim. Abruptly the figure half-turned and raised its hand as if signaling her to halt. What— Marin paused, unsure whether to heed the signal, wondering if this hesitation was a trap that would kill her.

The figure slowly drew back a hooded cloak, revealing no demonic creature but a man. Even in the darkness she could see the outline of a man's face, not the horrid countenance of a kayal. That one simple motion resembled the grace and efficiency of one of Torre Lavvann's silent signals, not the jagged, unpredictable movements of a vile entity on the wrong side of the veil. This person, whoever it was, turned his head toward her without hesitation, and Marin felt he was looking directly at her in the darkness.

Wait.

She froze, heart pounding, as the stranger beckoned her closer. Drawn in by something she couldn't explain, Marin lowered her bow, the arrow drooping in her hand. She stepped around the tree trunk and moved forward, apprehensive but fascinated—and feeling curiously safe.

"You have mistaken me for the enemy, my lady," said a soft male voice as she approached. There was something familiar about it. "What you seek is just ahead," he went on, voice falling to a whisper as she approached. "But beware—the creature is not alone. Your captain and the others are riding into a trap."

Was this man accusing her of something? Did he somehow know that she had planned to take this kayal single-handedly, or at least send it stumbling into Lavvann's ambush with her arrow between its foul shoulders? "How…how can you know this?" She kept her voice low but fierce. "Who are you?"

His voice carried an echo, like a song from a distant shore. "I once was with the Four Banners as you are now. My duties and allegiances lie elsewhere, but on this day we have a common purpose."

He offered his hand, and now Marin was close enough to see him better. Waves of light-colored hair reached nearly to his shoulders, his teeth were white, and his eyes had a sapphire glint, even in deep shadow. They shone with a light too wise, too bold and intimate for a man she was seeing for the first time. Then her hand was in his, and the touch felt so … familiar.

"I know why you are here, and I am not your enemy. I am a siri for the Rassan Majalis. My name is Hiril Altaïr, and I stand with you, Marin Hanani."

His words rang like truth itself. She trembled inside. "But … how do you know of me?"

He looked deep into her eyes and answered, "I have always known your name … my wife."

MARIN'S EYES snapped open.

The ship lurched in the rough waves and almost threw her off the bench. It was dawn at sea, and she'd spent the night on deck remembering. Or, it would now seem, slumped and dreaming. She had never seen Hiril's face in the shadows of the bay wood. That would have been impossible. She had only trusted his voice and the experience it carried. He'd known her name because he was a *siri*—information was his job. But he'd never called her his wife until much later. That had been the dream, speaking in his voice.

Marin stood and stretched away the ache in her muscles,

bracing her legs against the rolling deck. The night had been calm enough for her to drowse on this bench while trying to read her future in the stars. But now the sea grew choppy as a stiffer wind filled the sails, and her cloak was damp with spray, a dampness that seeped into her skin. She shivered a little, thinking of her warm bunk below, only to hear a familiar voice inside—her own voice—saying, "I've seen worse."

But had she? That was her old self speaking from a different time, much as Hiril had in her dream. Had she truly ever seen anything worse than this? The man she loved was gone from the world, and his ashes in her cabin provided no comfort. If anything, they reminded her of tracking the kayal, of those brittle scales that fell to the ground, eventually becoming one with the soil. Was that what lay beyond the curtain in the world of the Jnoun? Nothing but ashes?

The spray from another wave made it hard for Marin to think of dry, brittle things. The power of wind and sea hurled the little ship westward across *Baïr al-Zumr*, the Emerald Sea. She herself was a flake of ash, floating or sinking at the pleasure of the elements. Had she seen worse? Had she seen better? None of this mattered when she had no more purpose in the world, when the elements would decide her cruel fortunes.

Oh, but she did have one more purpose. Her year of mourning was ending, and she was on a pilgrimage in Hiril's name. She owed him this much.

After all, it was her fault he had died.

"FOLLOW ME," Hiril said.

Marin had just met this man, yet she knew there were no lies in his voice. He crept down the wooded knoll into darkness, and she followed.

The land guided their feet, leading them to a small southbound stream. They moved along its bank, navigating by the faint light of a dying sunset somewhere above the canopy of trees and clouds.

Her eyes alert for kayal, Marin followed Hiril closely enough to reach out and touch him. Everything about this man marked him as an expert tracker; still, this was her hunt, and her body remained tensed for a fight.

Deeper into the darkness they trekked. The woods formed a slender, crooked finger running much farther south than she had expected. Positioning the company at the other side of the trees would take considerable time.

Marin and Hiril moved in silent unison, focusing on the faint path. The trees thickened around the stream, forcing them away from the water and down into a shallow depression blanketed with fallen leaves. Both stepped carefully. Kayal had keen ears, and they were especially on the alert when they knew something was closing in on them.

The two trackers struggled up an incline to find the stream again. Here the banks were muddy and the channel deep. They bridged it with a fallen bough and began a steep climb. The trees thinned and the clouded sky seemed bright after the forest of shadows. The rain had stopped.

Then Hiril froze—except for the hand creeping to his shoulder for his bow. Marin crouched and did the same. They crawled forward, keeping behind ancient brambles at the edge of the tree line. Before them was a meadow some hundred yards across. Hiril pointed at a pine tree standing alone in the center.

The tree shimmered with a silver-white light, revealing several gaunt figures standing beneath its branches. At least two more stood guard with bows drawn at the opposite edge of the glade.

"It is an úathir ritual: The black arcana of burning and binding a tree spirit," Hiril whispered urgently. "We are too late to stop it."

Marin's heart hammered, nearly drowning out his soft voice. She knew enough about dark things to comprehend what an úathir meant for her company—a forest demon of terrible power, huge and vicious, ready to kill everything in its path.

"Look!" Hiril breathed in her ear. "They have already shaped it."

Marin's scalp prickled as an eerie crackling swelled into a deep, sus-tained cry. Pale green fire ignited the pine in the clearing, magical flames licking high, throwing the kayal's shapes into relief. The mournful wail pulsed against the clouds, echoing through the trees. A sweet-sick smell of burning wood and something else, something charnel, choked her breath and made her eyes tear.

The sound faded, taking the light with it. The celadon inferno left the tallest branches and retreated, stopping on the trunk a few feet off the ground. In the darkness after the dazzle of light, Marin saw a gray shape approaching the tree. The kayal-witch intoned a hideous chant as it thrust two V-shaped pieces of metal—monstrous arrow points longer than a man's leg—into the tree trunk where the green fire still burned. Amber sap poured out like blood from a wound, flowing down the arrow points into a stone basin nestled between the roots.

Marin's heart pounded. This demonic ritual must stop now. It was the only way to save her company. But even as the thought came to her, a hand fell on her shoulder. She looked at Hiril; he gestured for stillness. How dare he! But of course, he was right. Attacking now would accom-plish nothing.

The stench of scorched flesh hung in the air. The kayal-witch lifted white, mutilated fingers, the ones torn from Maeros's hand, out of the stone basin as the sap-blood glowed and writhed. A fleshy shape emerged from the basin, points of bone ripping through it, sprouting into an immense crown of antlers. The kayal-witch leaped forward, slapping a mask of bark into place below the antlers, and two red embers sparked to life in the mask's eye sockets.

The other kayal took axes to the pine's lower branches and set two of them in the rising column of molten amber, forming a pair of arms. The kayal wrenched the spears from the trunk and jammed them into the column to serve as legs. They attached the Prince's severed half-feet to the ends so that the thing could stand. Then they threw animal hides, rags, and forest soil at the demon, covering it with sorcerous armor.

Towering over the kayal, the úathir sprang to life with a growl of feral laughter. The kayal-witch embraced the demon and stepped back to shriek a command. The úathir turned and loped southward out of the clearing, branches snapping and smoldering in its wake.

Marin knew the demon was racing toward the riders.

Hiril turned to her, whispering, "You must warn the others." He pulled an arrow from his quiver and handed it to her. "Take this as I give chase. The kayal will flee when I attack. They will follow the úathir to the riders and choose to fight there." Hiril brushed his hand against Marin's fist as she clutched the arrow. "Fire it into the sky. The powder in the shaft burns red once the arrow leaves the bow. The company will see it as a warning beacon. After that, get to them as quickly as possible. We will meet there." Hiril placed a hand on her shoulder, urging her to go.

"But … the witch is the one I was hunting." Turning to him, Marin looked into his eyes and felt his strength flowing into her. "I know it," she insisted. "I can feel it was the one that took Maeros' fingers and feet."

He smiled grimly.

"I will go after the kayal-witch."

MARIN TREMBLED with rage.

Who was Hiril Altaïr to go after her prey? It was hers. She had tracked the kayal across the miles of Aeíx, followed it through the long, miserable day to this spot, sworn to her duty as a rider with the Four Banners. Who was he to take her prey instead? Just who was this man—he who had darted into the night to single-handedly ambush a kayal company still powerful with the dark magic they had conjured?

She couldn't see his arrows fly, but she heard the evil creatures shriek as one of their number fell, its head shattered by a powerful bowshot from her right. Two more of the things toppled, and the rest swarmed toward the far side of the glade, where branches still smoldered from the úathir's passing.

They were following the forest demon straight to Torre Lavvann's company.

Marin nocked Hiril's fire arrow, pointed it skyward, and loosed the bowstring. She rolled to the ground as a streak of brilliant red shot upward, coming up in a crouch and running around the clearing's edge as kayal arrows tore at the brambles that had concealed her.

Hiril had been mistaken. Some of the dark creatures had stayed behind to fight. And neither of the two coming to search for her body had fallen to friendly bowshots.

She faced them alone.

Marin forced away all thoughts of her company. Surely they had seen the fiery arrow. Indeed, she would be surprised if they hadn't been alerted by the úathir's piercing scream.

She was already moving to her left as she fired two quick arrows into the backs of the kayal who had come searching for her. Then she threw herself flat and rolled; the red flash of her warning signal had revealed glinting eyes in the branches of the lone pine tree, and as she'd expected, answering shots came from that quarter. They thudded into tree trunks a comfortable distance away as Marin continued to circle the glade.

She lined up her target in the dark, found the likely angle, aimed high, and released one powerful shot into the branches of the pine. Two kayal plummeted through the darkness and crashed to the ground, both pierced by the single arrow. She caught herself wondering if Hiril Altaïr had seen her skill. She also noticed there were no answering bowshots. Was it possible she had finished off the enemy in this place?

Sounds of battle drew nearer through the trees: the shouts and shrieks of men and kayal, the clash of steel, the thud of hooves. Had her company defeated the úathir? Were the creatures fleeing back this way? Marin doubted that a single wound would prove mortal to the kayal, and she would not have the injured rising again to join their dark kind in battle.

With blade in hand, she broke from the cover of the trees. The fallen kayal were moving as she came upon them; despite their injuries, they groped for their weapons. Without mercy, Marin plunged her sword into the first, and then silenced the second with a fierce blow to the neck. There were two more, fallen beside the brambles, and at least three more nearby that Hiril had taken with his parting shots. How many others? Were the rest caught in the skirmish that approached down the smoldering track through the trees?

Marin barely saw the kayal as it dropped from the branches of the pine and came at her with a long, jagged blade.

She hadn't counted on this one.

9

THE KAYAL attacked Marin with incredible fury.

Its blade sang through the air. She parried and riposted. The thing struck back, hooking her sword, forcing her arm aside. She feinted and gashed her enemy's sword arm with a twisting lunge. Blade dripping with black blood, she slashed again and lopped off its head.

She turned in a slow circle, calming herself. Five other kayal lay sprawled on the ground. The one that had taken Hiril's arrow through the head would never move again. Marin quickly dispatched the other four, then headed toward the sounds of fighting.

The smoking branches where the úathir had passed still stank of Maeros's charred flesh. Marin breathed through her mouth as she watched for signs of friend or foe. The battle sounds seemed to be moving farther north.

Except—

Something ran toward her in the gloom, too light for an unhorsed rider in chain mail, too fast even for Hiril. Marin raised her blade as the kayal appeared. Its blind haste signaled flight rather than attack—until the thing fixed its gaze on her. Even in the dark, its black eyes gleamed red. It raised a jagged blade, swerved and charged. Something about this creature—its scent? its hatred?—told Marin she was confronting the butcher she had tracked from Darós.

The kayal-witch.

And Torre Lavvann would spare it? Not while she faced it here alone!

Marin launched herself at her adversary, slashing deep into its *sword arm. But her enemy pushed back with even more fury than the one she'd fought moments earlier. It struck her blade as fast as she could parry. Saving strength while seeking advantage, Marin gave her enemy more ground as it tried to back her into a tree trunk. Her own battle fury gave way to a chill that spread from the pit of her stomach.*

She might not survive this fight.

Suddenly two arrows pierced the kayal from behind. With a grunt of shock and the snap of bone, it dropped its sword and fell face down, arrows protruding from its back and the base of its neck.

Marin dropped to her knees and closed her eyes, gasping. Footsteps pounded the forest floor, and she smiled at the welcome clink of chain mail. Someone gripped her shoulders. With a sigh, she dropped her sword and began to tremble.

"It is over," said Lavvann. Marin looked gratefully up at her captain. "Two are dead: Jarrle and Sarsca." His voice was raw with grief. "We will bury them this night."

"Brave men, both," said Marin softly. "I will miss them. But . . . did Hiril Altaïr reach you?" Worry sharpened her voice. "Have you seen him?"

"I am here." And so he was. Marin was unable to see how Hiril had fared in battle, but his step was heavier, and weariness weighed down his voice. "The rest of your company is running down the last of our enemies. The úathir was gravely wounded and its fire is flickering. It fled, but will not escape."

"We are in your debt, Hiril," said Lavvann. "But one more favor, if I may. Please stay with Marin Hanani while she gathers her strength. My duty lies elsewhere."

"Of course." Hiril waved a gracious hand. "See to your fallen soldiers."

Lavvann retreated into the woods, leaving them alone.

Hiril slid his hands under Marin's arms and lifted her to her feet. "You fight fiercely, Marin Hanani."

"I've seen worse."

"Have you, now?" A smile lurked in Hiril's voice.

An ominous gurgle interrupted them. The dying kayal-witch writhed, groping at the arrow in its neck.

Marin stared down at her enemy, grieving for her fallen comrades, sickened by the memory of the slaughtered prince. She kicked the creature onto its back, pushing the arrows deeper into its throat and chest. Its mouth gaped wide, and a stench of rot blew up at her.

It only fueled her anger.

"Your kind belongs on the other side of the veil!" she shouted. "Plague your precious Jnoun and leave us alone!" She almost picked it up and shook it, but the pallid, ashy skin looked diseased.

The kayal made a rough, gurgling sound as blood pumped from its wounds. It was laughing at her! Beyond rage, Marin lifted her sword. The red gleam flared in its black eyes, first at her, then at Hiril. Thick silence fell as a shadow lashed out in the darkness, stretching from the kayal-witch to coil around Hiril. A hollow, dead voice rang from the tendril of shadow.

"Little time will you live in peace. Then you will be cut down to rot, forever a lost spirit without release. Dark are the words I place on you."

The shadow faded. The kayal-witch's eyes went dull; its body collapsed on itself with a faint sucking sound.

"You have committed your last murder," Marin said, slashing at the carcass with her sword. Ashes whirled up from the kayal and settled again.

"Come, lady." Hiril took her hand, pulling her away. "Do not dwell on the hollow curses of a dying thing."

Marin let him lead, the day's exhaustion weighting her body like wet sand. The rain returned, rattling in the trees above them. All she understood was Hiril at her side. Marin promised herself that a curse would never rule her fate, but the thought of Hiril's death twisted a knife in her heart. She wished that the kayal had chosen her instead.

Hiril pulled her close, sensing her thoughts. Time stopped as they held one another under the woods' dark canopy, rain dripping around them but not on them. Marin wondered at that. She wanted the rain to wash away the foulness of killing and the uncertainty of what lay ahead.

Gently, tenderly, Hiril put his hands around Marin's neck and tilted her head back.

Then he kissed her.

70

THAT FIRST kiss was no dream.

Marin still tasted it on her lips, warm and promising, two years after that wonderful, horrible night. The memory lingered even as she held Hiril's ashes in her hands.

She had been standing at the ship's bow ever since they'd rounded the northern tip of Mornós. Both suns were high in the sky, dazzling her as she turned east to watch the Tayar Mountains rise out of the sea. Their sharp purple outline faded to soft lavender as the morning progressed, as the Hayl coastline rolled past the port rail and they approached the crowded ships' masts of Messinor.

Marin's bag, packed hours ago, lay at her feet. Beyond occasionally asking the sailors how soon they would dock, she said nothing. Her year of mourning ended tomorrow, and she still had ground to cover. It was all very well to lose herself in memories and dreams while confined to a ship, but now she focused her energy on the long walk ahead.

The ship sailed into the harbor, and soon she departed, walking onto the quay without a word of farewell, although she felt their curious eyes on her back. She moved along the pier, weaving her way around stevedores, merchants, and stacks of cargo. Foot traffic thickened as she left the waterfront and plunged into the heart of the city.

Like any port, Messinor was a lively place, bright with the colors of many lands, the music of many languages, and the aroma of many foods. Marin remembered that it had been some time since breakfast. She stopped to buy a wedge of cheese and small skin of local wine from a street vendor, eating her meal as she walked through the city with her eyes on the mountains beyond.

This was a peaceful place, in its way, and the simple pleasures of eating fresh food and being on a mission again nearly brought a smile to her face.

Almost.

Still she wondered, always and endlessly, what she might have done to prevent that curse from falling on Hiril. Throughout this year of mourning, it had been difficult to eat, to concentrate, to keep on pretending that she was whole.

"Why didn't you kill the wretched thing when you had the chance?" She had asked herself this question a thousand times. "What made you claim it as your prize? Why did you think you deserved one last word instead of simply cleaving its foul neck with your sword the moment it fell? Then it would never have come to this. He would have been spared. You would hold him in your arms right now."

Marin shuddered as she tormented herself with these questions yet again. It was the same voice with which she'd always said, "I've seen worse," but without the lightness of a casual boast. In the past year, that voice had accused her with the fierce edge that once challenged fate, now focused with all its scorn on her hesitation that night in the wood.

Hesitation that had cost Hiril his life.

"Little time will you live in peace, then cut down to rot," the kayal-witch had cursed him—and cut down he was.

The curse had come true.

11

MARIN WAS SILENT.

The memories were flooding back into her mind. How irreparably her life had changed. That fateful day played out once more in Marin's head as clear as it did the first time.

A messenger reached the door; his eyes were downcast and his hands were folded together before him in respectful sympathy. He'd just informed her that her husband Hiril was dead.

Marin had been at their home in Steffra when she'd received the news. What had been a pleasant evening alone had turned into the longest night of her life. The next morning, sleepless and still in shock, she was almost happy when another messenger arrived with a summons from the Rassan Majalis. Traveling to Ruinart was better than doing nothing.

After her ship arrived from Eliës, she was greeted in Cievv as a hero's widow. Officials and functionaries consoled her, invited her into their homes—but told her little about the hero's murder. Despair followed disbelief, and Marin grieved in solitude for days before agreeing to see any visitors.

It was weeks before Hiril's remains reached Cievv, and he was not cremated until some months after his death. Marin was, of course, puzzled by this, but all anyone would tell her was that it had something to do with how the assassin had marked Hiril's body. The Rassan Majalis's alchemists came and went, murmuring among themselves but saying nothing to anyone else. Finally, Hiril received the funeral rites reserved for a member of Ruinart royalty, although he was not a citizen of the kingdom. It was a sad and solemn occasion, and still no one discussed the circumstances of his death.

After the funeral, Hiril's ashes were kept for weeks in the royal family's citadel before Marin was permitted to take them away.

Meanwhile, she lived in two worlds at once—an inner realm of abject blackness where her spirit withered away, and a city of flowers basking in the glorious light of an early autumn. That world belonged to someone else, even though she walked through it every day. Her inner darkness grew; some mornings, despite the rich golden sunlight, she lay in bed as if waiting for a dawn that never came. The burden of staying in Cievv without her husband had become too much to bear.

At last someone arrived to offer her hope.

Torre Lavvann.

It was as if both suns had finally burst through the clouds. Lavvann's rugged face and gruff smile reminded her that she still had a place with the Four Banners, and that there was always work to do; and they could certainly use her help again. That was hope enough for Marin. The next day she left Cievv with her captain and returned to her company.

In the months that followed, Marin pursued dangerous paths with her brothers in arms. She rode north into Keafel beyond the Soller Mountains, to a gently rolling landscape of green and golden fields crisscrossed by strips of woodland. She hunted down ruffians and dark things without mercy, and fought fiercely in battle, no longer caring for her own safety.

Her company met with worried officials in the royal city of Hohnn, and at their bidding rode southwestward into the Tarkh Hills, a desolate region of high, rounded tors, broad ridges, and hidden vales. There, above the city of Limmún, Marin helped rid the area of a *behrraun*, a vicious predator that stalked and killed livestock and farmers. She nearly died in this fight, yet it seemed as simple as a child's game.

The Four Banners company boarded a ship to Cevar and lingered a while in the crown city of Enneri, its walls set on high cliffs overlooking the sea and the nearest of the Seven Islands. The rumored pirate attack never came, and Lavvann joked that Marin's fierce reputation had frightened them away.

The company sailed east to Nórra and then south to the island realms of Laval. They had no reason to make landfall on Aeíx this time, and Marin looked on the accursed island with bleak fury as they passed, hoping the outlaws and the kayal were busy slaughtering one another. Torre Lavvann saw the look on her face, and ordered her to take a furlough when they reached the kingdom of Falasan. There he knew a healer who might offer her help.

The healer's treatments relaxed and strengthened Marin's body but did nothing for her spirit. She craved a return to her company and its dangerous missions, but her next journey would be to Ruinart and Cievv.

The year of mourning was coming to an end.

12

MARIN LEFT her bed at dawn.

Beyond her window, the cityscape gave way to green hills that rose toward mountain peaks shaded violet in the early light. Other travelers had assured her that this road led to the shrine of *Sey'r an-Shal*—the Falls to Heaven. Many people came this way; the shrine was a source of drinking water for the lands below, as well as a place of pilgrimage.

The morning was clear and hot as Marin climbed the hills and wandered through forested valleys. Although she knew it was less than a day's walk, she became worried as the suns passed noon and the shadows inched westward.

At last, rounding a bend near the summit of a steep hill, she saw the source of the stream that her road had followed for much of the day. Water sparkled as it flowed from the mouth of a small cave and tumbled down several steep falls, each issuing from the pool above it. The shrine was a larger cave cut into the hillside beneath the highest waterfall. A long flight of stone steps led from the road to the shrine and the promontory above.

Marin climbed the steps as they curved around the topmost pool. It seemed like a sacred place, yet she felt no peace. One year ago today, Hiril had died. She had lingered in mourning until this moment. Something was supposed to change—exactly what, she still had no idea.

The shrine was cool after her day in the hot sun, its floor and walls smoothed and polished, echoing with the gentle splash of water. Cut into the stone floor were five shallow channels running the width of the cave. Five springs gushed from the rock wall to Marin's right, one into each channel. The water trickled across the cave toward the far wall. There, each trickle left its individual channel to join a wall of water that flowed upward as if ascending to heaven. Was it magic? Was it an illusion? Marin felt as if she should stand in awe of this miracle, and feel inspiration or be at peace.

She felt neither.

No matter. It was time.

The silver urn was cool in her hands, though it had spent the hot day under her cloak. Kneeling by the nearest channel, Marin drew a deep breath; it came out a sob. Her powerful, slender body curled around Hiril's ashes and slumped to the floor. A broken, breathless keening shook her. She'd wept often throughout the past year, but never like this, never with the desolation of a widow who finally knows—with the shattering of her heart—that she is truly alone.

The storm of emotion swept through her and was gone. She was empty again, her world filled with the noise of the inverted waterfall and the rapid beating of her heart.

She straightened and drew another long breath.

It was done.

As was the custom in most of Mir'aj, her period of mourning was at its end. Hiril had been born in a small village not far from this shrine, and Marin was carrying out his wishes that, should he fall, this should be his final resting place.

She tipped the urn, pouring the contents into the running water. Each particle of ash seemed to represent a moment they had spent together. All too soon the urn was empty—just as their time together had run out. With tears streaming down her cheeks and splashing into the channel, she watched as the water swirled his ashes away toward the far wall and into the waterfall that rushed up to heaven.

Even as a silver urn full of ashes, Hiril had been a presence in her life.

Now she was alone.

13

"SPEAK TO ME."

Marin pleaded beside the waterfall within the polished walls of the shrine, in the scent of wet rock, as if Hiril's voice could come to her just once more. Please . . . could he not whisper just a word?

She had carried out his final request, and according to custom, life would return to normal a year after his death—or at least move forward with some new purpose. Marin wanted to believe that here, in this place, at this precise moment, her pain could perhaps be transformed into something else.

But there was nothing here for her. Only the empty silver urn at her side. Only the watery silence of her solitude. Only her grief.

"Maybe Ala'i is not the one," Marin said aloud to the shrine. "There are other gods in this world that I can seek."

Though holding vast sway, Illam was not the only divinity in Mir'aj; there was also Jovah, Njambe, Himnnaríki, or Vijayu. Their practices might seem strange to her, but she had seen much on her travels; and she knew there were many ways in which people could worship and find solace. But in truth she knew this was an empty challenge to Ala'i—that professions of strong or wavering faith were nothing more than words intended to appease her loneliness, to justify the emptiness that Hiril's loss had left in her heart.

"There is no life for me," Marin said to the shrine. "Not anymore."

The water merely continued to rush by her. It could not react to her sorrow; it moved on without any care for her loneliness or despair.

Marin remained for another hour, thinking about everything—and nothing. The chamber darkened as the afternoon suns waned and shadows crept over the hills. She had spent enough time here. She would return to Messinor and wait there for her orders. Everyone knew where she had gone, and sooner or later someone would find a task for her. That would be her life from now on.

Then a chill came over her—and it had nothing to do with the cool breeze blowing past the waterfall as the heat of day diminished. It was something else.

Her hunter's instinct told her another presence lurked nearby.

Marin turned slowly, surveying the entrance behind her. She'd left her weapons in the city, along with everything else, and she felt trapped when she saw a man's shadow on the waterfall at the cave's mouth. Someone was standing outside, waiting for her to leave the shrine.

Let him come, she thought. *Today I welcome death with open arms.*

The shadow moved away.

A silhouette passed on her side of the bright waterfall, and a gray-clad figure came toward her. He was tall and thin, and he carried something in his hands that was clearly not a weapon. His movements suggested cautious respect, not battle readiness.

Their eyes met. His were as gray as his cloak, and his dark hair and thin mustache were shot with gray as well. Marin saw sharp intelligence in his face, but also the weakness of one who happily issues commands and lets others do the work.

"My condolences," he said in the formal tones of a bureau-
crat. "May peace be with you."

As he moved closer, Marin could see that he held something
in his arms.

Four books.

14

"WHO ARE YOU?"

Marin studied the man with the strange offering.

"My name is Nabeel Khoury," he said.

"And why do you trespass on my rite?"

Khoury hesitated, and then sighed. "It is a long tale—and one
that I must tell you, Marin Altaïr."

"How do you know my name?" she asked. "And how did you
find me here?"

"It is my business to know many things." Khoury made a gesture of apology at Marin's glare. "Ah … the timing of my presence
is suspect, I admit, but I knew of no other moment when I would
find you alone. Away from eyes that spy from afar—whether you
know of them or not. You are not safe. Not here. Not anywhere."

Marin rose to her feet, stifling a grimace at the stiffness in her
legs after kneeling for so long. "A woman I am, but most capable," she said, staring into the man's face. "This I can assure you,
Nabeel Khoury."

Khoury gave her a polite smile. "Hiril Altaïr was even more
capable than you, my good lady, and he is dead nonetheless."

Marin bristled. "As if I am unaware!" She picked up the silver
vase from the floor and shook it in his face. "Who are you to follow me into the hills, interfere with my pilgrimage, and warn me
of phantom dangers?"

"I am the *Rais* of—" Khoury began.

"So? How does this concern me?" she demanded, her anger
cutting his words short.

"May peace be with you, my good lady," he said quickly. "I did not come here to anger you. Hear me out, I beg you."

Marin breathed in and out, mastering her anger. "I am listening."

"I come from Havar—and I bring you proof of the danger that follows you."

"Havar?" The word caught in Marin's throat. The place where Hiril had been murdered.

"Yes, Havar. As I told you, I am the *Rais* of the sheikdom, and . . . " Khoury faltered.

"And?"

"I watched your husband die."

AN ECHOING roar filled Marin's head, louder than any waterfall.

"You . . . let him die?"

"Yes."

"And did nothing to stop it?"

Khoury lowered his eyes, his face burning with shame. "I did nothing," he whispered.

Marin's hand whipped forward, smashing him in the head with the silver urn. Khoury cried out and fell, the books scattering across the floor. She stared down at him, her chest heaving, thinking to kick his ribs until they broke and pierced his heart, or maybe to crush his throat with her foot.

Instead, she paced back and forth across the shrine, channeling her rage into each step. Of course she knew many ways to kill without a weapon, but this man was a witness to Hiril's murder, whatever role he had played—or had refrained from playing. Suppressing her urge to commit murder, she relaxed her grip on the urn, scooped a little water from the nearest channel, and splashed it on Khoury's face.

"Wake up and speak to me, Rais." Marin's voice was cold and level.

He sat up, grimacing. He touched his left cheek, sucked in a pained breath, and stared at his fingers.

"No blood," Marin told him, "but by tomorrow you will see a glorious bruise." She shook her head and gave him a mocking grin.

"I deserved nothing less," said Khoury in a low voice. "I am a coward."

"And yet you command the city guard of Havar? And does the sheikh know that you stand about doing nothing while men are murdered before your eyes?"

"When he so orders it."

Marin stared at him. "He...ordered my husband's death?"

"No. It was others. Those who are much more powerful than he."

Khoury hung his head once more, and Marin briefly considered striking him again. But there was more she needed to know.

"Very well, then. You were ordered to stand and watch. Who was his murderer?"

The man shook his head sadly. "Ciris Sarn."

Khoury's voice was quiet, but the words bit deep. Marin knew the name. Everyone did. Sarn had grown into a legend that haunted people's dreams. He was the most feared assassin in Mir'aj.

"Ciris Sarn murdered Hiril?" Marin sat on the floor next to Khoury. "But why would he do that?"

Khoury turned and made a sweeping gesture at the ancient relics scattered about the shrine's polished floor.

"For these."

16

MARIN DID not wait.

She sailed aboard the same ship on which she'd traveled east, booking the westward passage only an hour before it cast off for the return to Cievv. The purser had warned of storms, but Marin simply smiled.

The sailors were amazed by the change in her. Now she spoke with them, asking informed questions about open-water navigation and seeking news from faraway places. She did, however, keep her emotional distance and refuse to answer any personal inquiries.

Marin was on her way to Ruinart; she must now seek answers of her own. Although she'd hardly expected to discover her indirect connection to the dreaded assassin Ciris Sarn at the shrine of Sey'r an-Shal, it was better than no answer at all.

It was much better, in fact. The books she now possessed had changed everything. Nabeel Khoury was an honorable man—in his own way—and Marin knew this now. She owed him nothing less, despite his role in Hiril's death. After this year of mourning, his revelations gave her a purpose.

Vengeance.

Yet her vengeance needed a strategy.

Marin thought about this as the promised storm hit them shortly after they cleared Rimmn Island, as the ship bucked like a frightened horse, as the lantern swung crazily and spun shadows across the walls of her cabin. Her strategy must begin with the spymaster who had sent her husband on that last fatal mission. Ilss Cencova was a good man, shrewd and difficult to fool. He would surely want to know why she asked after Rassan Majalis' secrets. What could she tell him? She had a stormy ocean voyage to think about it, and she would need the time. Few widows sought the answers she wanted, and few widows rode with the Four Banners and struck fear into enemies' hearts. And, if Khoury was right, no one in all of Mir'aj possessed anything like what she carried in her cloak.

The four books.

What *were* these four books? She had to discover that, and whether they could help her destroy Ciris Sarn. She would have to do everything in her power, even if it meant playing false with those she trusted and respected.

In another lifetime, lying would have outraged her honor. But now it was just another arrow in her quiver, another means to an end.

Deception often hurt. Sometimes it killed.

Well, what of it?

She'd seen worse.

Part Three

A HUNDRED SORROWS

5.5.792 SC

7

EVERYONE HAS SECRETS.

Pavanan Munif knew this to be true. Today his secret had taken him away once more. A man like him didn't just wander into *al-Naffaq*—the Pit. No one did. At least not willingly. Munif was lured here, driven by a hunger over which he had little control.

Affyram.

His one vice.

His demon.

But he wasn't alone. Saffan had his boys. Dassai his whores. Malek too, and the Sultan. Munif was privy to them all.

Chased from his high tower in the *casbah*, Munif found himself again in familiar surroundings. At least he was getting better. In the past, when his habit had ruled his every waking moment, he'd practically lived down here. Now, Munif had weaned himself to just once a week.

Munif was tall. More than six feet, as most southerners were. His father was from the Kingdom, his mother was Rajani, born in Jaisvaran before emigrating to Qatana with her family. Munif's hair was dark brown, streaked with gray. He had penetrating green eyes and a hawkish nose. His prominent cheekbones were high, and his lips were thin. His almond eyes and honey-colored skin hinted of his mother. Ten years earlier he'd been rakish, but age and *affyram* had taken their toll. Still, Munif was a match for almost anyone and, despite his thirty-seven years—and his demon—he kept himself in formidable condition.

Munif was chief of the Jassaj agents in Riyyal, under the command of the Sultan himself. He reported directly to Emir Malek, the Sultan's youngest son. He worked almost exclusively under his own authority.

Not even Dassai could touch him.

Munif traversed the narrow, dark streets. His body trembled in anticipation. It was nearing the sacred festival of Eid ul-Fajdah, and he would play his part in the celebrations.

But first he needed a well-deserved break, something to placate his addiction and take the edge off the strain he was under.

Munif threaded his way through labyrinthine alleys and filthy cobblestone passageways, keeping to the shadows. He continued westward into the foreign quarter of Riyyal, finally reaching a great mosque that dominated the skyline of the city. Munif stopped for a moment, taking in the scene before him.

Here was the dirty secret everyone knew but seldom mentioned. Munif gazed in wonder at the immense abyss that stretched out below. It was surrounded—and hidden by—the Binais'r mosque. For all practical purposes, the Sultan's law ended where Munif stood. Below him, down in the Pit, was a world unto itself.

Beneath great wind-towers a circular path wound its way into the rock and sand. Expertly constructed platforms perched on the walls and extended over the hollowed-out earth. Crude dwellings had been carved into these walls. There were structures at the bottom of the gaping maw, shacks that served as dwellings for those unfortunate enough to have been lured in by the mirage that was Riyyal.

This city within a city was home to the dregs of Nujoom, Hayl, and Ungwara—even as far away east as Lasavísur in the cold lands bordering the Curtain of Night. Foreigners from these kingdoms had come in response to the promise of work—only to end up as thralls to the wealthy, forced to live like rats in cramped burrows. Those fortunate enough to be permitted housing in Qatana would often find themselves homeless should they make one small error in judgment, and be arrested for the most minor of infractions.

More often than not, these unfortunates were unable to buy their release. And then the Sultanate's agents, acting as pseudo-slavers, would purchase the condemned. But rather than being executed or mutilated, the guilty were transported like chattel to Riyyal. Once they had come there, only a lifetime of cruel labor could pay off the debt.

Qatani residents convicted of crimes would rather pay to be killed than be exiled to the Pit.

Munif took a deep breath and descended into *al-Naffaq*. The air became heavy and damp. The path, a serpentine route of loose rocks and gravel, was rough; in some sections it was very steep, and Munif was forced to ease his pace. He didn't want to slip and fall to the bottom.

"Damn!" he cried. Despite his caution, a small avalanche of damp stones slid beneath his feet and he nearly tumbled head-long down the precipitous track. "That's no way to die," he muttered, reestablishing a stable footing.

A little farther along, Munif paused to observe the sheer quantity of half-finished buildings—dismal sheds that the laborers here had yet to complete.

When he resumed his descent, Munif kept his eyes down, moving past the poor, the starved and forsaken.

Upon reaching the bottom of the Pit, he moved with singular purpose toward his destination, a squat structure consisting of a dozen small rooms.

There was little to worry about now. Plenty of time to indulge himself.

Munif approached the third door and was about to knock when another door opened at the opposite end. Two figures emerged and set off up the narrow path away from him. Munif stared at their receding backs.

These two were different from the rest.

They were Carac.

He knew all too well of their kind. The summoners would do anything to further their cause, including killing the innocent and sacrificing their own lives to ensure their violent purity—martyrs in the eyes of the people of Carac. Munif had lost them three months earlier, but now here they were, within reach.

His vice must wait.

Munif followed, keeping a safe distance. As he advanced stealthily, he noticed that the other denizens of the Pit whom he passed were on edge. Normally their eyes were lifeless voids, but now there was something different in them.

Nevertheless, he remained focused on his two targets as he began to ascend one of the winding paths out of *al-Naffaq*.

Munif looked into the faces of several more workers as he threaded his way past them. He could see it in their furtive glances. He could see it in their eyes.

They were scared.

2

THE STORM could not stop them.

Perhaps Munif would, however, before the end came. These thoughts plagued Donnò Galliresse as he stood on the rampart high above the city of Tivisis and gazed out at the emerald waters beyond the port.

From his lofty post in the Summer Citadel he could see the ancient paths wending haphazardly down to the sea. Galliresse watched the people below engage in trade as though it were just another day. But he knew that death would soon arrive in the harbor. He could feel that reality in the pit of his stomach; he fought the nausea that came with it.

Martyrdom would triumph.

A small man with delicate features and thinning white hair, Galliresse projected the aura of someone much more physically impressive. Beneath an air of placid introspection was a man of fierce competence. Already, at the young age of fifty-one, he controlled the greatest of the free cities in all of Givenh, perhaps the whole of Mir'aj.

As Lord of Tivisis, he held the highest position one could obtain unless born of royal lineage. Galliresse was proud of his accomplishments and the power he wielded.

The envy of Givenh and the islands of Miranes', Tivisis was unrivaled in its volume of trade. The city was open, vibrant, and fiercely independent. In the great port, numerous ships laden with wares from Qatana, Rajanahar, Zaraniz, and Khorbard kept the city's lifeblood flowing unabated.

Galliresse ensured that the merchant houses were given full leeway in exchange for the influx of gold arriving in the form of duty imposts. He knew that with this openness came certain risks. Due to the sheer numbers of people passing through its port, it was quite easy to 'become lost' in Tivisis—and there was a significant criminal element. To Galliresse, this was the cost of commerce.

Under his command, the city had gained even more autonomy from Givenh and positioned itself favorably in recent shipping treaties with Qatana. Even the Rassan Majalis felt the influence of Tivisis and seldom interfered on its behalf. There was too much gold to be made.

Yet, a dangerous cult headed by an influential cleric threatened this prosperity. The charismatic words of Ashraf Berdouni drew many to him. His message to the citizens of Tivisis was one of condemnation and abstinence. Not from carnal pleasures, but something much more mysterious: the banning of *Azza* in all of its forms.

Galliresse did not know the reason for the pronouncement, only that the message was beginning to take hold. Trade in *Azza* had given Tivisis its prosperity and independence. Oils, candles, incense, and more were made from the substance. Now the decree from Berdouni could destroy it all. Yet Galliresse let it go on.

He had his reasons.

Word arrived from the *misal'ayn* of Burj al-Ansour that two Carac summoners had set sail from Janeirah in the kingdom of Nahkeel. Galliresse was unsure of their exact purpose, but he knew that whatever brought them to Tivisis, it was not an act of mercy. Galliresse believed the rumors—that Carac was a forsaken place and its inhabitants harbored a love for dark, evil things.

He also knew of Pavanan Munif.

The capable Jassaj was on a ship sailing toward him, and Qatani spies were already in Tivisis, waiting.

"I wonder if their presence will be of any use," Galliresse wondered aloud. *Or,* he reflected, *if they will be able to affect the outcome of the events that are about to unfold.*

He did not know the answers.

3

MUNIF LOOKED up from the map.

In the half-light of the small cabin, a lantern swayed and flickered above his head. He felt a long, heavy swell roll beneath the hull as the dhow sailed deeper into the storm. Wind and rain-squalls buffeted the mast. Waves of green water crashed over the bow and poured across the empty deck. The ship climbed the face of a massive wave until it reached the crest and then plunged down, disappearing into the trough. Munif could hear the sound of timbers creaking, the popping of canvas and rigging as the dhow surged upward again.

The ship had been taking a beating for six hours.

The journey was taking a heavy toll. It had begun seven weeks before when he followed the two summoners out of Riyyal and hundreds of miles across the desert to the city of Janeirah.

Bending back down to the map in front of him, he traced his finger along the route both predator and prey had navigated to get here. They'd trekked northwest first into the Rab'al-Dourif and the sands of the Rim al-Sarab, which bordered the southern edge of Nahkeel. Passage across the Rab'al-Dourif was only possible through a string of oases, the largest of which was Waha al-Nurai.

In addition to battling the unrelenting desert, the men also managed to elude the Slen Thek, bounty hunters who had been tracking them from the onset. Naturally, they had no interest in the Carac other than the reward they would collect for their capture. Had the summoners been caught, Munif would never have known the true reason for their journey.

Fortune favored them however, as a sandstorm swept in, preventing the Slen Thek from making it to Waha al-Nurai. The Carac managed to slip away without being seen by the bounty hunters, but not without Munif.

An even greater threat lay ahead for them in Janeirah. Other, more dangerous foes were ready and waiting for them to arrive. The White Palm *badawh* passionately despised the people of Carac. They were prepared for a fight, but they were not interested in shedding blood. The White Palm wanted only the secrets the summoners carried with them.

Beyond the broken lands of the Rab'al-Dourif, the air was heavy with moisture from Zaraniz, carried inland over the green, fertile lowlands of the delta. This area provided abundant food for the kingdom of Nahkeel. The proud city of Janeirah stood here, at the mouth of the Dafna River. A place of burgeoning activity and of tremendous wealth, Janeirah was a waypoint to lands beyond the realms of Qatana.

Once in the city, the summoners sought passage across the Ras Mansour in one of the many merchant ships that sailed back and forth across the turbulent waters to Tivisis.

Ras Mansour was a treacherous shipping lane fraught with fierce corsairs, violent weather, and unseen shoals. Many voyages ended with cargo lost and travelers drowned. However, the allure of treasure and adventure incited many to gamble with their lives. As Munif knew, the two Carac he followed were determined to make the crossing with no thought for the riches to be made. They would not give up, and neither would he.

The dhow creaked once more, bringing him back into the moment. He tapped on the map, his finger finding Tivisis.

It was good to know where they were headed.

But it would have been better had he already discovered if this was indeed their final destination, or merely another way-point to somewhere beyond.

What lies ahead? Munif thought.

His resolve chased away any lingering doubt.

Quitting was the farthest thing from his mind.

FAJEER DASSAI chewed his nails.

The gnawing was a nervous habit, each fingertip a bloody crescent as he continued the assault. Dassai sat at his desk and mused over the plan as he had countless times before. Was Arzani good enough? Could he follow through completely? Did it even matter?

Dassai forced these doubts from his mind. After all, he had used lesser men for similar assignments. Certainly Arzani would prove equal to the task, and all would go well.

Where was the man? Fucking Mirani. Islanders—not a one of them could tell time to save his life. Still, Arzani was better than most, and had been chosen in part because of his close attention to detail. That, and he could be bought. Dassai had set the meeting in the evening, well after nightfall, to reduce any chance of delay. He didn't like to wait.

The knock on the door came an hour later.

"He's here." The voice from the other room was a low, raspy whisper.

Dassai quickly scribbled a note to himself. Setting down the *kalan* reed pen, he stayed in his chair a moment before he stood and made his way to the door. He turned the handle.

"Send him in."

Niccolo Arzani was tall, gaunt, and so pale Dassai wondered if he was perhaps a ghul or other undead thing. Black, tangled hair draped his neck and shadowed his eyes, framing a sharp-etched face with an angular nose and thin lips.

His ugliness served Arzani well; it allowed him to focus on his duties and remain free of sexual temptation. He'd been chosen by Dassai specifically for his post, and had become one of Galliresse's most trusted advisors.

"You're late," Dassai said as Arzani followed him across the room.

Arzani simply nodded, an apparent apology.

Dassai sat once more behind the desk. "So," he said languidly. "Tell me, did our lord take the bait?" He leaned back and awaited Arzani's response.

"Yes, and why should he not?" Arzani replied. "He has entrusted himself to the wisest of his counselors, and will rely on the expertise of the Jassaj to see that the summoners are stopped."

Arzani seated himself in the chair across from Dassai's desk. From a small table next to it, he took a glass of wine and sipped. He savored it with a sigh, nodding thanks to his host.

Cradling the wineglass in his skeletal hands, Arzani said, "He has great faith in you and Munif." He paused, allowing Dassai time to grasp the irony of his statement.

"Then all is as planned," Dassai said. "And you, my friend, will be our greatest benefactor." He ran his long, thin fingers through his cropped graying hair.

Arzani's lips twitched at the sight, but he said nothing.

"Do you have much concern that Munif and the others will live?" he asked.

"No; the end is near," Dassai said. "I have no doubt about this, assuming you have performed your task...flawlessly."

Arzani's eyebrows arched as he shot Dassai a quick, angry

glare. "I have complete confidence in those who I have placed in charge."

Dassai gave him a mirthless grin, revealing white teeth. "Then we have nothing with which to concern ourselves, do we?"

Arzani shrugged. "No ... no, we don't."

Dassai continued, "Three more Jassaj will join Munif once he arrives in Tivisis. These men are to follow the Carac to a safe house and then report back to Munif."

"According to your instructions," Arzani said.

"Yes, we will lead them to the old quarter and end it there. Munif and the others will trouble us no more."

Dassai continued to observe the other man's demeanor. He understood that Niccolo Arzani wanted to wrest control from Galliresse and place himself in his stead. However, Dassai wondered if he could actually succeed in doing it.

"I sense some doubt from you," Dassai said.

"What if something should go awry?" Arzani asked. "These men are not to be trifled with, especially Munif. Should they survive, you and I will be exposed."

"Your only duty is to lure them into the trap. Do not concern yourself with any other matter, my friend. The summoners and I shall attend to the rest. Leave the fate of Munif to me," Dassai said.

"For both our sakes, I hope you're right," Arzani said as he stood to leave.

Dassai paused for a moment, allowing Arzani to reach the door and place his pale fingers on the handle.

"Now ... as to the matter of my payment ... ."

PAVANAN MUNIF looked up at the lateen sails.

Twin triangles of white linen swelled in the wind as the dhow raced across pristine waters. The teakwood planks of the deck showed no wear from the rough weather. Only the rigging had suffered any damage from the storm, and that had been quickly repaired. From the bow he watched as a pod of playful dolphins swam in the wake of the ship.

The sight was as serene as any Munif had seen.

While not superstitious, Munif felt that a certain fate had guided the dhow's journey thus far. There simply was no other explanation for their survival. They'd been navigating around the Ras Mansour, leaving the Indigo Sea and sailing the main passage toward Tivisis. It was treacherous under the best of circumstances, marked by dangerous currents, deadly undertows, and perilous weather year-round. Beneath its beautiful aquamarine surface, broken ships lay in watery graves, torn asunder by the shoals that hid like wicked teeth beneath the surface of the Emerald Sea.

Then the storm had hit.

For two days strong winds and high waves had battered the dhow, taking a toll of all those aboard. Confined to quarters, Munif could do little but ride out the tempest. He was exhausted—the storm had sapped the last of his strength. Deprived of sleep, Munif felt weak and sickly. It was affecting his mood and motivation. Food, water, and fresh air hadn't helped. His mind and body craved something else.

But what he wanted, he could not have.

The first sun shone high in the blue sky; the second, a fiery orange crescent, was beginning to emerge from the eastern horizon. The rising heat was tempered by strong sea-breezes, a crisp wind blowing from the northwest. Munif could just make out a dark mass to the south.

Probably Rades, he thought.

If indeed he was correct and the dhow had not been blown off course, then they were near the island some seventy-five farsangs from Tivisis. If the winds held, they'd be there in three days.

The hold doors squeaked open, jarring Munif into alertness. The two summoners emerged, wincing at the brilliant sunlight. They had chosen to stay with the cargo rather than the crew—avoiding contact with the others aboard. Munif watched the two turn their faces to the sky as though in relief after the dark, dank prison below deck.

Munif edged closer.

He waited until they turned their backs to him, then slipped just inside the hold—partially hidden from view, but still able to listen to any conversation between the two. The first words were lost to him. The guttural dialect of their native tongue, Zaran, coupled with the ambient sounds of a ship at sea, made following the conversation difficult. Munif had studied the ancient language and knew it far better than most, but was nowhere near an expert. And there was nothing he could do about the popping of sails, creaking of wood, and slapping of waves.

He sighed deeply. This would be difficult—his focus was gone.

Munif strained to hear the taller of the two. From following them for weeks, he'd learned their names—both no doubt assumed for the passage. This one was Hersí.

"Thankfully...rains...stopped," Hersí said. "...rid our noses...stench...reach the city."

Munif noticed that the second man—Bashír—seemed grave. When he spoke, it was in such a tone that Munif himself was troubled.

"There are many...to stop us."

Despite their physical similarities—both had raven-black skin and wore long robes and cowls that concealed their bodies—Munif noted the marked difference between the two: Hersí appeared calm, while Bashír seemed anxious. Each man was a devout disciple of an ancient religion—fanatical to the point of murderous obsession.

"Do not be foolish," Hersí murmured. "...mission is guided by...more powerful than ours. Those...oppose us will suffer...consequences."

"...be little doubt...suffering will occur," Bashír remarked, rubbing his hands nervously. "... pray...not our own."

"We are well," Hersí said.

Munif noticed both men looked constantly up into the sky. Hersí pointed out over the sea. Munif heard him mention Tivisis, and then, amid the hushed jumble of words, the word *duty*. The shorter summoner listened intently; his nods appeared to placate Hersí.

Munif leaned forward, desperate to hear more, to understand better. He knew they were headed to Tivisis—this was certain. Beyond, however, remained unknown—thus he'd spent frustrating nights in his cabin, studying a map between bouts of nausea, unable to determine whether the city was the end of their journey or just one more stop along the way.

A shriek from the sky interrupted the discussion. All three turned as a scarlet-tailed tern landed on the rail not ten feet from Hersí and preened its feathers.

"Now that is a good sign," said Hersí.

"Some signs...not to...trusted." Bashír replied. Hersí spat over the rail, startling the seabird; it fluttered up for a moment and then came to rest again a few feet farther along the rail.

"Don't be a fool. A few clouds...not prophesy doom."

Bashír bowed his head and the two men moved toward the stern, continuing their conversation. Munif shook his head in frustration. It was impossible to follow them without rousing suspicion.

This was all he would get from them for now.

His quest for answers would have to continue.

6

"WE'RE CLOSE NOW."

Munif listened to the squat old salt with scarred cheeks. The mariner held a rope in his right hand and was coiling it around his left arm, all the while staring out to sea.

"Can't be more than five farsangs by my reckoning."

In the distance, Munif could see that the cobalt hue of the deep sea was beginning to warm into the soft azure common to the waters off the coast. The dhow continued its course through a deep channel. Though the depth was more than fifty feet, the water remained so clear that Munif could see sand and silvery-hued weeds moving with the current on the sea floor. Beyond the channel to the southwest, long, dark ribbons of kelp waved in the current as if bidding him farewell, as the vessel neared the end of its voyage to Tivisis.

The mariner pointed toward a shallow arc of limestone that extended into the Emerald Sea southwest of the mainland.

"Calanar Islands. You won't find them on most maps, though," the mariner said.

"Why is that?" Munif asked as he observed the tiny islands that dotted the surface of the sea.

"Because those who have houses there don't want to let anyone know 'bout them," the mariner replied. "Merchant lords and many a sheikh's mistresses—with more gold than sense. Least I've heard tell."

Grinning, Munif slapped the mariner's shoulder. "Probably true."

He knew the history of Tivisis well. The people here were justified in their pride. Warm, welcoming and vibrant—the city was unrivaled in its commerce, save perhaps for Riyyal.

As the dhow navigated between two of the smaller islands,

Tivisis came into view. The city appeared to be fashioned of silver and gold, with rooftops of sparkling gems: indeed, Pavanan Munif thought to himself, a crown fit for an empire.

Soon the ship found the harbor and Munif could see the marketplace beyond the crowded quays. The busy streets with long, wide walkways were alive with color and movement. Vendors hawked their wares, displaying rich, brightly hued cloth, mounds of ripe fruit, and birds of fabulous plumage from faraway lands. Even from this distance, Munif could see the glint of copper and brass. Everywhere he looked he saw myriad hues; and the scent of countless perfumes permeated the air. Maidens with veiled faces glided among the throngs of traders, sailors, and soldiers.

Munif watched as laborers on the docks unloaded vessels of every conceivable size and design. He could see longships from Khorbard, cogs from Ruinart, and caravels of the Rajani. Many of the ships bore scars from sailing treacherous passages to reach the city.

The end of the voyage was most definitely in sight.

Munif helped two others coil the ropes from the lateen sails as crewmen scuttled across the deck and up into the rigging. The easiest of the tasks was behind him; what lay ahead would be difficult. Once the ship was unloaded, the crew would be off to enjoy the pleasures and delights of Tivisis.

Munif shared no such luck.

There weren't any free moorings large enough to hold the vessel, and since their ship was third in line, Munif knew it would be nightfall before they set ashore.

The summoners, however, did not intend to wait.

As he watched, Hersí tossed three coins to the old mariner. He seemed to know exactly what the summoner had in mind, and when the captain was engaged elsewhere, he led the summoners to the back of the dhow where one of the tenders was already being lowered into the water. Hersí climbed down the rope ladder and claimed a seat at the prow. Munif watched all this, cursing under his breath. He would have to follow. Then he noticed Bashír standing by the rail, wearing a concerned expression.

Not good, thought Munif. He had counted on the two separating once they'd reached shore. Munif decided to go with Hersí.

"Wait," Munif called out to the mariner. "The boat can hold another."

He jumped into the tender and threw two *dirans* at the old man, avoiding the summoner's gaze. The mariner pocketed the coins before dipping the oars into the water.

Munif wiped his face with the back of his sleeve as he debated what to do next.

7

THE AIR was filled with a cacophony of voices.

Just beyond the dock, the port teemed with vendors; their booths, tents, and tables occupied every available space, creating a miniature city of their own. A confusion of scents and sounds overwhelmed Munif's senses.

He paused a moment to put each foot down several times on the solid ground, as if to be certain it was truly there. He kept his distance from the summoner—but close enough that he could still follow. Hersí walked slowly for several minutes as if he were trying to get his bearings. Munif took advantage of Hersí's momentary idleness and slipped into a nearby fruit stall.

Munif was finishing a slice of sweet melon, licking the juice off the fingers and wiping the corners of his mouth with the heel of his palm when suddenly Hersí took off running. Munif hesitated for a moment before tossing the melon rind away and racing after the summoner. He was well aware that Hersí, feigning languor, had been watching him all along. The chase took Munif down a narrow alley that avoided the central market, toward the more distant quarters of Tivisis.

As Munif followed, the foot traffic flowed easily; it required very little effort to keep the distinctive black robe in sight. Within minutes, the summoner came to a stop and knocked on the door of an undistinguished two-story building. Munif strained to see who had let Hersí in, but to no avail; he was unable to glimpse the entrance from where he was standing.

Sighing, Munif studied his surroundings in an attempt to identify where the chase had led him. He stretched, feeling the pulled muscles and pop of aging joints. An overwhelming urge to abandon his task hit him hard.

He could feel the sweat beading on his face, the dryness in his mouth despite the succulent melon; the slight tremor in his hands. And he knew his symptoms weren't due to the oppressive heat, or to fear.

No—there was only one reason for them, and only one solution.

Affyram would soothe his nerves—take the edge off a bit. He could partake and escape for a while. It would be easy to find a provider—surely there was one within sight of the building. The summoner wasn't going anywhere.

He had time—

It would be so pleasant—but Munif shook his head.

No.

The demon would have to wait.

"YOU ARE certain they remain unaware."

It was not a question.

Munif sat with three men at a table tucked away in the recesses of a cavernous coffeehouse. He had positioned himself against the wall, close to a small window with a clear view of the Laenidor Sacellum. The place was crowded, but no one had seen Pavanan Munif enter, save the three who offered him a chair. He looked at the men, each with dusky clothes and a hardened face—they could have been brothers.

They exchanged introductions, all false names to be sure. Munif waited until the server left the *cava* before speaking. His tone belied his noncommittal expression. He repeated his inquiry. "You're absolutely sure no one knows?"

Munif peered into the eyes of the man on his right. They were intelligent, cautious, ready. The agent's hair, like the others', was cropped short, his face dark brown from the sun and stubbled with a beard that had not seen a razor in days. He was dressed in drab clothing worn for too long without a wash.

"The Carac was not difficult to track, once we had the information from Burj al-Ansour," the agent said. "He's been under constant watch."

Directly across from Munif, the second agent looked up from his Tivisisí coffee. "Tonnás said the summoners would arrive within a fortnight. He was not wrong."

As patrons moved past them, the conversation took a more cautious turn. Munif lowered his voice. "What about the alchemist?"

"I allowed her to complete her work as instructed," said the third agent. "I assumed we needed the orbs to be taken at the same time as the summoners."

Munif thought for a moment before replying. "Yes, to make the case clearer for the Majalis. The ban remains in place, despite the passage of time."

The second agent scoffed. "Yet the wicked do not cease their wickedness, regardless of the consequences."

The first agent pondered a moment before looking up. "It will not be easy—taking them. This I know."

Munif shrugged and gave him a bitter smile. He felt on edge. "But we will. There are no options here. I've said enough—all here are capable, that is why you were chosen. It's time for you to leave."

The other three agents heeded his words, quietly departing

in unison and leaving Munif alone with his thoughts. He stood, and the room seemed to tilt sideways. His head swam and his stomach lurched.

"Damn, you look the a drunkard or fool," he muttered to himself. Shaking his head, he realized his next task would have to wait a while longer.

Munif would need every bit of his remaining energy simply to reach his room and fall into a much needed sleep.

9

THE SKY above Tivisis was black.

Across the city, thousands of oil lamps adorned the streets and bridges like strands of luminous pearls, each orb shimmering white-gold in the night. Over the rooftops and domes rose dim silhouettes of soaring spires, high turrets and slender minarets all but lost in shadow. Cool air lay thick and heavy in abandoned squares and parks. There was a pervasive hush—a whispering stillness.

Two shadowy figures moved silently through twilight corridors until they came to an alcove near the Chantry of Domòs, which concealed a narrow stairway to the catacombs.

Slowly they made their way down carved stone steps worn smooth with decades of use. The passage was filled with the sound of water trickling down the rough-hewn walls and dripping from countless cracks in the ceiling. The descent was slick and treacherous as the two made their way down to a small antechamber and then deeper into the tombs. With no fear or mistake, the summoners traced an unseen footpath through the labyrinth of caves and tunnels to a sunken cistern.

There they found it.

Cut into the eastern wall was a niche. As the hooded figures neared, the echo of their footsteps broke the silence of the cistern. Pale light pierced the darkness.

A door opened. They entered without a word.
Outstretched hands welcomed them.

70

THE NET was cast.

Munif caught a glimpse of the morning sun from the balcony. The whitewashed flat where he had slept was unadorned and simple, yet it was welcoming in its warmth, dryness, and stability under the feet.

Very soon now.

Word had already come to him that the ebony-skinned foreigners had remained stationary and isolated for the past day, recovering from the voyage. He was more confident now than at any previous time in the mission that he held the advantage.

After he breakfasted on bread with olive oil, honey and butter, along with a minted green tea and raw sugar, Munif took advantage of the ample floor space to resume his training regimen. He was happily surprised to discover that he'd lost little of his flexibility or strength despite the neglect of the past few weeks.

It was amazing, he thought, how rapidly he could recover with food and sleep. No longer apprehensive and distracted, Munif's spirits were renewed, his focus strong and determined. The call of *affyram* was fading.

He would not run after it.

Munif heard the sound of footsteps outside the door. He hurried over to it and stood by the hinges, on the balls of his feet, tense and ready. The handle turned and the door opened; Fajeer Dassai entered the room. Munif relaxed, but only slightly.

Dassai spun and raised an eyebrow at Munif's aggressive stance. He closed the door behind him and said, "Peace be upon you, Pavanan Munif. It's been a long time."

"Indeed, Fajeer, it has," Munif responded with a half-smile.

"You look rested. I see my aid has done you some good."

"Your help has been considerable—and well appreciated. I could not have survived without it." Munif padded barefoot to the small table where his pack stood open. He pulled out a linen shirt and put it on.

Dassai clasped his hands in front of him and ran his eyes slowly over the room while Munif finished dressing.

"I cannot claim the credit. I just act upon what is given me. I received word early on about the Carac and have been alert to their actions ever since. I am glad to see they've made it past the Slen Thek and White Palm. Had the assassins gotten to them, there is no telling how much it would have cost."

"If they would have taken the bids at all." Munif enjoyed the coolness of the tiles beneath his toes for a moment longer before shoving his feet into his worn shoes. He'd have to find another pair soon. "The Slen Thek, yes; the White Palm, highly doubtful," he continued. "The summoners would have been gutted and left as a feast for crows."

"There is little doubt that that is true," Dassai said. "But alas, they did avoid capture. They will be easy prey now."

Munif raised his eyebrows; even he was not that confident. "What do we know of their true plans?"

"Not much. I know little more than you—but I do think they're plotting something here in Tivisis." Dassai paused. Then, almost as an afterthought, he added, "Just what that mission is, I'm not sure, though surely it does not bode well." He frowned.

Munif could tell Dassai's mind was elsewhere. "And what of these containers they have requested?"

"Hmm, a diversion, perhaps? Or a means of escape? It's possible they've foreseen the actions of the Jassaj and have been told to secure it and use it against us."

Munif finished dressing. "Their powers are formidable; there is no mistake about that," Munif said softly. "And we must be prepared to defend against whatever they have planned."

"True, and that is why we must wait. We must learn a bit more before moving on them. Have the scrying sigils been marked?"

"Yes, on two of the walls in the flat. Though I suspect that they would take no chances and search the place. I can't imagine the sigils going undetected."

"And that is where you must learn to trust in me. Our man has been instructed to place false marks over the real ones. Once those are removed, the others will remain secure. The plan is safe and will hold."

Dassai is confident. Perhaps too confident? Munif wondered. Only time would tell. "So, we must wait until then?" he asked pointedly.

"Yes. You and your agents will lay the ambush as we gather the information from the meeting. I will give you the location soon, my friend."

"We'll be ready," answered Munif, glancing at the door.

Dassai acknowledged the unsubtle hint with a wry smile and turned to leave. "I expect nothing less from you, Pavanan." Dassai opened the door and stepped out. Just as it closed, he said, "Stay alert, and ready to leave at any time."

Munif remained silent.

11

IT WAS a bright, cloudless morning.

No longer confined, the summoners moved swiftly. They crossed Cannuan Square and followed a path that skirted the city wall and turned eventually into to a narrow, winding, upward-climbing street.

The old quarter of Tivisis clung to a hillside high above the sea. This was all that remained of the ancient city after the great earthquake centuries before. Crossing a wide bridge and leaving the thick stone walls of the new city behind, the summoners passed under the arch of the gateway and back four hundred years in time.

Tivisis was a place of stark contrast. Within the walls of the new city, great buildings gleamed, and the cobblestone streets sparkled with bits of embedded quartz. The old quarter was filled with dark alleys, twisting dead-end thoroughfares, and tortuous staircases. Few outsiders trod here.

High-walled houses—each hardly distinguishable from the next—cut a swath of stone across the skyline. Sunken streets hidden in the shadows were choked with debris. Even so, there were hints of beauty. At the top of steep steps, inviting doorways beckoned. Flowers overhung the balconies; fleeting glimpses of garden terraces, blossoming citrus, and pomegranate trees could be seen.

The summoners, immune to the surroundings, did not pause.

Despite being pressed in on all sides, the two, still cloaked in black, managed to weave their way through the crowded streets. Hersí was aware that some of the people shuddered involuntarily as they passed, and it pleased him. They needed a taste of fear.

The summoners realized that the timing of their arrival had been perfect, despite—or perhaps because of—the storm. They maintained a careful watch to be certain they were not being followed.

Each paid little heed to the murmur of commerce around them, taking care to avoid the many carts and stalls as they climbed farther up the hillside.

They continued past a deserted square, filthy and eerily silent. No horse-drawn carts traversed the narrow streets beyond. Even at the height of the day, the place was all but deserted, and crowded with shadows.

They crossed the street and entered a run-down, two-story house. They ignored the lurid offers from the harlots in the foyer and made their way upstairs to the second floor.

The hallway at the top of the stairs was squalid and dim. The wall coverings were peeled back to reveal etched warnings and obscene epithets. The worn floorboards exuded the unmistakable scent of stale urine. Drunken men and young girls long lost to innocence coupled in the shadows, their sinewy, underfed limbs intertwined in pathetic embraces.

Hersí led the way up the stairs with Bashír immediately behind, the carnal moans ringing in their ears. They reached the dimly lit door at the end of the corridor, and Hersí knocked three times. After a moment the door opened, and they slipped into the apartment.

They closed and locked the door behind them.

12

HERSÍ STUDIED his host through the haze of perfumed smoke.

Raviel Danoir was a short, rat-faced man from Sommel with gray hair and brown-yellow teeth. He scurried over to the solitary window and locked the shutters, then turned and peered into the shrouded faces of the summoners.

They responded by slowly drawing back their cowls. Danoir gasped; Hersí nodded in acknowledgement. It was obvious the man had never seen Carac before. Each of the summoners' skin shone like black lacquer, his head shaven except for a stiff tuft at the base of the skull. Both bore vivid ceremonial tattoos that began between their large amber eyes, crossed their foreheads, and continued down their cheeks and necks to disappear under the collars of their cloaks. Hersí knew their appearance had an unsettling effect on others, and it was no different now.

Danoir took a step back, his eyes darting from one summoner to the other.

"Carac summoners," he whispered. "Then the time has truly come!" He took a deep breath.

"It has," said Hersí.

"Your kind has not been seen in Tivisis for many years." Danoir glanced at the three wooden chairs beside his sloping table. "Forgive me, please sit down," he said, pulling out the chairs. "I was told you would arrive three days ago. I was beginning to wonder if you were coming at all."

"We were delayed by the storm."

Danoir grunted, seeming unsurprised. The summoners did not sit, but Danoir did and lit a pipe packed with sweet-scented herbs. "Tivisis has been overrun by spies," he said, "and the *sufis* speak. They know you are here."

"What of the containers?" Bashír said, approaching the table. "I trust you had no difficulty obtaining them."

"None beyond the risk of my life; such items are not easily come by," Danoir said. He nodded toward the corner behind the men. "They're in a secret compartment under the cabinet."

He started to stand, but Hersí held up his hand and walked over to the cabinet. After locating the hidden release, he opened the door in the wall, reached inside and pulled out two palm-sized, ornately decorated glass orbs.

Danoir stood. "I have been assured that they were properly prepared," he said. "The alchemist spared no effort. Each has been inspected many times."

Hersí set the orbs on the table and looked at them more closely. Danoir lit an oil lamp as Bashír joined them.

"What about the house?" Bashír inquired without looking away from their prize.

"It has been ready for weeks now," Danoir said.

Hersí reached into his robes and pulled out a leather bag. "Here is your remaining payment," he said, emphasizing the last word as though it were a pejorative. He opened the bag and pulled out a small vial. "There's also this," he said, handing the vial to the old man. "Use it if arrest seems inevitable. It is quick—and there will be no pain."

Danoir swallowed hard. "I ... do not wish to die."

Bashír's mouth curved into a smile devoid of deceit or falsehood. "One simple life—even if it is your own—is worth the sacrifice to ensure that the mission is completed."

Danoir's face paled. "Yes, for you, perhaps. But I must stay in Tivisis where I will be in constant danger. As for you, well ... you might not ... " His voice faltered.

Bashír's smile faded. "Then perhaps you had better take the vial now."

Danoir coughed weakly.

"Understand this," Hersí said. "You will welcome death should we fail."

Danoir nodded.

"Good," Hersí said. "We will depart soon. But first we'll rest and take a meal with you."

Danoir scrambled out of the way as the men shed their robes in preparation for the arcane pre-rituals.

Seizing the opportunity, Danoir snatched the leather bag from the table and hurried toward the door. As he reached for the handle, Bashír spoke.

"Danoir?"

The man turned. Bashír held out the vial. Danoir's shoulders slumped as he returned to the table. He reached out a shaky hand and took the vial, handling it as though it were a venomous spider.

"You'll need this ... just in case."

THE SUMMONERS were on the move again.

Pavanan Munif and the three Jassaj saw them leave the flat in the old quarter. The summoners turned the corner and hurried through an alley to the main thoroughfare with Munif and the Jassaj close behind.

Munif had a plan.

They would funnel the Carac to a dead end street where surrender would be the only option. The plan was simple, effective, and minimized any collateral damage.

Munif was sure of his intuitive abilities—and he always heeded them. Yet, an odd feeling of dread gnawed at him. He shook it off, attributing it to the persistent stress of the past several days. The plan he'd devised left no escape for the summoners—unless they could fly. There was no reason to allow a trifling uneasiness to distract him now.

Munif and his company maintained the farthest distance possible between themselves and their quarry in order to avoid detection. But he could not help noticing that there was something odd about the manner in which the summoners moved; their gait was not that of men fleeing from danger. They ran smoothly and with purpose. Neither looked over his shoulder. Neither seemed to suspect they were being followed. So why did it seem as though the Carac were leading them? Munif became anxious; a sense of foreboding continued to distract him.

A small object dropped from beneath the robes of one of the fleeing men. And then a second fell. Munif slowed down. The Jassaj passed him without pausing. One looked back with raised eyebrows and tilted his head, indicating that the quarry was getting away.

One of the objects had lodged in a muddy footprint. Munif stopped, noting the surroundings. They were in a narrow alley. A filthy grate ran along the edge of a walkway beside a tall building. Munif picked the object up gingerly, fingering what appeared to be pumice. There was a strange odor to it, similar to rotten eggs. It crumbled from porous rock to ash but was not hot to the touch. Something about the stone was familiar, but Munif could not quite place it. When he realized that the chase had gone on without him, he quickly set off to rejoin it.

He put on a burst of speed, hoping to regain precious seconds. He could see the Jassaj closing in on the summoners. They had trapped the Carac with no means of escape. The summoners paused briefly, then turned to face the three Jassaj.

Munif was suddenly aware of a change in the air. *Something is wrong,* he thought. And for reasons he did not understand, he made a sudden, unexpected decision. "I cannot be seen by the summoners," he muttered to himself.

"If you make one move, you will die," said one of the Jassaj to the Carac.

Then everything went terribly wrong.

14

"ALA'I PROTECT ME."

An inhuman scream erupted from the shadows of the cowls where the summoners' faces should have been.

Munif knew at that moment that he and his agents, not the summoners, were the prey.

The low screeching wail made the hair on Munif's body stand up in terror. From beneath the folds of cloth, a pulse of white-hot light issued forth and engulfed the Jassaj. Hot wind blasted past Munif's legs, to be sucked into the entities that rose before him.

He dove head first toward the filth-ridden grate, throwing it up and sliding under it, letting it clang into place above him. The fate of the other agents was out of his control. As soon as he slid inside the grate and tried to curl up, he realized it was not large enough to protect one person, let alone two. He felt warm blood flowing down his forehead as his head and shoulders collided with the stone wall. Even with his eyes closed, he could see the bright light, and he knew what was coming. He tried in vain to pull his legs under the grate as he curled into an awkward fetal position.

Munif could feel the rush of flames overhead. He heard the

piercing screams of the men as they burned alive. He tried to shrink back farther under the grate but the flames were too intense. He felt them lick at his legs below the knees, and he screamed.

Although the entire attack lasted a few seconds, Munif lay there much longer, swimming in and out of consciousness. His life passed before him: he saw himself as a child, running and playing with other children beside a small brook. Then, without warning, he faded back into reality and tasted the salty tang of blood.

Slipping back into a dream state, he saw himself as a young man courting his first love. They were on a swing in a garden and he was holding her hand. Munif remembered that incident vividly and the emotional turmoil that had resulted when the relationship ended. Again, he fell back abruptly into reality, and the acrid smell of smoke and burning flesh filled his nostrils.

Finally, he opened his eyes.

Although the pain had lessened considerably, Munif knew he was not yet out of danger. Uncontrollable shivering told Munif that his body was in shock. He had to seek immediate help, but he wasn't sure he could do so under his own power.

His arms were wrapped around his head. They were stiff and sore as he moved them to investigate the area below his knees. His lower legs and feet were still there. He breathed a sigh of relief that became a strangled gasp of pain. He couldn't see the injuries, but it felt bad. Despite this, he still had his duties.

He looked around in the dim light and realized he had miscalculated the size of the grate. The opening was below street level, and the place where he was lying, though cramped, could accommodate several bodies.

He began to roll slowly and carefully until he was flush against the back wall of the grate. His breath whistled through his teeth each time his raw skin made contact with the rough surface. Once he had righted himself, he reached up and gripped both sides of the grate. A noise outside sent him scuttling back down and away from the grate.

The time he spent waiting seemed an eternity. Munif listened as footfalls echoed on the stone. Someone had entered the terminus, walking slowly past him. Munif watched as a squat man inspected the remains of the other three agents. Munif could see the bodies were reduced to ash, their charred figures lying forever frozen.

The squat man seemed pleased with the results, and a swell of hatred surged within Munif. The man frowned and inspected the summoners' handiwork again. As he searched, he seemed to grow more frantic. Munif managed a grim smile as the man began muttering to himself.

"It cannot be! There are only three here? It's impossible."

The man walked in a circle around the charred remains of the three bodies. He knelt to scrutinize the scene further, his back to Munif.

"What can I do? I cannot tell him, I am a dead man if I do. The *Lamia'nār* had to work! There is no way he could have survived. He must have escaped somehow."

The man searched, looking into windows and peering down alleyways. Munif held his tongue and did his best to squeeze himself deeper into the grate. If the squat man spied it and happened to look inside—

The man let out a cry of frustration that bordered on rage. There was a clang of metal. Munif risked another glance outside, holding his breath.

The man had picked up a long, flat piece of metal that had been dislodged from one of the buildings during the blast. He poked at one of the agents' bodies until it fell over and shattered against the stones. He struck viciously at the remains, yelling in fury, until all that was left was powdery chalk.

Rage filled Munif. Still, he did not move as the man beat the remains of the second and third agent until they too were mounds of ash.

Munif closed his eyes and focused on his future—a future

built on retribution. He listened as the man continued to flail at the remains of the three agents, until finally he tired, panting harshly, catching his breath. Then at last he left, his footsteps fading into the distance. The alley grew silent.

Even in his anger, Munif knew this squat little man was not the source of the attack. He used his upper body to pull himself out of the grate. He lay on his back for a few moments to catch his breath and inspect the damage. He'd managed to escape with severe burns, but no muscle damage. The thin layer of linen that clothed his legs had all but disintegrated, and blisters had formed over much of the reddened skin.

He stood carefully and looked one last time at his fellow Jassaj. In honor of their service, Munif raised his hand to his forehead and whispered a prayer.

There was nothing else he could do.

They were all dead.

IT WAS just past midnight.

The two summoners slipped out of the room and moved into the hallway. It appeared to be abandoned save for one man sleeping propped against the wall, a bottle held loosely in his hand. The summoners crept past the drunkard and down the back steps out to a deserted back street. The night was cool, and there was a biting wind. The echoing refrain of fellahmin music floated into the alley. Although the Jassaj were dead, the summoners knew not to become complacent; so they set out in opposite directions in order to elude any other spies.

The men moved with purpose, knowing their final obstacle had been removed. Assuming Fajeer Dassai kept his promise, they would have no difficulty finding their way out of the city. Soon they would be in the safe house that had been prepared for them several farsangs northward, in the hilly lands beyond Tivisis. Still, they remained wary.

Hersí felt confident about their apparent success. He wondered briefly if the three Jassaj who'd been consumed by the magical fire had time to realize what was happening to them as they were engulfed in flames by the *unnālíí* spell. Secretly, he hoped they had; he had nothing but distain for the Qatani people. His kind, those from Carac, would no longer be viewed with contempt while the Jassaj were exalted. Their mission would garner the summoners both awe and terror.

As Hersí continued on his path, he thought about the discussion he'd had with Bashír shortly before their departure. Bashír fretted that the plan might fail and those who'd been pursuing them were not dead. "I'm worried about what will happen to us if they indeed live," he said. Hersí assured him that the Jassaj had not survived.

"The *Lamia'nār* consumed every living thing there," he assured Bashír.

Despite these reassurances, Bashír was worried about being caught and concerned that the entire mission was still at risk. And he was afraid that if they were captured, they would suffer a pain worse than that experienced by the Jassaj they'd killed.

It was a promise.

THE SUMMONERS traveled northward.

Darkness revealed little as the two summoners moved through the night, leaving the gates of Tivisis behind them. They'd spent the day in a flat on the northern edge of the city, near the Lisbarre Cathedral, Faliini Monuments, and the plaza of commerce. Many of the buildings in this quarter were reserved for dignitaries, and offices gave way to the houses of nobles and merchants. From dawn to dusk this was a busy thoroughfare with many people passing through it to the port and the lofty towers at Tivisis' core. Now the cobblestone roads were quiet and empty.

The summoners climbed the steep road that separated the mainland from the sea. Between two sets of rocky ridges lay a succession of valleys, and the road dropped into the first one to meander for some distance beside a slow-moving stream.

This wide valley was planted with fields of oats. These farms supplied Tivisis with grain; they kept bread on the tables of those who could afford it. As the Carac continued, the cobblestones gradually became more worn and broken, until a well-traveled dirt road stretched out before them. They kept to the main path running northwest, aiming for a series of steeply rising ridges barely discernible in the distance: the foothills of the Tayar Mountains.

At the center of the valley, a small village divided the fields of grain from the pastures set aside for livestock. The sole purpose of the place was to provide for the transport of freshly harvested foodstuffs to Tivisis.

A cricket chirped in the darkness. A bull snorted from a corner pen. A mange-ridden dog trotted up but quickly turned and retreated as it caught the scent of the travelers. The two men moved on steadily without stopping for rest or a meal.

They crossed a stone bridge over the Lialín River, making their way to the far side of the valley, where a steep, narrow path into the hills gave most travelers pause. The road was constructed with multiple switchbacks to prevent caravan accidents. The shadowy figures pressed on. As they climbed higher, the deep ebony of night receded, and the horizon showed the first signs of morning, lightening into shades of blue. As the stars faded, the summoners reached the top of the ridge. Below them stretched a spectacular panorama.

On the other side of the valley, stony foothills ascended to the precipitous mountains beyond. In the gray mist of morning, a

massive structure of rock revealed itself on one of the promonto-
ries. This was their destination, and now they began the arduous
trek down the ridge that would lead them there.

Down in the heart of the vale, they crossed a sturdy bridge.
Beneath them, a swiftly moving stream divided the valley. Immediately past the bridge, they left the road for a treacherous footpath through the woods.

It was here, among the trees shrouded in mist, that the men
spotted an abandoned building. It was a small stone house; it abutted several fields that spanned the distance between itself and the
great edifice that was their destination. They stepped inside, making no effort to announce their presence.

The house was much larger within than the dilapidated exterior had led them to expect. It consisted of two rooms, both empty.
The corners and the door frames were choked with cobwebs and
covered with a thick layer of dust. Hersí opened the shutters of a
large window and peered out. He could just make out the outline
of the stone fane at the top of the hill.

The fane near Burj al-Ansour housed many *fakirs* who sought
to become *misal'ayn sufis*. Lights flickered from small windows,
and Hersí realized they were candles placed there each day for
early morning devotions. Once the suns rose, the *fakirs* would
begin their day.

Hersí turned from the window and joined Bashír in preparation for the ritual. The Carac moved without hesitation, despite
the fact that neither had performed the spell previously. Hersí
watched in silence as Bashír knelt and drew the protective sym-
bols—looking closely for any mistakes. As Bashír drew the first
circle, with a second around it, they broke the silence briefly to
whisper an incantation.

Once the circle was completed, Hersí carefully drew the
two orbs from beneath his robes and set them in the center. He
returned to Bashír's side and knelt beside him.

Together they chanted the invocation.

17

FOR A few minutes, nothing happened.

Gradually, the room returned to darkness, save for the orbs, which began to glow fiery red. The summoners began the second part of the spell; the orbs pulsed more intensely with each new word. As they completed their incantation, the globes hissed and swelled. From their place within the protective circle, the summoners watched as a veil of copper smoke rose from each orb in the center circle. Slowly the smoke condensed, metamorphosing into two menacing shapes—damnable things wrested from the depths of a hellish abyss.

The two forms grew larger within the haze until they towered over the kneeling summoners. The mist of ash cleared to reveal two gigantic, demonic creatures. They appeared to be a combination of rat and boar, their bodies covered with leathery skin and wiry black hair. Curved, yellowish tusks protruded from their wart-covered faces, and their malevolent red eyes fixed on their masters'. The creatures rose slowly to their hindlegs. Both summoners noted that there were sharp claws on each foot. The demons made no effort to cross the crudely drawn line that kept them within the smaller magical circle.

One of the demons spoke, its hot breath reeking of decaying flesh. "You have called upon us, 'Those who know our true names'. What is it you seek?" Its voice was low and guttural, as if spawned from the very bowels of Nürr.

The summoners stood and faced the demons without fear.

"I offer a reward for your service," Hersí said as he pointed out the window. "Take the clerics and any others with them. You will find them laboring on the hillside. Kill them. Kill them all."

"This request commands a high price," the second demon said.

"The veil of the *shaitr* is lifted. You are free within the bounds of this world," Hersí said. "But," he continued, "for your part, you are to not spare a single life. Return here when you have finished … then you may call upon the others." He paused. "Leave utter destruction behind you … be ravenous."

The demons said nothing in response. Hersí sensed hesitation. Then the two creatures bared their razor-like teeth in a grimace. "Agreed," they said in unison.

Hersí closed his eyes for a minute and then, with a wave of his hand, he spoke a single word: *"Qatil."* With a great burst of speed, the two demons erupted from the center circle and leaped out the window. The summoners smiled.

The Carac would remain in the protective outer circle until the demons returned. They had a clear view through the window of what they knew was coming.

The demons charged toward the hillside.

RAHIB OMMAD was a sinner.

He allowed himself to commit just one transgression each morning. He would choose the plumpest dewberry from the best vine and eat it.

It was always only one berry—never two—and always from branches already straining under the weight of ripened fruit. In his mind, since he'd been doing this for several years now, it could hardly be considered a sin. Ommad admitted to himself that, in this, he did have a weakness. Still, he liked to believe he could atone for it somehow later in life. Even the *imams* had been young once, and he doubted they had been born without a few flaws of their own.

Ommad did his job well. He worked the vineyards and orchards of a collective famous for its grape and fruit wines. Profit from the wines allowed the clerics to expand their services and undertake more charitable projects. Over the years, this collective had focused on taking in young orphans, raising them with loving discipline, turning little street urchins and beggar-thieves into hardworking young men. Now, in an effort to do even more, the clerics were teaching rudimentary viniculture skills to the local farmers. In return, the farmers gave them produce, honey, and extra help during planting and harvest.

But the clerics were also hoping to dissuade others from burning or using *Azza*, despite the Rassan Majalis' strong endorsement.

From a young age Ommad had been taught that *Azza* offered protection from the Jnoun. For centuries the Sultans of Qatana had encouraged the burning of *Azza* as the only defense against the powerful entities that dwelt in the unseen realm. *Azza* took its name from its nature—it was said to be the very blood and essence of Ala'i, shed when he defeated the Jnoun and removed them from the mortal world. As long as men used *Azza*, the Jnoun could not cross the barrier. This practice had become commonplace in the islands of Miranes', perpetuated by pressure from the long line of Sultans.

Ommad had learned from the *imams* however that the legend of the Jnoun had been perverted. But because the lies had been repeated so frequently throughout the years, they had achieved the force of truth—hence it was common knowledge across the kingdoms of Mir'aj that *Azza* would preserve the barrier and prevent the Jnoun from crossing over.

In the predawn light, Ommad joined the orderly procession through the gates of the *sehan*. He was warm in his heavy wool garments, his hands clasped in the long sleeves as he savored the smell of the distant ocean. The group split in two as it reached the outer fence, half of the order setting off to toil in the vineyards, Ommad and the others to prune the orchards. He smiled to himself, already tasting the sweet tang of his forbidden fruit.

Ommad returned to the spot he'd left yesterday at the evening call to prayer. Working with expert precision, he pinched the cool, thick leaves with fingers permanently stained by berry juice. He lopped off branches with a tool he'd forged in seasons past. He kept it sharp, and it bit through thick branches as if they were slender stalks. The fields were silent save for the dignified shuffle of cloaks swirling through the long grass as other *rahibs* went about their tasks. Dawn brightened slowly into early morning as the first sun rose.

Then he saw it.

The dewberry was a fine specimen, red, glistening, and bulging with juice, outshining the others clustered around it on the branch. Today's private transgression would be worth any consequence, whatever it might be. Ommad smiled, imagining a whole orchard full of *imams* as secretly mischievous young *rahibs*, each stealing and savoring just one fruit. Just like this one.

Even as his eager fingertips brushed against the fruit, a shadow engulfed him. Certain he'd finally been caught at his daily delinquency, he turned with a guilty grin, expecting at least a glint of humor behind the frown.

Ommad's grin gave way to horror when he saw what cast the shadow. Behind him loomed the thick, hairy back of a demon as it scooped up a nearby *rahib*—was it the soft-voiced Jamid from Sarahin?—and snapped the boy in two with strong jaws before he could even scream.

Without thinking, Ommad dropped to the ground and rolled beneath the briar. Deep instinct told him to make himself as small as he could. Also without thinking, he held the handle of his pruning tool in a soldier's grip. Where had he learned that?

Workers shrieked all around him, their familiar voices unrecognizable with panic. The demons attacked mercilessly, killing one *rahib* after another with the power and speed of lions and the dark intention of something much worse. Defense was impossible. No one had time to shout warnings; there was nowhere to run. With no belief that this could ever happen, and with no training in how to react, the *rahibs* stood helpless, stumbled blindly in circles, or crashed into bushes as the demons cut them down, tearing their bodies apart with tusks and claws. Screams reverberated through the valley, rising to unearthly wails or dying in wet gurgles. Everyone was slaughtered—peaceful clerics and hardworking farmers, even the group of orphans housed at the collective. The demons did not distinguish between holy and mundane, young and old, contented and ambitious. All fates ended in a scatter of broken bones and shredded flesh. Blood stained everything.

A few *rahibs* working farthest from where the demons began their slaughter understood what was happening. They ran for the safety of the fane's walls, robes snapping behind them, mouths wide with terror. But the demons were on them long before they reached the sanctuary, cutting them down as a scythe harvests wheat.

One young *rahib* tried to clamber up a tree. A sharp claw caught him in the back, cleaving gashes so deep his viscera bulged out between the severed muscles. As he hung head down from the tree, his entrails slithered along the lower branches and trunk, landing on the ground in a warm red pile.

Blood spilled between the cupped hands of another *rahib* as he knelt, rocking on his heels, trying to hold his mutilated face together, making the soft braying sound of a newborn camel. The demon turned as if irritated by the noise, swiping at him again from behind. The *rahib* slumped forward, his face striking the hard earth, an arm tearing free.

The demons bit, tore and slaughtered their way across vineyard and orchard, working with savage efficiency until every one of their prey had been mauled, maimed and bloodily killed. The corpses of the fallen lay strewn across the landscape, and the footpath was a crimson river.

The creatures surveyed their work with fiery eyes and twitching noses. Blood spotted their yellowish tusks, and their hides frothed with rank sweat. They paced among the vines, bushes, and trees, searching the carnage for any trace of movement. If a voice moaned or a foot twitched, they crushed and ripped the body, scattering its parts.

Ommad cowered small and still beneath his low-lying bramble, but not quiet enough. In shock, he'd hunched motionless as a stone during the slaughter, but in the ringing silence after the final death screams, he began to tremble. He was still clutching his pruning tool like a weapon when the huge clawed feet stopped in front of his hiding place.

The foliage jerked away, catching Ommad's robes and dragging him upright. The demon inspected him, determined that he was alive, and raised a clawed hand.

"No!" Ommad wailed, slicing the air with his pruning tool. The sharp edge caught the demon's wrist, digging into leathery skin. The creature paused for an instant, looking almost puzzled. Then it twitched its wrist, snapping the iron blade, and followed through with its blow.

Ommad's pain was brief, his final cry short.

19

THERE *WERE* others.

Twelve, to be exact. While Hersí and Bashír had been sent to Burj al-Ansour, they were not the only ones charged with this mission. They were each given this rare opportunity—a gift, to show the unbelievers. A true hand, not of some god that turned his back upon his children, but of *Pamankar,* the harbinger of things to come. He was destruction and despair, and they, the Carac, were his messengers.

Each of the summoners was at peace with his actions. Indeed, if tradition or training had permitted, they would have grinned like giddy boys. They were the true children of the god, the chosen ones. An adolescent looks to his parent for guidance and support, desiring to be true, faithful and obedient. And so the summoners basked in the approving glow of *Pamankar.*

Their actions were fair, they were just ...

They were *right.*

Before the second sun rose above the Curtain of Night, all the lands of Miranes' felt the power of the Carac. The hungry Ruwar demons ignored the panicked screams and pleas for mercy from those they hunted. Once summoned, they were ruthless in delivering the message: *Do not stray again.*

The summoners watched calmly as the creatures, bloodied from slaughter, paused in their rampage.

From their position within the protective circle, the Carac could see the outline of wine-terraced hills as the first sun began its ascent from behind them. As they watched, the demons returned. They stood in the clearing as if waiting for one final order. Hersí nodded in approval. Once full daybreak arrived, all evidence of the demons would disappear, banished to the darkness of the abyss. However, the new day had yet to fully appear.

The demons circled the house, coming together again at the open door. Neither man offered any challenge; they were content to watch the dawn break over the ridge.

"The first sun has still not risen," Bashír said, looking out the window. Just then, the entire ridge of the steep, rocky hill began to glow with the sunrise.

"And we will not see the second ever again," said Hersí, his voice low and calm. "Our duty is complete."

Bashír bowed in silence and steeled himself against the baying of the demons outside.

"Are you ready?" Hersí asked.

"Yes."

Bashír nodded again. The summoners cast one last look at the new sun. As they knelt and began to erase all traces of the protective circle, the silence deepened.

Their timing was perfect.

A faint tinge of a different light became visible on the distant horizon: the rising of the second sun. As he rubbed away the last of the protective circle, Hersí felt a shift in the air. Bashír stiffened beside him. The room was charged with tension as the demons neared the doorway, baying in gleeful anticipation.

The summoners would be allowed just enough time to finish the final part of their mission before departing for paradise.

It would occur with the full emergence of the second sun.

The demons separated as they approached, each choosing a summoner. Simultaneously, Hersí and Bashír lifted their arms in supplication, heads back, their black hoods slipping from their heads.

They welcomed the sun's gentle warmth on their faces.

WORD OF the slaughter had reached the city.

The bold architecture of Tivisis, the winding pathways, the terraces and wide courtyards, all faded into shades of gray as Munif moved with strong purpose. It had begun to drizzle, the last heaving breaths of some faraway storm, but the rain did nothing to alleviate the blanket-like humidity.

Munif walked steadily, his soaked outer shirt tied around his waist to cool his burns and hide his raw legs from sight. His pants and shoes had been ruined by the fiery blast, and he'd discarded both in the alley where he'd nearly been killed.

The pain of his wounds cried for relief. The familiar trembling and terrible thirst had returned. He needed *affyram*!

Munif had decided to shadow the squat man, knowing it would lead him to his target. Steeling himself against the agony and the hunger of his addiction, Munif was able to maintain a good distance without losing his target.

As he passed a darkened market, he made a quick detour and

obtained a pair of low shoes and a couple of blankets, tossing money at the vendor without counting it, his eyes remaining locked on his prey. With the wool cloth wrapped around his face and body, he felt more confidence about moving unnoticed in the streets and staying dry in the inclement weather.

Munif was hurting, but the pain ran much deeper than the injuries inflicted by the Lamia'nār. Despite the shortcomings of men and their rulers, Munif believed in the Jassaj—he trusted in the cause for which he fought. Now his faith was shattered. One of his own had turned against him, a brother-in-arms whom he had trusted completely. The more he thought about this, the angrier he became—fueling the energy of pursuit and eclipsing his yearning for *affyram*.

Munif could not get the screams of the dying out of his head. Their cries of confusion, terror, and dismay were forever etched in his mind: the wave of fire igniting them, the heat consuming their bodies. When Munif had looked through the grate, he'd been greeted by the horror of their remains—they'd been caught in mid-action.

Then the traitor had shown himself. Now that man was just up ahead, leading the way to his master—someone Munif knew could only be one person.

Fajeer Dassai.

The heavy mist turned to a soaking rain as Munif continued to shadow his prey through the streets. Munif was sure the man wasn't a professional. There was no sign of tradecraft; no sudden stops to stare at some meaningless item, no random turns to catch a glimpse of a too-familiar face. Munif shook his head. The fool didn't check even once to see if he was being followed. More likely, it was just greed which lured the man in too deep with the help of Dassai. But the job wasn't complete. He would go to his employer to report his failure, and would find out then just how expendable he was.

Pavanan Munif would use the employer to track down Dassai. He knew he must not let Dassai escape from Tivisis. Munif still needed to get word to the *misal'ayn* at Burj al-Ansour and alert Qatani authorities of the betrayal. But the location of the tower was miles away from Tivisis. By then, Dassai could have slipped away.

Once Dassai learned of Munif's survival, he would not be safe; all trust was now gone. To make matters worse, Dassai had many spies in place, and they would be used against Munif.

Over the years, Munif had come to know of key flaw in Dassai—he was a man who often overreacted and panicked easily. In this state of heightened fear, he would make mistakes.

If Dassai eluded him here, Munif would have to get to Burj al-Ansour and alert Riyyal before Dassai's lies could.

Munif had his own doubts.

21

RAVIEL DANOIR paused.

Winded and exhausted, he had finally reached his destination. His shoulders slumped.

It would be over soon.

The horses could smell him. Danoir made his way past the stalls, his shuffling feet destroying the carefully raked pattern in the dirt of the shedrow. Around him, he could hear the sound of disturbed animals. Hooves pawed nervously at straw bedding, and tails swished in agitation. Danoir could see the bared teeth, the tossing of manes. One trumpeted in defiance. Danoir wished he had the horse's courage.

In the rear of the stable was a tiny room with a small oil lantern that glowed brightly. A young boy lay sleeping on a cot nearby.

He prodded the boy roughly, startling him awake. Danoir pointed to the door, and the boy hastily got out of bed and left the stable. Danoir licked his lips and waited for his fate. He could feel his throat tighten. His heart thumped against his rib cage.

Niccolo Arzani stepped through the door, his robes hidden by a richly embroidered black cloak. He regarded Danoir with an ill-disguised sneer. Danoir opened his mouth to speak, but Arzani's venomous tone stopped him. "It failed?"

Danoir nodded, awaiting the tirade.

"Tell me everything you know."

Danoir explained it all, from the scream had he heard down the street, the three—not four—ash statues of the Jassaj, and how he couldn't find Pavanan Munif anywhere. Arzani remained silent as he listened. When Danoir had finished, Arzani reached into the folds of his garments. Danoir winced as the advisor tossed something at him, but he caught the object by reflex. He knew without checking that it was a bag containing the remainder of his payment. He licked his dry lips. "You must … I need refuge!"

Arzani was already shaking his head. "No, Danoir. I cannot give you sanctuary. Get out now. If you are seen in this city tomorrow, you will be tried and hanged as a criminal. You're finished in Tivisis."

Danoir stood with his mouth open for a moment before shutting it with resolve and turning on his heel. His best option was to leave tonight.

There might not even be enough time to gather his things, but his mind eased as he realized he had escaped with at least one possession.

His life.

22

MUNIF WATCHED from the shadows.

Unaware of the Qatani spy just a few feet away, the squat man quickly packed clothes into a canvas travel bag.

Danoir was so absorbed in packing—so relieved that he had escaped death—that he didn't react as Munif moved silently closer. He didn't turn even as Munif pulled his blade and stabbed him at the base of the neck.

Munif ran it through, hard and downward, severing bone, flesh and nerves. He could hear the muted gurgling of blood pouring into the man's throat. The death spasm was strong, clamping down as Munif struggled to pull the steel blade out. Danoir fell to the floor.

Munif paused, his senses alert.

He'd followed Danoir to the stables, hoping to overhear the conversation, but was unsuccessful. Still, it was clear the conspiracy went very high. Many had to be involved—perhaps even the lord of Tivisis himself. After Danoir left the stables, Munif followed him to his rundown flat and waited until nightfall.

Munif searched the disheveled room, but found nothing of use. He kicked a scattering of coins away and then thought better of it. With the lifeless eyes of Danoir staring back at him, Munif searched through the dead man's clothing, finding a small vial. He pocketed it, then gathered up the coins and dropped them into a small pouch.

Finding bread and water in one of the larders, he ate wolfishly, hoping to satisfy the pangs of hunger he'd been feeling for the past hour. The coppery smell of the man's blood did nothing to put off his appetite. When Munif finished, he rummaged through the wardrobes and found some linen cloth that he could use as bandages for his wounds. They would be loose on his legs, but not cumbersome.

One traitor down, one more to go, he thought.

Munif knew exactly where to find him.

23

ARZANI RETURNED to the house.

The house was located in the Palace Quarter between the Summer Citadel and the Palazzo Condesta. A labyrinth of alleys surrounded it, cut off from the rest of Tivisis by a high stone wall. Within were the residences of powerful merchant lords, city officials and magistrates, and a host of foreign emissaries.

Constructed over the course of centuries, every street in the Palace Quarter was framed by ancient buildings that circled each other in ever expanding rings. The streets were paved with hard brick, the sharp edges long eroded by endless streams of passing feet. The fronts of the buildings had once been whitewashed, but had darkened over the years to the dirty gray of chimney soot and neglect.

Toward the center, near Regent's Square, the streets became much shorter than those running along the outside edge of the quarter. Though it looked random, in fact it was a defensive measure put into place long ago. The twisty, narrow streets would prevent attacking soldiers from forming into large groups, stringing them out and subjecting them to ambush from any one of the dozens of passages that cut through the circular streets.

It was hopelessly confusing to newcomers, but Arzani knew exactly where he was going.

He opened the door and entered, scanning until he found what he sought—an entry to what he presumed to be the cellar. Pushing the heavy oak panel aside, he paused a moment to let his eyes adjust to the complete darkness below. Soon enough, his eyes had focused enough for him to see dimly, but he held the handrail and stepped gingerly down the creaking wooden steps. A curious mix of damp, musty, and sweet wine smells lingered in the air.

Reaching the bottom, Arzani strode forward, ignoring the old wooden racks holding dusty, forgotten bottles of wine. At the back of the cellar a drafty hole in the wall led to a well-built tunnel. Within minutes, he was sidling through a secret entrance on the lowest floor of the citadel.

Once in his private chambers, he scribbled a message and went to find a courier to pass it on to Fajeer Dassai, who he knew would be awake, even at this hour.

He did not have long to wait.

24

"WELL."

Arzani eyed Dassai. "It appears we have a problem. Pavanan survived."

He held up his hand as Dassai began to speak. "We don't know how, but his body was not among the dead," Arzani said, adding, "However, it is possible that he was behind the others and survived the blast, only to succumb elsewhere later."

Dassai ran his hands through his hair and shook his head. "No. No, that bastard lives, I can feel it. Damn him! We should have had someone there to take care of that possibility." His face flushed with anger. "You should have been better prepared!"

Arzani shifted in his seat. "It is pointless to lay blame now. It is done."

Dassai glared at him for a moment longer before heaving a sigh. "At least the Carac were successful. Their mission is achieved. Fear and panic will reign in the streets. On the other hand, we must do what we can to deal with Pavanan's escape. You must convince Galliresse that Munif acted of his own accord, killing his fellow agents and betraying the people of Tivisis. Make him wary of the intentions of the Jassaj and even the motives of the Sultan. Pavanan Munif must be blamed. It is the only way. Make him a wanted man throughout Givenh and all of Miranes'."

Arzani nodded. "It will be done."

He stared as Fajeer Dassai began to pace frantically, plotting his next move. "Yes. This will work. But showing that the Rassan Majalis was at the heart of it may serve us even better." Dassai pointed at Arzani, his eyes boring into the advisor. "You must make sure that Galliresse believes this comes from the Rassan Majalis and the Sultan of Qatana. Givenh will be convinced to turn against them."

"But will this not make Galliresse look incompetent as well?" Arzani asked.

Dassai shrugged, but did not look away. "What you do to undermine him is of no concern to me. Succeed, and this may seat you as the new Suffet of Tivisis, and all can still fall into place as I have planned."

Arzani's eyes gleamed with anticipation.

Dassai gave him a devil's grin. "Need I state clearly what will happen should you fail?"

The other man's eyes dulled as he contemplated the word.

"I must leave." Dassai said abruptly, spinning away.

"Where are you going?"

Dassai paused at the door. "I am of no more use here. My presence is a threat now. Tell Galliresse that I am returning to Cievv for a full account of the attacks. It would be best for him to believe it. You can reach me in Dorré if there is need. There is still more work to be done."

He slipped into the corridor, leaving Arzani to puzzle out his meaning.

Arzani knew Dassai would not return.

25

MUNIF WAS READY.

He'd closed in on Dassai. It hadn't taken long to find him. Munif perched on top of the bridge, watching as Dassai neared, oblivious. With perfect timing Munif leapt down on him.

Dassai's legs buckled. He fell hard on his hands and knees, grunting as the breath was knocked out of him. Rolling clear, Munif didn't give him a chance to catch a gulp of air. He punched both his fists down on Dassai's back, then flipped him over and slammed a knee into his chest to hold him down. "Fajeer, Fajeer," he said in a mocking tone. "That has always been your failing: you never look up."

Ignoring Dassai's struggle to breathe, he crossed his arms, grabbing the cloth around the man's neck with both hands, further choking off Dassai's windpipe. Munif took great delight in the look of surprise and pain on Dassai's face.

Dassai closed his eyes. "It is ... too late ... to stop it."

Munif suddenly went cold, relaxing his grip. "Too late to stop what?" He shook the prone man.

Dassai sucked in a breath. "The Carac went to ... They summoned ... just before dawn." His eyes opened and there was such finality in them that Munif recoiled. "It is done."

Munif looked up in horror as light from the first sun painted the sky red. Dassai took advantage of Munif's loosened grip, slipping both arms within Munif's, breaking the chokehold. Before Munif could react, Dassai slammed the heel of his left fist into his opponent's chin and pushed Munif's shoulder with his right hand. Munif crashed backward onto the pavement.

Still struggling to breathe, Dassai scrambled to his feet, giving Munif time to recover. Within seconds, they were facing each other again.

Munif struck first, shoving with his left hand and then striking Dassai in the throat with his forearm. He tried to slip his arm
under Dassai's shoulder to throw him back to the ground, but the
attack had slowed him. Dassai easily avoided the move, pushing
Munif off balance and scything his right leg at Munif's ankles.

Dassai connected cleanly, sending Munif crashing once again
to the street. Shards of pain stabbed through him as the blisters
on his calves burst open. Munif fought to stay conscious as agony
swept over him and blood flowed down his legs.

Dassai chuckled. "You also tend to distract easily. And,"
he said, sneering, "it appears you did not escape the fire
unscathed."

Dassai's voice had come from somewhere to his left. Munif
fought to regain his sight, frantically blinking to clear the fog.
He pushed himself upright and found Dassai looking at him, a sly
grin on his face.

"It's true," Munif said. "I didn't escape the fire unscathed. But
you won't escape here unharmed, either."

Dassai's smile dissolved as both men squared off once again.
Munif, struggling through pain that turned the edges of his vision
red, knew he did not have much energy left. Maybe enough for one
last strike, but that was all. It would have to be a killing blow.

He balanced himself the best he could, locking the fingers of
his right hand. With a tremendous scream born of pain and fury,
he launched himself at Dassai, the hard edge of his hand slicing
toward his foe's windpipe.

Too slow. Mere inches from his target, Munif felt his outstretched arm pushed away as Dassai easily sidestepped the blow
and locked his hand behind Munif's head, forcing him to look
toward the ground.

It seemed to take hours for Dassai's knee to come up. The first
blow crashed into the left side of his chest, cracking three ribs.
Munif would have fallen down yet again but for Dassai's grip.

The second stroke took him in the chin, and this time, Dassai let go. Munif's head snapped back, and as he fell he could feel teeth cracking and blood flowing from his shattered mouth.

Once again on his back, he stared toward the sky, feeling the blood pooling in the back of his throat. He could hear Dassai, but he could not move, let alone breathe. Dassai stepped into his view and looked down at him, his face shadowed as the first sun's rays lit him from behind. Dassai shook his head and waved in a mock salute. "Farewell, Pavanan Munif. Before the day is done, Tivisis will no longer welcome you. You have become the betrayer of its people—and you will be punished. Yes, you will."

Munif wanted to scream in protest, but the words did not come. Dassai stepped over Munif and disappeared, leaving him on the gravel.

Dassai was gone. The fight had cost Munif everything but his life, and even that was in question.

Pushing unconsciousness aside, Munif pulled himself together. He sat up, wincing against the pain and spitting his mouth clean. Running his fingers over his ribcage, he easily located the injury. Holding his side with his right hand, he used his left to lever himself to his feet.

Munif was grateful that Dassai had not bothered to take his weapons or his coins. He took off his robe with great care and folded it. Before he could do anything else, he needed to find a place to heal.

Beaten and betrayed, Munif limped away from the palace gate.

He also failed to notice the shadow that separated itself from the wall and began following him.

Part Four

WANTED

13.10.792 SC

7

CIRIS SARN was a marked man.

He was weary of his life and actions. The past plagued him, every day a living reminder of fate; cruel and twisted. His hour of judgment would come, soon perhaps. He would pay dearly for choosing this path. But for the present, Sarn had other, more immediate concerns that involved both his employers and his enemies.

Taking a moment to get his bearings, he adjusted the cloth that covered his mouth, the light fabric damp with sweat. Many travelers used facial coverings to protect themselves from the heat of the suns. It also served to keep his identity hidden from prying eyes.

Sarn neared the gates of Marjeeh, another powerful and wealthy sheikdom that stretched along the coast of the Crescent Cape. After killing one of Dassai's men in Pashail, Sarn had fled north—ignoring both Oranin and Havar where Dassai would no doubt be expecting him to return.

The spree of assassinations he'd committed in the last six months put him at constant risk— reckless retaliations against the machinations of a dangerous mind. But Sarn had no choice in the matter. Dassai dictated his actions, and the curse prevented him from doing otherwise. He was weak and vulnerable, and could not change anything. Yet.

He left the caravan road, soon coming to the southern gates of the city. Two guards stood there, bored with inactivity, their swords lying in their scabbards. Sarn pulled the scarf even more tightly around his face as he shuffled past them. He knew he could kill them before they could draw steel, but he preferred not to.

Neither of them gave a glance as he passed by them.

Continuing on, he soon came to a narrow aqueduct bordering the road. Farther along, a flat stone lay in the shade of a palm tree. Many others used this place to obtain clean water. Sarn dipped his waterskin into the aqueduct, filling it, then taking a large swallow. It was somewhat cool, and instantly revived his parched mouth.

Sarn contemplated his next move. He had thoughts of going farther north to Tanith where he owned a *riad*, but even that might not be safe; there was a good chance that a trap had been laid for him there. His safest course of action would be to seek refuge in Marjeeh, at least for the time being.

He contemplated the available contacts and safehouses that might be available there. His thoughts wandered to the vineyards. Recalling them brought back unpleasant images of its destruction and the confrontation with Dassai, followed by his killing of Hiril Altaïr. He gritted his teeth and shook his head as if to empty it of the unwanted memories. To this day, Altaïr's murder unsettled him. The actual killing did not bother Sarn so much as the reasons why. It had set off the series of vicious slayings by his hand, all strands in the web of Fajeer Dassai's sadistic schemes. And what part did the books play in this; what did Dassai want with them? *Should I have done what I did, leaving them there for someone else to find?*

Dassai had played Sarn to kill Altaïr, but failed to realize that Sarn could play the game just as well. A smile crept across his face. However, what had occurred in the months that followed weighed on the assassin. He was a marked man, the reward for his capture so high that there were all manner of potential takers. Jassaj from Qatana and the *siris* of the Rassan Majalis were expending every effort to apprehend or kill him.

Sarn was unaccustomed to the threats. He felt like a fool now. Dassai was not even in the same class as himself. And yet ... and yet, he'd succeeded in his designs. Sarn had been too complacent, too obsessed with finding peace. He'd allowed his single-mindedness to lapse—and had paid dearly for that mistake. So had his father. And Jannat.

He'd never been introspective; Sarn believed that his actions were made easier by avoiding self-examination. However, he'd spent more than twenty years under the thumb of Dassai, and even though he now possessed the key to his freedom, the goal seemed as elusive as ever. Was life more choice or destiny? Perhaps it was more plan than happenstance? These thoughts had, of late, interfered with his ability to focus, but the killing of Altaïr lingered with him the longest.

His mind filled with more questions than answers. Sarn knew he must abandon this self-inquisition if he was going to avoid his pursuers. No one in these lands mourned Hiril Altaïr personally; however, Sarn was sure that the *siri* was valuable and many would seek to avenge his death. Dozens, if not hundreds, were waiting for the assassin to make a fatal error. Sarn knew they would never stop hunting him.

He'd been on the run before. This was different. The stakes were raised, the gold too much for the greed that gripped the hunters. Now he was forced to spend his own wealth to keep safe. He would kill, if necessary, to remain in the shadows, but the less bloodshed now, the easier it would be to stay hidden. The question Sarn needed answered most was, where should he go next?

Sarn refreshed the waterskin once again, then wearily dragged himself upright. Resolved, he turned north, following the road into the heart of the city.

Perhaps he knew where to go for help, afterall.

SARN'S DESTINATION lay just within the walls of the city.

Flanked by tall square towers, Sarn moved quickly, passing through a labyrinth of dark corridors toward the north gates. Near the fortifications were the homes of wealthy merchant families, brilliant white *riads* hidden within a sea of palms, their fronds shading the green lawns and well-watered gardens. The lands beyond the walls were flat, covered with orange groves and date orchards that stretched toward the distant hills.

His eyes darted into the shadow above the scarf still pulled tightly across his face, glancing occasionally at the rooftops. His senses were at maximum alert. But he saw nothing.

While Marjeeh was not as familiar to him as the other sheik-doms, Sarn kept a number of reliable contacts in the city. He continued through the narrow streets and the bazaars jammed with traders selling their wares and street urchins looking to steal them. Sarn followed the road to the secluded house of Lueih Taghmaoui, an influential merchant.

Sarn rang the bell, letting the scarf drop. A servant answered, glancing inquiringly at the assassin. A look of abject fear came over his face; he slammed the door. Amused but not showing it, Sarn waited patiently. When Taghmaoui finally opened the door and saw his unsmiling visitor, his greeting was simple. "Shall we drink tonight in solemnity or in celebration?"

"A bit of both," Sarn replied. "But mostly in silence. I don't want to talk. I just want to drink myself to sleep." Taghmaoui motioned him inside, and Sarn welcomed the feeling of security that washed over him.

Taghmaoui did not project the manner of the wealth he possessed. Neither obese nor gaudily dressed, he wore light robes over a body well toned for his years. Women swarmed to his side, and offers of companionship—both legitimate and perverse—were always forthcoming. No one, as yet, suspected him of nefarious deeds, leaving him free to entertain as he wished. And so, as the heat of the day gave way to the chill of night, the two men passed a bottle between them until the fire grew cold, their eyelids heavy, and their breathing even.

He and Taghmaoui were not friends; they were something far more—men who understood each other. Someone Sarn could trust when he needed it most.

That time was now.

3

SARN WAS ALONE.

While Taghmaoui went out on business, the assassin slept. It was well past midday prayers before he finally woke. The house was empty, the servants having fled or hidden in their quarters. Sarn found the kitchen and ate there.

It was early evening when Taghmaoui returned and greeted him with genuine pleasure. Two servants soon followed, carrying baskets filled with various breads, cheeses, and several bottles of wine.

Taghmaoui also brought news. "A Rassan *siri* has been seen in the city," he said between bites of bread and sips of wine.

Sarn listened nonchalantly, leaning against a chair, a mostly untouched glass in his hand. He already was aware of this information but feigned ignorance, nodding slightly.

It was a game the two men had played for many years. At times, Sarn had had reason to employ Taghmaoui. He was a successful businessman, after all. Sarn was satisfied just to hear the information from the merchant, knowing the service would in some way be repaid, just as he was certain that this current hospitality would prove profitable.

Sarn took a piece of cheese from the table, swallowing it whole, then raising both wineglass and brow in his host's direction.

"It appears that the Majalis and others are seeking the assassin who murdered a man named Hiril Altaïr. They will pay handsomely for information leading them to the killer."

"This is true," Sarn said.

"And is it true that you have also been marked for death?" Taghmaoui asked carefully.

"Yes, but," Sarn replied, "I am worth much more alive." He smiled as sipped the wine.

"The danger will increase the longer you stay."

Sarn caught the subtle hint. "Why would they go through all that trouble just to capture the murderer of a spy?" he asked.

"This man was no ordinary spy," Taghmaoui answered. "It is said that he carried valuable documents. These were stolen upon his death."

"There appears to be an abundance of spies about," Sarn said with a smirk. "Those pursuing Altaïr's killer—and those lamenting lost opportunities in Pashail." Sarn could see Taghmaoui's look of surprise.

"Hiril Altaïr was of considerable importance to the Rassan Majalis," Taghmaoui responded, instantly becoming more serious.

"So it seems," Sarn said. "Though I care little for politics, word has it that Altaïr was valued by both the Rassan Majalis and Qatana."

"True, my friend. But more important, the information he carried elevated his status even more. Now many want to avenge his death because they feel cheated out of what was stolen."

"What do you think?" Sarn asked.

"I do not know what was taken—all that matters was that this information was not found. Altaïr was killed for their own reasons by whoever ordered his death; whatever he carried, they did not want it to reach the embassy."

"And hence the great effort expended to take his assassin out," Sarn said.

"Yes, and there are plenty of takers, depending on whether they seek the information for love of king or lust of gold."

"And what of those who desire both?"

"Pity them, for they will lose the race. Their passions are diluted. Those whose appetite is pure—for good or greed—have the greatest strength."

Sarn finished his glass of wine and poured himself another. He took a sip. It was some time before he spoke again, his voice reflecting his exhaustion.

"Where do I go?" Sarn asked. "How long before I am found again? Tanith is no sanctuary, yet I believe that is where I'm being led."

"I don't follow," Taghmaoui said, as if alarmed.

"I'm a puppet on a string. Fate is not in my favor; it's held in the hands of others." Sarn took another sip and smiled sardonically. "Perhaps it's held by no one."

"There are those I can contact who may be able to offer you aid. But you cannot stay in Marjeeh for long."

Sarn could not pry deeper. *It's obvious the merchant feels at risk,* he thought. *He's probably also worried about revealing the names of his contacts.* Sarn had to decide whether the merchant was now an asset or liability—and he had to do so without direct attachment to the man himself.

Sarn realized that if anyone were to profit from these recent events, it would be Taghmaoui delivering value to Sarn—not gaining anything from him. The merchant had made his alliance with the assassin many years before; but the past would be meaningless if Taghmaoui felt he could benefit more by turning Sarn over to his pursuers.

Sarn's eyes never left the merchant's face. *So what is it, Taghmaoui?* he mused. *Are you an ally, or a threat?*

It was obvious the merchant was thinking the same thing. Sarn's eyes dropped to his wineglass for a moment. He looked up at the merchant again. "So, it is possible, then?" he asked.

The merchant visibly relaxed. Sarn had done the right thing.

"'Can it really be done?' would be a better question," Taghmaoui answered. He sliced some cheese and crammed it into his mouth with a piece of bread. He continued talking while he chewed. "There are other killers to catch, but more gold is wagered in your favor than otherwise. They say you're to be feared because you have no heart."

"I had a heart once," Sarn said. "It was of little use to me."

Later, in bed, Sarn thought about the evening's conversation. He was glad he'd left the past alone, and he was pleased that Taghmaoui was willing to help him despite the lure of reward. He could not stay at the house long and upon his departure would have to proceed carefully, with so many still hunting him.

How much time did he have left? Sarn wondered.

Then he fell asleep.

THE BATHHOUSE bursar was dead.

Only one other thing was certain: Sarn wasn't the executioner this time. He'd merely found the body.

After breakfasting on strong coffee, date-nut bread, and sweet figs drizzled with syrup, Sarn had left the *riad*. His dreams had been plagued with cruel images and haunting memories of his father, the emaciated and mutilated figure staring at him with dead eyes. Sarn needed the daylight to comfort him.

His walk to the fortifications that surrounded the city was uneventful. His thoughts ran from his father and the talisman Barrani had given him to the conversation with Taghmaoui, then to Rimmar Fehls.

He'd forgotten about Fehls. Sarn had used the man before. Fehls often served as a go-between for Sarn and Dassai, even sometimes for the Sultan himself.

He'd last seen Fehls more than a year earlier. The man had proved valuable in leading Dassai away from Sarn during his affair with Jannat. Long before that, Sarn had brought the man into his web of contacts. Sarn's bribes had been enough to win Fehls over, and he'd played to the man's greed. He couldn't rely on that forever, though. Sarn would have to be rid of the curse soon or take a chance on Fehls's weaknesses.

The number of people he could trust—never a great many—was slowly shrinking, and he could feel his enemies tightening around him like a noose on his neck.

Sarn headed to one of the many bathhouses that dotted the city. He had a contact at the Hamam al-Hannah, a man who could deliver a message. Sarn would have to risk it. He needed Fehls again.

He walked quickly, with calm purpose, avoiding eye contact with others as he passed them on the street. When he arrived at the *hamam*, he hung back a little to assess the area. All was clear. He advanced furtively toward the entrance.

Sarn slipped into the small room through a window that extended across an entire wall. It was then that he found the bursar's body. Leaning down, he placed his hand on the man's neck, his eyes darting around the room, scanning for any movement. The flesh beneath his hand held no heartbeat but had not yet cooled, and the blood that pooled beneath the man's head still oozed, soaking into the tiled floor. The bursar's life—and his killer—had departed just moments earlier.

Sarn stood up silently, his face impassive while his mind worked furiously. *Another assassin at work here.* Sarn pressed himself against the cool wall and moved to the window, scanning the street and nearby buildings. He'd not seen any movement on the rooftops, and the only other way into the *hamam* was from the rear. Sarn moved silently through the deserted hallways to the back of the bathhouse and approached the door, alert and ready. Grasping the handle, he slowly opened it and peered out, his face nearly two feet from the crack in case of an attack. From his position, he could see the dim alley. The silhouettes of several people were visible; they seemed oblivious to the murder of the bursar.

On the second-floor terrace of the opposite building, two doors were both shut. Again it seemed that no one had been alerted to the killing. Sarn knew the assassin had to be nearby—most likely still in the *hamam*.

Nothing was coincidence. Someone was trailing him closely, forcing his hand. Preoccupied by his thoughts, Sarn had let another take the advantage. Now he was in danger again.

Ready for an ambush, Sarn waited until the alley was empty. He closed the door behind him and moved away from the bathhouse. He had to work quickly, before a patron stumbled on the bursar's body.

The narrow alley led to a cobbled street. The opening was bracketed on both sides by painted terraces topped with stone balustrades and pots overflowing with flowers. The placid scene contrasted starkly with the scene of death that he had left behind.

Sarn knew there was someone hidden just out of his sight. He couldn't take any chances. Whoever it was would soon die.

Seconds later, Sarn was upon the would-be assassin, thrusting a thin metal blade neatly into the base of his skull. The man slumped forward, sprawling in the alley's entrance.

Sarn hid just inside the passage, hoping the body would serve as bait to draw the other killer into the open.

Would it work?

SARN WIPED his blade.

He moved away from the body into the shadows and returned to the *hamam*. With his skills and his heightened senses, he had no need to search for his prey. He merely needed to stand still and detect the changes in the air, the emanations from stone and earth, the sound of heartbeats.

Within a few seconds, Sarn was satisfied that he was the only one drawing breath inside the room where the bursar lay dead; and he realized that the other assassin was somewhere else, waiting for him.

While he knew of only the bursar, there could be others somewhere in the many chambers of the bathhouse. These hidden forces concerned him; whether one or many, they were a threat until he could identify them. However, he was confident that he could evade them. Sarn's birthright of hatred had fueled his hunger for death since he was a young man. Over the years Dassai had tranformed him into the most lethal assassin who served the Sultan.

He smiled, thinking back upon the irony that had led him to his current situation. Sarn had lost his mother at birth. He grew to watch his father become a shell of the man he once had been. Mired in depression and guilt, Sarn began to loathe Barrani, and to hate his stepmother even more. The whore had married his father only to get close enough to bed the dignitaries and the merchants who frequented Barrani's tailor shop.

Sarn knew his stepmother despised him. He tried to convince his father that the woman was a leech bleeding him dry. But no matter what evidence the boy presented to his father of the woman's true nature, Barrani was too stubborn to listen.

Finally, Sarn stumbled on the excuse he needed. Coming home from the bazaar one day when he was eleven, he found his stepmother in bed with another man. His father was away on business for the royal family. In a fit of rage, Sarn lashed out with his unharnessed powers and brutally injured the man.

His stepmother's screams shook him out of his fury. As she tended to the terror-stricken man's wounds, Sarn threatened to kill her if it happened again.

That had been his mistake.

He should have killed the bitch right then.

In fear of her life, his stepmother revealed Sarn's power to one of the Sultan's viziers. Soon after, Sarn was taken away from the only home he had known, and away from a father whom he grew to despise more every day.

His birth-mother was a *Para*; female elemental spirits brutalized by greater Jnoun such as the Jinn, Jann, Marid, and Efreet. All such elemental beings were bound to the world. The Jnoun did not have free will and could not enter Paradise, thus escaping the bounds of Mir'aj—therefore most were jealous, spiteful, and harbored hatred for the mortals whom they, on behalf of Ala'i, had originally created.

Often *harem* Jnoun such as *Paras* attempted to flee to the mortal realm to escape their suffering, seeking out kind-hearted males to marry. Sarn's mother had chosen Barrani. She transferred her soul into her unborn child and upon his birth, she died—but her spirit lived on in the body of her half-elemental child. She had been powerful for her kind, and Sarn held a strong link to the unseen world.

Knowing his unique birthright, the Sultan ritually bound Sarn, who was thenceforward cursed to be an assassin in the Sultan's household.

The rest of his formative years were spent under the guidance of Fajeer Dassai, from whom he learned the art of killing.

Tajj al-Hadd, a shadowy organization known only to the Sultan and a select few within his circle, raised children who showed promise as ruthless killers. It was there that Ciris Sarn learned to fight. It was also there that he learned to harness his Jnoun power, learning to guide it under the watchful eye of Dassai.

Sarn had proved to be one of Dassai's star pupils; he was destined to be the best. Once unleashed, he proved to be unstoppable. Working under the twin command of the Sultan and Dassai, Sarn dispatched political enemies, dignitaries from neighboring kingdoms, merchants, and crime lords. He became known as the *Kingslayer.*

His career had not been without its mistakes. The first began when he was assigned to kill a man in the court who had been deemed a threat to one of the Sultan's advisors. Sarn was twenty-four at the time, and had already earned an impressive reputation. He'd followed the man home and discovered that his target's wife was his stepmother. She had remarried; Sarn would discover moments later that she had given birth to four children with her new husband.

Although Sarn had been commanded to kill only the man, he'd been overcome by such blind rage at the sight of his step-mother that he killed her, too, along with their children. When it was over, he'd stood in the middle of the man's lavish living room, panting heavily, covered in blood.

He remembered looking around, seeing the lifeless bodies of his target and his stepmother—and the discarded bodies of the four children, hurled about the room and shredded like rag dolls.

I was supposed to kill this man and make it look like an accident, he'd thought. *What have I done?*

He'd fled the scene, knowing that he would face certain death when his carelessness was discovered.

When Dassai found out, he was furious. Despite that, how-ever, he had not had Sarn killed. The assassin was too valuable.

Sarn lived on, doing his duty for Dassai, all the while plotting his escape. Several times he'd tested Dassai's strength by disappearing for days, or even months, at a time. But he was always caught.

Not again.

Sneaking away from the front entrance to the bathhouse, Sarn made his way down several cross streets before pausing. Marjeeh was teaming with people who wanted him dead. Since his arrival, the main gates to the city had been placed on the highest alert and guards were checking everyone who tried to enter or leave. In the time since he'd ended his visit with the merchant Tagh-maoui and returned to the city, the number of patrols had tripled. Was the merchant already dead, with betrayal on his lips?

The noose was tightening.

6

JUST A little longer.

Certainly the night could offer him cover. But darkness was still an hour away. Sarn continued to wait. Left with his thoughts, he turned his focus on the firestorm of plotting against him. He had to eliminate this threat and get out of the city soon.

By now, someone would have found the two dead bodies. The alarm would be raised—quietly—all over the city. The authorities would be looking for a killer. It was possible that one of those hunting him would recognize Sarn's handiwork.

Despite his anxiety, Sarn knew escaping during the day was too dangerous. So he postponed it until darkness arrived.

From ancient times the sheikdom of Marjeeh had been a city of pearl merchants. As the late-afternoon suns waned, Sarn could hear in the distance the voices of loungers congregating on roof-top coffeehouses. Somewhere to the east, beyond the crowded buildings, a pearling fleet was anchored in the harbor.

Sarn hid in a walled garden of one of the city's many opulent mansions. He'd watched this one for several hours to confirm his first impression: there was no one living there at present. He rested his back against a fountain, the water of which flowed down from the holding vessel into a shallow pool.

Though the sheikdom was quite wealthy, with many rich inhabitants, but there was a poorer quarter of the city as well, where paint peeled from walls and windows were covered with oilcloth. The pungent odors of cooking and of human waste offended sensitive noses. The affluent merchants had long since moved on to locations that were more desirable.

That was where his pursuers would expect him to go, to hide among the squalor.

But Sarn knew he was safer among the rich.

As night fell, he abandoned his temporary haven. He continued into the market quarter, its wide streets empty and still, dimly lit by flickering oil lamps. When dawn arrived, this place would be teeming with activity. Merchants would badger passersby to purchase their wares, shouting incessantly as they wove their way through the crowds that passed from one end of the market to the other.

Sarn paused at the door of a small shop, its window decorated with indigo silk. He removed a length of soft, pliable metal from his cloak and bent it into the shape of a key. He slipped it into the lock, and it clicked softly. He gently pushed the door open.

Inside, Sarn quickly gathered a bundle of cloth, and some matting, floor screens, and wooden crates. As he knelt in front of the assortment, he thought back again to his youth. It was only in desperate times that he used such alchemy. Slowly, rhythmically, he began to chant, the arcane words flowing freely. As he gathered more energy from within, his hands began to tingle and his head felt as though it were separating from his body.

The forces he called began to pull up on his spirit. The room lit with a flickering glow, and he felt a sudden heat burst from the floor in the middle of the room. Sarn retreated to the far wall, his eyes dazzled by the glow, as snakes of fire climbed into the darkness.

Sarn covered his face with his sleeve and steeled himself to wait until the fumes within the shop became a dense cloud, forcing all of the air into the fire. Choking and gasping, he felt his way back to the front door and went outside. The tenants above would wake in horror to billowing clouds of smoke. He continued slowly down the deserted street, allowing the arson to serve as a screen.

At the first corner he stopped and turned to watch as the street filled with people. City guards came from everywhere, shouting instructions and yelling for water. A woman in a nightdress wept while children stood motionless, entranced by the flames. Sarn turned and walked through an open archway, continuing calmly down the street as people raced out of their homes and rushed past him.

He made his way to the other end of the quarter, walking more quickly now. He passed more shuttered shops, turning at each corner, weaving his way from the center of the city toward the walls. He did not delude himself that his escape had gone undetected. Somewhere, someone would know the fire was a diversion, and would know it had been started by alchemy. It was only a matter of time—hours, perhaps—before he could expect the silent shot of an arrow or the thrust of a blade in the darkness.

How soon would it come?

7

NO EXIT.

There were four gates out of Marjeeh, one for each wall that kept Sarn contained. Each would be on alert and well guarded. He would have to find another way.

He eased his pace and ambled along the darkened street toward the west gate. Oil lamps flickered for some distance, ending at one of the walls he'd have to scale to get out of the city.

He ducked into the entrance of an alchemist's shop that advertised itself on the wall with faux arcane sigils. The entryway was deep, more than adequate for his needs. He took a vial and a small glass square from within his cloak. From the vial he tapped out several drops of blue fluid onto the glass plate. Swirling the cerulean liquid with his finger and reciting another incantation, he trained his eyes on the glass as he held it out toward the empty street.

He could think of at least three people who were trying to kill him, and there would be at least double that number tracking him now. Everyone would suspect Sarn. He knew that.

Sarn concentrated harder on the swirls of blue before him,

waiting for an answer. He stood motionless, hidden from sight by the deeper recesses of the doorway. Only occasionally did he avert his gaze from the glass to relieve eyestrain. Otherwise, his focus was direct and intense. Before long he was rewarded for his patience: he detected movement. The spell produced a flutter in the darkness, nothing more, but it had revealed everything he needed to know.

Sarn nodded wordlessly, wiped the glass clean and returned it to his pocket. He continued to wait in silence.

Whoever was pursuing him was likely questioning his own security. He could not be sure what had happened to Sarn. He knew his foe could not stay concealed much longer.

True to his expectations, a moment later Sarn saw movement in the shadows. A dark figure took a tentative step forward, moving out from the protection of the darkness. He stood motionless on the walkway, his eyes sweeping the street and the shops.

Sarn averted his gaze from his enemy—a tactic he employed frequently whenever he wanted to prevent someone from guessing he was being observed. Sarn waited a few moments until his adversary turned to scan the opposite end of the street. Without wasting a moment, Sarn stepped out from the doorway, reached for the rough stone of the archway above him and, hand over hand, began silently scaling the wall. He positioned himself directly above the doorway and watched as the spy stalked silently below.

The man crept along, cautiously searching each doorway before moving on to the next. He paused to peer down an alleyway and then continued along the buildings, unknowingly inching ever nearer to where Sarn waited, perched above. Sarn had little doubt that a dagger was tucked beneath the man's belt.

As his opponent searched the doorway directly beneath Sarn's feet, he released his hold on the wall and dropped, wrapping his legs tightly around the man's body. The man whirled and clawed at his belt for a knife, but the force of Sarn's sudden weight on his shoulders sent him crashing to the ground.

Before the man could draw his next breath, Sarn's hands closed around his neck. There was a sound like the snapping of a dead branch, and the man stopped resisting.

Sarn crouched over the man and watched with amusement as the fool gasped his three final breaths. Sarn stripped the corpse's pockets of their contents but left the blade untouched in its scabbard, a sign to others that he was on to their game.

He rose to his feet. He knew everything done here was under the bidding of Fajeer Dassai. He gritted his teeth.

Sarn's only chance was keep resisting Dassai's plotting. He surveyed the wall, estimating its height.

There was no choice but to escape to Tanith.

THE SKY showed promise.

In the early morning light, the first sun cast a scarlet blush across a landscape of soft rolling hills covered with olive groves and vineyards. Soon, the second sun would race across the heavens, a blaze of molten gold that would chase away the last stars. A trio of small aquamarine orbs faded from the sky, along with the first pale moon of winter.

Sarn sat with serene interest, watching the stars fade in the pastel sky. Although he could sit for hours and study their courses, he knew it was time to depart.

He headed first for Taghmaoui's second home an hour outside of Marjeeh, and rested until just before daybreak. The house was smaller than the merchant's residence in the city, but was neat and clean. An olive tree shaded the front entrance, ripe fruit threatening to fall to the stone walkway below.

He went to clean up, finding the bathroom in a tiny alcove off the main room. A pitcher of water and a basin lay on the countertop, and he used both to clean his face and hands as best he could. Moving on into the kitchen, he made himself a simple but satisfying meal of camel-milk cheese and sweet-potato bread. He also drank freely of water to prepare his body for his upcoming trek. Sarn knew that the roads were no place for him to be traveling in the light of day, but he did not want to depart for Tanith without bidding his host farewell; he would wait for Taghmaoui to wake up. In the meantime, he would savor the respite that Taghmaoui's hospitality provided.

Taghmaoui appeared beside him soon after dawn, and did not seem surprised to see that the assassin had entered sometime during the night. His greeting was warm, but Sarn noted the strained smile on the merchant's face. "I trust your stay has been a comfortable one," Taghmaoui said, in a tone that sounded strangely cautious.

"You are a true friend, Taghmaoui," Sarn said carefully.

"My houses are your houses . . . as always."

"As ever, you have done well by me—and this service will not be forgotten," Sarn responded. "I will leave for Tanith tonight."

In obvious relief, Taghmaoui let out the breath he'd been holding, and Sarn smiled sardonically. "The city is a danger, then?"

No man was more in league with Marjeeh officials than Taghmaoui. His in-depth knowledge of the city's current status was exactly why Sarn had gone to him before departing. His host did not disappoint him now.

Taghmaoui cleared his throat, sounding nervous. "Late last night, before the winehouse closed, two men came into the place, asking questions." At Sarn's nod, he continued. "They were asking about you. I spoke to them as you asked."

"From the Cape Cities or elsewhere?"

"Qatana, I suspect. These men showed no papers. Perhaps the Rassan Majalis."

The assassin evaluated this information. It was altogether probable, he thought, that the two men were *siris* who had been tracking him since he'd left Pashail. It was likely at this point that they did not know he'd left the city. *I killed one of them last night. Then again, the men Taghmaoui is speaking of could simply be consulate agents trying to find their man's killer. It was also possible that the two men were sent by someone else not directly involved but acutely aware of the circumstances and the reward.*

In any case, Sarn knew he must leave no trace of his departure from Marjeeh.

He studied Taghmaoui for a moment and considered his options. *How much further should I involve this man, who is in many ways a friend?* Eventually, the network of spies would track Sarn to this house. It was unlikely the merchant would come to physical harm; he was a skilled bladesman in his own right, and several of his servants had been corsairs and cutthroats in the past. His manservant was rumored to have once been a skilled assassin, though not as adept in the trade as Sarn.

As for trouble with the law, Taghmaoui's distinguished position in Marjeeh was secure. As long as subsequent visitors to Taghmaoui's estates found no trace of Sarn, it was unlikely he would come to harm. There was no reason to put the merchant in further jeopardy; the man might be useful in the future.

"Once I am gone," Sarn said, "you have taken care to see that there will be no complications?"

"Most certainly, as I always have. You will have safe passage northward to the border, but from there you must travel at your own risk."

"I understand. My thanks again to you, as always," Sarn responded.

"A blessed farewell, until we meet again."

9

HE NEEDED to stay off the road.

Sarn looked back from outside the stone walls as he departed the ancient vineyard. He had to walk; his horse had been taken from him in Pashail. She was valuable, and he knew Dassai would keep her for himself. Still, it didn't make the trek any easier.

His plan was follow one of the caravan roads north to Tanith, more than fifty farsangs distant. The journey was long, and he would most certainly be tracked.

Sarn's steady pace just within sight of the road carried him deep into the evening light. The road curved gently past caravanserais, shrines, and thickets of cork trees. The prized trees were well tended, but they offered Sarn some protection from the sight of travelers, and from any possible threats.

There were fewer caravans to follow at this time of year, and he saw only the occasional rider during the day. Night had arrived, but the lingering heat had not yet cooled when Sarn decided to stop. He ate some fried cakes and drank pomegranate wine. Once the light of the moon was bright, Sarn set out again.

As he continued north over the course of several days, the vineyards and orchards began to thin out, with wilderness encroaching, protecting the road from the suns' heat but increasing the risk of other dangers. The land rose slightly, dotted with small hills and shallow valleys. Sarn approached the southern end of a shallow depression, dry from the lack of rain. The *hassi oued* marked the boundary between the sheikdoms of Marjeeh and Tanith.

Despite the arid conditions, Sarn was skilled enough to find clean water and wash away the dust of the road. He filled his waterskin before pressing on. It was another five days to the city walls of Tanith. Now the road climbed again, more sharply this time, leading him to an upland scattered with brown grasses and little in the way of green vegetation. Amid the scrub, red-tinged rock formations held shallow caves that would shelter him from the twin suns. Sarn pressed on, his feet following the furrows of past rains.

The air cooled significantly in the darkness of night, and nocturnal hunters began their search for prey. Sarn listened as the distant cries and dying screams pierced the blackness. No animals stalked him, however, giving him a wide berth; one predator can smell another, and Sarn's scent communicated danger. Nevertheless, he was not a fool; he kept a blade in each hand as the hunters killed and the hunted died.

Sleep would come slowly, and Sarn's thoughts returned to his youth that had shaped the man he was now. Sarn shuddered. He hated his memories—they were painful, like knives twisting in his gut.

As he lay on a bed of damp heather, he wondered what he would find in Tanith. A safe haven, he hoped. Jassaj from Riyyal, certainly. Who trailed him now? A *siri* who had traced his travels from Pashail? Haradin, perhaps? It was difficult to say with any certainty.

Sarn gritted his teeth. One thing was certain. The lone tracker who followed him now—that hunter would not survive the journey. Sarn pondered how to kill the man, and settled on the means most familiar to him.

Two hours later, he closed his eyes.

70

SARN SLIT the man's throat.

Blood spurted from his neck, soaking the ground crimson. Sarn's ambush had been flawless, silently coming up on the man from behind and cutting the man's throat from ear to ear. Cold.

Vicious. Perfect.

The man's slashed throat gurgled horribly as he fought, twitching, until finally he slumped, his dead weight dragging Sarn's arm downward. Sarn pulled the blade away and released his grip. The man's head lurched forward, his mouth open in a voiceless scream.

Sarn searched the man's garments. *Slen Thek.*

He disposed of the bounty hunter's body carefully in the early morning and continued his journey northward. He watched the stars fade away in the light of dawn before he rested.

After sleeping for four hours, Sarn crossed a series of dry washes that sloped steeply down from the rugged peaks to the sea.

The trek was laborious. Sarn moved through the high bluffs above a caravanserai and savored the aroma of food carried on the wind along with the wood smoke. It was this scent, or perhaps the comforting presence of others, that made him stop—despite the danger—and light a small fire in the shelter of a thick clump of young walnut trees. He warmed his thin hands over the flames and ate his meager rations.

Sarn carefully unfolded a parchment map and studied it in the dim light. Though the map was weathered and torn, he could decipher the images. The lands that bordered the sea roughly resembled a curved scimitar. The long perimeter of coastline fronted the Crescent Cape. Just inland lay the rugged Haffal Mountains which formed a similar line, preventing the desert from encroaching. The wealthy sheikdoms maintained their fortunes within this thin, sheltered boundary. Tanith was the northernmost of these lands, where the mountains and the sea converged.

Although he'd covered more than half the distance of his journey, Sarn estimated he was still ten farsangs south of his destination. If he went any farther west, he would have to move through rough terrain and low mountain passes; traversing them would be difficult. Staying close to the Ras'mal Hari, he would make better time but risk a greater chance of discovery. *Keep to the road,* he thought. *It will be quicker. I have nothing to fear but death, and that I've never feared. I've only feared the shackles of life.*

He was nearly finished with his meal when the hair on the back of his neck rose in warning. He immediately stepped on the fire and doused the flames. He sat in darkness and watched the embers die.

Sarn's nerves prickled at the sound of horses' hooves pounding along the road. He moved to a different area within the thicket and watched for the approaching rider.

A dark-robed figure on a white horse appeared out of the night. The rider pressed on without hesitation.

Fortunately Sarn had extinguished the campfire soon enough for the telltale smoke to dissipate. With his keen vision, Sarn could just make out a long, sheathed sword carried over the rider's shoulder, and the glint of chain mail covering the rider's head. He was not a *siri*; they were less inclined to wear mail, and they always kept their weapons hidden. Sarn was still being hunted.

Once he was certain the rider had moved on, Sarn returned to his camp and knelt by the dead fire.

It would be a cold, dark night.

11

SARN PAUSED.

A day had passed since he saw the rider. He stood on the fringes of broad, fertile green fields. Groves of date and olive trees and orchards of citrus stretched into the distance. To the west loomed the last of the rugged mountains, curving around toward the cape north of the city. Two small rivers moved northeastward where they emptied into the sea. He was close now.

Sarn could just make out a few distant towers of Tanith, topped with banners that shimmered in the breeze. Sarn had inherited a keen internal compass from his mother. He had crossed this way many times before, as sure of his direction as migrating fowl.

The northward road skirted the wide plain. In low places, cane stalks with sharp-edged, leafy tops grew six feet high, while solitary, exotic, jade-colored fig trees towered above the fields. He'd seen no one since the rider in the woods the day before. His provisions were exhausted.

The suns were setting on the sixth day of his journey as Sarn crossed the last of the bridges fording the two rivers. He reached his destination late, and paused to wait under cover of night. Although most others feared the dark, he was at ease in the shadows. It was the place he knew best.

He waited for the appropriate time to enter the city. Though the darkness allowed him to move stealthily, he remained cautious. This was how he had survived for so long—and the reason so many feared him.

Sarn stood watching the faint, familiar outline of Tanith's outer walls. The city gates were still open. Were they waiting for more riders to approach the city?

He would have to wait until morning.

Daybreak carried the paired suns over the ridges and the flats, laying waste to the shadows and warming the earth with glowing pastel light. The alabaster walls of Tanith faced a horizon washed in shimmering glare.

Sarn navigated a course through the gate. Beyond was the center of the city, where the slender minarets and golden domes of the palace stood outlined against a brilliant cerulean sky. He heard the sound of bells on the wind.

A great citadel rose in the west like a spike hewn from the living rock. The high walls of the *casbah* that surrounded the citadel loomed over the rest of the city.

Tanith lay like a jewel upon the hilt of a curved sword.

12

"KEEP IT moving! Come on now!"

A voice called out from the gate, growing louder as Ciris Sarn drew nearer.

As he entered the gatehouse, the gatekeeper's gruff voice rasped out of the turban that shadowed his face. "Why must we always be kept waiting? For once, I should like to see someone properly prepared." He was short and rotund; he did not glance up as Sarn came closer.

Sarn slid a small brown stone bottle along with his identification papers across the official's table. "Because if it were not for people like me, your daily routine would be even more mindless."

The man was visibly shaken as he recognized the assassin. "Ah, it has been too long, my friend," he said. He thumbed through the papers and stamped a page, then quickly thrust them back toward Sarn.

"Not that long," Sarn said. "Three years."

"It is not the same here now," the gatekeeper said. "But surely you already know that."

A young assistant departed through the rear archway. Sarn waited, knowing that the boy would return with more officials. He'd deliberately chosen this time of day to enter, because he guessed the trap would begin to close as soon as the older official recognized his face. The fat man appeared disturbed by Sarn's presence and, for a moment, said nothing.

"You will please stay here," he finally said. "My assistant will bring back the customs official."

Sarn was prepared for this. He walked calmly to an open window overlooking the bridge. It was hot inside the gatehouse, and musty with the smell of camel shit and sour milk.

"Who will he bring back?" Sarn asked.

"Does it matter?"

"It does matter. Because unless there has been a legitimate complaint made against me, I cannot see why I should be treated as a beggar or thief."

"Ciris Sarn, if that is truly your name, I have no personal problem with you. You have passed through these gates many times through the years and have always been kind to me. Nonetheless, your name means more these days, and you know this to be true. Your presence here can mean only that you are fleeing from something and want to use our city as a hiding place."

"Are not all men hiding from something?"

"Ah, yes, of course. I'm usually trying to hide from my wife." He grinned. "As I said, for me, there is no concern. However, others see differently than I. And they have far greater power."

"So a pack of jackals have come seeking an easy meal, have they?"

The gatekeeper nodded. "Your work has not gone unnoticed. Rumors abound; and even if what they say is untrue, I can't keep you from being interrogated."

So the assassin waited, his eyes ranging over the tranquil water below. The warmth of the midday sun quelled the comfort of the morning breeze. More than just the temperature had begun to rise. Irate voices filled the air along with the scent of coriander and smoke. The meridian bells rang out, issuing the call to prayer. A few moments later, the inspector came in.

"You are Ciris Sarn?" asked the elderly man. Sarn did not recognize him. He had olive skin, grizzled, unkempt hair, and weary, deep-set eyes. "It seems we have not had the fortune of meeting before this day. It is my pleasure to do so now."

Sarn nodded. The inspector pointed to a small table and two empty chairs; plainly, he intended to conduct a more detailed interview. The man spoke in a punctilious manner as he thumbed through Sarn's papers. "So you choose to come back to Tanith now?"

Sarn nodded. "Yes, I have a house within these walls."

"Indeed…" The inspector paused, staring down at the papers between them, then leaned back in his chair. "To see you in person is all the more intriguing. You are, as they say, a legend in Tanith, and elsewhere, no doubt. It comes as a shock to see you face to face."

"I'm just a simple man, much like yourself—but on the other side of this table."

"If you wish to believe it as such, I suppose. However, I know you. The other men who have seen you here know you, and so do all who dwell within the walls of Tanith." The inspector straightened and leaned forward, putting his face near Sarn's. "Now, tell me the real reason you have returned … *Kingslayer.*"

"I am here on business," Sarn said evenly. "To get answers to lingering questions that concern none but myself."

"Or could it be that the disturbance you left in Marjeeh leads you here?" the man countered.

"I have no knowledge of any matter in Marjeeh," Sarn replied flatly. His eyes bored into the official; the man shifted uncomfortably.

"So after three years you return?"

"Am I not entitled to return? After all, I keep residence in Tanith."

At this the inspector frowned but said nothing. He signed a few documents and grudgingly granted the assassin entrance into the city.

Sarn turned at the door. "Thank you," he said without malice. "You have been very … wise."

He had expected more trouble. The grizzled official had admitted that the entire city knew of his deeds.

So why had it been so easy?

The answer came swiftly.

Dassai. He'd told them to allow Sarn's entry. So he—and his henchmen—would be waiting for the assassin inside the city.

So be it.

Sarn exited the tower and gazed at the suns sinking toward the horizon.

Yes, Tanith was a beautiful place.

13

SARN SHUT the door.

He left his *riad* in the soft violet light of early evening and made his way to the forecourt of the Biar-ben hostel.

The message he'd found among the papers the inspector had given him indicated the location of the meeting. It also made clear there should be no delay.

A lane of polished stones led to the center of a wide court-yard where a fountain sprayed gently into a pale blue circular basin. Tall palm trees were silhouetted against the purple sky, and brilliantly hued barbary blooms filled the warm, still air with sweet floral perfume. The richness of this city in the midst of the parched land sent a wave of pleasure to Sarn's weary mind.

Subdued lighting filtered from copper lamps that hung beneath latticed arches. A path of inlaid mosaic led to the dining hall.

Despite the inviting surroundings, Sarn found himself treading lightly, as though he could sense the presence of someone unseen. Those who'd followed him into Tanith would be better prepared and deadlier than the assassin he'd dispatched in Marjeeh. With each one he killed, the next would be stronger.

He passed through the wide, open doorway and stepped into a lofty room with a domed ceiling supported by long, slender beams. The effect was astonishing—as though the ribs and frame of an ancient sailing vessel had been inverted and carefully placed atop the walls. The room was lit by great, heavy lamps and hung with tapestries depicting past naval battles.

Few of the low, round tables were unoccupied. A lively murmur of conversation and laughter filled the room. Dishes and bowls clinked and clattered, chairs scraped, and pretty young women with large round trays traversed the raucous crowd, stopping just long enough to slap the hands that had strayed too far from the tables. Sarn quickly took in the scene before threading his way between the tables.

He could sense the dark eyes that watched him with veiled curiosity.

There were few outlanders in Tanith at night. The inner city was almost entirely inhabited by the wealthy and their servants. There were few winehouses or shishas, and fewer visitors. The foreign quarter lay outside the walls, and was an altogether different place.

Sarn had always been impressed by the subtle charm of the clean, cobbled streets and the flat-roofed, whitewashed houses with their brightly painted doors and elaborately decorated windowsills.

Set high into one of the many hills, the dining terrace overlooked the city and the sea. It was also less well lighted than the main hall inside. Sarn made his way toward a table occupied by two foreigners and settled into a low rattan chair across from the men. From this position he had a clear view of the entire area while remaining in the shadows.

One of the men motioned to a young girl dressed in white. She came forward with a bottle of red wine, poured a glass for Sarn, and scurried away.

"Say something, Ciris. It has been a long, long time."

"And to what do I owe the pleasure?" Sarn asked without meeting the man's gaze.

"Such a lovely place Tanith is," the man said, ignoring the sarcasm. "One could stay here forever, I think."

"I've thought the same thing."

"I'm certain you have, Sarn. Yet, you do have certain obligations that must be met. You still remember those, do you not? You are needed in Riyyal."

Sarn sniffed the wine, swirled it in the glass briefly, and took a sip. He tasted it, then turned his head to the side and spat the small mouthful onto the stone floor. "Whatever allegiance I owed to Qatana has been long since paid in full. I owe you nothing."

The Tajj al-Hadd *askar* watched as the wine ran along the cracks in the stone. "On the contrary, you have a duty to us as long as we need you. There is nothing you can do to change it."

Sarn met the man's gaze for the first time. His eyes were black pools of hatred, though his face never changed. "Perhaps. But I can reach across this table and cut both your throats before either of you says another word. Then you will have no need to worry about any of my so-called obligations."

The second *askar* laughed. "Do not be rash. Do you think we're so foolish as to come unprepared?" He leaned close enough for Sarn to smell his scented breath. "There are a dozen soldiers trained on you as we speak."

Sarn could not resist the urge to glance around the crowded restaurant. He saw no one with a weapon. Perhaps the man was bluffing. "Maybe so. But it will matter little in the end. Both of you will die before me."

The two men remained silent.

"Ah, yes, I have forgotten," Sarn said. "You are bound to these assignments as well, with no choice of your own. You are nothing but a messenger. What makes you think that I would not prefer death?"

"Because we have been through this before, and you have always obeyed your orders. I see no reason why you will not do so again."

Sarn pushed back his chair. He was tired; the journey had been long. "I grow weary of this conversation."

"Be at the port tomorrow morning, or you will not live to see the first noon sun," the first man said.

Sarn's eyes burned again.

"Until the morning, then," he responded.

KHOLED NAJIR listened to the entire conversation.

He sat at the next table, dressed in the manner of a merchant. His eyes gleamed. He had not been this close to Ciris Sarn before. *Could he actually do it?* Certainly not in the presence of the two men seated directly across from the assassin. In addition, there were others lurking about unseen. They would be keen on killing Sarn as well, should the assassin fall. *No.* He would wait for a better opportunity.

Sarn had eluded the Haradin many times, and a number of the assassins had been slain by his blade. Najir wanted to see Sarn die now—tonight—but that would not happen. The risk was too great. He had to remain in the shadows, keep his disguise, follow the plan, and comply with the Emir's orders.

Najir glanced around the room. His disguise was convincing enough that no one questioned his presence. Today, he was Hanif Masood, a textile merchant from Calilif.

Despite the temptation, he only looked at Sarn from the side. He did not want to make eye contact with the assassin, as Sarn was the only one in the room who could penetrate Najir's disguise. One look at his eyes and Sarn would recognize the killer within.

The rest of the people here were sheep, oblivious to the wolves around them. Najir's skin was dusky, but it would be assumed that he was of mixed blood. No one would suspect he was Haradin.

Very few people here knew much about the Haradin, other than that they were fierce, ruthless warriors from the deserts of Qatana. Unlike the Slen Thek, who were killers for hire, the Haradin were soldiers of a secret army sworn to protect the Sultan.

According to rumor, centuries ago they'd become autonomous. They knew no boundaries, and crossed freely from one kingdom to another. Territory did not hold them. Ideology was their center—and they grounded themselves in it.

Their training included not only tracking and live capture, but also mastering the skills of the spy and assassin: disguise, weaponry, poisons and antidotes, and ambushes. This was Najir's great challenge—a personal mission.

One of the most feared skills of the Haradin was the ability to adapt and change tactics, which was why Najir was able to sit casually—unremarkable and unnoticed—at the adjoining table and observe Sarn's meeting with the *askars*. It was also why three additional Haradin hid nearby in the square, waiting for Sarn and the two men to come by after their rendezvous. The *askars* would pass through the square on their way to the next destination. Sarn would follow without their knowledge. And the Haradin would close the trap on the assassin.

Najir watched and waited, staring off into space as though he were a scholar contemplating philosophical problems and their solutions. From the corner of his eye, he watched as Sarn finished his business and abruptly stood. As Sarn stepped past him, he could see the rigid set in his jaw, the flash of hatred in his eyes.

Hmm, that is interesting, Najir thought.

He waited for Sarn to exit the room before getting up to follow. But he would observe Sarn's movements only to confirm that he was setting off in a false direction—around the inn and over to the other side of town—to throw off the Jassaj spies.

Once he was satisfied that his target had performed the expected maneuver, Najir quickly returned to observe the agents. They finished their wine, left the dining room, and proceeded west toward the outer city.

He suspected he would have to wait only a few minutes before Sarn took up the same trail. The sooner, the better; Najir had taken little rest or food over the course of this task, and it looked to be a while longer before it was over.

It was worth the wait.

SARN PLANNED his move.

He knew he was being followed by at least two men, and perhaps more. Tension had mounted during his conversation with the two *askars*, and he was frustrated that his plans, so carefully conceived, now had to be abandoned. He discarded all emotion; he filled his mind with the cold detachment that had always served him well when there was need for swift action.

Sarn glanced at the sky. Soon the rising moon would flood the mountains and the tall towers of the citadel with a silvery light. The narrow streets of the inner city were a tracery of shadows. He moved quickly but cautiously as the dim light suddenly became a ebony maw directly before him. The scent of fruit trees wafted by him as he followed the merchant and the two *askars*. He carefully crossed one more avenue and hesitated as he looked into the inky blackness.

The throughway had ended in a dense grove of glass-bloom trees. These trees were popular for their unique blooms that, beginning in late spring, covered every inch of the tree. When the blooms fell they hardened, becoming brittle like ultra-thin glass. Children loved to run through the fallen blooms in a cacophony of crunching sounds. By fall, the petals would disintegrate into fertilizing dust, essentially cleaning up after themselves. Sarn would have to be especially careful here, using every bit of his trained stealth.

He stepped into the darkness.

The entrance to the grove was completely devoid of light. He saw the faint flicker of candles in the windows of distant houses. Somewhere ahead of him he heard the crisp, delicate sound of dead blooms shattering. He lengthened his strides.

The sound of the distant voices alerted him and he halted, listening, but he could not see the *askars* or the other man. Sarn began to move in, stepping with the utmost caution, shifting larger blooms with the side of one foot before setting it firmly on the brittle shards, and then proceeding likewise with the other. The grove was pitch-black on either side of him, but the darkness began to fade as the moon rose. He watched as the *askars* reached the opposite side of the park and passed into the dim light beyond. He paused to survey the scene.

Where was the other man? The merchant?

The air was full of the warm, sweet fragrance of the gardens that spread out in all directions from the central path. The sky, powdered with stars, was losing its rich, velvety purple as the crescent moon rose higher. Sarn, however, was conscious only of an oppressive unease in the atmosphere.

While he considered his next move, his concentration was shattered by the faint but unmistakable sound of a heavy object rolling along the ground. He hurled himself back against a tree and gripped the bark, bracing himself and instinctively shutting his eyes.

His foresight paid off. Massive spiderwebs of brilliant, blue-white electricity crackled through the trees, filling the copse with frantic, flickering light. Sarn felt the impact on his chest, but the tree absorbed most of the blow, leaving him unhurt. Had he kept his eyes open, his night vision would have been completely destroyed, leaving him vulnerable to attack.

As he stepped away from the tree, he heard and then saw a figure running down the path away from him.

Ignoring the crunch of the brittle petals, he began to move toward the man. He'd taken only a step when another figure appeared out of the darkness, running in a half-crouch. Sarn realized he was in the middle of an ambush.

Before he could react, he heard the slight whirring sound of a thrown knife. Luckily, it missed his chest, skimming across the meaty part of his left bicep. A sharp lance of pain shot through him. Sarn stifled a curse, but the wound was not life-threatening. Painful, yes. But not debilitating.

The incapacitating charges, followed by the thrown knife, confirmed the identities of his attackers.

Haradin.

The Haradin assassin charged. Sarn plucked the knife from his belt and stood, mind focused, blade aimed at his attacker's throat. As the assailant closed the gap, he spun and launched himself into the bushes, hurling something in Sarn's direction. Sarn saw a spherical object hit the ground and roll toward him. Unable to use the trees as cover this time, he stepped deeper into the shadows. The object exploded within a yard of him.

Sarn was momentarily stunned, but the sphere had otherwise not affected him. Realizing he was running out of time, Sarn closed his eyes and muttered under his breath, extending a finger toward the assassin's hiding place.

Globes of light streamed from his outstretched hand, gathering together like balls of quicksilver until they became a mass of pulsating brightness. The Haradin howled in pain and fear, his eyes seared from the blast.

Sarn finished the spell and then slipped even deeper into the trees. The light would remain for several more seconds—more than enough time for him to make his escape.

Behind him, he could hear the Haradin hunting for him in vain. Soon he reached the edge of the park and fled into the darkness.

Sarn was gone.

Part Five

INSTRUMENTS OF DARKNESS

4.12.792 SC

7

PAVANAN MUNIF traveled east from Tivisis.

He felt that good fortune was with him as he entered the cara-vanserai on the outskirts of Riannis. A week had passed since the ambush in Tivisis, and he was still on the run.

Fajeer Dassai had left him broken and betrayed. The pain of Munif's injuries had brought the urge for *affyram* roaring back with a vengeance. Twice he'd had to resist the impulse to venture into an *affyram* den. How simple it would have been to simply buy his dose and pipe, allow himself to be led deep into the darkened building, and lose himself to the *annka*. Each time, though, Munif resisted. It was a battle, and the pain he'd suffered was almost unbearable. It was the toughest fight he'd ever had to endure.

Munif had hoped to post a message at Burj al-Ansour, but he felt the danger was too grave to make the attempt. Traveling in that direction was too hazardous. He was certain that Dassai and Arzani would expect him to head north toward the *misal'ayn*—or west from Tivisis back to Ruinart. They would be waiting to hem him in.

Instead, he'd traveled by foot eastward from Tivisis. He stayed away from the Inni Qawr, hugging the coast; it took longer, but it was much safer than taking the caravan road. Six days later he reached Riannis.

There he booked passage on a ship bound for Hayl. Though the island kingdom was a rival to Givenh, the borders were open, and the two realms were on friendly terms with each other. He secured passage as discreetly as possible, and paid well to stay off the manifest. Slipping past the small custom house was not dif-ficult and did not cost him any more of his dwindling coins.

His first task upon landing in Mourejar on Courós, the southern-most island in Hayl, was to find a *hakima*—which he quickly did.

One look at him and the healer ushered him inside her cramped quarters, demanding that he strip and bathe. She was a kind, elderly woman with sharp blue eyes. She bound his broken ribs and applied a salve to the raw skin on his legs. In addition, she supplied him with clothing, waving away the extra coin he offered her.

He'd felt better soon after his visit with her. Not completely; that would take time. The idea of visiting an *affyram* den was still foremost in his mind, but the salve the healer had applied had dulled much of the pain. He hoped it would continue to stave off discomfort while he decided what to do next.

Munif feared being in a city. Too many eyes could see him; too many mouths would betray his whereabouts for a fee. But he had no choice.

The streets were well maintained, having been designed for carts and carriages. While it was easy on his quickly healing legs, the trek through the city was not kind to his spirit. He spent his waking hours brooding about his betrayal and picturing the deaths of the clerics on the hillside near Burj al-Ansour. His thoughts constantly turned to Dassai, making him ever more sullen. He knew Dassai had more dark designs and was intent carrying them out.

Just before nightfall, he spied a caravanserai in the north of the city. Although he was not hungry, weariness weighed heavily upon him. He needed to find a place to rest and find relief from the pain of his wounds—if just for an hour or two.

Only then could he continue.

2

NIGHTFALL DEEPENED.

Munif knew he was carelessly consuming an excessive amount of wine. He'd found himself entering the caravanserai without even looking at the name of the place. As he found a chair at the bar and took the first sip, he realized with some displeasure that he had to try to avoid falling into a drunken stupor. The road that lay ahead of him was long. But, he reasoned, partaking of wine was better than slipping into the depths of *affyram*.

Munif shrugged. The hour of his departure mattered little anyway; no one waited for him back in Riyyal. He had never married. He'd been in love several times—passionately, foolishly, and fondly—but none of his romances had ever led to marriage. He lifted his glass and toasted his lost agents.

Cheers accompanied the twanging of strings, rising to a raucous chant that echoed to the high beams of the bar. The pain in Munif's head pounded in time to the music, and his stomach churned. It was time to go. He'd been here for hours now, and it was late.

He rose cautiously from the chair, planting his feet firmly on the floor. The room spun slightly when he closed his eyes, but it was not as bad as he had thought it would be. His training with the Jassaj had included learning to function while drunk or under the influence of drugs. Despite his altered state, it would take a lot more than what he'd consumed to incapacitate him.

As he tried to slip away through the crowd, friendly but strong hands grabbed him and pulled him into the revelry. Cheerful drunken faces peered at him through the pall of smoke. Someone shoved a glass of the house *arak* into his hands. Munif glanced down at the milky white liquid and looked up at the young man who'd staggered in front of him. "Nushing can be sho bad when you have a good drink," the man slurred. "Forget your troublesh. If there'sh no sholution, there cannot be a problem."

Munif smiled broadly at his newfound acquaintance's words. As the crowd threw their arms around him and welcomed him into their circle, he realized he'd needed this night of revelry at the caravanserai, this night of song and drink. It kept his mind from dwelling on bitter thoughts.

He'd never expected failure when he'd pursued the two summoners. He was disturbed that there might be betrayal within the ranks of the Jassaj. Munif was a proven agent—a master, in fact. He was proud of his accomplishments. However, he wondered if his faith in them had been completely misplaced. The enemy had managed to elude him, thanks to Dassai. They'd completed their mission and brought terror to Burj al-Ansour and the Mirani kingdom—all because of Fajeer Dassai. Dassai had turned bad, and Munif had been unable to stop it. He'd succeeded before in similar situations, but this failure—this he would always remember. Even while he was drunk, the faces of the fallen haunted him.

"Damn," he muttered.

"Wallowing in self-pity, huh?"

Munif looked up and realized he'd been deposited into a corner of the room. Now he sat next to an old barkeep, his face permanently etched with the years.

"I am Khaleed Sudairi," the man said. "Who might you be?"

"Just a traveler trying to make his way in the world."

"So are we all." The man laughed. "Just make sure you keep your head out of the arak so you don't drown in misery."

"I appreciate your concern for my well-being," Munif said.

"It is nothing," the barkeep said, waving his hand. "I think of everybody's well-being. It is part of my trade."

"I see."

"Will you be staying here? You should. I see in your face that you feel you must go—like a cart horse straining at the traces. But there's not much hope you'll ever reach your destination—

whereever that may be—in your current state. Your best bet is to leave in the morning."

"I'm not as bad off as I look, my friend."

"The festival in the city will make the roads crowded and difficult to pass," warned Sudairi. "It will be nearly impossible even for one with his wits about him."

"To tell you the truth, I'm glad of the respite. I really am. But I'll be even happier to leave."

"I've done more than enough prying for one night," Sudairi said with a smile. "I wish nothing but the best for you."

Munif wished he could agree. He would take his leave and journey to the harbor. From there he could make for Darring. Another uncertain crossing to distant islands made him wary.

Munif set down his empty glass and was about to leave when he realized the revelers would try to stop him again; they would want him to stay and continue the party. He'd best depart as quietly as possible.

Or he could give them something to distract them.

He spotted a man on the other side of the crowd whose gaze was directed away from Munif. He looked like a *rawi* who'd come to entertain the revelers with his stories. Munif surmised that the man was waiting for an opportunity to acquire an audience.

Munif set down his glass and climbed onto the nearest table. A cheer echoed through the caravanserai, but he lifted his voice above it. "I beseech the fine men around me to hear the call of an important duty!"

"Don't be turning serious, now, stranger," one cried. "Let's keep it light."

"Let him speak," Sudairi chided them. "No matter what he has to say, it's his right to say it."

A brief quiet settled as Munif addressed the group again.

"I speak of the important duty of men who drink! Men who drink must listen to other men who drink!"

Drunken roars of approval from his audience. Munif paused.

He had no idea what to say next. But the noise was increasing again, and he knew he had better work quickly or risk losing his audience altogether. "We also have a duty to listen to those who have important tales to tell," he went on. "There's an *rawi* before us who wishes to bring us sweet music—or perhaps a poet's sorrow." Munif placed his hand over his heart and bowed slightly from the waist—his best attempt at conveying sincerity—which, he hoped, would elicit a respectful silence from the crowd. "We should grant him respect and listen to him."

From his vantage point, Munif watched as wisps of smoke gathered in the heavy air. The glow of candles and oil lamps was all that kept the room from utter darkness. Shadows played in the corners, accentuating the already forlorn ambience. The night wind whispered menacingly beyond the windows. He was content, for the moment, to be safe inside with the *arak* and his comrades. Right now, even failure did not seem quite so bad.

The *rawi* seized the opportunity Munif had provided. "Thank you, kind stranger," he said, then turned to address the gathering. His sharp, clear voice rang through the smoky air. "I do indeed have a tale to tell.

"In the city of Cihharu," he began, "there lived a tailor who had the good fortune to be married to a beautiful wife. The two shared a strong, mutual affection. One day while the tailor was at work in his shop, a filthy street urchin sat down at the door and began playing on a timbrel."

Chairs scraped along the floor, and voices faded to a murmur as the revelers settled in for a good story.

"The tailor was pleased with this performance and decided to take the boy home and introduce him to his wife. He hoped the urchin might entertain them both that evening after dinner. He proposed this to the boy, who accepted the invitation. And the tailor—"

Munif was entranced by the stranger's black eyes and enthralled, as were they all, by his dramatic delivery. Truly this man had the gift of storytelling.

As the *rawi* continued his tale, keeping the audience's attention on himself, Munif took the opportunity to leave.

He slipped out the door and into the darkness.

3

MORNING WAS NEAR.

The stars were just beginning to vanish as the horizon grew
lighter.

Munif estimated he had an hour more before both dawn and
he would reach the city again. Once there, he could find passage
on one of the ships moored in the harbor. Then he would be off
to Tammós.

He was drunker than he would have preferred, but he had
not had enough wine to silence the swiftly growing alarm. As he
rounded a corner in the narrow lane, he sensed something behind
him. He turned and saw a shadowy figure moving toward him.
His heart hammered in his chest as he thought, *Just my luck—I'm
careless one time and Dassai's fiends find me.*

The figure drew nearer. Munif was almost sober from fear.
Realizing he could not flee, he chose the only alternative. He
charged at the figure. Just as he was about to shove him to the
ground, the stranger's palm struck a glancing blow across his
upper arm rather than his face.

Despite his muddled brain, Munif realized he had to end this
fight quickly. No stalling, no circling; his actions, in his condition,
would be too predictable. He began to shift back and forth, acting
more inebriated than he really was, hoping to lure his attacker
with a false opportunity. Then he took a wild swing, advertising
it as plainly as possible by preceding it with a loud grunt.

The feint worked: the stranger sidestepped him easily. Munif
allowed the motion to pull him forward as though he were off

balance, and the assailant stepped toward him. Munif's left foot landed solidly on the ground, and he immediately kicked back with his right, catching the man high in the shin. He followed this by bringing his right elbow up in a weak but distracting blow to the attacker's chest.

Now they were face to face again; Munif gave the man a swift punch just below the sternum, keeping the movement short. A hiss of breath let him know the stranger had definitely felt it, but the jarring impact awoke the old pain in his ribs.

Munif kept himself low and his forearms up to protect his damaged midsection. A fight like this would end with him on the ground; and he knew if the stranger were to get the advantage even once, he would lose. The assailant attempted to grab him, but Munif stepped as far back as he could to draw the man forward. With a sudden lunge, he launched himself. He threw short, furious punches into the man's torso, then tried to knee him in the groin.

The other man smashed both fists into Munif's back, driving him down. As Munif dropped to his knees, he brought his right forearm up between the other man's legs, hoping for a disabling shot. His adversary stumbled back.

Before Munif could find his feet again, the stranger held up his hands. "Enough," he gasped. For several seconds he did nothing but breathe. Gulping air, the stranger half-groaned. "Pavanan, stop!"

He knows my name! Munif spent a few moments feeling exhaustion take over his mind and body. Then, wobbly as a newborn colt, he pulled himself to his feet. The stranger recovered more quickly, but this time when he advanced, he held out his hand.

"Forgive me, my friend. I've been trailing you since Tivisis. You know me."

"I know you?" Munif was still on guard. How could he know this person?

The figure nodded. "Yes."

As he drew nearer Munif got a better look at him. He drew in a sharp breath as dim moonlight illuminated the man's face. "Prince Nasir! How?"

Nasir aït-Siwal nodded. The man who'd been thought lost in the desert—who'd gone missing during the 500-farsang Cibaq al-Bahr race and been presumed dead—was swathed from head to toe in a light-colored *abaya*. His skin was weathered, his face deeply lined. His eyes held deep secrets. "Calm your nerves," Nasir murmured. "You are one of the few who knows that I am alive. Not even my father is aware."

Munif nodded slightly, then mustered enough energy to ask, "Why? Why the attack?"

Dawn was approaching rapidly, and in the waxing light, Munif was able to recognize Prince Nasir's countenance more readily. He still wondered how the Prince had been able to remain hidden for more than eight years, though the Prince's features, which were remarkably ordinary, would make it easy for him to blend in with people anywhere in the kingdom.

"I wanted to see if you were worth saving," Nasir answered.

Munif blinked in surprise. Nasir smiled. Slowly, Munif began to smile too.

He grasped the Prince's hand in a warm grip.

THEY ALL thought he was dead.

The air was blisteringly hot, and a sandstorm was about to move in with a furnace blast of wind from the east and a blizzard of white sand. Shielding his eyes, Nasir stared across waves of blinding white dunes that rose hundreds of feet in a glistening sea of gypsum sand.

There was no shelter.

No time.

He dismounted, dragging his horse behind him, laboring toward the summit of the dune. The suns dimmed as the deafening roar swelled at his back. He reached the top and raced down the other side just as the full force of the storm hit. His horse snorted in alarm and reared as an avalanche of sand nearly swept them both off their feet.

Hot wind and blinding sand flung Nasir down the slope. He struck an exposed block of limestone, and his legs buckled. He plunged forward. His hand slipped from the reins and he fell over the edge.

He crashed hard in front of a shadowy opening.

His horse was gone. He struggled to his feet and moved toward the looming blackness. Even with his vision obscured he could see that this was not a cave. He knew the legends of the desert, which told of whole cities and civilizations lost—swallowed by the sand. He struggled into the darkness, while the wind tore at him in one last attempt to consume him.

A wave of sand swept over the opening and cascaded down. He wavered, overcome by a sudden feeling of dread and the weight of unnatural sleep. Haunted images drifted through his mind.

This will be my tomb, he thought—and remembered no more.

That was eight years ago.

NASIR GAZED at the sea.

He was a changed man. After years in the oasis of Waha al-Ribat, Nasir was compelled to leave for Riyyal.

The journey was imperative.

Rumor had it that his brother, Malek, was likely to be the next successor to the throne. Their father, Raqqas Siwal, was old and weakening. As the firstborn, Nasir was to have become Sultan upon their father's passing. But when he went missing, the succession had been thrown into disarray. Malek was seen as cruel and corrupt. But there were few others of royal blood who held favor with the Sultan in Qatana.

Nasir stood at the rail, lost in memories of the past. The years he'd spent in exile had not only healed him physically, they had cleared his mind, giving him a different perspective on the royal family.

He knew that he was presumed dead. Hewad Sareef, his savior in Waha al-Ribat, had been feeding him the information. Sareef had also been keeping Nasir's true identity concealed from the others in the oasis. They knew him only as an unlucky merchant who'd been rescued in the desert by the nomadic *badawh* during the height of the vicious sandstorm. He'd used time to his advantage and said little about his past, merely nodding in vague agreement—or sometimes apathy—whenever the topic turned to the sandstorm or his rescue from it.

There was an old tale of a man who had wandered for years in the desert. Mad with thirst, he had succumbed to illusions of immense struggles among the heavens. Nasir had suffered no such hallucinations, but he had seen the path he must choose.

He reached into the folds of his cloak and pulled out a parchment. He unfolded it.

Sareef had drawn the map years before. "If you take this western route," he had said, tracing the line on the map with a gnarled finger, "it will lead you to the northern coast. From there, you can set sail to Cievv."

Cievv was his destination. It was there he would meet with Hiril Altaïr.

He'd come across the literary relics in a forgotten city that had been unearthed during the sandstorm. He'd found shelter in its ruins, where the ancient walls had provided some relief from the storm. While he waited, he'd wandered through the abandoned chambers. There he discovered four manuscripts, leather-bound and set on a small niche chiseled in the stone wall. He'd opened them, but they were written in a language he couldn't decipher.

Although he couldn't have said why, he took them—he felt compelled.

He dug himself out of the ruins in the days that followed and made for the al-Ribat oasis. After a day in the blinding desert heat, he collapsed. His last thought as he lay baking in the suns was, *I am truly and hopelessly lost.*

When next he remembered, he woke in a white-walled room. Curtains fluttered in the windows. He lay on a large bed with sheets of fine cotton. He tried to sit up, but a woman dressed in a *hajib* urged him back down and gave him a sip of water. Nasir accepted the water gratefully, and in the days that followed, he learned what had transpired.

White Palm, a *badawh* people, had rescued him. They'd found him and brought him back to Waha al-Ribat where they'd nursed him back to health.

The White Palm took solace in elaborate rituals, praying to Ala'i for recognition and comfort. Their words flowed like poetry, weaving an intricate pattern as they spoke.

They'd found the books. In the weeks of his recuperation, Nasir learned that they not only understood the language of the text, they were descendants of the people who had written the words.

They told him a little of *Waed an-Citab*, the Books of Promise. This involved the blood of Ala'i, called *Azza,* used in lamps, among other things, across the lands of Mir'aj for over nine hundred years.

As the son of the Sultan of Qatana, Nasir was well versed in the kingdom's stance on the burning of *Azza*—it kept the Jnoun, the evil spirits that dwelt in the unseen realm, from breaching the veil that divided them from Mir'aj.

These books were a contract between the tribes of Jnoun and the Sultans of Siwal.

After much discussion with the *badawh*, Nasir had suggested that if the Books of Promise were turned over to a trusted *sufi*, perhaps the truth would be revealed. Nasir was in no condition to make the journey to Havar, and asked therefore that the manuscripts be sent to Tariq Alyalah.

His wish was granted. Meanwhile Nasir remained in Waha al-Ribat, learning the beliefs and customs of his *badawh* guardians and regaining his strength. His goal was to meet with his trusted *sufi* friend, learn more about the ancient texts, and find the missing fifth book.

Nasir sighed. The twin suns shone bright in the western sky. Footsteps sounded behind him, and a moment later a weathered hand gripped his shoulder. Nasir smiled. It was Pavanan Munif.

"We are close?" Munif asked.

"Yes. Tomorrow, I think, if the wind and weather hold," Nasir replied.

"Fajeer is somewhere on the island. This I know."

Nasir turned to Munif.

"And we must find him."

THEY CHOSE a place near the river to rest.

After they landed on Tammós the night before, the Prince and Munif had made camp in the hills above Dorré. Nasir had told Munif little about his time in exile, but Nasir was clearly uncomfortable among so many people, and Munif had his own reasons for staying clear from contact. By silent agreement they avoided the city.

The following morning they set off, traveling hard throughout the day, stopping only to eat modest rations or to drink their fill of water. There was little time to sleep, and they held only the briefest of conversations.

Finally, at dusk, and Nasir moved them off the road. "We're close now," he told Munif. "It's time to rest before tomorrow."

They came to a stand of chestnut trees within sight of the great stone bridge that spanned the Culnn River. The river was wide and fast, with tremendous boulders thrusting above the raging water. The road on its opposite bank led to the city of Aley.

Munif didn't know why they were traveling to Aley, or for that matter why they'd sailed to Darring. When he pressed for more information, Nasir explained that Fajeer Dassai held a residence in the hills. Aley was noted for its *masyafs*; grand summer houses belonging to powerful nobles and wealthy merchants. It was likely that Dassai would be here as his third wife kept a *masyaf* in the city. There was no telling at this point how close they were to Dassai, but something in Nasir's eyes gave Munif a glimmer of hope.

In the dim light they spied a small clearing beyond a thicket. Avoiding the clearing, they hiked into a dense, tangled area within the brambles, which provided them with seclusion for the evening. Nasir pulled out a thin bedroll and spread it on the ground. As Munif did the same, Nasir spoke out of the darkness. "We will light a fire and have a warm meal at daylight. We don't want to attract unwanted attention tonight. For now, we should try to get some rest."

As Munif lay down, he contemplated the impossibility of sleep.

That was his last thought of the evening.

LIGHT CREPT over the hills.

They slept soundly for hours despite the hard ground and the chill in the air.

Munif woke to the sweet smell of hardwood burning and fresh food over a fire. He looked around for Nasir, and saw him sitting some distance away, eating what that looked like roasted rabbit. Munif sat up. He glanced toward the first sun, which was rising, and realized how late it was.

Prince Nasir shook his head. "You haven't missed anything.

I got up only a little while ago. I took the liberty of finding us breakfast." He indicated several pieces of rabbit that lay steaming on a flat rock.

Munif joined the Prince and joylessly ate his fill. After they finished their meal, Nasir lay on his side and looked at Munif with a neutral expression.

"What happened to you?" Munif asked. "The official word was that you were killed in a sandstorm during the Cibaq al-Bahr race."

The Prince nodded. "That is only partly true. The fact that I am here proves that I did not die." He chuckled.

"Obviously not. But why didn't you return? Why did you wait so long to reveal yourself?"

Nasir hesitated. "While I was lost, I discovered ... revelations." Munif could see that Nasir was choosing his words with care. "It was dangerous information. It has taken me this long to verify it."

"What kind of—"

Nasir changed the subject. "You were told that an attack was to be carried out near Tivisis. What happened?"

Munif's mood darkened. "I was betrayed," he said. "I tracked two summoners to the city, where I was nearly killed." He quickly told the Prince what had happened to him.

"You know for sure who it was?"

"Yes. Fajeer Dassai."

Nasir nodded. "And you are aware that the summoners you tracked were only one pair of several?"

"Yes." Munif had learned of other dreadful attacks as well. He sat staring off into the thicket that so effectively concealed them.

"I can tell you little more now," the Prince began. "Only that the information you were given came from me."

Munif turned to him in surprise. "From you? But how? Why?"

Nasir nodded. "Later. I will reveal more in time."

Munif stared at him, dumbfounded, and Nasir continued. "I have been watching you, though you've never noticed me. You followed the summoners, while I tracked their hunter."

Munif's thoughts turned to Dassai. "How can it be that such deception is allowed to exist?"

"At one time, Fajeer Dassai was just as dedicated to the Sultan as yourself, but at some point he was lost, obsessed with power and wealth. This plot of his began years ago, even before I went missing. Needless to say, he garnered support quickly from my brother, Malek, who made a deal with Dassai that when our father died and Malek became Sultan, Dassai would gain control of the Rassan Majalis."

"Was your brother responsible for your disappearance?"

"No. That was an honest and unforeseen occurrence. I really was lost in that sandstorm. What I've just told you is what I've learned from careful investigation. Sources told me that Dassai saw his opportunity when I failed to return, and began forging a stronger relationship with Malek. Now they are inseparable."

Munif sat wide-eyed. "You say you came upon this while in the desert—but you didn't tell me how—"

"You were discovered through Dassai's actions," Nasir said. "And already know more than most ever will."

Munif tried to remember a much younger Fajeer. Yet he could not recall a time when Dassai had left his post, or had had any interest in the Rassan Majalis.

"Dassai is very clever, and it has taken tremendous effort to reveal his intent," the Prince said. "However, it is now time to rein him in."

Nasir spoke so confidently, so matter-of-factly, that a chill ran down Munif's spine. "And what is his intention?"

"Fajeer Dassai wants to control the Rassan Majalis as well as my brother—to be the true power behind the throne, and thus all of Qatana. He used my disappearance to get close to Malek. He's been influencing my brother, who, in his desire to succeed our father as Sultan, devised the attacks in Miranes'.'"

"Emir Malek arranged those attacks?" Munif felt the betrayal sink deeper into his gut.

"He did—acting in collusion with Dassai."

"I still don't understand the reasoning behind the attacks."

"Fajeer is one of the most powerful men in the Kingdom. He is very close to the Sultan of Qatana. He knows that my brother is more amenable to furthering the interests of the Sultanate—and he can persuade my father to do anything. Dassai persuaded him to spread the story of my demise, which guarantees my brother the crown."

Munif saw the connection immediately. "And that guarantees Dassai a willing and able puppet."

Prince Nasir nodded. "You see the seriousness of the situation."

Munif sighed. "I do."

IT WAS some time before Munif spoke again.

More questions formed in his mind, but he could not bring himself to speak. He wanted to know everything, yet he did not want to dominate the conversation.

Nasir smiled grimly. "There are places within the palaces of Riyyal where even I am forbidden to tread."

Munif knew he had to be satisfied with that response. Yet, one more question nagged at him. "Why have you allowed me aid you?"

Nasir shrugged. "I thought it was the best thing to do at the time. I was there when you tried to stop Dassai from leaving Tivisis, wounded and in anguish over the loss of your fellow agents. I saw your efforts to put a stop to the plot. When it was over, I wanted to give you an opportunity to redeem yourself. I must tell you, however, that it is only in your own eyes that you have failed. I commend your efforts. You are blameless with regard to those unfortunate events."

Munif's eyes welled up with emotion. He closed them, overwhelmed with relief. It was a balm to his spirit to hear those words. As Nasir waited quietly, he took a few moments to regain his composure.

Munif turned his thoughts to the troubles at hand. "You have my word that I will assist you to the end."

The Prince nodded in approval. "Through the years there have been numerous plots against the Rassan Majalis and the Jassaj—yet never from someone so high within the Sultanate. I still do not know the extent of Dassai's plot. Nevertheless, it is time to put him in the noose. He will never realize the extent of our knowledge—even at his last breath."

"What else can you tell me?" Munif asked.

"While in Tivisis, Dassai had a meeting with two men we believe to be key players in the plot. I believe he comes here to further incite terror. Just what action remains unclear, but is something that we must prepare for."

"Similar to what happened in Burj al-Ansour?"

Nasir nodded. "I believe so, done to cause panic and chaos, so that he can gain favor by seeming to resolve it."

"Is that possible?" Munif said.

Nasir shrugged. "Despite his efforts, he cannot subvert the Rassan Majalis. They will maintain control in spite of him," the Prince said confidently as he extinguished the fire. "The Rassan Majalis is too powerful to oppose. They will not stand for subversion, even from one of the Sultan's own right-hand men."

"So you knew he would come here."

Again Nasir nodded. "Yes. We believe so."

"You've been gone eight years, but you keep saying 'we.' Are others assisting you in tracking Dassai?"

"Yes," Nasir said, smiling slightly. "I do not wish to divulge their identities at this time. But yes ... I've been aware of Dassai and Malek and their plans for some time."

Nasir sighed, his features going grim. "I sent out messages in the hope that it would reach certain allies. They never did help us, and I was informed that Dassai played a part in intercepting the couriers. They are lost now."

"Lost? Who is lost?"

Nasir avoided the question. "Later. We must prepare to leave."

Munif sat silent, pondering this new information. With renewed vigor he sprang into action, putting away his bedroll and helping to douse the remaining embers. Soon their packs were ready and they stood together with the river before them. He smiled. It had been a long time since he had felt this confident.

Nasir glanced at him. "Are you ready?"

"Yes," he said. "I'm ready."

They crossed the bridge and followed the road toward Aley.

MUNIF WAS WEARY.

The path had taken them to the east coast of Tammós, across a steep divide covered with trees and scrub. A westerly wind blew from the sea, bringing heavy fog and relentless drizzling rain.

He lay beside Nasir on the sodden turf of a steep hill, thoroughly soaked, hidden from the road below by a small boulder. An outcropping behind them formed a small cave, which offered partial shelter from the elements.

Nasir had insisted that they stop there above a nondescript little village. All seemed peaceful, yet the Prince refused to leave. When Munif questioned the decision, he simply said, "More will be told in time."

They waited in silence. A gray veil slowly descended to obscure the landscape. Both knew that once the rain had passed, a fierce wind would follow. Munif was beginning to doubt that the sorry conditions were worth the cost.

"We are in danger here," Munif said.

The Prince nodded. "Yes. But there is a larger threat ahead without the information I seek."

"From whom?"

Turning his gaze from the village, Nasir said, "The *imam* here is an old friend. He has shared information with me that makes me cautious."

From their shelter, Munif and Nasir had a clear view north to Aley. They maintained constant watch over a path that led south a little distance before descending a second hillside and passing out of sight. That hill was covered in low-lying scrub, and its slopes were scattered with pine trees. Thorny brambles hindered their view—and their comfort. The rain changed to a foggy spray that blew incessantly into their faces.

Munif was an expert in wilderness survival, but after traveling for days with Nasir, he had come to realize that the Prince was as well-prepared as Munif.

Before long, Munif heard a faint noise behind him. A stranger slid adeptly down an embankment and picked his way through the underbrush toward Munif.

"Rest easy, Pavanan," the Prince said. "This is the man I spoke of. Itani Hayyek has been waiting in the village for some days now."

The *imam* was tall, with dark hair and strong aquiline features. He was dressed in the simple yet functional garb of a cleric. He was probably tied to the *rahibs* who'd been slaughtered near Burj al-Ansour, and Munif winced as he visualized the atrocity.

"I see the track is as active as ever," the *imam* said in a voice that wove seamlessly into the sounds of wind and rain. "The light will fade once the worst of the weather arrives."

Munif shrugged. "You'll get no sympathy from me. While you sipped sweet wine beside a warm hearth, I was freezing my ass off here."

"True enough, but you were made for this," Hayyek countered with little remorse. "Just look at you."

Nasir could not help but smile. "I'd be glad to get some rest and leave you behind. I'll think of you while I warm my hands in front of a roaring fire, and pray you don't catch a chill."

"Thank you for those kind thoughts," the *imam* said, producing a small flask. "I'll be warm enough for a while yet."

Nasir snatched the flask from him and took a sip. "Has sharing been eradicated from your extensive list of virtues?"

"Not completely. The weather does cut to the bone, does it not?"

"We won't see anything tonight," Nasir said. "We may as well leave him here to watch until morning."

"No one has moved along the trail in some time," said Munif, "and the old hut outside the village is long since deserted."

The *imam* nodded and settled to his watch.

Munif stretched and motioned to Nasir.

"Show me where I may find that warm fire."

THEY WAITED.

Munif and Nasir returned to their observation post just after the first sun's dawn. At some point during the night the rain had stopped, leaving a thick mist to filter the suns' rays.

Itani Hayyek lingered with the two men. Munif enjoyed the *imam's* dry wit and quick retorts. After about a half-hour, the cleric carefully stretched his back.

"Well, I doubt you heathens have any more use for my services this day. I'm off to get dry and have some–"

Suddenly he dropped beside Munif and bent low, looking off into the distance. Munif followed his gaze, peering through the thick vegetation. A massive shape lumbered along the road that descended into the vale from the north. They could hear low growling, and something akin to a dog's high-pitched whine. The thing approached and moved past the abandoned house.

Munif could not believe what he was seeing. Twice as tall as a man and nearly as wide as the road itself, the creature walked on two massive feet. Its thick skin was a dull dark gray, and black fissures scored it all over, like mud that had dried in the sun. Pavanan Munif had not believed he'd see such a thing in his lifetime.

The Kúrrūl had a young girl tucked beneath one arm; she was trying vainly to break free. It was plain to see she was exhausted; her screams were so weak he could hardly hear them. Directly below her, the demon's fist clenched around a massive spear— a twenty-foot-long tree trunk sharpened to a point at one end. In its other fist it dangled three human heads by a knot of hair. Munif shuddered as it passed below him and went on its way.

"So the rumors are true, then," Munif murmured as he weighed the situation before him. "I never would have believed it if I had not seen it myself."

Nasir shook his head. "To conjure up such creatures—" he muttered. "Dassai must have used considerable magics to set Kúrrūls on the loose. He'd need a legion of Carac to conjure up those vile things." Nasir studied the back of the demon as it receded from their view. Hayyek sat quietly, but his lips moved in a silent prayer.

Only a handful of summoners had the power to break the binding of the world and unleash the Kúrrūl, and the monster's presence could mean only one thing: someone very dangerous had either forced or persuaded the demons to act. Few creatures were as strong and cruel as these, and where there was one, there would be others.

As the suns rose and the mist cleared away, Munif and Nasir watched with the *imam* as three more demons came from the direction of the village. Farther off they could hear the sounds of men and dogs foolishly giving chase.

The three men watched in horror as the grisly scene took shape below them. The first demon tossed one of the pursuers effortlessly against the wall of the house, so hard that a scattering of stones fell onto his writhing body.

As the demons drew nearer to Munif's hiding place, another villager stabbed with a sword at the second creature's legs. The demon turned and the man backed up against a tree, dropping his broken blade. He let out a muted scream as the demon's great ax descended upon him. The massive weapon tore through his skull and clove his body in two, embedding itself in the exposed roots of the tree between the man's feet. The halves of his corpse fell to either side, and his organs emptied out across the ground. The Kúrrūl barely paused before continuing up the path.

A man screamed in pain as a Kúrrūl hacked off his hand. One of the dogs lunged at the third demon's groin, whipping its head back and forth, growling fiercely. The dog's teeth could not puncture the demon's flesh. The demon reached down and clenched its fist around the dog's body. Suddenly the dog ceased struggling. The last sounds it made were the crunch of its collapsed ribcage and the dull thud of its body hitting the ground.

The first demon turned, making a swift motion with its hand, and the three moved south on a path that led them below the onlookers.

Munif noticed that a group of four women had run out of the town toward the woods. They managed to avoid being spotted, racing through the scrub, not daring to look back.

Near the point where the women had left the path, a lone figure fled the village at a dead run. A Kúrrūl followed the man, easily overtaking him. It rammed a sharp branch into the man's back. The point exited through his chest, and the demon lifted the man into the air, then flung him violently to the ground. Munif hoped the man was already dead as the demon pinned his head down with its gargantuan foot and jerked the tree-spear free.

A fourth demon joined the first three on the road. Munif's stomach lurched. As he started to turn, a steady hand held him still.

"Wait. We're not moving yet. Watch!"

Minutes passed as the demons moved slowly south, unhindered, following the road directly beneath the horrified watchers. It was then that Munif thought his eyes were playing tricks on him. The first demon's left side shifted and blurred.

Nasir set his lips close to Munif's ear and whispered excitedly, "Look at the right arm of the second one. They're not true Kúrrūls. It's all a clever deception. They're Haríís—changelings—experts in shape-shifting."

Munif glanced at Nasir and asked, "Are they worse than the Kúrrūls?"

Nasir shook his head as the third and fourth Haríís lumbered by. "No. They can take on the characteristics, the strengths, of the thing they feign to be—it's a true change of form. But they have weaknesses. Still the survivors will report that demons killed those men, and there'll be no reason to doubt them."

After the last Haríí had vanished from view, Nasir stood up and motioned to Munif and the cleric. "We need to get back to the village. Dassai no doubt wants to be certain the news of the demons' rampage reaches the *misal'ayn,* and is then relayed across Miranes' and back to Qatana. Hayyek and I will deal with the Haríís. You must find Dassai. Keep him alive if you can, and hold him until my return.

"Now go!"

11

NASIR AND the *imam* followed the Haríís.

They knew that the fiendish creatures could not maintain the strength and size of Kúrrūls for long; they would have to change. They also knew that the Haríís would be weak and disoriented once they transformed back to their own lithe forms.

Nasir and Hayyek hunched over in an attempt to remain dry. Their labored breathing beneath their dirty, sweat-drenched robes was the only discernible sound. The air's chill had beset them without mercy since the outset of their journey, and the deepening darkness only made it worse.

With every moment that passed, the Haríís were less able to hold their false shape. Their forms blurred as the strength of the spell waned.

Hayyek began to move, drawing a short dagger from beneath his robe, but Nasir stayed his hand.

"Patience," the Prince whispered. "Soon."

After a short wait, the changelings reverted to their natural shape. They blinked nervously, eyes darting in their dark-red, horned heads. Their thin arms, each ending in a three-fingered, clawed hand, twitched as they glanced about.

"Now!" Nasir yelled, flinging himself forward, unsheathing his sword.

The momentum of his charge speared the first one through the chest. Bright green blood gushed as Nasir wrenched the blade out. He whirled and slashed another across the throat as Hayyek drove his dagger through the third one's ear. One last upward thrust from Nasir's blade ended the fight.

The two men stood panting, staring at the strewn bodies.

"I doubt the villagers will believe they were Haríís," Hayyek said weakly. "Still, one cannot be sure."

"Once they've seen the bodies, they will be convinced," Nasir replied. "It's getting late; let us try to get back tonight."

"We still have to get to Aley to aid Pavanan."

"Let's not worry about that yet," Nasir said as they moved on. "He is very capable. If Dassai is there, Pavanan will not lose him again. In the meantime, pray the rain doesn't flood the ground here."

"I do know how to pray my friend," Hayyek said.

12

MUNIF WAS close.

He traveled through the rolling hills, staying in sight of the road. Using the suns as his guides, he worked his way skillfully to the spring where the three of them had set up a camp. Their gear was still stowed at the base of a tree near the water's edge. Taking a fair share of the food and water from one of the packs and leaving the remainder for his companions, he made his way to Aley.

By late afternoon, the hills and the thick scrub gave way to cultivated fields and fertile vineyards. Gnarled beech trees grew here and there, and the flora became more varied. Munif passed through a vineyard, ignored by the workers as they tended rootstocks and repaired trellises.

Munif alternated between a steady trot and a hurried walk, driven by his need to seek both the truth and his addiction. Contrary to what he had thought, the gnawing need for *affyram* had not diminished; in fact, it had grown stronger. Sweat beaded his forehead—not solely due to his exertion.

In Aley he might find what he sought.

As darkness fell, he moved closer to the road, knowing the third moon of winter would not provide enough light to guide his way. Finally he reached the whitewashed wooden bridge that spanned the Danui river.

Aley had long been known for its beauty and its many summer houses. As Munif crossed the bridge, he caught his first glimpse of the city's legend and its original reason for being: the dark silt of the island's soil and the gypsum sands of the river passed over each other, creating ever-changing patterns. *Sufis*, mystics, the curious, and the desperate flocked to observe the strange shapes that seemed to metamorphose into meaningful images and prophetic scenes.

Aley had grown from these mystical beginnings. At first a select few were drawn here by the desire to study the images in the water. They'd erected a shrine on this spot, and soon gathered a following. Not long after, merchants had moved in to provide for the pilgrims' needs.

Over time, the sect had died out, but the shrine remained and the town expanded. Seeking a way to keep Aley prosperous, the citizens began to hold an annual summer festival with an open market. A wealthy merchant had purchased land on a low hill overlooking the town, south of the river. He'd erected a *masyaf* on the crest of the hill overlooking Aley. Locals said that he'd found his fortune by reading the patterns in the river. Soon other wealthy families followed suit, building beautiful summer houses in the hills. One of them had been Dassai, who chose this place for his wife Cala.

Munif reached the *masyaf* just after midnight.

13

MUNIF HAD to be careful.

The merchant who'd built the elegant home was long gone, but his house had become a well-known retreat for Dassai. Munif knew Dassai was inside. There could also be any number of his men surrounding the place or ferrying messages back and forth to the *misal'ayn*.

The path took Munif past several summer houses to the gate of Dassai' house. Moonlight made stealth difficult. He sharpened his ears to listen for danger, but heard nothing but the sound of buzzing insects.

Picking his way carefully, he circled the small city, darting from one concealed position to another, staying upwind of the dogs whose baying he occasionally heard. The perimeter of the *masyaf* was planted with a coass hedge of green cypress for protection and privacy; closer in, extensive gardens lay hidden in the night.

Nasir had told Munif that he had others watching the summer house. There was no sign of them that Munif could detect. He pulled himself over a stone wall and slipped stealthily across the cropped lawn.

Even in the darkness, he could make out the shapes of manicured shrubs, topiaries, and fruit trees standing no higher than his head.

He kept low to the ground, using whatever cover he could find. Finally he came to a small tree covered with auburn and golden leaves, its branches erupting from the trunk and cascading down to the ground. He carefully pushed aside the branches, mindful of the crisp, noisy foliage as he entered its interior—where he saw the figure of a man leaning against the trunk, staring at the house.

Munif knew immediately that something was wrong. The man had failed to turn toward the noise. He could not possibly be sleeping in that position. Munif touched the agent's shoulder with his hand, whispering, "So, is he still in—"

The spy's head lolled unnaturally for a moment before detaching with a sickening snap and falling toward Munif. Instinctively, Munif reached out and caught it. The glossy white of dead eyes stared back at him. Munif suppressed the churning of stomach acid that worked its way into his throat, and spun around, searching for the enemy.

He saw no one.

THE MAN had been dead for several hours.

The blood was dark and congealed. His head had been almost completely severed, probably by a razor wire or a butcher's blade. Even more disturbing, the assassin must have held the agent's head there for some time to keep it from bleeding outside of the body. There was no pooling of blood and little to detect even on the spy's back, chest, or shoulders. Instead the blood had been forced to flow down from the severed neck stump into the man's innards.

Munif confirmed this as he felt the bloat around the agent's midriff. The feet and hands were also swollen.

Munif propped the man exactly as he'd found him and carefully replaced the head. As quietly as he'd come, he exited the hiding place, stealing closer to the house. He kept to the garden paths, mindful of places where he could disappear into the flowers if necessary.

Near the rear entrance he saw lights shining through the second-story windows. He pressed as closely as he could to the side of the house, kept at bay by the hedge. He followed the perimeter around two corners until he came to the front entrance. There he found what he was looking for: a second-floor veranda jutted out above the main entrance. An identical structure hung directly above it on the third floor.

He nodded in satisfaction. Experience had shown him that few people—or their servants—ever thought to lock upper-story doors, especially in the front of a house; they believed that no thief would be so conspicuous. Since this was the main entrance, it was also the most elaborate, with tall, stately evergreens on each side, and pillars covered with frescoes. He reached into his satchel and extracted simple shoes, which he slipped on. The soles were very rough, created by pinching with clever barbs, forming ripples along the entire length. He also wore thin gloves made especially for this purpose, with a small lip on the end of each fingertip to catch and hold ledges. He climbed quietly, using a tree as cover, and rolled over the railing onto the terrace.

He checked the door and, as he'd hoped, it was unlatched. He had entered an unused bedroom; a dressing gown was laid out carefully on the bedspread. He moved quickly to the other door and cracked it open to peer into the hallway. There were no lights save one shining under a door diagonal to him. Directly across was another, darkened door.

He stepped quietly into the hall and padded over to the door where the light shone, and knelt and pressed his ear to the door. He was able to understand only some of the murmurs that came from behind it. An unfamiliar voice was difficult to make out, but Dassai's clear tenor carried easily to Munif's ear.

"You and the other will wait here for the return of Pavanan. Those who choose not to side with us will aid in your ambush. They must be led to believe that I remain here and that the meeting set for tomorrow will take place as planned."

There was a sound like glass being set on wood, then Dassai's voice continued. "This will not be an easy fight. The man is a master—and if you underestimate him, you do so at your own peril."

The other man's voice rose and fell, and Dassai responded. "Don't worry about that. If he survives, any message he sends from the *misal'ayn* will be received very differently in Cievv."

"The rest will turn or fall," a third voice said. "Make no mistake about that, Fajeer. Everything is still well in hand."

There was a rustling of cloth, and then Munif heard Dassai's voice again. "Good. My work here is done. I will leave for Ruinart and prepare to address our friends."

Munif knew he had to take Dassai now or never.

"MEOWRRR ... "

The sound came from directly behind where Munif was kneeling. It startled him so much that he nearly lost his balance and fell against the door.

He glanced behind him and saw a rather large, striped gray cat staring at him inquisitively. He turned away, and the cat came closer, meowing more insistently and with a significant increase in volume. He waved a threatening hand at it, but the cat was oblivious, and apparently hungry. It let out a caterwauling that could have been heard throughout Aley.

Footsteps approached behind the closed door, and Munif knew he was out of time. He stood quickly and stepped toward the door. As soon as it cracked open, he kicked viciously, snapping it back into the face of the person behind it. He kicked again, this time following through with his full weight, shouldering the door aside. The man behind it looked up in surprise, cupping his face with both hands as blood gushed from his nose. Munif reached out and grabbed him by his hair before he could collect his wits, and slammed him into the edge of the door, knocking him unconscious.

No one else was in the room.

Munif ran through the nearest door; it led to a sitting area. Dassai was there near the windows, with his back toward Munif. He was searching frantically for something in a large pouch.

Munif crossed the room at a dead run and slammed into Dassai's back. Dassai fell headlong over a table and crashed into the window frame. The bag fell away, but he had something in his hand. Munif got his feet under him and backed away. Dassai was still stunned, so Munif changed direction and raced toward yet another door. The force of his charge broke the handle, and the door fell away to reveal a darkened bedroom.

Munif sprinted across the room, slammed the door open, and reentered the hallway. The third man he'd heard just moments earlier was nowhere to be seen. Neither was the cat.

Munif ran down the hall. Reaching the other end, he checked the first door and found it latched. He turned to try the opposite door when a long sharp metal blade appeared with a resounding thwack in the frame near his head.

He spared a glance at the fast-approaching figures just as one of them pulled his hand back for another throw. Munif didn't wait for another knife; he reversed direction again, hoping the first door's lock was weaker than his shoulder.

He found himself in a massive, unlit room. A platform bed took up most of the room, and the heavy curtains around it were moving. Sounds of confusion and fear confirmed that the bed was occupied.

Time slowed as he weighed his options and then acted on them. He closed the splintered door and moved past the bed to the windows, where he saw a terrace. A money pouch lay on a dresser, and he took it, slipping it into one of his pockets. He opened the door that led to the veranda and stepped out. He glanced down and saw dark water nearly thirty feet beneath him.

The *masyaf* had been built so that one wing abutted a deep stream. Over time, the stream's banks had eroded, and subsequent owners had been forced to add supports and stones as the water's edge encroached upon the house. Now the stream flowed directly below.

His pursuers came barreling through the door. Munif had only a moment to judge where the deepest pool was below him. He swung his legs over the railing, sucked in his breath, and jumped, keeping his body vertical but his legs loose beneath him.

He hit the water with force enough to pull his feet out from beneath him. He felt his back brush against a sharp rock, and he let his breath out slowly as he fought the current.

The instant his head broke the surface, he started swimming, trying to get to the opposite shore. He heard something splash into the water near him, and then his feet touched bottom and he half-swam, half-slogged to the opposite bank.

Heart racing with a mixture of fear and relief, he found a path and made his way to the outskirts of Aley. A stable was situated conveniently on the road that led out of town. Slipping into the empty shedrow, he inspected the curious heads peaking out over the half-stall doors until he found what he was looking for—the intelligent face of a blood-bay gelding. Quickly he opened the door, seizing the horse's halter and vaulting onto the bare back.

Within seconds he was out the door and moving away from the stable, pausing just long enough to throw the sleepy-eyed stable-boy a sopping wet but heavy bag of coins.

He had to find Nasir before it was too late.

Part Six

REVELATIONS

28.2.793 SC

7

THERE WAS still time to kill her.

The summit of the hill was a tapestry of color, carpeted with wildflowers and fragrant herbs. Two dark figures looked down at the twisting path that emerged from a dense expanse of maritime pine and chestnut trees and stood unmoving as a red cloaked traveler passed below. This strange climate might have its charms in afternoon sunlight, but after a day of careful travel through the blowing drizzle, these desert dwellers had no affection for the place. They were silent and withdrawn, their faces grim. Each wore a long, hooded *bishlah* that billowed in the stormy air. Beneath the cloaks were layers of ink-black linen.

They had tracked the woman for most of the day, shadowing her path, keeping her in sight as she set a course through the hills above Cievv, keeping their distance to avoid giving themselves away.

They had studied the maps upon their arrival in Ruinart. They knew the paths she would likely take. Only when the time was right would they seize what she possessed: the Books of Promise.

Both figures remained on the hill after she'd passed from sight, winding steadily upward, following the path toward them. Afternoon was slipping into evening, and the clouds were breaking at last. The western sky glowed orange as the second sun dipped behind the purple masses of the Soller Mountains. In the twilight, the sky had become a stunning canvas, a mosaic of pastel colors and subdued contrasts. The desert dwellers were unmoved by the beauty, keeping their eyes on the bend in the path just below them. Night would fall soon. Even if the clouds blew away, a waning moon and a scattering of stars would be all the light they would need.

They found comfort in the darkness. Darkness made it easier

to strike. If this wasn't the spot, they'd find another. Perhaps they would close in on her from two sides. The best strategies were fluid, not set in stone.

The veil between worlds was as thin as gossamer. The two figures saw no change in the land around them, but their hearts knew. Soon—very soon—the barrier between Jnoun and men would be gone. Then there would be a reckoning—retribution against all who did not believe.

They would burn.

All of them.

2

MARIN BIT her lip.

The scene had played out continuously on the voyage from Messinor until the ship docked in Cievv. Sometimes it took the form of a charade; other times, it seemed that nothing less than complete honesty would succeed. Again she wrestled with the words in her head. How would she say what needed to be said? Which words were right, and which would doom her efforts? Even the serene views from above the unwalled city failed to comfort her, and she delayed her meeting with Ilss Cencova yet another day.

From the crest of the hill Marin slowly descended a series of loops and switchbacks, coming at last to a little bridge over a swift-running stream. Still below her, she caught glimpses of where the path entered a belt of green trees and eventually rejoined the web of footpaths leading back to the city.

Would she return there tonight? She still didn't know what she would say to Cencova. Perhaps she needed another day after all.

The incline was steep, its gravel slick but posing no real danger for an experienced hunter. The day's rain hadn't been heavy enough for water to pool between the stones. She was more than halfway down when the path skirted a wide scarp and bent away from the hill, nearly doubling back on itself. As she moved, she felt the subtle approach of an ominous presence—a hint of malevolence. Instinct drove her toward cover, but there was nothing here above waist height. She was exposed.

Quick, light footsteps approached from above and below. Someone without her training might not have noticed them yet. Marin dropped into a crouch, drawing her sword. She backed silently into a low wall of heather and gorse, peering between the stems to see a figure emerging from the shadows below. It was tall and menacing, its face hidden in a hooded cowl. Another figure appeared from above, hugging the scarp as it edged out into the open. This one wore the same dark *bishlah*.

There was only one reason for them to be here. They were hunting her, just as Khoury had warned.

"She is near, I know it." A man's voice, speaking in Rumes'. "Have a care."

"We should have killed her and taken them days ago," said another man's voice. "We could do it now."

The quiet words hung like shards of ice in the evening air. Marin crouched motionless, thorns poking into her back. She gripped her sword tighter, the other hand resting on a pile of loose stone. The two men stopped before her, scanning the hillside.

"And yet we cannot."

"Why? Why must we wait for an order?"

"Because our duty tells us so."

Marin knew by their dialect they were from the south. *Qatana.*

"All things in time, my friend. Matters such as this require flexibility." This one had to be from Riyyal, Marin realized. His presence was commanding. "Both plans and risk will be rewarded in the end. Set aside your fears and doubts."

"Have they called on Ciris Sarn to come? He cannot be trusted, but their minds are clouded."

"Do not speak his name," said the man from Riyyal.

The other snorted. "Haradin fear no one. Why should we curb our tongues?"

"He is not in Ruinart. This I know."

"Then we must not wait any longer. Kill her now."

Marin could almost see the tension in the air.

"Soon," said the one in charge.

"It is not enough to say 'soon.' I must know when."

There was a pause. Marin held her breath and turned her head slightly for a better view. One of the black-clad Haradin shook back his sleeves. His olive-dark fingertips traced silvery threads in the air—luminous and ghostly, a spider's web of dark alchemy. The strands wrapped together in small circles, and each circle became a mirror. As the mirrors took shape, the man gathered them in his hands. It was too difficult for Marin to see any more, for the Haradin stood with their backs to her. She remained still lest they catch a reflection of her movement.

Then the one from Riyyal spoke. "Do you still doubt?" His voice was full of venom.

Marin's fear grew. Her mind raced and her heart pounded. She stared at the arcane mirrors as they faded away into the twilit air, trying to decipher whatever alchemical mystery her pursuers had discovered.

"One thing I do not doubt," said the other Haradin with cold amusement in his voice. "We are not alone here."

He turned, pointing a finger directly at her.

3

THE ONLY way out was forward.

Marin's sword was already drawn and the Haradin were still reaching for theirs as they rushed toward her. She leaped to her feet, pulling free of the gorse, her other hand clutching the stone on which it had rested. She met her assassins with a vicious swing of her blade. She ducked slightly as she followed through, feeling the air part over her as one of the Haradin narrowly missed her with his own curved sword. Marin stayed low, tucking her blade beneath her, and drove forward into the first Haradin. She knocked him over, slamming his knee with the rock as she rolled forward and sprang to her feet—just as the second assassin came at her, swinging his scimitar.

She parried his thrust, grunting at the impact as the blades clashed and shot sparks. Metal locked on metal, the fighters pushing against each other with desperate strength. Marin risked a backward glance. The one she'd knocked to the ground had staggered to his feet, a bit unsteady on his injured knee, raising his scimitar above his head. Turning back to the Haradin she'd already engaged, she yielded with her blade and then pushed, knocking him off balance for just a moment.

It was enough. Marin moved quickly, her sword ringing against his as she spun and slipped behind him. She put her foot in the small of his back, shoving forward so that the man tumbled into his partner. She hurled the rock at the back of his head. Then she broke free and rushed downhill along the switchback.

Looking to her right as she rounded the next turn, she saw two menacing shadows racing down toward her. One was limping and the other weaving as if stunned, but they outnumbered her and their legs were longer than hers. She plunged recklessly off the winding path, somehow keeping her feet while crashing down a steep slope, blurring past exposed rock and wild growth. Marin winced as branches and thorns caught clothing and struck exposed flesh. Her face, arms. and legs stung with scratches.

The sky was still light above the ravine, but the darkness at the bottom blinded her. She gulped for breath and tried to listen over the pounding of her heart. There was no disturbance on the hillside above, and the sound of water at her feet was peaceful. The stream rushed through the darkness, flowing fast and probably clean. She bent down and splashed cold water on her cuts and scratches, and paused to listen again.

Still no sounds of pursuit.

Marin's eyes adjusted to the gloom. She followed the streamlet as it trickled beneath towering pine trees with branches bending low over the banks. She ducked under them, pine needles and nut hulls crunching beneath her boots. The tunnel of branches felt like a hiding place. Or a trap.

She moved on. The incline was much less severe than it had been on the hillside, but she did not slow her pace. Beads of sweat streaked her brow, running down to sting her eyes.

After a time the stream poured over a mossy waterfall and ran alongside a more visible footpath. The ravine broadened into a valley, and the twilight brightened.

Marin had to rest. She was breathing in ragged gasps. Her heart raced with fear and exertion.

Then she felt them, and a moment later heard them.

Who else could it be but the Haradin? And they were approaching quickly.

She'd stayed too long. Cursing silently, she set out once again.

Panic carried Marin faster and farther than she thought exhaustion would let her go. Her feet pounded the forest path, but she could not feel them. Breath tore in and out of her throat. Still the Haradin chased her, maybe closing in, maybe just running her to death. She stumbled over something in the path, lurching, barely keeping her feet. Yet she dared not look back.

She needed sanctuary—some place that would offer her both rest and protection from the assassins.

Then she knew.

"I will see him now," Marin told herself. "It makes no difference whether I have the right words."

She knew the house of Ilss Cencova was near. Reaching it was her only hope. There would be a high wall, a sturdy gate, and sentries standing guard. Inside would be a place to rest, water or wine to drink, and a man who would listen carefully to whatever she said.

If the Haradin let her reach him. She felt them on her heels now, although she would not risk a glance behind her.

Was this it?

Marin saw a trickle of light spilling out between the trees to her left. She leaped off the path by the stream and struggled up a gravel incline with what felt like the last of her strength.

Sanctuary.

A single man stood before an arched *qoos* of stone, dressed in armor and holding a long spear. The sight of an ally unlocked her voice. Her scream was more like a whimper.

"Kill them—"

She dove behind the stunned guard and fell to the flag-stones.

"Them! Out there!" she gasped furiously, pointing toward the stream. Why was he staring at her instead?

Marin raised her head and looked past him. No one had fol-lowed her.

They were gone.

"MARIN? It is you."

The words came from behind her as she stood in the court-yard. She knew without turning that it was Ilss Cencova. She rec-ognized the assurance in his voice and the solidity of his tread on the flagstones.

"I am sorry." Marin turned wearily. "You must think me mad."

"Well, you certainly know how to make an entrance."

Marin looked at him as he stood silhouetted against the door-way. Cencova was of average height, but with broad shoulders and thick hands that bespoke power. Though he still moved with youthful fitness, she saw the years etched on his face as he stepped into the lamplight of the courtyard. Time, worry, and decisive action had lined his brow and cheeks like a beach worn down by the tide. Thick hair spilled from the top of his head and down his neck; he flicked it out of his eyes with the casual gesture Marin remembered so well. His chin was hidden under a thicket of unkempt hair. When she had first met him, the flowing mane and beard had been mostly black. Now, only a few dark hairs wove through the gray.

"I was told you were in Cievv, but waited for you to come to me in your own time," Cencova said. "I heard your rather interesting dispute with the guard and came myself to see the assault on the house."

Marin smiled. "He thought me mad, too. I cannot blame him for that." She blew out a sharp breath. "I bring news."

"It would definitely seem so," Cencova said. "Come."

He motioned for her to follow him into the house. The great hall echoed with their footsteps. The high-windowed room had seen its share of banquets and councils but now seemed more of an armory and warehouse. He led her down a side passage filled with the clatter and smells of a nearby kitchen.

"You will be staying for supper, of course," Cencova said over his shoulder and moved on without waiting for an answer.

Turning a few more corners and descending a short flight of stairs brought them deeper into the house. He threw open a door and waved her in. Marin relaxed a little as they entered a cool, quiet chamber with a gilded fountain bubbling gently in the center. White marble benches circled the cascade of water. Cencova offered her a seat, ladled water into a pewter cup, and handed it to her. He watched her drink gratefully.

"You must tell me why you've come," he said, breaking into her silence. "It has been over a year now since I saw you last."

Marin sighed. "I come seeking answers...about Hiril and why he was killed."

Cencova leaned forward, his high forehead wrinkling in thought. "We know Ciris Sarn was his killer," he said carefully.

Marin paused, her mind racing. *Ciris Sarn.* She had never seen the man, yet vividly imagined running her sword through his chest. But there was a conspiracy far deeper than the deeds of one ill-famed assassin. Did she trust Cencova enough to tell him about the books?

She took a deep breath. "What if you were to learn," she began slowly, "that everything you had been taught—everything you have trusted and believed in since the day you were born—is a lie?"

"What do you mean?"

Marin studied Cencova and finally reached the decision she'd struggled with for days. She had no choice but to tell him all that she knew. It was clear this evening's attack was an effort to steal the manuscripts she kept in the hidden pocket of her cloak.

She looked into the spymaster's eyes and saw in him nothing but a deep commitment to her. He'd been devastated when Hiril was murdered. He'd confided in her at the funeral. She'd wept in his arms.

She must trust him.

"Before I tell you what I have learned, think about this for a moment." Marin's words flowed smoothly now that she had decided to speak the whole truth. "What if people that stood to profit from your ignorance conspired to keep you ignorant? Not just in this or that, but in every aspect of your existence."

Cencova frowned. "I'm listening. But I don't—"

"Think on this, then. What if someone showed you the ways in which you had been deceived? And showed you also that your father and his father and many who came before had been taken in by the same lie? How valuable would the truth be to you? Would it change your life? Would that lie reshape your world, or would you choose to disregard it and carry on with what that you already know?"

Caught up in the excitement of sharing her secret, Marin no longer felt exhausted from her escape, and her cuts and scratches no longer stung. She watched Cencova, waiting for a response.

After a moment, he shrugged. "These are very deep questions. I suppose I would have to know more."

Marin nodded and went on. "What if, after realizing the truth of those deceptions, you chose to respond to that truth?" Her voice rose with confidence. "What if you began studying history and wars and politics, and you discovered that, like a string of pearls, key moments in time were not random—that they'd been crafted with skill and care? Suppose you came to understand that certain people had intentionally created history as we know it—told us all an impossible tale in order to keep us completely ignorant of the truth?"

Cencova's expression remained neutral. "What are you implying, Marin?"

"Only this." She flicked a fingernail against the cup in her hand, and it rang like a bell. "Everything you know about the history of Mir'aj has been rewritten to suit the purpose of those in power."

"What do you mean, those in power?" Cencova gave an irritated frown and didn't wait for her answer. "Listen, a deception on such a scale—a conspiracy of the size you're describing would be...well, impossible. Too many people would know...would *have* to know the truth."

She said nothing, waiting for him to finish sorting through her words.

"Look," he continued, "I'm not sure I follow you. Just what are you getting at? Even if what you're saying is possible, what kind of consequences . . . what could possibly be at stake?"

"The fate of every living person in Mir'aj."

5

THIS TIME, Cencova looked astonished.

As she finished the tale, Marin saw the impact her words had on the spymaster.

She'd begun with her visit to the shrine where she'd paid her respects to Hiril, and described her conversation with Khoury, who had given her the books. She told of her journey to meet with Cencova here in Cievv, and today's attempt on her life after she postponed her visit.

Cencova looked pained when he heard of her indecision. "It is my fault, Marin. I should have done something long ago."

"What do you mean?" Marin asked.

"I was the one who directed Hiril to seek out Tariq Alyalah and learn if what he possessed was as powerful as we suspected. Your husband was to meet the *sufi* at Burj al-Halij. Everything we discovered after his death led us to believe that he was murdered before this meeting came to pass."

"When did you suspect Sarn?" Marin demanded.

"From the beginning. But—"

"The evidence was clear."

"Yes . . . and no. The manner in which Hiril was—" Cencova broke off and looked carefully at Marin. "Let us say that it was unlike his other murders. The method was quite different. Sarn wants us to know it was him."

"So the investigation led you elsewhere."

"The trail widened so far that we made no further progress. It kept coming back to the assassin. Yet Sarn eluded us. Until now." Cencova's voice turned grim. "This changes everything. There is nowhere he can hide."

Marin set her cup on the fountain's ledge and reached deep into her cloak. "I am placing my trust in you," she said. "There is something I must show you."

Slowly, almost fearfully, she brought out the books one by one.

"Ah," murmured the spymaster. "I suspected ... but scarce did I believe ... ."

All of the books in Marin's hands appeared to be the same, yet somehow each was different. They exuded a sensation of ancient wonder and knowledge while looking as if they had come new from a bindery. The palm boards of each book were sewn with silk into lambskin bindings, protected from wear and the elements with a slipcover of rich brown canvas. The black calligraphy, written in a language neither she nor Cencova could decipher, stood out as if freshly inked on the creamy pages.

Marin shuddered at the touch of powerful magic as she placed the books on the bench next to her. Each looked the same, appeared to be the same size. But each was different.

They *felt* different.

The first one's cover seemed gritty to the touch; the second slightly warm; the third damp. The final book had a feeling of weightlessness as if, despite its heft, it could float away like a feather in the wind.

Marin and Cencova sat in quiet awe, picking up each book and, running their fingers along the covers, leafing through the pages.

"These are what my husband died for," Marin finally said.

Cencova nodded.

"What are they?"

"*Waed an-Citab* ... the Books of Promise," he replied softly.

"What is their history?"

Cencova told her.

6

"YOU HAVE been carrying the greatest lie ever told by man."

Even as he spoke the words, Marin could sense Cencova's struggle within himself.

"If what you just told me is true, and if the things I already know are true," he continued, "certainly these texts you have brought me are far from ordinary."

"So the trail of bloodshed would tell us. Too many have been slaughtered—Hiril and others—for these to be merely ordinary." Marin gestured at the books. "I am being hunted because of them. No, they are much more than ordinary."

"Yet even with the relics that, against all odds, now lie before me, I remain skeptical," Cencova said. "Without greater proof, I cannot be certain. The burden of indictment for holding these books falls heavy on our shoulders if we pursue this to the end."

"How so?"

Cencova sighed, bowing his head and running his fingers through his hair. Looking up, he smiled wanly and put his hand on Marin's. "We have a decision to make, Marin Altaïr. The easiest course would be to destroy them now. Burning flames or the depths of the sea could make it seem as if these books had never existed. The old order of things would remain in effect."

Marin nodded.

"However, given the power we both sense in them, I'm not even sure they can be destroyed. Look at their age." He ran a wondering hand over one of the books' cover. "They hardly seem old. And if we could dispose of them, what possible magic might we unleash? And do we allow this charade to continue, a society built of lies piled upon lies? Yet . . . if we topple that pile of lies, what consequences do we face?"

"I agree with you," Marin said. "We must decide, but what?"

Now that they were talking, the whole thing seemed impossible despite all that had occurred. Cencova knew much more than she had guessed. Indeed, he seemed surprised only that she had brought the books to his house. Magical as these volumes felt, could they truly be the root of ... everything?

The plot was too great, the years of widespread deception too mad to consider. If someone could prove that the Books of Promise held such lies and that a conspiracy of untold dimensions had existed for centuries, then kingdoms and councils would fall as the conspirators were crushed. Who would rise to take their places? The ripples of this discovery would spread across Mir'aj in ever-growing, unpredictable ways.

Who could invent and spread such intricate lies? How could such lies take root in every aspect of society? The scope of this thing went beyond imagining. Diabolical factions, unnatural monsters, assassins and saboteurs all perpetuated the lies under whose orders? It could only be someone with unequaled power and influence.

The Sultan of Qatana himself. There could be no one else.

Once Marin put a human face on this madness, the picture in her mind shifted into something more believable. Just as Khoury's news of Sarn had finally focused the rage she felt at Hiril's death, laying the vast conspiracy at the Sultan's feet turned it into a knot Marin could unravel.

Maybe.

She resolved to try.

Cencova studied her for a few moments and then shook his head. "This cannot be settled without time and careful thought. I now wonder whom I can trust to help us make these dire decisions," he murmured. "Whom do I go to?" He reached out and squeezed her hand. "And, there is the matter of Ciris Sarn and what role he plays in all of this."

Marin's eyes flashed. "For that reason alone, I will not stop. Vengeance will fall upon the assassin, and I shall deliver it."

"Marin, do not be so hasty."

She ripped her hand out of his grasp. He stared back at her impassively.

"Hear my words," he said. "We do not know what part he has in it."

"He is nothing but a killer!"

"True, but a highly successful one. From what I know of Sarn, he wields terrible power."

"But—"

He raised a hand, silencing her. "Neither of us can fathom it, but it is there. Sarn does not kill without reason."

"He kills because he is paid to kill."

"You are correct. Someone paid for the assassination; Sarn just carried it out. You risk losing the trail to your true enemies if he is killed."

Marin shook her head fiercely. "He is my only enemy. If I see him, he dies."

"Your hatred blinds you, woman." Cencova's tone was harsh, suddenly that of a strategist instead of a friend. "Don't you understand? He is a link. Through him we can learn everything we need to know."

Marin would not be mollified. "As long as he draws breath, he mortally offends me. I will wash with his own blood the profit he made from killing Hiril."

Cencova sighed heavily. "I understand your anger, Marin. But you assume too much."

"Such as?"

"That he killed Hiril for gold."

"Why else would he?"

"Why?" Cencova's bushy eyebrows arched. "Information. Power. Perhaps something else."

"His motivation does not matter to me."

"Perhaps not. At least, not at this moment," he said. "But there is much more to decipher about this whole business. I need time to think."

"I will go alone if I must," Marin said, lowering her head. She had come here hoping for—what? Something different from this. Her long day and desperate evening caught up with her. Her shoulders slumped and a sob escaped her.

Cencova reached out a gentle hand to wipe the tears from her cheeks. He spoke in softer tone.

"Give me three days."

7

MARIN'S POLITE and friendly mask was slipping.

Her patience would be the next thing to go.

After Cencova ended their discussion and gave her supper, he sent her to the city with six guards to escort her through the hills. They met no obstacles along the way, nor did trouble find Marin in the Rassan Majalis' safe house where they hid her. Two of the armed guards never left her side—except when she needed privacy to relieve herself or bathe.

Cencova needed time to draw up a list of those he could absolutely trust, and then contact them. Marin knew this difficult task could take longer than three days and had no idea when she'd meet with the spymaster again.

But she would not be idle. Her year of mourning was past, and she would not sit waiting for danger to come again. Why wait? If there were any assassins lurking in the city, whether her pair of Haradin or some others, she would find them and take them on. After all, she knew something about hunting enemies in cities, too.

Of course, her guards would not permit this if she made her plans known; or, at best, they would insist on coming along. Either way, they were inconvenient. Marin needed a way to escape from them.

She found one.

The wine was strong and excellent, and she convinced her guards that drinking alone gave her no pleasure. Fierce and deadly as she could be, Marin was also a beautiful young woman. Neither of these men had wives, she learned—and neither could resist her subtle charms.

She entertained them with war stories from her Four Banners campaigns, filling their cups again and again until they stopped noticing whether she filled hers. At length, both were snoring lustily, one with his head on the table, the other stretched out on a bench. Marin blew them each a kiss on her way out of the room.

She stepped into the street, head clouded with the wine. Her night vision was slow in coming, and she felt as if she were swimming or flying instead of walking. But she had her sword and her confidence. Even drunk, she reasoned, she was more than a match for most sober men.

Marin strode purposefully through the streets of Cievv, a city that never slept. She scoured the winehouses, coffeehouses, temples and brothels looking for Qatani foreigners who might have recently arrived.

"So you're saying that you don't remember anyone at all this past week?" she demanded of yet another innkeeper. "You know Qatani, yes? Maybe Haradin? Olive skin, black clothed, dangerous assassins?"

The man grunted. "So what if I did?" he said, not looking up from his accounts.

She placed one hand on her sword and slapped the other hard against the wooden counter that was keeping him alive—for now. His head snapped up, and he went pale, as though he stood before a judge about to pass sentence.

"N-no, my good lady, there have not," he stammered. "Not been any . . . I mean, yes, I don't remember . . . I mean, no, no Qatani have lodged here since winter!"

"Thank you." She flung the words at him like a curse and pushed back out to the street. An ocean breeze tugged at her hair and made her feel more awake. "Craven fuck," she sneered at the door. Maybe he heard her. Who cared?

She stood outside the inn for some moments, surveying the cramped streets and the people—revelers, tradesmen making late deliveries, petty thieves or unfaithful husbands going about their furtive business. She savored the heady scents of late-night meals, aromatic wood smoke, and fruity wines, all carried on the sea air. It was a fine night to be drunk in the streets, although she felt a stab of sadness that all these people, all the people of Mir'aj, in fact, had no idea they were living a lie.

Marin carefully set off in a direction that swept her along with the crowds, choosing an indirect route to her bed. She'd been in the streets for hours and was no closer to learning anything about the men who had attacked her in the hills. The wine-inspired excitement of outwitting her guards, of being free and on a mission, was draining away. Now she felt sober, sleepy and exasperated.

Pulling her hood firmly around her face, she blended first with one knot of people, then another, making her way back to the safe house. She kept her ears open to their chatter. Braggarts and fools, that was all they were—dull, ignorant men, of no use to her.

What a waste of effort.

It was not until she slipped back into her chamber and had thrown off her cloak that she finally conceded defeat. Wherever the assassins were, they'd hidden well. Nothing short of chance was going to bring her any closer to them. Cencova certainly wouldn't help. He had greater concerns.

The guards still lay where they'd fallen, snoring merrily. The one at the table had a hand wrapped around his cup. Marin found her bed and fell back against the cushions, drained in mind and spirit. But the tension that had driven her through the streets, poised for a fight, was still with her. It could be a while before sleep found her.

What had she been thinking when she went on this reckless

little adventure? She had no clue about her attackers beyond what she already knew: they wanted the Books of Promise, they were involved with Sarn, and they were versed in the sinister secrets of dark alchemy. Beyond that, instinct had failed her tonight. As she lay in bed, mind still reeling, she felt as if she'd failed Hiril as well.

She realized she was caressing the empty space next to her. She turned her head and softly stroked the pillow, remembering the touch of her fingers on Hiril's smiling cheeks. Words of endearment rose to her lips, but what came out was much different.

"I must find him," she whispered. "I will slice him open and cut sinew from bone. He who is worth less than nothing took your life that was beyond price. I will turn the sea red with his blood and burn his corpse in a cauldron hotter than both suns."

When she finally fell asleep, the pillow was soaked with her tears.

IT WAS almost midnight.

Ilss Cencova rose from his table, snuffed the candle, and left the room. There were always reports to read and ways to interpret them, he thought as he descended the back stairway, wrapping his cloak around him. But some of the most valuable information could not be committed to paper, at least not yet.

The stairwell was dark, and anyone watching the rear of the house would have a hard time seeing him open the door and step into the night. He crossed the back garden, crept silently through an outer gate, and stayed in the shadows of the alley until he came to a back road. The nighttime revelry never reached the part of Cievv where Cencova kept his office, and his dark cape and intimidating manner made him an unlikely target for suspicion— as long as he walked with confidence.

He followed a dim, quiet route to the harbor, where he made for a private slip far from the busy freight depots. Once there, he crossed the stone landing to the hidden stairway that led down to the moorings.

Standing alone in the dark, Cencova knew instantly that he was being watched. He did not turn but shifted his stance to acknowledge the contact. On the quay above him, someone softly whistled a few notes of one tune, then another, then a third—a prearranged signal to assure him this was indeed an intermediary for the Majalis rather than a solitary sentinel descending the stairs to stand beside him. Each man was well hidden within the shadows of his clothing, and both stood facing the water.

"We have news," the agent said.

Cencova grunted acknowledgement, and the contact continued.

"There is proof that the attacks were sanctioned by Ciris Sarn, and that he headed to Riyyal."

Cencova finally spoke. "Does Sarn seek to usurp the throne himself? I cannot believe he carries such weight."

"Sarn's purposes are unclear, but do not underestimate his strength or reach. The Sultan is dying. Nasir is lost, and Malek is weak. Who will inherit the throne? Perhaps Sarn has some unseen control over the matter. Then there is Fajeer Dassai. What part does he play in this? Too many unknowns. We must narrow our focus."

"What does the Rassan Majalis wish of me?" Cencova said.

"Everything possible must be done to capture Ciris Sarn. Find him. Take him alive. The *siri* are at your disposal."

Cencova remained silent for a time. Distant chimes marked the late hour. "Any hope of aid?" he finally asked.

"The conspiracy runs deep. The Jassaj are also involved. Pavanan Munif acted under Sarn's authority while in Tivisis. He must be taken as well."

"Which *majals* know of the plan?"

"Very few," said the agent. "We're afraid it will get back to the conspirators. It is a small stable that knows about this." He looked back up the stairway. "Will that be all?"

Cencova debated whether to tell them about the arrival of Marin and the books. He chose caution and held his tongue. "Yes. That is all for now."

The agent bowed slightly in Cencova's direction and ascended the stairs. His footsteps faded quickly as he moved off down the quay. Cencova continued to gaze at the black waters, waiting. He heard footsteps coming toward him and the voices of a man and woman passing above his head. He waited until they boarded one of the ships farther out before making his way back home.

There is still someone else I need to see, he thought.

9

MARIN CLOSED her eyes against the fierce light.

Her head pounded as she lowered it into her hands. She willed the pain away and tried to focus on something useful. Her mind swam with all the random facts and baseless rumors that had come to her attention since her journey to Ruinart began. If she could just organize them into a useful pattern—

Someone stirred next to her, groaning slightly. Without opening her eyes, Marin knew it was one of her guards, standing wearily on either side of the bed where she slumped. She felt some remorse for him, but not much.

They had all been sleeping off their debauch late in the morning when someone banged with unnecessary vigor at the door. It was Cencova's messenger. He raised a disapproving eyebrow at the staggering guards who admitted him, and at Marin sitting blearily in her bed, trying to make sense of the interruption. The spymaster would see her now, and she must make haste despite her . . . condition. The man shook his head at the guards and departed.

They escorted her through the streets without a word, shielding their eyes against the light, flinching at the midday bustle. Marin could tell they were embarrassed by last night's unprofessional conduct, and wondered if they knew she had slipped away from them. Mostly, though, she focused on navigating the overwhelming sounds and smells of Cievv in the impossibly bright daylight. In a corner of her mind, she wondered if Cencova had found out about last night's wine-fueled search of the city and wanted to have words about that—or if he was ready to continue the conversation begun at his house three days ago.

Because of his work with the Rassan Majalis and the *siri*, the spymaster maintained a number of rooms in the city, and conducted his business first in this one, then in that one. Only a select few knew how to find him on any given day. The place to which Marin's guards brought her was in a wealthier neighborhood where the streets were mostly quiet except for well-dressed, orderly servants going about their errands. The flat was two flights up at the back of a handsome, spotlessly clean house.

The antechamber's windows overlooked the harbor. It was a clear day, and the sun streamed in. Marin could have asked one of her guards to pull the curtains, but decided against it. Calling Cencova's attention to her condition might start the conversation off badly.

Instead, she sat with closed eyes, thinking about the Books of Promise and the vast conspiracy spun around them.

"There is always an answer," she told herself. "It is just waiting to be found."

That had been Hiril's guiding philosophy. So far, she was still seeking any answer at all. Lies were thick on the ground wherever she looked. Who among the powerful were doubling their allegiances? Who suspected whom of betrayal? Marin knew that she could become a suspect herself.

"What if Cencova talks about me?" she wondered. "What if I gave myself away last night, and he has decided to give me up?

How many already know I am here?"

She smiled bitterly at the thought of such things. She knew in her heart that her motivation would always remain pure: Hiril's enemies were her enemies. No jewels, however they glittered, and no sword, however sharp, would deter Marin from her mission.

She lifted her head at the sound of an opening door. A man stood before her. He was not a guard. Obviously he must be the spymaster's assistant. His face was expressionless, and Marin felt a surge of excitement despite the painful pounding in her head. The man cleared his throat.

"He will see you now."

"SARN MUST wait ... for now."

Marin had almost relaxed after Cencova handed her a small cup of strong coffee and made pleasant small talk that included nothing about last night's impulsive behavior. Both had ignored the four Books of Promise sitting on the table at his elbow. But at these words, the color drained from her face, and her head began to pound anew.

"Why?"

Had she been feeling more like herself, the word would have burst from her in a scream of rage. Instead, it came out in a meek whimper.

"You have another mission first." Cencova's tone was firm.

Marin said nothing.

"You must confirm the authenticity of the books."

Again she was silent.

"We must know this before anything else," he went on, "but it will be a difficult task, Marin. You must seek the Sha'ir of Aeíx."

"Aeíx?" Marin grimaced. "Do you know how much I hate that

place?"

Cencova gave an apologetic shrug. "I understand why you might. Nevertheless, that is where you'll find this particular *sha'ir*."

"And what is a *sha'ir*?"

"An elemental witch. One who delves into the lore of the Jnoun."

"And this sorcerer can prove that the books are real?" Marin asked.

"I believe so ... yes."

Marin hesitated. This was not where her quest was supposed to take her. How did it bring her any closer to cutting off Ciris Sarn's arms and legs and spitting in his eye while his life bled away? She was beginning to understand, however, that other people's strategies would postpone this satisfaction. As long as they didn't rob her of it altogether, she would accept the choices they gave her.

"Well enough," she said wearily. "What must I do?"

"It will be dangerous." Cencova looked at her with some concern. "I know you are not yourself today, but I want you to reach this decision with a firm grasp of the risks. The Sha'ir of Aeíx has an evil heart, and may kill you rather than reveal the books' contents."

"I may be suffering this afternoon," retorted Marin, her face growing hot, "but I assure you my grasp of this matter is as firm as anyone could wish. You will not let me kill Sarn until you have unraveled the lies that wrap themselves around those." She gestured at the four books stacked on his table. "This accursed bitch may provide me with answers, or perhaps she will murder me. That is the risk I will take."

Cencova was silent for a time.

Finally he nodded and pushed the books across the table toward her.

"The ship is nearly ready.

"You sail tonight."

11

SHE HAD been here before.

Marin had ridden across the island with the Four Banners. This was the place where she first met Hiril. Where the dying kayal had cursed his future. Where they fell in love for the last year of his life. She had hoped to never set foot on these shores again.

At least there was no rain this time.

It wasn't a long journey from Darós, but the coast road was treacherous. The land that faced the sea was rocky and dry, the soil consisting of limestone rock and rough sand. Ragged hills rose above sheer cliffs. The suns' reflection off the crags made the landscape gleam white as Marin followed a narrow path to a desolate ridge. It was shaped like a skeletal finger pointing west, a command to leave this island and flee far away.

All who lived on Aeíx feared this spot. They were afraid of the *sha'ir*, and believed that she regularly stole and ate the bones of the dead. Marin wondered how such a bright landscape could conceal something so dark.

A few hours out of Darós she reached the opening of a tunnel—a forbidding maw, black against the white rocks around it. She drew closer, remembering the spymaster's warnings. "The place is riddled with tunnels, and the witch dwells somewhere within them," Cencova had said. "I am unsure of which one. None living has seen her lair. Tread carefully."

Marin approached the entrance cautiously, her pace slowing as she peered at the dark hole in the shining landscape. The light of the second sun let her see fifty feet into the tunnel. She could just make out three caverns splitting off from the main entrance. Beyond that, the daylight would not go.

She lit her lantern.

Marin had little doubt that each of these caverns led to other tunnels and pits, winding deep into the rocky point like a rabbit's warren.

Cencova's warning echoed in her thoughts: "She may kill you rather than reveal the contents of the books." Marin had accepted that choice. If she died, her life without Hiril would be that much shorter. If she succeeded, Ciris Sarn was that much closer to dying at her hand.

"Either way, I win," Marin reasoned to herself, moving into the darkness.

12

VOICES OF the dead taunted her.

Marin shuddered as dark words and strange images resonated in her mind. She knew it was a spell, a barrier of magic against anyone who attempted to disturb the *sha'ir*. She knew Aeíx was becoming more of a fell place with each passing year, and this enchantment felt like the root of everything else that plagued this miserable island. Angrily she ignored the ghost voices and their whispered fears. She wouldn't let these things stop her.

Marin went deeper into the cave. She paused at yet another fork that led to three different tunnels. Since she'd walked into the darkness with lantern held high, all of her choices seemed to come in threes.

Up to this point, the air had been cool and still. Now there was a faint hint of rot. She took a step closer to the tunnel on her right. The odor of rot grew stronger.

Here. This tunnel.

Marin entered, ready to face the witch.

An overwhelming odor of excrement and decay assailed her nostrils as she moved deeper into the tunnel. Marin doubled over and retched, her body recoiling from the charnel stench. She fought the urge to turn and flee, forcing her way deeper underground with her cloak over nose and mouth.

Time passed, the foul stench growing with each minute. She willed herself to ignore it. The books lay in a deep inner pocket of her cloak, their presence reassuring her like protective talismans. The cool air gradually gave way to a warmer, damper atmosphere, tinged with the reek of sour milk.

Marin paused briefly in her descent and suppressed a shudder. Her hand gripped the handle of a short-bladed saif. The lantern's dim flicker barely reached ahead of her now, and she relied more on sound and touch to guide her way. She breathed evenly and deeply through her mouth, calming herself. Walking into danger was nothing new to her. Keeping an inner calm had always kept her alive on these missions.

So far.

A distant light grew, beckoning. Sensing she was close, Marin pressed forward.

She paused at the mouth of a cavernous room with stalactites jutting like fangs from the ceiling. Shadows flickered on the walls. A faint tinge of smoke masked the stench of decay, making her eyes sting. The light came from thousands of foul candles dripping greasily from ledges and crevices in the walls.

She took a cautious step forward, dropping the cloak from her face and gripping the hilt of her sword.

Across the cave, something stared at her with predatory eyes. She could feel its hunger and hatred before she saw what it was. A wasted figure sat on a throne of what seemed to be polished limestone. It was a hag wrapped in a raven-black *abaya*, and she had the look of someone expecting a guest. At her feet lay an opening like a shallow grave, where a blue light burned with a smokeless flame.

Taking a deep breath, her muscles coiled and tense, Marin entered the vile lair. After a few more steps, she could see that the *sha'ir's* throne was actually made from weathered rosewood and bleached bone.

A voice spoke, making her skin crawl.

"Come closer, my pretty thing," the hag said.

13

"DO YOU know of these relics?"

Marin held one of the books in her right hand. Her left hand never strayed from the handle of the saif. She had stopped ten feet from the witch, not daring to come any closer. "There are three others. They were found together."

The *sha'ir's* gaze flicked to the book Marin held, then settled on her face. "Where were they found?" The voice was thick and gurgling, with an edge like tearing parchment.

"It matters not," Marin responded, suppressing a shudder at that unsettling sound. "They are here now."

The hag's dark eyes fixed upon Marin with penetrating force. They carried the same magical charge that Marin had ignored when she first entered the tunnels.

"Strong, too, I see." Marin heard envy and admiration in the words.

"Yes," she agreed, and meant it.

The *sha'ir* smiled, baring puffy gums and blackened teeth filed needle-sharp. A shiver of fear raced down Marin's spine. Yes, she was strong, but fear was essential, too—it had kept her alive many times.

"Relics, you call them. And you can't read them, and want to know what they mean. Why should I share such secrets with you?"

"It is important to me," Marin said, which was the truth.

"And what will you give me in return?"

"You may feast upon the bones of a ruthless killer," Marin said in ringing tones.

The witch's horrid smile widened even more. "Ah, yes. Yes, I would love that. But I need more."

Of course she would. Marin knew that anyone who proposes a bargain is at a disadvantage.

"What's that?" she asked neutrally.

"I will tell you the secrets of those books. But after you kill the assassin, his soul becomes mine."

"As you wish." Marin bit back a smile. She cared nothing for the soul of Ciris Sarn, and if this meant further torture for him after she took his life, so much the better.

"And," rasped the witch, "the books themselves become payment as well. All four of them."

Marin's mind raced. Despite her personal mission to kill Sarn, she understood that, to many, the Books of Promise held far more value than the life of one miserable assassin. Who was she to trade the fate of the world for her own revenge?

"Well?" The hag's grating voice became even more unpleasant. "The Four Books. Yes."

The witch was her only choice. Maybe gaining the knowledge of what was written in the books would make the books themselves unnecessary. Cencova could find a solution to the problem. He must—because she had to take this chance. "Agreed," Marin said at last. "They are yours once he is dead."

The *sha'ir* made a chilling sound that was perhaps a sigh of pleasure.

"But now you will translate them," said Marin. "You agreed."

"Yes, yes. Come to me."

Marin hesitated. Words might shield her, but physical contact with this loathsome creature would be far more dangerous.

"Do not fear," the *sha'ir* said, her smile turning the words into a mockery. "I have no ... desire for you ... just yet." She beckoned with a bony claw.

Marin moved closer, Cencova's dire words flitting through her mind once more.

"Your left hand." The *sha'ir* gestured again. "To seal the bargain."

Marin reached across the flickering blue pit, ready to lash out with her sword if she sensed the slightest threat. The hag enfolded her hand in fingers that felt like those of a desiccated corpse, but pulsing with unnatural life. They clamped shut with an explosion of pain. Marin cried out and jerked her hand back, eyes flicking to the cut that ran across her palm from thumb to smallest finger. The hag grinned, her long nail tinged red. Marin took a step back, unmindful of the blood running from the wound.

The *sha'ir* made arcane gestures above the pit and uttered words in a language Marin didn't recognize. The air between them shifted and almost took form.

It was a dark presence, shapeless yet threatening.

"Our bargain is sealed," the *sha'ir* said. "The Evil Eye is on you, always watching. If you fail to deliver those four books as agreed, a curse will fall upon you. The mark on your palm will disappear when I've been paid in full."

What have I done? Marin thought.

The *sha'ir* held out both hands, her bony fingers twitching with impatience. "Now, give them to me."

Trembling, Marin handed the books to the witch.

MARIN COULD not understand the words the *sha'ir* uttered, but the sense of ill magic grew stronger.

Brilliant red light flashed behind the witch. Marin threw up her hands to protect her eyes, but the sight of her bleeding palm reminded her that she needed to watch everything. Flames roiled behind the throne, and Marin lowered her hands in time to see— something—emerge from the fiery pall. She forced herself to stand her ground and breathe.

A shape of infernal fire loomed behind the *sha'ir*, the flames from the top of its head blackening the ceiling. Marin shrank away from the molten giant. Its blazing eyes were impossible to meet. They swept across the cavern, passing over the *sha'ir* and settling briefly on Marin.

She knew what this thing was. An efreet. A hellish spirit, known for its brazenness and evil. Efreeti—born of flame. Marin had heard that they were cunning, malevolent, with a burning hatred for mortals. Was the *sha'ir* actually strong enough? Would she be able to control what she'd called up? If not for the books now in the hag's shriveled hands, Marin would have fled.

"What do you wish of me?" the efreet asked. Its voice was deep, melodious, compelling—yet still inhuman. And certainly not to be trusted. Marin felt a chill despite the intense heat.

"To glean the knowledge contained in these ancient texts of wisdom." The witch held up the Books of Promise.

"I will do your bidding," rumbled the efreet, "with the promise of more essence of the dead."

"I know what sustains you." The *sha'ir* smiled as she flicked a sidelong glance at Marin. "It shall be done."

What? Marin stepped back as a spike of fear stabbed through her stomach.

The hag actually laughed. "Do not fear, my pretty thing," she said. "The efreet gains its strength through *Azza*, not through you."

What followed might have lasted only a few moments or half the night. It was a dream or hallucination outside the flow of time. Throwing foul-smelling objects into the blue fire and chanting in a voice like the death cries of tortured animals, the *sha'ir* performed a ritual that invited the efreet to possess her—yet when the Jnoun tried to enter, a pillar of flame reaching out to consume the witch, she fought it as if fighting for her life.

It was horrific. Marin fought her own body's compulsion to run from the stinking cavern.

She stayed. She would not leave this place without the Books of Promise.

Thrashing in what could have been a dance or a death spasm, the *sha'ir* flung herself at the walls of the cave, knocking statues from the ledges, flapping her black *abaya* against the floor when a falling candle set it alight. The efreet was her partner in the dance, bright as a sun, insubstantial as smoke, laughing madly as it tried again and again to merge with her body. Suddenly it pulled back, threw her against the cavern wall, took a running leap and effortlessly plunged into her, its immense fiery bulk simply disappearing.

For a moment all was still.

The *sha'ir* sat propped against the curving wall. Her eyes were open, staring blankly at Marin.

Then she spoke.

The voice was not her own; it was the efreet.

"The books . . . give them to me."

There was irresistible command in that voice. Marin felt her feet move; they brought her to the throne where the hag had left the books. She picked them up. The ancient magic she felt when she touched their covers seemed more alive than ever. She was amazed, but the amazement belonged to someone else. The efreet's mystical essence was transforming her into a puppet. Would she ever be herself again?

Marin thought about killing Ciris Sarn, and the hatred was satisfyingly familiar. Yes, she was still her own creature.

While she was lost in reflection, she had walked to the *sha'ir* and placed the books in those bony claws.

She pulled back. The dry old skin was burning hot.

The *sha'ir* lifted the first manuscript and paged through it, running swift fingers over the black calligraphy. Marin expected the palm boards to singe and curl, but nothing happened. The witch sat hunched on the floor of the cave, skimming her way through one book, then setting it down and picking up another. She flipped through the pages and reached for the third.

With the efreet's attention turned away from her, Marin

came back to herself. It was quiet in the cavern. The stench was hideous, and her body ached as if she'd been standing for hours, tensed for flight.

The *sha'ir* set down the third book and picked up the fourth. She went through this one more slowly, whether paying closer attention or fighting off sleep, Marin could not tell. At long last, the hag finished the final book, made a neat stack of all four, and held out the *Waed an-Citab*, her dark, empty eyes staring through Marin.

She took them, careful not to touch the hands again.

Then the efreet spoke.

IT WAS GONE.

Impossible words were still ringing in her mind.

Marin had braced herself for the efreet's huge fiery shape to burst out of the *sha'ir* once it had told her what the Books of Promise held. But there was no fire to be seen, other than the guttering candles that lined the cavern's walls. A wisp of the efreet's essence undulated from the hag's body with a flash of light in colors Marin had never seen before. It faded as if retreating into the distance, crossing back into the unseen realm of the Jnoun. The *sha'ir* jerked once and slumped forward like a dead thing.

Marin stood watching, as she had for hours—disgusted, exhausted, and realizing that she could now flee. The books were still in her hands. She hid them once again in the folds of her cloak and turned to leave.

"Well?"

The witch struggled to her feet, looking careworn and irritable. "Now you've learned the secrets," she said, her raspy voice sullen. "Are you satisfied?"

"Yes," Marin said.

"When Ciris Sarn is dead, I will know." The *sha'ir* wagged a finger at her. "Whether he is slain in Qatana or Miranes' or anywhere else, I will see. And I will command his soul." Her smile was all pointed teeth and puffy gums. "Then you will deliver the *Waed an-Citab* back to me. And I will keep them."

"Yes," Marin said. "That is our bargain."

"Wait," the *sha'ir* told her, turning abruptly. "A trace of the efreet's flame lingers within me." She reached into a wooden box on a nearby ledge and produced what looked like a glass eye. "This will tell us if it said all there was to say." Holding the round object in her right hand, she slammed it with surprising strength into the palm of her left, pressing and grinding until the smooth glass was embedded in her flesh. Revolted, Marin looked on.

The orb pulsed with the same impossible colors the efreet had flashed when it vanished moments before.

The *sha'ir* raised her eyes and fixed Marin with an menacing stare. "There is a fifth book," she rasped. "I shall have this one too."

"A fifth book?" Marin shook her head. "I know of only four."

"There is a fifth," the *sha'ir* repeated. "The efreet knows to be true. Bring it when you return."

Marin stood a little straighter. "May I remind you of your own words?" she said coldly. "Four books, or nothing. Was it not our bargain?"

The witch clenched her bony claws, nails clicking on the glass orb embedded in her palm. "Do as I say, pretty bitch," she spat.

"I am not bound to this!"

The *sha'ir* thrust her face toward Marin, her features contorted into a mad grimace. Her breath stank of carrion. "You will bring me the fifth book!"

"Never!" Marin shouted and ran for the mouth of the cavern.

The *sha'ir's* feet slapped on the stone, closing in fast.

Too fast.

16

MARIN BURST out of the cave into the glare of sunlight.

Both suns were already well above the eastern horizon, and their reflection off the white limestone ridge was blinding after a flight underground.

She sat gasping on the nearest boulder, clutching at the stitch in her side. If the *sha'ir* emerged from that black opening in the rocks, Marin would be defenseless.

But the hag did not appear. Indeed, Marin had run so fast and hard through the fetid darkness, lantern thrust in front of her to keep from crashing into the tunnel walls, that she had no idea when the witch had stopped chasing her. Maybe the *sha'ir* had thought to slow her down with the onslaught of malevolent whispers and nightmare images that haunted the caverns, but the assault on her mind had only made Marin run faster.

She looked around as the painful heaving of her breath slowed. This white finger of rock, jutting into the sea from a desolate coastline, was the most beautiful thing she'd ever seen, especially under a blue morning sky with gulls screaming and wheeling above the surf. It was good to be alive, to see where she was, to breathe clean air again.

Marin patted the deep fold within her cloak where she had hidden the books. Yes, they were still there. She laughed in relief at not having to go back into those caves and look for them.

Her lantern was still burning brightly in the daylight. She extinguished it and set it on the ground. Her saif was still at her side, too, and she gripped the comforting shape of its handle.

Taking inventory of her possessions, enjoying the sunny morning, calming her pounding heart and heaving chest—the simple pleasures of here and now were so much better than the images that would haunt her mind if she let them. The efreet, its frighteningly beautiful voice coming from the hag's vile mouth, had told her things that mortal minds were not meant to comprehend. To recall it now would be too close to the terror she was trying to escape.

Escape. Yes, she must get away from here.

Marin rose to her feet, picked up her lantern, and set off down the slope. It was still early in the day, but she intended to reach Darós and her ship as soon as possible—to be well out to sea before night fell again on this cursed island.

It was best to think only a few minutes or hours ahead. Facing the horrible truth could wait until she was with someone she trusted.

When the path between the boulders met the coast road, Marin turned her face to the south and began to run again. One hand rested on her sword and the other clutched the lantern like a weapon. She felt ready for whatever dangers this land might hold.

Until an armed figure stepped in front of her as she rounded a sharp bend.

Her sword was drawn and swinging through the air before she recognized her foe.

It was Torre Lavvann.

17

"YOU LIVE."

Marin smiled as she saw the look of relief that washed over Lavvann's face.

"Indeed, Torre, I do." It was the only response she could manage. She sheathed her sword.

"Is something chasing you?" The Four Banners captain stepped to one side, peering around the bend behind Marin.

"Not yet." Marin's smile faded. "But I wish to be far from the shores of Aeíx by nightfall."

"An excellent plan!" said Lavvann, grinning. "Come."

He spun on his heel and strode off at a brisk walk. Marin fell in beside him, comforted by the familiar clink of chain mail.

"Did Cencova send you?" she asked.

"He did. He knows my long history of saving your life."

Marin snorted. "Why not just put us on the same ship? Fewer sailors to pay."

"He knew I would be finishing some business just across the channel, and sent one of your sailors to collect me."

"Why were you on Inníl?"

Lavvann shrugged his broad shoulders. "Greedy brigands, timid royals—the usual tales." He gave her a sidelong glance. "And why are you on Aeíx, which we all know is your least favorite place?"

"I like it less than I did before," Marin sighed. "And I'll like it still less when I return yet again."

Lavvann's lips curved in his familiar ironic smile. "I suspect you have a story to tell me, Marin Altaïr."

"Suspicious, are you?" she shot back. "Well, maybe I do."

And if so, where would she begin? She trusted her former captain with her life, a trust he had confirmed on many occasions, yet there were parts of her story about which she was still unsure. But even as she deliberated, Marin found herself beginning the tale, her tongue loosened by the ocean air and the comforting presence of her old mentor. It was such a relief after her encounter underground with the *sha'ir* and the efreet.

She told him of meeting Nabeel Khoury at the shrine of Sey'r an-Shal, of her resolve to kill Ciris Sarn by her own hand, of the Haradin's attack in the hills above Cievv and—finally, because her story made little sense without it—of the *Waed an-Citab*, the Books of Promise.

The efreet had told her exactly what they were: contracts between a long-ago Sultan of Qatana and the four tribes of Jnoun. That would explain why one book felt like fire, one like water, one like sand and one like air. The contracts were an agreement to slowly destroy the curtain between worlds, although the efreet had been vague as to the method of destruction. Over the centuries, the Sultanate had worked steadily, using its supreme authority to fulfill the terms of the contract.

And if Marin was to believe the words of a Jnoun whose hatred for mortals was legendary, the contract was nearly fulfilled.

She and Lavvann reached Darós without incident and boarded the ship in silence. Marin had hoped that sharing what she knew with an old friend would make the knowledge easier to bear. It had not.

A world where Jnoun roamed free was not a place in which mortals could live.

SOMETHING WAS pounding on the ceiling.

Cencova ignored it even though Marin started from her chair at the sudden noise.

"Large men are throwing flour sacks and kneading dough," he told her.

"What?"

"Bakery. Upstairs," said the spymaster, pointing casually upward. "People wonder how I can work here, but in all honesty, I don't even notice the noise any more."

They sat in another sparse flat, to which Cencova's guards had conducted her after the ship docked in Cievv. The half-basement room lay near the heart of the city, its sunken windows just above ground level in an old garden in which the bakers left their broken wheelbarrows, empty crates and other rubbish. Alley cats patrolled the area, suggesting an active mouse population.

"So, Ilss, have you nothing to say?" demanded Marin. They had been silent for some minutes before the distraction from above.

"I have much to speak of," Cencova told her. "But if you refer to the report you just gave me about your meeting with the Sha'ir of Aeíx, I must think awhile before I say anything."

Marin growled, rose to her feet, and began to pace the room.

"I will, however, say something else. Something I believe you want to hear."

She stopped and turned to look at him.

"There is a lead. You will have your chance soon."

Marin stopped breathing. "Go on," she said.

"A man was captured in Riyyal." Cencova's brown eyes caught the light of a sunbeam slanting down into the room, and appeared to burn from within. "He is not from the kingdom; rather, he is from Tanith. Yet he has dealings with the royal family. This we have good reason to believe. The Jassaj have never informed us of his actions before." He waved a dismissive hand. "We are only now learning his true motive for being there. One thing is certain, however. He was to meet with Ciris Sarn."

Marin's heart leaped as she imagined coming upon Sarn from behind and striking off his head with her sword. But she kept this emotion out of her face. Instead, she spoke deliberately. "So you do bring good news, then." She pursed her lips. "Go on."

Cencova paused and looked into Marin's eyes. When she remained silent, he continued.

"There is a way to get you close to him."

Marin stared calmly at him as if he'd never spoken. She turned and walked to the window, watching as one of the cats inspected a stack of rusty baking trays that leaned against the wall. He could see the tension in her shoulders.

"Tell me," she said.

"I shall very soon. A week, two at the most. There are others who must be gathered to aid you in this mission. You cannot do it alone. And Marin—I know you would try."

She did not answer. She watched the cat lunge behind the trays and then back out, a mouse squirming furiously in its jaws.

The cat turned to look Marin in the eye, and trotted away with its prize, tail held high. A strange feeling overcame her, a wave of emotion so strong that she felt faint. Then she recognized the feeling: hatred. Hatred raged within her heart. Perhaps it was consuming her spirit as well.

"Again I wait," she said in a low voice. "This is too much to ask."

"And yet you must," Cencova said. "I am with you in this matter, and I want you to trust me. There are two sides to this. Can I trust you, Marin?" He waited for her to speak, and then sighed. "Patience. You will see this out to the end; however, you must obey my words when you do so."

She met his eyes but said nothing.

"Marin, do you understand?"

She remained silent.

19

THE MAN waited.

It was dark and there were no windows in this private sanctuary hidden deep within a network of cloistered buildings. Only a few torches burned in sconces. It was common for family members to spend time in solitary reflection, sitting motionless in a dim chamber. But only someone intimately familiar with the deceased would realize that this particular man was not here to mourn. He was here to find Ciris Sarn.

The sanctuary's door opened and a tall figure joined him. Had this second man been a mourner, there would have been a quiet greeting between the two. Instead, the first man spoke abruptly.

"Where is the spy?"

The newcomer peered through the gloom. "I do not know." His voice was heavily accented. "He said he would come."

"I am here."

Both men started as a shadow separated itself from an unlit

stretch of wall.

"I sat here all this time with you in the room and did not know it," said the first man angrily. "What child's game is this?"

"You *majals!*" The voice mocked them from the darkness. "How much else escapes your notice?" A short silhouette walked toward them, moving with muscular grace. "My orders were to find both of you. Now you are each here. Let us begin."

"You are a Jassaj spy," snapped the second *majal.* "Let us remember who works for whom."

"And let us not bicker like old women." The first *majal* waved his hand impatiently as he spoke, voice betraying a slight accent. "Torre Lavvann is preparing to leave for Riyyal."

"Hmm." The spy sat on a bench that faced theirs. "What of Pavanan Munif?"

The second *majal* made an irritated noise. "There are many irons in the fire; you are but one of them. We need you here."

The spy said nothing, but bowed his head slightly to acknowledge he understood. The second *majal* continued.

"We have an unforeseen problem. A man who was once valued is now a threat to our goals: Rimmar Fehls. He cannot be allowed to live. He is far too willing to compromise. There is no telling how much information he gave to the *siri* holding him." He leaned forward and pointed a finger at the spy. "The group you join must not know anything about Fehls' mission. Either you or Sarn must kill him before he decides to talk."

"It will be done," the spy agreed. "But where is Ciris Sarn?"

The first *majal* spoke. "Sarn is on his way to Riyyal. You will hear from us when you get there. Arrange for the *siris* to be kept out of the way while you greet Sarn."

"But what if he has already spoken?"

The first *majal* made a dismissive gesture. "Do not concern yourself with things you cannot control."

"But I am concerned," the spy said defiantly. "What about Fajeer Dassai? Weeks have passed with no word from him."

Awkward silence fell as the *majals* considered this. Fehls might have been willing to betray the Rassan Majalis without a qualm, but his loyalties were obviously to Dassai.

"Again, you need to dismiss these worries," the first *majal* finally answered in a brisk tone. "Fajeer's duties often take him down uncharted paths. He knows his own affairs well."

"I think your plans go too far," the spy growled. "At some point a loose string will be found—and then the ball will unravel. We're all marked for death if that happens."

Suddenly the second *majal* leaned across the distance between the two benches and brought his face close to the spy's. The smaller man stared back at his employer, unsure how to react.

"Listen, and listen carefully," the *majal* said with a growl in his voice. "Should you fail, then death will be the kindest fate you could ever know."

"Everyone dies," the spy said.

The *majal* sat back with a sneer. "Just get to Riyyal."

ANOTHER SHIP, another crossing.

And this time, Marin had company.

The Ruinart coastline swung from starboard to stern as the ship turned southwest, catching a favorable wind that would take it to Janeirah. Marin watched the sunlit sea through the porthole as she stood in the small galley. She assumed the straight-backed, respectful posture of a Four Banners soldier on review for some minor king—though her uniform was much different.

She wore a long, flowing robe that covered her from head to toe. Her hair was pulled back tightly beneath a hood woven of fine fabric. Marin suspected she looked very different from most Qatani women, yet this was how they dressed, and how she would dress while in Qatana. Beneath the robe a garment of lighter material clung to her body. Pockets on the inside of the robe could hide various weapons.

"Marin, I'd like to present your travel companions," said Cencova.

He stepped aside and held his hand out to the first man, fit and muscular with a shaved head, pointed chin, and eyes of different colors—one cerulean blue, the other a light amber, like the sap from a spring tree. "Silím Rammas," said Cencova.

Rammas bowed slightly, acknowledging Marin as she stepped forward. She stared into his mismatched eyes for a moment and saw in him a hint of both loyalty and dedication. His size, stature, and sharp chin reminded her painfully of Hiril. She dipped her own head in greeting and backed away.

Cencova moved on to the other man. "Adal Hussein," he announced. Hussein was a truly handsome man, with chiseled features and flowing black hair tied back in an intricate knot. He was shorter than Rammas, the same height as Marin, but burly and athletic. Hussein was more generous with his bow, and Marin wondered if he might be mocking her. She approached him as she had Rammas but halted a few steps back. His brown eyes, which should have been comforting with their rich color, had seemed to look at the world—and at her—from an amused, uncaring distance.

After they had spoken briefly about their mission in Riyyal and started to go their separate ways, Marin pulled the spymaster aside.

"Is this Hussein a cruel man?" she whispered. "I felt as if I looked into the eyes of a predatory animal."

"Well, he is certainly not to be trifled with," Cencova admitted, "but I trust Adal. I assure you, we were fortunate to have secured his services. Indeed, he would have been my choice for your companion if we needed only one."

"He appeared to mock me," Marin said slowly. "Is it because I am a woman? Because I was married to Hiril?"

Or because, she thought without saying, *he is amused by my claim on Sarn's life?*

"That is his way," Cencova told her. "Hussein may not be the man everyone would choose as a friend, but he is the most valuable comrade-in-arms you will ever meet."

"I can think of one better."

"Ah, let me guess." Cencova's brow furrowed, but his eyes twinkled. "You are thinking of Torre, correct?"

Marin glared at him. "Must you mock me as well?"

"No mockery at all." He smiled, raising his hands. "Only delight that you led the conversation where I was about to take it."

Marin raised an eyebrow, waiting for him to continue.

"He will meet us in Janeirah."

21

THE SWORD gleamed in the sunlight that flooded through the porthole.

Marin stood in her private cabin, a privilege accorded her as the only woman aboard, and considered the familiar blade in her hand. This sword had been in her family for countless generations. Before coming to her, it had belonged to her father; she'd claimed it when he died. She was the first woman of her line to carry it, and in her hand, it had bested enemy after enemy.

She recalled with fondness her captain, the man who'd taught her to wield this sword in battle. She would never forget Torre Lavvann's leadership of the Four Banners company. She thought of all the time he'd spent teaching her how to survive in the wild, and how he'd patiently trained her to be quick on her feet, engage without fear, and outwit her opponent. He'd taught her to be dangerous.

Marin's lips tightened. "I wonder if I'm as dangerous now,"

she murmured, considering how, except for her brief skirmish with the Haradin in the hills above Cievv, she hadn't been in a battle since she embarked for Sey'r an-Shal with Hiril's ashes.

She took a fighting stance.

All of her attention flowed into the weapon itself—its remarkable design, its perfect weight, its flawless balance. A familiar fire rushed up her sword arm and through her veins—the fire of battle readiness that Lavvann had taught her. It was still here.

"Now for proper attire," she said to herself.

Lovely and exotic as her traditional costume was, it was all wrong for swordplay. She threw off the long robe—that was easy enough, although she would have to figure the movement into her reaction time—and considered the lighter garment she wore underneath. No doubt it was comfortable enough in the desert heat, but nothing about it would deflect an enemy's blade. Indeed, a sword-point could tangle in this fabric, which would be more hindrance than help.

She knelt before the ancient wooden trunk from which she'd taken the sword, its lid propped open against the bulkhead. Hiril had presented this trunk to her as a souvenir from the hoard of a shipload of corsairs that he'd brought to justice. She swallowed a lump of pain as she traced the gold inlay inside the lid. The corners of her eyes pricked, and she blinked in surprise. She thought the tears had died along with her heart, but sometimes memories of Hiril would catch her off guard.

Her sword's brown leather sheath lay at the top of the trunk. She blew away its coating of dust, revealing thin veins of gold that swirled over the surface. The precious metal wound around embossed letters that spelled out *Fend Amarra*—a creed she no longer recognized as her own.

Marin set the sheath aside and removed the remainder of her gear from the chest, setting each piece on the floor beside her.

Her worn green cloak would be of no use under the Qatani

robe, but she would wear her tunic, which was the same forest green as the cloak but of a lighter fabric. As always, it would conceal the thick leather jerkin she wore beneath it, her answer to chain mail, which was too heavy and confining. Her soft calfskin leggings would be part of the outfit. Her leather gauntlets were likely to be out of place in Qatana, and as much as she disliked the soft-soled slippers Cencova had given her, they were probably more practical than the tall, dark-stained boots that had served her well on so many previous missions.

Last of all was the hunting blade, a treasured gift from Lavvann. She set this carefully beside her sword, her fingers tracing the ash-colored ~M~ burned into the ivory hilt. Lavvann had personally carved, polished, and shaped it to fit Marin's small hand. It seemed to pulse warmly under her touch—as if a remnant of the kindly artisan's life force still dwelt in his creation.

Her eyes softened as she considered the blade. Lavvann could chide her all he wanted; she knew with certainty that he loved her as a daughter. She smiled as she recalled Hiril's jealousy before he understood the true nature of Marin's relationship with her master.

Marin sighed. Such was the bittersweet past. The future awaited her—as did the unknown.

"Let Cencova provide guardians if he wishes to assuage his guilt," she murmured. "Rammas and that Hussein are not going to change my fate." She looked at her sword, her hunting knife, and the usable parts of her old uniform. "These are all I need for this journey—these and Torre Lavvann."

"You will meet Torre in Janeirah," Cencova had instructed her. "He will guide you through the desert to Riyyal. In addition, Sallah Maroud, a *siri*, will join your company. They will provide both aid and protection; do not fail to heed their advice."

"I will do my duty and finish it," Marin told him. Those were the words he needed to hear. She had a duty of her own, and she repeated it to herself yet again.

The minute I see my opportunity, Sarn dies by my hand.

Ciris Sarn, be warned. Don't fear these men; it's me you should be afraid of.

I'm coming for you.

Part Seven

THE SKIN TRADE

11.3.793 SC

7

ILSS CENCOVA stared out the window.

Watching the late winter rain falling outside, he was weary of looking at a gray world. It was not yet spring. He was besieged; there were few he could trust. So many people pursued so many different agendas that trying to find the truth was nearly impossible.

Cencova shook himself out of his thoughts and turned again to his desk. With a sigh, he eyed the sheet of parchment that lay before him. The message written on it had left him stunned.

He read the brief summary again, searching for clues as to why this had occurred. The message had come from Nasir. It stated that Fajeer Dassai was the person who had initiated the plot against Tivisis to threaten the Rassan Majalis. He hoped to also cast blame on the Sultan Raqqas Siwal and convince the Rassan Majalis that Qatana conspired against the trade council. Dassai was coming to Cievv with more of his lies, intending to find an audience that was willing to listen.

Cencova stared down at the words again, clutching his head in his hands. The message concluded that Pavanan Munif had no part in this—he was faithful and could be trusted. Cencova's heart chilled with the knowledge that his suspicions of Munif were unwarranted.

Cencova studied the letter again, hoping that perhaps running his fingers over the words could make their meaning clearer. Who else conspired with Dassai? How deep did the deception run? He dropped the parchment and leaned against the desk, staring across the room.

Cencova wished that this was all a dream and that he would awaken to find that none of these things had ever happened. He did not know whom to trust anymore, and the crushing weight of it all made it difficult to breathe.

Dassai is coming to Cievv.

He needed more from Nasir, a better explanation. Hopefully another message would come, and soon. Cencova closed his eyes and breathed slowly, struggling for focus. His next course of action was to get word to Donnò Galliresse in Tivisis and tell him of treachery within his own house.

Only after word was sent would Cencova settle down to wait.

2

GALLIRESSE'S HANDS trembled.

Breaking the seal, he skimmed the document; certain words leapt off the page.

They were hunting the wrong man.

Fajeer Dassai was the deceiver, the plotter behind it all. Pavanan Munif was innocent of any wrongdoing, and indeed was their best hope of capturing Dassai. It was also clear that Tivisis itself was threatened from within. Someone had been turned against the city by the lure of wealth and power. Galliresse choked on the acid taste of dread. It was worse than he'd feared.

Several thoughts struck Galliresse at once. How could this happen? What if Munif was mistakenly imprisoned, exiled, or executed? Was Galliresse a capable leader? Would the king replace him, and would shame fall upon him? Galliresse was relieved he did not have a family; no wife or children would have to suffer with or because of him. He would lose his position, his house, his lands—everything he had worked so hard for.

He was a necessary sacrifice, nothing more. Someone would have to be responsible for the lax governance that had allowed Dassai to execute his horrific plans—and that someone would be Donnò Galliresse.

Something else crept into his mind, something dark and pervasive. What if this was a lie as well? Was Cencova more worthy of trust than anyone else? Galliresse shook his head. He was being fed lies. All information was being passed through his advisors, and he believed in them all. There was no possible way this could happen ... Unless ...

"It could only be you." Galliresse spoke aloud. "Niccolo." He clenched his fists so tightly that his nails dug into his palms. A bead of sweat dripped from his brow. Shaking off the sting of betrayal, he forced a smile onto his face. Oh, how he wished he knew where Arzani was right now. He envisioned the blade he would use to cut the bastard's throat. An ironic laugh escaped him.

Trust was a fickle thing, he supposed. Here was a man for whom he would lay down his life. They'd forged a loyal, important friendship—and Arzani had thrown it away. What had he hoped to accomplish by helping Dassai?

There would be time to think upon this matter later. It was not in Galliresse's nature to act rashly. No, he needed to exercise patience and plan carefully. Something from the past would turn up and help him plan his future, he was sure of it.

Galliresse needed hope—a thing that was in short supply.

PAVANAN MUNIF did not wait long.

His evening meal had just been set before him when he glanced up to find Prince Nasir in the entryway. Munif sighed in relief.

Nasir sat opposite him and spoke quickly. "I'm afraid you won't have time to finish your meal, my friend. Dassai is no doubt headed to Cievv, and our ship leaves within the hour. His route takes him around the island. From here, with any luck, we should arrive at least a day before him, but there are many risks still before us."

Munif swallowed the piece of roasted lamb without chewing, and gulped down the last of his wine. In the past few weeks his appetite had returned as his wounds healed. His hunger for *affyram*—always persistent, always whispering to him from the recesses of his mind—had never left him. He wiped his mouth and stood to leave, but lingered for just a moment to mourn the meal he was about to abandon.

Nasir stood as well. "We will have him. Mark my words."

As they started toward the front door, it swung open. Two large men burst through it, filling the room with their bulk. More of Dassai's hired killers.

Nasir swept his arm across a tabletop, grabbed a plate and threw it at the invaders. They ducked, and the delay gave Munif and Nasir an opportunity to flee toward the rear door. On his way out Munif tilted a table on its side, throwing the men to the floor.

Munif followed Nasir silently, the two hurrying along a back street. The slow pursuit lasted only a few minutes. They both knew that the two men following lost their element of surprise and would quickly give up the hunt.

Nasir pointed along another passage, toward the west. Beneath the pale lamplight the two figures were a dim blur moving past the stone walls--their footsteps echoing on worn stone. The Prince paused to look around a dark corner, listening intently for any sound coming from behind. There was none. They waited for a moment before continuing across the street. Their destination was just ahead and they were not about to be caught now.

Nasir and Munif raced to the stables.

DONNÒ GALLIRESSE stood quietly.

He stayed near the top of the ancient stone steps and scanned the city of Tivisis lost in his thoughts.

He longed to see the day when a man's honor could not be

sold for his weight in gold. He touched his spindly fingers to his thinning white hair. His legs felt heavy, as if he carried all the cares of his people. He was not a gullible man, yet he had been acting like one. He would gladly give up every coin he earned for the news he so desperately needed to hear: that Pavanan Munif had succeeded and Fajeer Dassai was dead.

Galliresse walked into the open court that looked out over the city. In the distance, the lavender skies met the sun-kissed sea. For millennia, the long, narrow inlets and waterways surrounding the city had provided safe haven for mariners during storms. The crystalline blue-green waters lapped gently against the sharp white rocks. Across the land, the green hills with their abundance of vineyards surrounded the city like jewels in a crown.

Sadly, the beauty of Tivisis served only to remind him of his mistakes.

The citizens here were open and trusting. They often greeted strangers as if they had been long-lost family. Galliresse sometimes thought they were fools for failing to appreciate the delicate workings behind the city's serenity. Now he wished, as they all did, that he knew the face of the cruel man who had awakened them from their gentle sleep and introduced them to harsh reality. He shook his head slowly and heaved a sigh. Galliresse wanted to believe his leadership was essential to this city. He needed to discover who had caused all of this to happen.

But where to look?

NICCOLO ARZANI was in Cievv.

Unfortunately the news did little to lessen the anger that seethed in Galliresse's heart.

Galliresse retreated to his favorite spot overlooking the city. He ordered his agents to survey the streets and look for others involved in the conspiracy. He was not certain how long this would take, or whether there was anything to be found. They had to at least try to act on this information.

Arzani had been discovered two days ago. He had approached the council halls of the Rassan Majalis, delivering more of Fajeer Dassai's lies. Galliresse assumed he had done this in order to keep the pressure on Pavanan Munif.

Correspondence between Galliresse and Cencova proved fruitful—Arzani had been followed on the chance that he would lead them to other conspirators. And indeed, he walked right to them.

Galliresse was now convinced that Fajeer Dassai was the mastermind behind the attacks. He was manipulating Arzani and many others. It seemed that truth had eluded them all.

Dassai was infamous even here, where people whispered of his ruthlessness. He coordinated a vast web of spies, collaborators, and criminals. He had the ear of the Sultan, his son, and even the assassin Ciris Sarn.

If this information was even partially true, Galliresse still had a chance to redeem himself in the king's eyes. He had nothing else to lose. At least failure met with death was a better prospect than failure met with dishonor and humiliation.

With his spirits slightly restored by these reflections, Galliresse began to regain a sense of hope. Would it be dashed again? He knew the answer then, as surely as he knew his age. He was sadder, but he was also wiser. Galliresse had already been stabbed in the back by an invisible blade that cut deeper than any poisoned dagger.

It would not happen again.

6

THE HOUSE was empty.

Niccolo Arzani lingered in the shadows of the trees nearby before venturing to the front door. It was a short walk from the winehouse over the bridge, but it was enough time for him to become anxious regarding his next course of action. There was no sign of Dassai or anyone else, and that only made his decision more difficult.

Steeling his nerves, he picked the lock and opened the door. The waft of cold air from within startled him as he stepped across the threshold. It told him the house had not been occupied for quite some time. His footsteps reverberated across the hardwood floor as he crossed the great room. He descended a short flight of stairs into deepening darkness.

Arzani felt his way along the walls until his eyes adjusted to the dim light. He found a small kitchen and began fumbling through drawers until he located the stub of a candle and a tinderbox. He lit the candle, and although it provided a dim light, it was better than the dark. He made his way up the stairs to either confirm or assuage his fears.

Dassai had been gone for days, if not weeks. Arzani wandered the empty rooms looking for answers. It was clear that Dassai had yet to return. Would he ever?

Arzani, with little else to do but wait, used the remainder of his candle to light a fire in the hearth. Tired, cold, and hungry, he sat down heavily on the soft bed and surveyed the room. The light from the fire, along with what was left of another candle he'd found on the writing desk, revealed a grand room full of intricately carved wooden furniture, long, elegant floor runners, and delicate tapestries. He had this in Tivisis, but now it was all in jeopardy. He was out of options; he despaired of what to do next.

He lay back on the featherbed, his head resting on the down-stuffed pillows. He wanted to feel that luxury one last time before surrendering it in both heart and mind.

Arzani fell into a deep sleep.

ARZANI AWOKE, confused and unsure of where he was.

It was dark. The embers were dying, and the room was quite chilly. Suddenly, there was the slightest of noises—the soft click of a door latch.

Someone was coming through the front door.

Arzani gathered his wits and slid off the side of the bed near the windows, opposite the door. He waited for a time behind the linen curtain before realizing, with some degree of chagrin, that he was silhouetted against the milky luminescence of the moonlit sky.

He mentally prepared his justification for being there.

It would have to be convincing if he was to stay alive.

THE DOOR was unlocked.

Munif thought it odd that the entry would be open. He'd come here after receiving word from Cencova that this was the house of Dassai and that Niccolo Arzani had been seen here. He nudged the door open with the tip of his sword and stood back as it swung inward, prepared for whatever might lunge out at him. When nothing but a cool draft greeted him, he stepped carefully inside.

Munif entered the room quietly, gliding along the wall near the hearth with his sword still drawn. Immediately he saw a man partially hidden behind the bed. It was not Dassai.

The man stepped forward.

"Fajeer, I'd hoped to encounter you here."

Munif recognized the voice in an instant. He turned toward the embers to hide his face, and lowered his sword.

Arzani rose from behind the bed. "I have delivered your message, but I fear the plan has failed. Now I cannot return to Tivisis. I would most certainly be arrested."

Munif knew he could not afford to waste such an opportunity. Kneeling before the hearth, he stirred up the embers with the tip of his sword. He heard Arzani approach behind him.

"Take me back to Qatana with you. I have skills that will prove useful to you. I can assist you once Malek assumes the throne and you control the *majals*."

Arzani's tone told Munif that he had revealed everything in this desperate bid for survival. Munif stood but kept his back to Arzani. "You have told me more than you could possibly know," he sneered, then pulled back his hood and wheeled to face him.

"Impossible," Arzani whispered, even as the sword ran through him.

9

IT WAS RISKY.

Munif placed a hot coal in the bowl of water and elixir he had prepared. Although he'd often coped with such situations, this time fear crept in. He must do this alone.

Munif jerked the linens from the bed and, stepping over the still warm corpse, carried them into the water closet and spread them on the floor. Then he went back into the bedroom. It was both tiring and gruesome to undress Arzani's body. He dragged the naked corpse into the water closet and rolled it onto the bed linens.

With a practiced hand—and his exceptionally sharp knife—

he cut away at the flesh of the dead man's face, allowing for extra room along the jaw line. Munif, despite what the alchemist had promised, remained skeptical that the elixir would fasten the mold to his own face and transform him into an exact likeness of Arzani. There was no room for error. And even if the elixir did perform as promised, it would be an unpleasant experience—no matter how convincing the mask might be to others.

Arzani's skin came off easily. Munif was grateful for that. Sometimes, the alchemist had told him, if the cutting and peeling process took too long, the blood and other fluids between the face and skull would become sticky. The skin would lose its inherent bonds—and the facial structure that makes each person unique would be compromised. Then he would look more like a leper than a double.

The bed sheets prevented the blood from spreading out in a gummy pool on the floor. Munif rinsed the ghastly mask with care and placed it on a shelf, then picked up the bowl of now transparent gel and smoothed the warm sticky substance through the interior of the shell. He mentally counted off the seconds before lifting the mask of flesh carefully and—steeling himself—leaning forward into it and closing his eyes.

As the viscous material touched him, he recoiled inwardly. His stomach churned. As he pressed harder, however, there was a flash of heat and the cold skin warmed, becoming like his own. He found a small hand mirror and checked to make sure all portions of the face were now living tissue, albeit temporarily. The mask would last for days, if not weeks.

He returned to Arzani's corpse and looked it over carefully. There was very little muscle on the frame. That was fortuitous; the mission that had begun in Riyyal many months ago had worn Munif down. But he was slightly taller than Arzani, and he could not reproduce the narrow shoulders by mimicking the dead man's stance. There was no way Munif would pass for Arzani by simply wearing his face.

Swearing under his breath, Munif held the stiffening arm still while he sliced the forearm open all the way down to the thumb. Pulling the skin back, he lodged the tip of his knife in the space between the wrist bones and pressed down firmly as he twisted the blade. The maneuver chipped off a single piece of glistening bone. Dropping the arm, he went into the bedroom and pulled a vial from his belt pouch.

He added a pinch of powder to what was left of the gel in the bowl and watched as it returned to its liquid form. He added the bone to the bowl and waited for it to dissolve.

Although he'd used similar elixirs in the past, he wasn't exactly sure what to expect. He lifted the bowl to his lips and drank deeply. The vile taste made his stomach heave again, but he closed his eyes and willed himself to wait for the effects to take hold. Suddenly it seemed his nerve endings were on fire; the pain that coursed through him was more agonizing than any he had previously experienced. Terror seized him; Munif opened his mouth to scream, but no sound came from his throat. He knelt at the foot of the bed and gripped a bedpost with both hands to keep from thrashing.

Eventually the pain receded. Slowly he regained his senses, until he could stand. The transformation was complete.

Now all he had to do was clean up the room and wait.

For the next several hours, Munif practiced reproducing the timbre of Arzani's voice until it matched as closely as possible. Fortunately, the tone and timbre weren't unique, but it was a difficult task to perform from memory. Next he spent some time rehearsing the man's inflection and regional dialect. "Only his mother would know the difference," Munif murmured.

Also during this time, he disposed of Arzani's corpse and made the bed. He practiced with his sword, adjusting to the new skin.

Finally, as dawn approached, Munif heard a door open and steps echoing through the house. Stashing his sword where he knew it would not be discovered until he returned, he replaced the blade with Arzani's thin saif.

Rather than meet Dassai in the bedroom, Munif chose to take himself downstairs to play an agitated and fearful Arzani; he knew that Dassai would be less likely to rid himself of the man if he begged.

Let the game begin.

70

"WELL, NICCOLO, I must say this comes as a surprise."

Fajeer Dassai sounded amused as he stood on the threshold. "I had no idea you had the courage to stay. Perhaps I should just bleed you where you stand." Dassai spoke these last words in a conversational tone as he knelt before the hearth—just as Munif had hours earlier.

Munif had met Dassai while descending the staircase, wringing his hands and looking as small and worried as he could. He did not approach Dassai, preferring to remain as far from him as possible without provoking suspicion. He allowed Dassai to lead the conversation, and when he did speak, he spoke each word precisely in an effort to mimic the timid Arzani. Dassai had retrieved a bottle of wine and poured himself a glass before turning to the fireplace.

Munif had no doubts that Dassai was planning to kill the man he thought was Arzani. Munif was confident he could take Dassai off guard—laying him open for a killing blow. But that was something he no longer wanted to do. There was much more to gain now. Munif had to improvise; he chose his next words carefully. "Please. I can do nothing but ask for mercy and an opportunity to prove myself not utterly useless. Allow me to be your escort."

"I do not need you. I need people on whom I can rely. You failed me in Tivisis. You failed yourself by letting Pavanan Munif survive. What good are you to me?"

Munif did not answer right away, stretching out the silence as an admission of Arzani's guilt. Then he breathed in deeply and released the breath slowly, as though he had just come to a decision. "Should I fail you again in any way, I will take my own life." He said it with conviction.

Munif waited while Dassai pondered his words. Dassai replaced the poker beside the fireplace and stood. Munif felt some of the tension leave his body as Dassai turned and smiled at him. It seemed that Dassai had thought of a use for Arzani after all.

Munif did not smile in return.

77

"JUST A little longer."

The words echoed through Munif's mind. He was still sealed within the flesh of the man whose life he had taken. Thus far Dassai seemed not to suspect the deception.

He paced as he waited for Dassai to rejoin him. Dassai had ordered Munif to stay in the house while he met with someone in the city. Munif would have to be patient and have faith that his revenge would come soon.

An alchemist had once told Munif that when a person assumed the identity of another—especially through these means—that identity would begin to consume him. The essence of the dead would remain behind, attempting to hold on to what it knew, unable to let go of the life that had been taken prematurely. Munif had begun to believe it was true: the longer he remained within Arzani's skin, the more nervous he became. Always confident and in control, he had begun to question everything about himself. He worried that should he remain Arzani for much longer, he would have difficulty remaining sane.

Dassai appeared. "All will go as planned, Niccolo," he said with delight. "I have given enough reason to suspect the Sultan and Ciris Sarn. They believe the Sultan is unfit to rule. I have convinced them it is time for Emir Malek to take the throne."

"How is this possible?" Munif tried to keep the concern out of his voice. He wondered if he would be able to carry out his own plan in time.

"The *majals* are much more powerful than you believe," Dassai answered. "They control the trade in *Azza* and thus the very wealth of Qatana. Without the council, Qatani influence in Mir'aj will wither and die." Dassai walked to the chair. Munif wanted desperately to run him through—to end it right there and then. But he could not. Despite all of his fears, the game must still play out. But time was growing short.

"What's wrong with you, Niccolo? You look ill."

"No ... no ... I'm all right."

"Do you not have faith? Was I wrong to keep you?"

"No, not at all," Munif replied in Arzani's tenor. "I have bound my fate to yours. And despite any misgivings, I do believe that you will receive what is justly coming to you. I am more worried about my health than your plans, Fajeer." He began cautiously to walk toward the stairway. In truth, he felt as though a knife had stabbed his innards.

Dassai made no effort to conceal the contempt he had for his companion. "You are fortunate I still happen to need your services," he sneered. "Otherwise, I would have the pleasure of gutting you myself." He turned his back on Munif and walked to the window.

Munif stood, slightly amused by the irony of that last statement. *It will be more than your flesh that I will take from you,* he thought.

Just wait and see.

12

A PALE moon gleamed across the landscape.

Ilss Cencova stared out the window, his back to Nasir, as he struggled to control his emotions. "I was never certain whom I could trust," he said. "I was told Pavanan Munif was the man responsible. I questioned this allegation, but found myself unable to come up with any explanation that would absolve him or conclusively lay the blame on anyone else. Only after your message came did I know whom to believe."

"I'm sorry, Ilss." Nasir spoke softly. "It was difficult to find a *sufi* capable of getting word to you from Darring. I promise you can trust Pavanan with your life."

"And what about Marin Altaïr?" Cencova turned to Nasir, his eyes filled with fear.

"She and the others will meet Prince Malek and Ciris Sarn in Riyyal. Marin is our only chance to recover the fifth book and the proof it will bring." Nasir hesitated. "My family will be disgraced, but it is the only way. I hope that a greater future still lies before us."

Cencova shook his head. "I promised myself on the grave of her husband that I would let nothing happen to that woman. Tell me, how do I live if she dies?"

"I know it is difficult, yet this is no time to dwell on such questions," Nasir said sharply. "Marin and the men you sent are more than capable of handling themselves in the face of danger. In the meantime, we have other pressing concerns."

"Such as?"

"Fajeer will seek to turn many in the Rassan Majalis. They will not know whom to believe. This chaos favors him—he is more cunning than you will ever know. Still, it is my hope that Pavanan Munif will prevent him from succeeding."

"I hope so." Cencova walked around to the side of his desk

and picked up a parchment. "This message came earlier. It is from Pavanan."

Nasir took the parchment and read it. "I am to meet him at Miráshel tonight. It says, 'Beware: looks can be deceiving.' An odd thing to say."

"Indeed." Cencova sighed and sat heavily in his chair. "But there must be a reason. I will alert as many as I can about the current situation."

Without another word, Nasir turned and left the room. Cencova looked out at the gray afternoon and thought of all the mistakes he'd made that had led them to this. He vowed that Fajeer Dassai would pay. He longed to be the one who ran his sword through the traitor's heart.

If Munif didn't do it first.

13

"WOULD HE come?"

Sending the message to the Prince had been an exercise in stealth and cunning for Munif. Dassai kept a keen eye on his companion, watching for any mistake that would provide a reason to call him on his promise to end his life.

It was apparent that Dassai had little patience for Arzani, and a great deal of distaste. Munif didn't blame him. Arzani had been a man with a soft backbone, and Munif did not at all like the person he was impersonating. He had never had time for a man who believed the best way to get through life was to ingratiate himself with whoever happened to be in charge. Yet the more time Munif spent within Arzani's flesh, the more he sensed he was being swallowed by Arzani's mind.

Could it happen? he wondered. *Shall I become Arzani, and simply continue living as him, without any memory of my previous life? What will happen to me? Will I have any awareness that I'm destined to live*

the remainder of my life as someone else? Or will my spirit become sepa-
rated from this body, and be sentenced to an eternal hell?

As he ruminated in this fashion, he realized this ruse could not last much longer if he was to maintain any semblance of sanity.

In the end, Munif found a courier who would do anything for a few coins; he sent the boy off to deliver the message to Nasir. He only had to threaten to cut off one of the boy's ears to swear him to secrecy. Dassai's ill humor kept most of the servants at arm's length, and they rarely approached him unless necessary.

Munif was more than a little concerned about leaving Dassai's side for any length of time, despite his desire to see the Prince again. He felt the man had become unstable. Dassai was drunk with power—and with him in that state, no one within his reach was safe. Munif worried that Dassai might simply tire of Arzani's insipid whining and decide to kill him to relieve the boredom. However, it seemed Dassai was keeping Arzani around for some as yet unknown purpose.

It was late when Munif went to meet with Nasir. Dassai had finally fallen asleep, much to Munif's relief. Of course, it helped that he had plied Dassai with glass after glass of wine. After an hour, Dassai had relaxed enough to brag openly about his cunning in arranging the summoners' massacres in the Mirani kingdoms. He had been especially proud of the innocent blood that had been shed. He spoke of his control over Prince Malek, his disdain for the Sultan and the entire royal family, and the incompetence of the Jassaj and *siris*. "It is only a matter of time," he slurred just before he nodded off.

Dassai had arranged a meeting with several members of the council. Soon he would convince a sufficient number of the *majals* to kill the Sultan.

Munif mulled all this over as he approached the Miráshel. He hoped Nasir was waiting for him.

As he entered the park he saw the Prince leaning against a statue of white stone. As he tried to raise his hand as a sign to

Nasir that he was approaching, someone grabbed him by the shoulders and pushed up against a tree trunk. Cold, rough ridges of bark dug into his back.

"Niccolo!" Nasir hissed. "Another plot you willingly serve, I see. Whom are you paying off now for his favors?"

Munif laughed and said, "So, tell me what you really think of me, my Prince."

Nasir jumped back, confused.

"What's going on here?" Nasir ran his hands over Munif's shoulders. "Is that you, Pavanan?"

"Yes, it is," Munif said, chuckling. "Thank all that is good, I can finally speak to you. And I can talk to someone as myself rather than that spineless worm whose face I wear."

Nasir looked at him with wonder. "How?"

"I discovered the location of Arzani with the help of Ilss Cencova. I killed him and used his skin as a disguise. These have been the darkest days of my life, my friend."

Nasir threw back his head to laugh heartily, then remembered where they were and stifled it; he spoke seriously and quietly. "I can imagine. What have you discovered? Where is Fajeer?"

"I am safe for now," Munif said. "He still needs men he thinks he can trust."

Nasir raised his eyebrows in surprise. "It's a brave thing you do, Munif. I admire it."

"He suspects nothing. He is at his house, asleep—passed out, actually. However, not before he shared with me the details of his upcoming meeting."

Munif told him where he thought the location with the *majals* might take place. "I cannot believe they can actually do this, hold a gathering of such treachery in the very chambers of the council."

"Once we're certain of the exact time, we'll make our move," Nasir said carefully. "There must be a reason he needs Niccolo there. I sense that he may have a sinister plan for you."

"So do I," Munif agreed. "I find it difficult to believe he has allowed the man to live this long. But I cannot expose myself too soon. I must allow this meeting to take place."

Nasir nodded. "We will be there with you, my friend. That I promise."

As Munif made his way back through the darkness, he hoped Dassai had not noticed his absence.

Soon he would know for sure.

FAJEER DASSAI was wide awake.

Munif entered the room to find Dassai stoking the meager fire in the hearth; he did not look up when Munif walked in. For that, Munif was grateful; he was not certain he had managed to suppress his shock upon seeing the man absolutely unaffected by a night of heavy drinking.

"Nice of you to return, Niccolo," Dassai said. "Where were you?"

"I . . ." Munif noticed that the chair was gone. "I went out for a walk to clear my mind, Fajeer." Munif hesitated, checking his voice as he spoke, hoping he had not resumed his own inflections after speaking with Nasir. "I assumed you were resting for the night," he said.

"Heed this warning," Dassai spoke evenly as he stood and picked up his sword from the table. "I am not a drunk, nor do I sleep deeply." He stood in front of Munif. "It would take something much stronger to leave me unconscious."

The perspiration on Munif's upper lip was real. The slight tremor in his legs was not something he had feigned in order to match Arzani's likely reaction. He was truly afraid for his life.

Dassai laid the flat of the blade against Munif's neck. "If I thought for one moment that you might cross me, Niccolo, I would take off your head with one swipe of this steel. I would not wait for you to fulfill your promise to me and take your own life. I have no such patience. Do you understand me?"

"Ye–yes . . . yes, I do. I have done nothing to betray you, I swear!"

Dassai smiled a tight, humorless smile and put the sword down. "That's good. I still see a good future for you, my dear man. And I would very much dislike it if I should have to change my plans at this late date." Dassai sheathed his sword and set it back on the table. He turned toward Munif and let out a burst of hearty laughter. "Don't look so frightened, Niccolo. I said a great future lies ahead for you. You will soon see." The smile disappeared, and his eyes narrowed. "Now let me be."

Munif turned away and sat on his bunk. When Dassai returned to the hearth to stir up the fire, Munif furtively studied the sword on the table. He pondered its precision and its beauty, and considered that it must be ready for whatever might happen.

Here was yet another opportunity for him to murder his nemesis. But he knew that he must not kill Dassai now. He must wait. Dassai was not stupid; he would be expecting that Arzani would be foolish enough to challenge him. He was always watchful, always poised for action.

No, this was not the time for vengeance. On the other hand, neither would there be anyone sleeping here tonight.

Of that Munif was certain.

CENCOVA WAS relieved.

Until the Prince informed him of the meeting, he had no way of knowing that Munif was at this very moment wondering if Dassai had been completely truthful, or if he had been feeding Munif false information as a test of his mettle. For Cencova, this would be his opportunity to avenge the murder of so many—

Hiril Altaïr foremost.

Cencova arranged a force of *siris* and an alchemist to close the noose around the traitor's neck. They planned their strategy with care, mindful of all possible contingencies. The only thing they did not plan for was failure. They had come too far for that to be an option. If they did not succeed in stopping Dassai, everything would be lost. Dassai would rule through his puppet Malek.

As the first sun rose above the horizon, Cencova and Nasir felt very much alone. Since neither had a propensity for idle conversation, they watched the sunrise in silence. Each man considered his life up to this point. They agreed that they had had good lives—and that whatever sacrifices they were about to make were worth it, when they considered the many blessings they had received throughout the years.

Behind them, a horse snorted. They turned to see Munif mounting the steed he had borrowed from the stables. Munif glanced their way, and when he had confirmed they were observing him, he turned the horse away from them and crossed his fingers behind his back. This was a familiar signal. It meant something had happened; there might be problems.

Nasir and Cencova went over to where their own horses were stabled. They ducked behind a large bale of hay just as Dassai came out of the house. Through a space between the bales, they watched as he sprang onto his horse and kicked it into a gallop. They would have to put plenty of distance between themselves and Dassai so that he wouldn't notice them following.

Now, as they watched, Dassai and a group of men who had come to meet him moved up the road away from the city's center. Then, from the east, they spied a large number of men also riding toward Dassai. Dassai waved a greeting as they joined him.

Cencova recognized some of the men and was dismayed. Fajeer Dassai's lies had indeed succeeded.

Cencova and Nasir followed the riders at a distance for some time, counting the numbers of men ahead and watching for new arrivals. They agreed that if they could gradually move up behind the *majals*, they would not likely be recognized. They were dressed plainly enough that they could assume the identity of servants and ride along unnoticed. Dassai would not know they were there until it was too late.

There was much left to do.

The council hall rested in the hills above Cievv. The look and design was more fortress than a place of commerce. The sessions were adjourned for another two weeks so Munif knew traffic to and from the hall would be sparse. As both men rode and closed in on their destination, each knew that Dassai was wise in his timing.

As the main procession passed under the archway leading into the immense labyrinthine of buildings, Dassai veered away from the group and the main entrance.

"There is someone who I must consult with before the meeting starts," Dassai said after leading Munif to an elaborate structure which was windowless and had only a single door leading inward. "I will come for you in two hours. Stay near, is that understood?"

"As you wish," Munif said.

The door opened and Dassai entered, leaving Munif alone with the horses. He knew this was the perfect opportunity to meet with Cencova and Nasir. They could prepare the *siris* for impending confrontation. A few minutes later Munif and the others were reunited.

"I think it is time to bring in the alchemist," Cencova said, "I have an idea that may just work in our favor."

"Tell us what you have in mind," Munif responded.

16

THE CIRCULAR chamber was massive.

It had four entrances, each accessed by a long flight of polished stone steps that descended into the dimly lit room. Immense marble columns of various colors and grains supported a stunning silver dome. A single sconce on each pillar held an oil lamp, providing illumination for the chamber.

Carved high on the walls were words in the ancient language of Náhk: *Tueil Acaran Mehl Sirion.* The phrase, which meant *Hope Is the Wellspring That Flows Within,* had long been adopted by the Rassan Majalis.

Above, on the interior of the dome, a mural depicted the heavens and the earth: the suns, moons, and stars, and the lands and seas of Mir'aj. Intricate patterns were etched in the stone floor. At consistent intervals, laid out in a great ring, were dozens of chairs. At the westernmost point of the chamber, like the setting in the ring, was the High Seat reserved for the *majal* who had been appointed to oversee the Rassan Majalis.

Munif was tense with anticipation.

He had never been in this place before. According to tradition, only members of the council were permitted in the chamber. There were no tours for the curious, and those who occasionally tried to approach the High Seat were gently but firmly ushered to a small area just outside.

Dassai walked just ahead of Munif, his confidence evident in his gait. Munif so longed to run a blade through him that he was visibly shaking. For the past week or more, his every thought had been consumed by the moment when he would slay Dassai and the manner in which it would be done. He paused for a moment, placing his hand on the wall to steady himself. He wondered if everyone in the room could hear his beating heart; it was pounding in his own ears. Sweat dampened his upper lip and forehead.

Dassai glared over his shoulder, making it plain he would not tolerate Arzani's weakness. Munif lowered his hand and concentrated on keeping his gait steady. Though he was trained to feign sobriety even while extremely intoxicated, there was little he could do to counteract the dizziness that always hit him when he was anxious or stressed. As he fought to restrain the shaking in his hands, he was mildly heartened to reflect that this show of emotion would help him impersonate Arzani more accurately.

Munif casually inserted his hands into the folds of his robe and felt around until he had confirmed—for the third time in as many minutes—the presence of a small vial. Cencova had obtained it from the alchemist and had instructed Munif and Nasir in its use. Munif rolled the small cylindrical container between his fingertips, carefully avoiding contact with the sharp metal tip of the lid. Once it pierced his skin there would be no going back. The spell would last only five minutes, and he was still not certain when to use it. Should he release it too soon, the alchemy would wear off before their plan had sufficient time to succeed. After five minutes, it would cease to protect him from the thing that Cencova was going to unleash on Dassai and the others; he would be just as blind as the rest.

He decided he would wait to use it until Dassai spoke his first words.

He walked slowly down the steps, taking in every detail of the hall. Of the chairs, only eight were occupied. The High Seat was empty. He did not recognize the faces but knew each person there represented a threat. These were the men whose vast wealth held sway over the various kingdoms of Mir'aj. Munif was certain that even though they weren't directly responsible for the slaughter of the *rahibs*, dozens of innocent victims, along his own agents—these *majals* had approved of the outcome. It was all done to increase the consumption of *Azza*. Therefore, their own wealth could only increase.

Munif contemplated the nature of greed. What kind of a man bullied his way into riches so vast that he'd never be able to spend them in his lifetime? It was far better to be a man of humanity than one of avarice.

It seemed a sacrilege to allow this group of tyrants to use the sacred chamber for their rapacious schemes. Munif's hatred for men like these ran deep. The only thing that kept him from springing into a mad frenzy of action was his awareness that the results would be far better if he waited for the right moment.

Dassai walked to the center of the hall and waved his hand, indicating that Arzani should stand behind him.

"Say nothing if you want to live," Dassai whispered.

MUNIF WATCHED.

Dassai was across from him preparing to negotiate with the eight figures seated in the chamber.

Munif's fingers squeezed the vial as he fought the urge to fidget. He wished it contained *affyram* instead.

"It gives me great pleasure to have been granted audience in this splendid hall," Dassai began. "I come bearing news of a grave plot, one that originates with the highest authority of all: the Sultan of Qatana." Dassai looked around him, visibly pleased with himself.

Munif pressed his thumb hard against the needle-like tip of the vial. He turned it upside down in his palm and felt the cold sting as the fluid entered his bloodstream. His vision began to dim as Dassai continued his speech.

"There is a tremendous and nefarious force at work. This force seeks to undermine our livelihoods. Do you agree?" Dassai paused as the attendees murmured their support.

Munif was nearly blind now and could make out only the

faintest of light and shapes. He could no longer see the seated men, nor could he see Dassai, who was directly in front of him. He began to panic, realizing that without his sight he could not confront the man who was his last hope for retribution.

Dassai continued, "The Sultan plots against the council, to weaken its foundations." He paused. "My proposal is simple. The time has come for Sultan be removed and his son Emir Malek placed in his stead, under my control."

Munif couldn't believe what he was hearing. Dassai was advocating the assassination of the Sultan.

One of the council members rose and gestured the others to silence. "With all due respect, Fajeer Dassai, while I believe you have our best interests at heart, I have to admit that I am grave doubts." The *majal* paused; his colleagues all nodded in agreement.

"Your skepticism is understandable," Dassai said. "But I bring proof."

The *majal* who had spoken murmured to his colleagues. Munif grew tense with anticipation.

The *majal* broke off his conversation. "Very well, Fajeer Dassai. Give us the proof and we will bring this matter to the full council."

The words drove a dagger through Munif's heart.

ILSS CENCOVA knew it was time.

He looked across the chamber. Behind every column stood a *siri* at the ready. Cencova and Nasir had brought their men in through the building's four entrances; each man had silently taken his position after Dassai and Munif entered.

Nasir stepped from the shadows. Each of the men held a slender rod of platinum three feet in length. Cencova made eye contact with each one. The agents advanced from behind the pillars, readying themselves for the fray. Cencova had great confidence in the agent's capabilities.

Cencova turned to face the column and looked up at the casing that surrounded the lamp. His target was a small round opening. Reaching up, he inserted the rod into the opening and let go.

He had released their most powerful defensive weapon. A swirling energy swallowed the platinum and consumed the fire. A pulse of blinding white light bounced off one pillar, only to hit the next and the next.

The light continued to intensify, expanding to the summit of the dome. Shards of brilliant white rained down upon the chamber. There were screams of shock and terror, then of agony.

Cencova raced down the steps. Like Pavanan Munif and the rest, he had taken the alchemist's antidote. He could see perfectly well in the dazzling light. Bodies were scattered on the floor, writhing and whimpering in pain.

Cencova performed a quick head count. There were six . . . seven . . . eight. Where was Dassai? *Damn it all, has he escaped again? impossible!*

He looked again, scouring the chamber. His heart beat wildly. There was no sign of Munif, either; both had vanished.

79

FALLING STARS showered upon them.

The effect that was both magnificent and devastating; Munif was grateful the potion had performed as promised, allowing him to see normally amid the luminescent maelstrom. After his initial surprise and wonder, he turned his attention to Dassai.

Dassai drew his cloak over his head and crouched down. He scuttled behind the nearest council chair, and then ran swiftly toward the steps leading up to the southern exit.

Munif hastened in pursuit. It was the first time, he realized, that he'd ever seen Dassai try to escape anything. The light was growing stronger as the effects began to wane.

Dassai paused, waiting as a *siri* rushed down the steps toward him. Dassai leaped. The agent, caught off guard, tumbled headlong to the chamber floor. With all the speed he could muster, Dassai ran up the steps and out of the building.

Munif clambered over the fallen agent and went after Dassai. His normal vision had almost completely returned, and he could see his prey as he ran across the wide field of winter grass adjacent to the chambers. He sensed Prince Nasir following, still wrapped in his scarves.

Dassai jumped over rows of manicured shrubbery and trampled beds of flowers as he flew past the edge of a garden, following a stone path that led down toward a river. A low bridge with three arches spanned a brook that fed into the rushing current.

Dassai slid down an embankment and ran under one of the arches. Munif was right behind him now and, when Dassai paused and turned, Munif thrust his sword into Dassai's midsection.

Shock and surprise replaced Dassai's perpetual sneer as he looked down at the blade lodged in his abdomen. Munif grimaced and twisted the sword, and Dassai screamed. He slid down against the wall of the archway and looked up at his enemy.

"There is more to you than I would ever have thought possible, Niccolo Arzani," Dassai said. He coughed, a deep, racking sound. Bloody spittle spattered his chest and thighs.

"It ends right here, Fajeer. You are a dead man."

Dassai's voice rasped with strain. "Why? Without me, you are no more than waste, discarded like a whore's birthing sac."

Munif twisted his sword again. Dassai screamed anew. "Indeed there is much more to me than you imagined. I'm going to purge your body of its spirit, so that it can slither down into the abyss where it belongs. But first, there's something I want you to see."

Munif pulled a small razor from his pocket. With the precision of a butcher, he sliced the skin of his forehead. Blood and clear fluid trickled down his face as he watched the horror dawn in Dassai's eyes.

Dassai tried to pull himself up but fell back. "What are you doing? You're mad!"

Munif jerked the loose fold of skin downward, peeling back the layer of Arzani's living flesh. Ripping it from his face, Munif flung it at Dassai. He smirked as Dassai vomited blood, and wiped away the lingering bits of membrane with the hem of his robe. "So now you see, Fajeer Dassai. This is the vision you will take to the grave, to remember for all eternity."

Munif stepped back as Prince Nasir approached. Nasir's face was concealed by a scarf that covered all but his eyes. Dassai craned his neck to see him.

"And one more thing," Munif said, stepping aside and nodding at Nasir.

The Prince removed his scarf and stepped closer to the dying man.

Dassai looked up at Nasir, his eyes boring into the Prince's. "No, it can't be!" he cried.

"It is a pleasure to watch you die," Nasir said.

Dassai began to shake uncontrollably. At last Munif withdrew his blade.

Seconds passed as Munif savored the death throes of his most hated enemy. He was determined to stay until Dassai drew his last breath. The moment he was dead, Munif would speak of him no more; retribution had been served.

Nasir clapped his hand on Munif's shoulder, looking pleased. "It is done, Pavanan."

20

HE LOOKED UP.

Only a trace of silver remained as the moon Isíll waned in the evening sky. Cencova sat on the highest tier of stone steps that surrounded a wide reflecting pool. This place had always brought him a sense of calm. He came here whenever his life seemed to be headed in a direction that required reflection and solitude. Had it really been only a year? Each new season had marked a change.

Tomorrow, the sun would shine and new life would stir. Cencova did not know what the future would bring, but he was glad this struggle was nearing its end. He was eager to see Marin Altaïr once again, but it would have to wait.

She was somewhere in Qatana. He hoped she was safe. Her plan to use the books as a bargaining chip to lead Ciris Sarn and Prince Malek out into the open was admirable, but Cencova knew Marin Altaïr well. He knew that if she could lure Sarn out, she would kill him.

Cencova had warned her that the books must not come into Prince Malek's possession. It was plain Ciris Sarn would attempt to retrieve the books for Fajeer Dassai, with the purpose of continuing the lie. Cencova believed that Dassai's meeting with the *majals* was further proof of a conspiracy. It had nearly succeeded.

Prince Nasir had gone back into hiding. It was still uncertain what the consequences of Dassai's deception would be; therefore Nasir had slipped away shortly after Dassai uttered his last word. He'd told Munif where he could be found and then was gone.

Pavanan Munif, a man whose loyalty had been questioned, had proved in the end to be true. At first blamed for the failure in Tivisis, he'd ultimately prevented Fajeer Dassai's plot from succeeding. Cencova had no doubt that, had Dassai won his gamble, he and Prince Malek he would have run Qatana into ruin.

The Books of Promise remained a secret from the world.

Cencova knew the heart of the secret was contained in the fifth book. The greatest lie ever—

No. Too many lives were at stake—including Marin's. Whatever it was, opposing forces would do everything possible to keep it hidden. They would stop at nothing.

Perhaps that was for the best.

Although Cencova was proud of the stand he'd taken, he harbored serious reservations. The damage was already far-reaching, and he doubted it could be reversed. Now there was doubt where none had been before. Fajeer Dassai had been a clever schemer, true enough, but how could Dassai's plot to remove the Sultan have even happened? Why had his greed not been squelched? Could it occur again with someone else? The effects of his actions would linger—and it would be some time before all was right again.

"I thought I might find you here," a soft voice whispered.

Jolted from his thoughts, Cencova leapt out of his seat, nearly falling headlong down the rows of stone steps. A hand reached out and steadied him. Cencova turned to see Nasir standing at his side, his expression serious.

"Nothing is yet decided?" Nasir sat down beside him.

"Not yet," Cencova said. "The *siris* will seek out any who shared Fajeer's views."

"And what is to become of Pavanan Munif?"

"He has proved both capable and loyal in the highest degree. Should he wish to remain, no one will prevent him."

"Good," Nasir said.

Cencova sighed. "I blame myself for failing to see through the false accusations that shadowed him for so long."

"Don't let it bother you." Nasir laid his hand gently on the elder man's shoulder. Then he stood. "Well it is goodbye for now, I must leave for Tivisis. We will speak again soon. I wish you the best in all of your efforts."

"I wish the same for you," Cencova said.

21

EVENING APPROACHED.

The first sun had dropped just below the highest peaks of the Soller Mountains, a cauldron of molten gold beneath dark gray clouds. The air cooled quickly as the afternoon faded into night. It would be weeks before the spring weather gave way to summer. People still wore warm garb as they wandered about the city of Cievv.

Ilss Cencova left his home and entered the city to dine with Pavanan Munif. The afternoon session of the Rassan Majalis had just ended, and he watched as robed and cloaked figures returned, scurrying in different directions. He was in awe of how they'd managed to come together and make swift, precise decisions.

Despite this, he felt sullen. He hoped to see Marin soon. A wave of guilt passed over him as he remembered the murder of her husband. Cencova had watched as Marin fell into a grief so deep he thought nothing would ever pull her out of it, and devoted her life to the sole purpose of exacting revenge on the assassin who'd killed her husband. She was like a star that shone too brightly and quickly burned out from within. She cared for nothing in the world except the death of a single man; she didn't even care for herself.

He was never certain if he'd made the right decision to send her away, but in the end he'd let her go. He felt that she needed to go in order to save herself. Perhaps she had.

The random slaughter was both cruel and brilliant. Fajeer Dassai had known exactly what he was doing by creating terror among the people. Still, Cencova shuddered when he considered the manner in which Dassai had pursued his goals. *Why are the innocent always the victims?* He knew the answer as soon as the question came to him: *Because it was the easiest course to take—and one that would have the greatest effect upon others.*

He found Munif already seated at the coffeehouse. Cencova was saddened to think that he'd once doubted the man. He wondered where they would all be now if he'd allowed himself to be guided by his intuition and dismissed the charge against Munif. Perhaps he would have discovered Dassai sooner, and the events that followed could have been prevented.

In reality, he knew that this would not have stopped those who were corrupted by power. It was useless to wonder at all the possibilities. Heartache and turmoil were behind them, and it was time for Cencova to move on. He was unsure of what he would be moving on to, but he would cope with it as it came.

The same could be said for Pavanan Munif who had, at last, bested Fajeer Dassai. Cencova sat across from him, still struggling with emotion.

"Do not be so downcast, Ilss. My face will heal." Munif grinned.

Cencova laughed, his mood lightening immediately. "Of course it will."

"I hope you feel better, now that this is over."

"I am sorry not to have trusted you from the beginning. I have no excuse." Cencova shook his head sadly.

"Ilss, stop it! It's not going to help if you let this dominate your thoughts. Fajeer is dead."

"You're right . . . and I know. Still, it's a weakness of mine."

"It's understandable. There were so many webs of deception—you could not possibly have been expected to be certain which of us had been turned. When such news comes through distant sources, it becomes even more confusing, I'm sure. Don't worry any longer. I would have done the same thing if I had been in your place." Munif leaned forward. "There's another thing to consider. Ciris Sarn's role in all this."

Cencova had to consider that. How much did Sarn actually

know about what was happening? Did he have any clue as to what Dassai had been perpetrating—or was he merely another pawn in the game? Cencova suspected the latter. Although he did not know Sarn personally, he knew the man was intelligent enough to avoid being taken in by deception. And if he did realize what was happening, he would demand a much higher price. Cencova suspected that this was the case with Sarn.

A life wasted.

"I wonder about this myself," Cencova said, pressing his fingers together under his chin. This familiar gesture seemed to comfort Munif, and he leaned back in his chair. "It would not surprise me to learn that Fajeer tapped Ciris Sarn to kill Prince Malek and the Sultan as part of his plan. A bit of blackmail, if you will."

"So the *Kingslayer* is innocent?" Munif asked.

"A man like him is never totally innocent, but something like that."

"It's possible. I guess," Munif said. "But Sarn will execute Fajeer's orders only if in the end it serves his purpose."

"True. Killing the Sultan may give Ciris Sarn his freedom. Perhaps then he will disappear, never to be seen again."

"Unless Marin finds him first."

Cencova fell silent, his thoughts turning toward Marin.

22

DONNÒ GALLIRESSE WAITED.

He crouched in a narrow passage off the Royal Road in the Gardens Quarter of Tivisis, away from the prying eyes of passersby and the ill-fated lovers who rendezvoused amid the shadows.

He wasn't sure why he thought of fate now; he'd always believed himself to be a rational man. Yet here he was, soon to have a direct role in the way it acted on the world. Galliresse still couldn't fully believe what he'd been told, what he must now do. Fate had turned her head, and justice must be done.

"You alone?" a gruff voice asked behind him.

Galliresse nodded.

"Here is the official sanction," the man said, setting the letter in Galliresse's hand. "I'm to make sure you acknowledge the bearer's authority."

Galliresse broke the seal and unrolled the parchment. As he read, his eyes narrowed and he sucked in his breath. Though he'd known what the letter decreed, he gasped at the enormity of it.

"He is at the Hajjirin Masjid. In the library. Make sure he is dead."

Galliresse was still shaken. Over the past few weeks, his appetite dissapeared and he'd become frail. Galliresse was a shell of a man, gaunt and hollow. He knew that they would take action because of his failures. Eventually they would seek him out. All his thoughts were consumed by this reality. They would make him carry out the task himself, just to prove his worthiness.

Could he really do it? *I am no assassin.*

Galliresse was trapped in a maze of lies and deceptions woven by others. He had no control over the outcome. The way was chosen for him.

"Yes, I know how this works. I have signed such orders myself." It was unlike Galliresse to lose his temper or his faith; and right now he was dangerously close to losing both. He felt the heat rising in his face, but he was not afraid.

Galliresse heard the man behind him cough and then ask, "Do you not believe? I sense some doubt in this. We have provided you with the truth. If you cannot carry out your duty, tell me now. The King in Givenh and the Rassan Majalis will find another to take your stead."

The words hit Galliresse hard, and he felt his jaw clench. Doubt had managed to get the better of him. Again. "No. If it must be done . . . it will. And it will be done by me," he said.

"Think very carefully about what you are planning to do. We know the struggle that must be going on between your head and your heart. But you cannot falter in this. Our future, yours, mine, the citizens of Tivisis, and all Mirani depend on it. Do not let your legacy go to waste."

"I . . . understand . . . " Galliresse's words trailed off, leaving him alone with his thoughts. For all he knew, the messenger would soon be his executioner. "It will be done tonight."

"Very good," the man said. "Meet me back here at midnight. Bring proof it has been finished."

"I will," Galliresse said.

23

THE LIBRARY was empty.

Prince Nasir sat on the soft cushions. A stack of books lay on the table before him. His mind was filled with trepidation; the return to Riyyal would be long and dangerous. But the treachery facing him after that would no doubt be even greater.

Though his father was ill, he still commanded considerable authority. His brother Malek would be difficult as well—Nasir's hope rested in Marin and the others' ability to stop him. But Nasir would bring an army along with the knowledge that would change the course of history, and right a wrong that had for too long been a burden upon his people and all others in Mir'aj. This knowledge would give him strength and carry him through to the end.

After visiting with Ilss Cencova, he'd left for Tivisis. Nasir needed to learn about the mistakes made in the city which led to the horrific events that followed. He hoped to speak with Donnò Galliresse—the Suffet of Tivisis, a man Nasir met a decade earlier. He wondered if Galliresse would remember the Prince. He wondered if Galliresse was still an honorable man. Afterward he would leave for Nahkeel and there meet Pavanan Munif. It was good to have a friend to share the journey, and Pavanan was close to him now. He would need him again before long.

Their last conversation was still clear in his mind. "Get some rest," he'd told Munif. "You are going to need it. We will wait in Janeirah for word of my brother's fate. Regardless of whether he comes back, I will gather our allies to return to my home and face my father."

"And if Malek is there?" Munif asked.

"If my brother is there, I will deal with him," Nasir said.

Soon, for the first time in more than eight years, he would stand in his father's presence. But not to kneel with tears on his cheeks in front of the frail old man. No—it be to see an injustice finally righted, to see his father one more time before he died.

Prince Nasir stood and sighed. He needed to feel the cool night air and clear his mind. As he moved past the table he stopped suddenly, startled by the sight of Donnò Galliresse standing close by. "Your Honor. What brings you here? This is a surprise."

"No, it is me that is surprised, Prince Nasir. When I learned of your return, I did not think it possible and had to see you before my own eyes." Galliresse's frame partially blocked the exit, and Nasir was struck with instant foreboding. *Something troubles him, I can see it in his eyes. This—*

Nasir saw the blade in Galliresse's hand as he stepped forward, grim-faced. "I have no choice. Please forgive me."

Nasir took a step backward, but it wasn't enough.

Galliresse was on him quickly. The struggle was fierce but brief. Minutes later, Nasir was sitting upright in his chair, as still as a statue. His eyes were open, and his tongue lolled from his mouth. His pure white robe was splashed with red.

In the distance, the door to the library closed.

Part Eight

SANDS OF TIME

1.4.793 SC

1

RIMMAR FEHLS was a beaten man.

Malek aït-Siwal could see that as the man slouched on a stool in the cell. Fehls had been captured without incident and brought here quickly.

The Emir could sense that Fehls was ready to tell him anything he needed to know about Ciris Sarn. He could see it in the man's expression, in the worried eyes. He'd known that Fehls had been helping Sarn from afar, but he'd said nothing for more than a year, keeping tabs on their actions, waiting for the right time to make his move. Now everything was coming to a head, and Fehls was finally in Malek's custody. His next step was to use the spineless rat to his advantage.

He turned from the small window in the door and nodded to the guard.

Fehls, a tall, thin man with olive skin, looked up when the guard unlocked the door. Malek could see the fear in his tired eyes—the sudden recognition of the man who was here to see him. He stood and began to move to the far side of the cell. Malek raised a hand and shot him a warning look. Fehls stopped.

"Leave us," Malek said shortly.

The guard bowed and left.

Fehls whispered hurriedly, "I told them *nothing* . . . I promise—"

"You have suffered a great deal without surrendering your loyalty. I will see that you are rewarded," Malek said. "However, there is more that you must do."

"Of course," Fehls said fervently. "Just ask."

"I have been informed that there are men who would stop everything that we have planned."

"Release me and I will kill them all!"

"I believe you would, but no . . . at least, not yet. There is still a bit more of the game left to play."

Fehls nodded slowly, never taking his eyes off Malek. "What do you wish me to do?"

"I need you to help Ciris Sarn gain entry into my father's private chambers."

Fehls said nothing. Malek watched him intently. He knew Fehls had a close connection with Ciris Sarn—that the assassin would trust him. He would be able to convince Sarn to return to the Sultan's palace and obtain the key he needed to break his curse, especially if he thought Fehls was working on the inside.

Finally Fehls spoke. "What makes you think Sarn is here for the Sultan?"

"Does it matter?"

"Are you that eager to attain the throne?

"Perhaps."

"What if I refuse?"

Malek sighed. "Rimmar . . . you and I both know what Sarn desires more than anything else. The Sultan can provide that. We also know that soon I will be Sultan." He paused, allowing his prisoner time to comprehend what he had said. "I am simply asking for a favor—one that will benefit us both."

Fehls nodded. "You're right. Very well. I will get Sarn inside."

"Good. I will make sure the guards bring you a meal before you are released." Malek stepped out of the cell. The keys were still in the lock. Carefully he re-latched the door and brought the keys down to the main room. He tossed them to the guard, who caught them deftly. "Give him some food, and then release him before the suns set."

The guard nodded.

MALEK STEPPED OUTSIDE.

The sky was clear. Shimmering on the horizon, the spring suns had not yet set over the white desert sands beyond the city of Riyyal.

Prince Malek had learned from Dassai that Fehls was involved with Sarn. The man had worked with the elusive killer before, not only in Riyyal but in Tanith as well. Malek also knew that Dassai had driven Sarn to Riyyal, forcing his hand, leaving him no choice but to kill his father. Malek would give the assassin the last piece of the puzzle that he needed—but not until he had performed one final task.

He relaxed for a few moments in the sunlight, basking in the hot air that blew in from the desert.

Everything was falling into place.

3

CIRIS SARN caressed the talisman in his pocket.

The five threads made his fingers tingle. Just thinking about being in Riyyal once again, this close to the Sultan, who held the key to breaking his jinn-curse, made him anxious.

It was time to end it once and for all.

Sarn had little trouble getting into the palace; his long-standing ally Fehls, who'd given him directions to the Sultan's private chamber, had provided him with the appropriate access point.

"Kill only if absolutely necessary," Fehls had implored. "Do everything within your power to avoid contact with anyone in or about the palace, and do so only if that is unavoidable." Sarn had nodded understanding.

Sarn made his way through the city, inside the *casbah* walls and toward the palace like a weapon shot true to its target. He wove through narrow passages and passed street merchants in the bazaars, sharing the cobbled roads with men on horseback. Sarn kept his gaze averted from everyone, a damp cloth wrapped around his face to cool it and conceal his identity. Despite his skill, he needed to be extremely cautious.

He stopped under a palm tree. Across the road stood the high wall of the Sultan's palace.

Access onto the palace grounds was easy. Upon scaling the wall, he wove stealthily through myriad paths, keeping to the shadows of the trees and the ornate walls. He hid in the shadow of an immense statue and watched one of the many palace guards as he paced up and down. As soon as the guard's back was turned, Sarn slipped into the palace, keeping close to the walls. He made his way through the lower floor of the vast residence until he found a deserted foyer. From there he climbed the winding staircase to the Sultan's chambers.

There was only a single guard at the entrance to the royal apartments. Sarn waited in the shadows of the stairway, watching the guard. At the toll of the evening bell, the guard moved away to make his rounds of the upper floors. Then Sarn made his move.

Like a wisp of wind, he glided up the remaining steps and across the hall to the doors that led into the Sultan's chambers. Once inside, he turned his attention to the figure lying swathed in blankets on the bed in the center of the room.

Sarn approached the bed slowly, his heart pounding.

At last.

THE SULTAN looked up at the assassin with terrified eyes.

Sarn pressed his hand over the Sultan's mouth, silencing the scream before it began. The blood drained from the old man's face.

Working quickly, Sarn pressed a fishbone needle into the Sultan's lower lip, thrusting it through into the upper lip and pulling the thread tight. The Sultan thrashed in the bed. Sarn pressed his hand down harder on the Sultan's mouth. "Quiet, or you die!"

He stitched the Sultan's mouth closed, droplets of blood forming at each tiny puncture wound.

When he was finished, Sarn reached into his bag and brought out a handful of salt. He sprinkled it over the Sultan's bloodied mouth and spoke the words of the spell that would unbind his curse.

The Sultan's eyes rolled back. His body shook violently, his arms and legs flailing in wild protest.

Sarn held him down on the bed and waited, but the Sultan did not speak the word of response to his spell.

A spike of alarm pierced through him. Something was wrong.

The chamber doors flew open behind him. Sarn spun around as a dozen armed guards rushed in. He grabbed his sword and faced them as Prince Malek entered the chamber. "Put your sword down, Ciris. There's no need—"

Sarn grimaced, raising his blade over his shoulder in a defensive posture. "Stand back or your father dies."

"He's not my father," Malek said. He gestured toward the bed. "The man behind you is a commoner from the city of Riyyal who looks—quite extraordinarily, actually—just like him. Did you not realize you had walked into a trap when your incantation met with no response?"

A flash of anger pierced Sarn's thoughts. He felt his face flush with embarrassment. He had, of course, realized his error— seconds too late. Suddenly, Fehls came to mind, and he realized who had betrayed him.

"Come, lay down your sword," Malek said. He gestured for Sarn to relinquish his weapon. "We aren't going to kill you— and you aren't a prisoner. On the contrary . . . I have an offer for you."

Sarn lowered his sword cautiously. He glanced at the whimpering figure on the bed and saw that the Emir had told the truth. The man on the bed was just a decoy who bore an unsettling resemblance to the Sultan.

The anonymous target of Sarn's methods continued to make mewling noises as he squirmed, his hands clawing at his ruined mouth. Ignoring what he considered to be merely an expendable tool, Malek stepped forward. "My offer is simple. At this moment, a woman waits for word from me. She carries with her four books. You may remember those from when Dassai ordered you to kill a spy named Hiril Altaïr. You left them there."

Sarn frowned. He had placed those books beside the body in direct violation of Dassai's orders. Now his rebellion against Dassai had come back to haunt him. "So they are important, then," Sarn said. "How did she get them?"

"That should not concern you. What should be of interest is the woman's identity. She is the widow of Altaïr—Marin."

Sarn displayed indifference. "How does this concern me?"

"This is what I want you to do," Malek said. "I will give you the freedom you seek." He paused. "But only *after* you bring the books back."

"Where is this Marin now?"

"She is here. In the city. Doubtless looking for you."

"I see." Sarn replaced his blade in its scabbard.

"There is one other thing," Malek said, holding up his hand.

Sarn frowned. "What?"

"You cannot kill her," Malek said. "Not yet at least. I want you to guide me to her."

"You will accompany me?"

"Yes." Malek sneered. "There is another book that was not in Altaïr's possession. Marin knows its location—and I will convince her that she must lead us to it."

"The question is, will she trust you?"

The Emir's eyes gleamed. "It will be her duty to seek it out. I can convince her that the books are important to the Kingdom—that they were stolen by Dassai, and that Hiril Altaïr, acting on behalf of Qatana, was attempting to return them when he was killed." Malek's voice grew soft. "That will provide some kind of closure for her."

"Where is this place?"

"From what my sources have told me, it's near the Waha al-Ribat."

Sarn glowered. Just getting to the oasis would be difficult. Somewhere in the desert beyond was the hiding place—and that was said to be infested with not only Jnoun, but ghuls as well. "And you think she'll find it for you and then just let you take it for yourself?"

Malek shrugged. "There is nothing to be concerned about."

Sarn scowled. "If this book is guarded by ghuls, discovering it will release them. You are aware of what will happen?"

"I am." Malek matched Sarn's glare with his own. "That is not my concern, and it shouldn't be yours. You're perfectly capable of defending us."

Sarn thought about this. His only goal was to end his curse. However, releasing the ghuls could prove dangerous to everyone, himself included. Was the risk to his life worth it? Yes, he decided . . . because what was his life anyway, as long as this curse was part of his existence? He'd often wondered if death would be better. "So I lead you to this woman, and she leads us to where this fifth book is. What are your plans then?"

"Once all of the books are in my possession, you can kill her—and anybody else in her contingent. Then I will give you the word so that you may be free of your curse."

It took only seconds for Sarn to decide; even with the inevitable release of the ghuls in the equation, he must agree.

The ghuls would be ravenous when released; they would maim, or kill every living thing within reach.

"I accept."

SARN REFLECTED for a moment.

The events he had witnessed ran repeatedly through his mind. It was then he saw Rimmar Fehls.

Sarn followed him, making his way through the crowd. He watched as Fehls entered a small residence. Sarn waited. In a few moments, Fehls came back out and continued up the street. Sarn waited for a time before entering a broken-down flat. The walls were bare and stained with smoke and ruddy brown mildew. The room was devoid of furniture save a few wooden crates that still bore the faint odor of rotting fruit. Deep ruts ran the length of the hardwood floor. Sarn found nothing out of the ordinary and left.

Fehls was easy to find, readily picked out of the afternoon crowd by his appearance and gait. Sarn closed in, unnoticed.

Sarn observed a change in Fehls's posture and knew that Fehls suspected he was being followed. Considering whom he'd betrayed, there was only one person he should fear. He knew Fehls's heart would jolt—all men's did—when they encountered the assassin. He also knew that Fehls would desperately try to remember all of his training but then realize how futile it was. There was only one chance for him now—escape. But Sarn was not going to let that happen.

Fehls knelt suddenly and pretended to pick up something

from the street. As Sarn watched, he looked about the fruit market until his eyes stopped at a small passageway leading east toward the network of alleys. It was across the street from where he knelt, and he appeared to be contemplating his options.

Sarn took advantage of Fehls's indecisiveness to approach him and grip his shoulder.

"Walk with me to the end of this street. Take the corner," Sarn said calmly. "Two buildings down, you will open the first door on the right. Be calm and do nothing to indicate that you are under duress. Do not attempt to flee. If you resist, I will bleed you where you stand." Feeling the man's terror, and with his arm companionably around his shoulders, Sarn urged him along. Sarn chatted to him of inconsequential matters, smiling the entire time.

As soon as Fehls stepped inside the door Sarn had indicated, Sarn struck him in the back of the head. He dragged the limp man up a narrow stairway to a small windowless room. Sarn locked the door and waited.

Eventually, Fehls tried to stand, but then slumped back onto the floor. "I sense a betrayer in my midst," Sarn said.

"No, that is not true! I helped you gain access to the Sultan's palace! That is all I did."

"I gained access . . . but it was a trap."

"I did not know. I swear!" Fehls pleaded.

Sarn shook him once by the shoulders, hard enough that Fehls's head banged into the wall behind him. "I have a suspicion that there is much more going on—and that you know something about it. There are shadows cast around you that betray everything you do."

Fehls was silent.

"You haven't asked me how I escaped. Aren't you just a bit curious about what happened to me? Or why I am here now? Instead of in the palace prison?"

Fehls whimpered a few syllables, but Sarn, furious beyond anything Fehls could have witnessed, raised a hand, and Fehls stopped sputtering. "It's too late, Rimmar. It's too late to convince me you knew nothing about it."

"I . . . I know you are to lead Prince Malek to the desert to meet Marin Altaïr." Fehls paused, and Sarn noted that he chose his words carefully. "It is said she possesses relics of great value."

"And how would you come to know this?"

"I'm just trying to stay alive!"

"Well, if that's what you really want, tell me more!"

"The woman who possesses the books believes you killed her husband, as well as others . . . and that you sent summoners to kill the clerics in Givenh. They believe *you* are behind it all, but none of them knows why. They believe you plan to usurp the throne for yourself. I was told to maintain this facade. Nothing more."

Sarn admired his efforts to provide a reasonable explanation. But he also knew that Fehls was lying; he knew even more than he had just revealed. Sarn could torture the confession out of the man, but the result would be the same; he'd either kill Fehls for lying or kill him to keep him from telling the truth.

Prudence dictated that Sarn assume the worst; Fehls had betrayed him. But he respected his betrayer enough to end his life swiftly.

Sarn drew back his fist and Fehls flinched, but not quickly enough. Sarn's fist turned into an open palm. The pick concealed in his sleeve slapped into his palm and entered Fehls's forehead just above the bridge of his nose. Sarn pulled his hand back with some difficulty; the point of the steel had gone all the way through and exited through the back of Fehls's skull.

The dead man slumped to the floor.

Sarn wiped the blood from his hand and looked down at Fehls's lifeless face.

He felt nothing—nothing at all.

6

MARIN ALTAÏR was sullen.

She had waited four days in Riyyal with no word from the Emir. She was at the mercy of his whims and did not know whether or not he would accept her offer.

The plan was risky, using herself as bait to lure out Ciris Sarn. The Books of Promise were part of the bargain. Malek would gain possession, and she would get the assassin.

Marin knew the value of the relics—her husband and many others had died because of them. But only she knew where to find the fifth book. This was the sole reason she still lived. Malek needed her.

Yet, every day Marin received from a courier cryptic instructions to go to a different location and look for a message.

The messages had all been the same.

Wait.

She went alone, leaving Torre Lavvann and the others behind. From the caravanserai, she took advantage of the shadows cast by the towering whitewashed buildings as she passed through crooked passages and crossed over arched bridges of stone.

Riyyal was a city of water. It was impossible for her to imagine such a verdant place so far removed from rain. Yet there were an endless number of canals, fountains, and pools throughout the city.

Marin turned down another secluded side street and quickly found the *madrasah*—the destination given to her by today's courier.

Marin navigated a system of stone passages and ornate galleries within the building until she reached a great chamber. In the niches on both sides of the room were sculptured reliefs of the revered ones. Above the openings were arched windows, each stretching more than twenty feet in height. On the floor, centered beneath the painted murals, was a sculpted scene of children kneeling in reverence. Each prayed with a pledge basin at his side as the first Sultan of Qatana looked down upon them all. Marin paid little attention to the scene; she had not come to pay tribute, only to find the message left for her.

Beneath the basin of the third kneeling child was a loosened stone and a notch in which she could insert the tip of a thin steel blade.

There was no writing on the envelope. Carefully she fit the block back into place. Looking around quickly, she broke the royal seal and gingerly extracted the ivory parchment.

Tomorrow at dusk Ciris Sarn will escort you and your companions from the city. You will find him waiting at the Fountains of Ilmiyyah near the western gates of the city. He will be your guide to Waha al-Ribat. From there you will lead him to your final destination. Once the books are in my possession, you may do as you wish with the Kingslayer.

Marin read the message again; *finally*. She knelt on the floor, let her shoulders slump and her head droop, and allowed the torrent of emotions to wash over her. She hoped that by letting them overwhelm her now—where she was alone and private—she could prevent them from betraying her when tomorrow came.

"Soon, Ciris Sarn . . . soon, I swear it."

SHE WAS READY.

Marin led her group to the western gate. Beyond Riyyal the horizon was fading into a canvas of pastel shades painted by the setting of the second sun.

Marin found Sarn at the fountain. After so long, it all seemed to happen in an instant. One moment she was anticipating her encounter with the assassin, and the next, he stood before her. Beside him stood another man dressed in fine silk; the style of his head scarf identified him as a member of the royal family. Was this the Emir?

Marin looked into the eyes of the man she intended to kill. This was not the baleful, hollow-faced demon she had expected to confront. He was tall, with broad shoulders and high, chiseled cheekbones. He might be considered handsome were it not for his eyes. His cold black stare chilled her to the bone. She felt her heart leap, and her knees weakened.

Sarn led them away from the city just as the second sun set.

"TELL ME."

She looked at Torre Lavvann as her former captain entered the tent. He was as direct as always.

"Tell me."

"Sit," Marin said, "and I will."

"I need to know." Lavvann studied Marin. "What did you learn from the *sha'ir* that you are keeping from me?"

"The books contain the truth about the essence of Ala'i: a truth that appears to contradict everything you or I have been taught to believe, that proclaims it all to be a lie that may already have doomed us."

The implications of this gradually became apparent to Lavvann. "What else?" he asked.

Marin held out her left hand, exposing the unhealed scar in her palm. "The *sha'ir* while possessed by the efreet revealed the location of the last book. I can find it. It will be revealed to me when we are near to the location."

Lavvann leaned forward with interest. "How so?"

"A binding spell. Powerful magic that will aid us. However the four books are to be hers when the fifth is found."

"I see." Lavvann nodded.

"We must find it," Marin said.

Lavvann looked troubled. "These books have been kept secret for a reason," he said. "I am not sure if they should be found."

Marin sighed and said no more.

9

THE SHIMMERING of the mirage hid the danger.

Marin and her companions were five days into the desert and ten days away from reaching the oasis when they were ambushed.

The attack seemed to come from all sides. The camels strode along at a steady pace, with Silím Rammas in the lead to scout their route. Adal Hussein brought up the rear, with Marin in the middle of the party. Prior to departing, she had donned a white flowing garment of light fabric that covered her body from head to toe and shielded her from the harshest rays of the suns. Her headdress provided her head and face with little relief from the stifling heat. The books were concealed in the inner pockets where they would be protected from the elements. Her sword, in its scabbard was ready for use at an instant.

The wind had intensified, pelting them with sand. They covered their faces, turning their heads away from the stinging blast. Their camels slowed, pushing on against the gale. Rammas called out from the front of the party. "This is just a short squall! It should blow over quickly."

"We can hope!" Marin exclaimed.

Before long, the wind was screaming like a jinn unleashed. The blowing sand provided all the cover their attackers needed.

Their assailants came at them suddenly but were still far enough away that Marin and her companions had time to prepare. Swords and bows were drawn, and everybody prepared for a fight. The four men that Cencova had sent to accompany Marin encircled her. Sallah Maroud strung an arrow to his bow and took aim at an approaching rider. As they drew nearer, the wind died, the airborne sand settled, and Marin could see the Haradin.

She muttered an oath under her breath as they came closer. There were eight of them. Rammas and the others followed Maroud's lead and pulled bows and arrows from their packs. Marin winced at the blinding flash of sword blades and scimitars as the Haradin approached.

Their arrows flew.

Marin drew her own sword and let out a piercing cry as the arrows hit their targets. Three Haradin went down. The other five continued their charge, and the battle was on.

Marin dove ferociously into the battle, meeting one of the Haradin with a flash of her blade. The assassin's arm dropped to the sand, blood gushing from the stump of his elbow. Rage deafened her to the sound of steel against steel, to the cries of anguish. Her sole focus was survival.

Her companions matched her fury as they fought alongside her. Before long, all five of them had drawn their mounts into a rough semicircle and successfully fought off the remaining assailants. Panting from the exertion, they dismounted and snatched at their water skins.

Around them lay the slain bodies of the assassins. Their blood stained the white sand red. The Haradin horses had scattered and were lost to a predictable fate in the desert.

Lavvann sheathed his sword. "Is anybody hurt?"

"One of them sliced my arm pretty badly," Maroud said.

Marin and Rammas tended Maroud's wound. They bound his arm, and Marin smiled at him. "Don't worry."

"I won't worry, Marin," he said. He smiled. "It cannot go easy, it never does."

"There will be more," Marin said. "Either Haradin or White Palm. Word has spread of our coming."

"That is probably true," Malek said. "We need to leave quickly."

He was right. The faster they moved, the sooner they could reach the oasis, and possibly avoid more hunters. But too much exertion was even deadlier. The desert itself was unmerciful— even more than a legion of assassins.

Once they had collected their belongings and bound their wounds, they resumed their journey west. Sarn was at her side in an instant, as if he were keeping a close watch on her.

She let him. *I am keeping a close watch on you, too, Ciris Sarn,* she thought. *And the first chance I see, I will spill your blood all over these desert sands.*

None of them spoke.

70

DANGER CLOSES *from all sides.*

She kept her thoughts to herself as off in the distance, Marin saw two figures on horseback.

It had been two days since the Haradin attack. They had not encountered anyone else; nevertheless, they had not let down their guard. They were wary of other *badawh* and cutthroats.

Since the ambush, the heat had become even more brutal.

At the height of the day they were forced to take shelter, setting up tents to shield themselves from the suns' heat. Lavvann sent Hussein ahead a short distance to scout out the road for them. He returned with periodic reports during their progress, and they adjusted their pace accordingly.

The last report had come two hours ago. No sign of anyone, and by their best reckoning, they were alone.

For now.

11

SARN WAITED.

Several hours after the others had gone to sleep, he watched as Marin approached his tent.

She entered silently, carefully moving aside the folds of cloth that hung across the entry. She paused for a moment, as though she could feel his eyes upon her.

She is beautiful, thought Sarn. The way he felt about that startled him. Women did not usually affect him in that manner.

Sarn lay on his left side, wrapped in blankets, his head opposite the entrance. As she peered in the dim light, he moved slightly, shifting as though in sleep.

He admired her courage in entering his tent, and watched as lowered the flap quietly behind her. She took several small, careful steps closer and then hesitated. Slowly she reached for her blade. Sarn rolled into the shadows, vanishing from her sight. She froze, looking about wildly.

His eyes met hers as he stepped away from the dark wall of the tent and approached her menacingly.

Sarn had known that at some point, one of these travelers would try to end his life. Marin was the one whom he had suspected from the start. Earlier that night he had spied her venomous glances as they ate together.

After all, he had killed her husband, Hiril Altaïr.

Sarn saw her flinch, fully expecting a lethal blow, but he did not approach. Instead, he was content to watch the emotions play across her face—all but fear.

He continued to stand silently, waiting for her next move. Whatever weapon she had hidden behind her back remained there.

Sarn underestimated no one. While it was true that most assassins were men, there were women just as capable; and Sarn knew that they were, in some ways, superior. A woman tended to be more driven and relentless than a man. Female assassins were dedicated, deceptive, and ruthless. These qualities made them extremely lethal.

He had expected the worst from Marin, but he quickly determined that although she was capable of killing, she was not a killer. She was different. Yes, she was fair and cunning, but not cold and shallow. Something in her eyes told him she was much more complex than he could have imagined. He decided to spare her life tonight.

But he knew he would kill her eventually.

12

"DO YOU think I'm a fool?"

Marin went still. She recovered quickly though, hoping that her disappointment and uncertainty were not perceptible. She brought her empty hands up in front of her and murmured, "No, no, of course not. I heard sounds and feared you might be ambushed by some unseen attacker," she said, flinching as she realized how feeble it sounded even to her.

Sarn lit a candle and continued to study her. She could swear his lips quirked. "So, you were worried about my welfare? I hardly believe that . . . and yet to take my life now would seem to be an even greater folly."

Her chin rose involuntarily as the anger boiled up inside again. "You know nothing about me or my motives," she whispered.

He regarded her for a moment. Did she wait for his attack? Did she hope he would end her life quickly?

Sarn sighed and raked his fingers through his dark hair. He straightened and beckoned to her. "Come, sit—let's talk. We haven't spoken much, and I could use the company." He sat at one end of the tent, thoughtfully leaving a place for her near the doorway, as far away from him as possible.

The irony of this invitation did not escape her; she stood for a moment, indecisive. Finally however her shoulders drooped and she sat quietly.

She looked around, then said, "I have watched you use magic—the false image of yourself when you battled the Haradin."

"It's a simple spell, a protective illusion."

She raised an eyebrow. "But the use of arcane—even trivial—magic has serious consequences for the one who weaves the spell, doesn't it? Isn't that why there are so few who can do such things?"

He nodded, seeming unsurprised by the question. "True. It is said that one will first wither from within and then age outwardly from its continual use. Yet for some reason, be it a boon or a curse, I suffer little of this effect . . . at least, on the outside," he said wryly, as if to himself.

"Are you jinn-born?" she asked.

The look that passed across Sarn's face was brief, and to the untrained eye, undetectable. It told her that her guess had hit home.

"I will not burden you with my past tonight," he said. "I wish to hear of yours."

"Mine? How could that possibly interest you? My deeds pale in comparison to what you have done." She made no attempt to hide the contempt in her voice.

"How is that? Your possession of the books tells me you are important."

"I once had a future, but that was taken from me. Though it can never be replaced, I seek to right some of the wrongs done." Marin paused and said, "The books will give me the chance to change this."

"Then we share a common bond. Let hope we see it done, then," Sarn said.

The shock of his words resonated in Marin. Looking at him, she knew he could see how she felt—and she could see his emotions, too.

He was pleased.

13

MARIN SHIVERED.

It was the following morning, and the company continued its trek to the oasis. Marin was still reeling from her conversation with Sarn.

Sarn had awakened everyone at the crack of dawn and was silent as they all packed their horses for the day. He didn't say a word to her. Instead, he quietly fed and watered his horse and then consulted with the Emir away from all the others. They traveled six hours before stopping.

They reached a caravanserai without incident. The owners provided them with bedding, cheese, and bread. Marin heard the metallic clink of coins being exchanged. Somehow, she did not fear for their safety. In truth, Marin wasn't sure what she felt anymore.

"You'd better get some sleep," Sarn told her. "We have a long trek still ahead of us."

"A week?" one of the others asked.

"Yes."

"The path is becoming more difficult to follow with each passing mile," Marin said.

"Finding proper passage from this point onward will not be easy," Sarn warned her. "But don't concern yourself. I know the way."

Marin allowed herself a small smile.

"I am not afraid," she said.

SOON.

Marin knew that her confrontation with the assassin was getting closer. It was impossible to keep from brooding on it.

She told Sarn little. He had been successful in getting information out of her, but she'd revealed only what she wanted him to know, weaving fact with fiction. Sarn had listened, nodding. The closest she'd come to Hiril's death was a brief mention of a spy dying in Havar. For a moment, Sarn's eyes glinted, as if he'd realized she was alluding to her late husband. But she'd moved on quickly, changing the subject to how she'd gained possession of the books that Malek sought to possess. Sarn had questioned her about that, and the answer she'd given was the same as before. "I came across them accidentally." Sarn had nodded, seemingly accepting her explanation.

At some point during their conversation, Marin had found herself relaxed and even at ease with Sarn. His voice was soothing somehow. "My birthright has been more of a curse than a blessing," he said. "Everything I have undertaken has been because of it."

"So you are a servant, then?" Marin asked. She doubted this would draw out a confession, but thought it was worth a try.

"In a cruel way, yes," Sarn answered. "There is a man named Fajeer Dassai. He is close to the Sultan and Prince Malek. I am at the mercy of him and ... others ... " Sarn faltered. She detected a furtive movement as he touched something in his pocket. " ... a tool for the Sultan."

"And you must do as they command?"

"Yes."

"Why?" Marin pressed him. "It seems that you would be a slave to no one."

And then Sarn told her more than she ever would have expected him to reveal. He told her of his mother, and of the veil between the mortal world and the realm of the Jnoun—how in certain instances the barrier broke or tore, allowing these elemental creatures to slip through to Mir'aj. He told her of his father's marriage to such a being.

Marin was silent, awestruck by his narrative. He went on to explain that he was both human and Jnoun, begotten of his father's seed and nurtured in his elemental mother's womb, hence the mystical blood that flowed through his veins. "My mother died in childbirth," he said. "My father later married an ambitious whore whose only desire was to use him to get at the wealthier men of the court." He told her about the rage he'd felt over her neglect, how she'd arranged to have him kidnapped from his home and delivered to the Tajj al-Hadd. He spoke of his rage and the result of his uncontrollable actions.

"What happened?" Marin asked.

"I killed her lover," he confessed. "She witnessed the attack and discovered my secret."

"And she found a way to get rid of you."

"Yes," he said.

He revealed the training he'd received in the Tajj al-Hadd from Fajeer Dassai. He told her how Dassai had groomed him from an early age to do his bidding, how he'd become a virtual slave to Dassai because of his blood. He explained how the seeds of resentment festered. "I am a pawn to the Sultan of Qatana."

Marin remained silent.

"Yet . . . someday . . . I might live in peace," Sarn said. "But only upon the Sultan's death can this occur."

"For you to be free, the Sultan must die?"

"Yes."

His revelations subjected Marin to an onslaught of conflicting emotions. When she returned to her tent, she had a new perspective on her husband's killer. On the one hand, revenge for Hiril's murder still drove her, compelling her to complete her task. On the other, she'd discovered, like it or not, a newfound compassion for Sarn.

She tried to shake it off, but try as she might, she could not rid herself of the feeling.

Her sleep that night was troubled.

MARIN MUTTERED a curse.

She had told more lies and used more trickery in her attempt to avenge her husband's death than she ever would have imagined. She should not have listened to Ciris Sarn last night. She should have excused herself as quickly as possible and returned to her tent.

No one should have to endure as much as she had—no matter what their crime or what they'd suffered in life. She hated Sarn because she needed him. She needed him to save her from *becoming* him.

Marin and her escorts rode behind Sarn and Prince Malek, making good time in the blaze of the double suns. Off in the distance, mirages shimmered along the endless horizon, seeming to float over the blinding white sand. Sarn had told Marin this morning that the oasis was only a day's journey away.

And when we find the last book, she thought, *will I have the conviction to kill you?*

Rammas shook his head as if reading her thoughts. "It doesn't matter anymore. You know what we must do."

Surprised, Marin found herself nodding.

She secretly hoped Sarn had heeded her request.

16

DARKNESS FELL.

As the second sun set, they made camp at the base of a large sand dune. Malek and Sarn sat huddled together away from the others.

"We'll stay at the oasis only long enough to regain our strength. The location of the treasure will not be far away," the Prince said. "And when we are finished, we return."

Sarn nodded. His mood was reflective and troubled. All day he'd been lost in thoughts about Marin and the potential consequences once the book was found and the ghuls were released.

"She will lead us," Malek continued. "When we reach the spot where she will unearth the fifth book, I will move quickly. One slash with the blade, and her blood will spill out onto Rim al-Jass."

"And the others?" Sarn asked, already knowing what the answer would be.

"Surely they will not be too much for you to handle. I will help once I've killed Marin."

"Releasing the ghuls will be our foremost concern," Sarn said. "The men who accompany Marin will no doubt fight them, but I can't guarantee your safety." He looked at the Emir. "It's possible that their strength will be too great even for me."

Malek smiled. "I have confidence you will defeat them. Don't concern yourself with it."

Sarn nodded. "Then once it's finished, you will give me my reward."

"Yes." Malek smiled. "And then your curse will be lifted."

Sarn nodded. This promise outweighed any other decision he could make. His glance darted toward Marin's camp. He'd been thinking about what she'd said to him. Now her words brought back memories of Fajeer Dassai and the actions that ultimately had sent him on this path of fate. That single act of rebellion—stealing the Books of Promise and laying them beside Hiril Alta-ïr's body—had brought them into the hands of the woman whom he knew to be Hiril's widow.

"Follow my lead," the Prince said. "And do not fret. Our journey will end soon."

Sarn nodded. "I'm ready."

17

WAHA AL-RIBAT.

Ahead of them they could see a ring of jade floating in an alabaster ocean of sand.

Despite the welcoming oasis, Marin was lost in visions of her encounter with the assassin. That she was a trained warrior of the Four Banners was still true, but she was first and foremost a woman.

She felt the pain of those who needed nurturing. Upon hearing Sarn's life story—how his adolescence had been spent, the treachery of wicked men, and his search for peace—her entire body had become exhausted with inner turmoil. Here was a man who was not at all what he seemed. Sarn was no demon; he was a mortal tormented by memories and dreams—and a curse.

Sarn had told the story of his time with Fajeer Dassai in the tone of someone making a confession. Dassai had taken him so far beyond the border of humanity that he'd ceased to be salvageable. Marin could do nothing to bring him back from the darkness—and she could not let go of her hatred of that evil.

After reaching the oasis, Marin chose to be alone. She spent a good deal of time at night ruminating over their conversation. She had shown Sarn some sympathy but could not, under any circumstances, allow herself to tell him her own story. She had also been careful to not say anything that would cause him to suspect her true intentions. She knew that anyone who had been held captive long enough usually ended up feeling some connection to those who held him. She also realized that by leading Sarn and Malek out into the desert, she had put herself and her entourage in mortal danger.

Little more was said between the two of them in the following days. Their conversation defined their uneasy relationship. It was in their eyes when they met, in their touch when they brushed against each other. Very clearly, it said that one of them would not walk away from this alive. Marin was determined to be the survivor.

At last they were ready to leave the oasis. Although they faced danger once more, they were refreshed and eager, ready to ride to the finish. Marin looked into the eyes of her companions and knew they all felt the same way.

The end was near.

THE SUNS were beginning to set.

As they approached the dunes, Sarn motioned for Marin and the others to hang back. She and her company stopped and watched as Sarn and Malek rode between the dunes toward a low hill. Sarn dismounted and knelt.

For a moment Marin was struck by the stark emptiness of the desert and the feeling it aroused in her. *Serenity.* This place was imbued with it. For miles in all directions were nothing but undulating dunes in a graceful, shifting sea of white sand. Beyond, and everywhere surrounding the lost oasis, the Rab'al-Athar was devoid of life yet eager for death. Marin understood now how so many could be taken by this presence, overwhelmed by a the powerful spirit of the place.

Many lives had been lost here, overwhelmed by the elements. It was said that the winds of the desert often carried the voices of the dead. Marin shivered. She could almost hear the shrill cries of those disembodied voices all around her.

That life could exist in a land so forsaken defied logic. There was a strange power in the desert that could lead a traveler to believe the only way out was death. And indeed, many who had crossed that barren ocean of sand had taken their own lives simply to be rid of the menacing magic that surrounded them.

Yet north of them, in the direction from which they had come, was an oasis so beautiful that it brought instant hope for redemption. If the traveler, weary and demoralized after endless days of journeying through this unforgiving wasteland, could only know—even as his final hope withered—that such an oasis lay just with reach, he might hold on. However, Waha al-Ribat was not known to many, and few ever succeeded in reaching the place.

Even when Marin had drunk in the serenity of the green oasis before she left it again, she could not shake the sense that this was not the journey she had bargained for. She knew terrible things were about to happen here in this temporary haven—things that would change the meaning of beauty for her forever.

She observed Sarn as he knelt upon the sand and realized that he, too, was apprehensive.

They were close now.

19

SARN STOOD at the top of a dune.

He looked out over a vast sea of shifting sands. It was the third day since they'd left the oasis; they'd been traveling since early morning. Marin had told them they were close now. He'd meandered along behind, talking with Rammas as Malek led the way up the massive dune and then stopped.

Sarn knew that Marin was standing behind him, watching him carefully, but he did not acknowledge her presence. Did she suspect him? Had she known all along that he had killed her husband, and was seeking revenge? He dismissed the thought. After all, how would she have found out? Sarn had committed Hiril Altaïr's murder in the absence of witnesses. No, he reasoned, she couldn't possibly know. Nevertheless, Sarn sensed she was far more dangerous to him than she appeared. And that angered him. Was she to cut his life short even before it truly began again?

"I do apologize for my behavior," Marin spoke softly, and her remorse seemed genuine. "I am sometimes too outspoken for my own good."

"If you were not outspoken, you would not be Marin Altaïr." He immediately regretted his placatory tone.

"Of course, I understand." Marin stood beside him and followed his gaze. Sensing his discomfort with the awkwardness of the moment, she provided him with an opportunity to recover his dignity by offering a compliment. "Once we have the final book," she said, "can you also control the weather and bring good fortune to our return?"

Sarn smiled tightly. The twinkle in her eyes suggested she was teasing him. "And you think I could not? Am I not Ciris Sarn, the *Kingslayer*?" he said mockingly. "I control all things that I choose to control."

He felt Marin stiffen beside him. This was an interesting woman, and he longed to learn more about why she had chosen such a dangerous path in life. Surely she could have been anything she chose to be. She was beautiful and charming, and it was difficult to imagine a man who would not be drawn to her. Yet, something about her seemed strangely familiar. Marin Altaïr was a woman, but she was also something more.

She wanted to ask him something; Sarn could sense the unasked question hanging in the air.

"Tell me why you killed my husband."

But she said nothing.

20

IT WAS HERE.

Marin knelt over a perfectly round etched stone set in the sand. How can this be, she thought. How can it just show up like this? The desert should have swallowed it ages ago.

Although not devoid of beauty, it was not something one might seek to possess. Three feet in diameter, it sealed a smaller opening sunk in the desert floor. Prompted by Malek, Sarn joined them, and together the two of them brushed the sand away from its surface, slowly uncovering it.

"It has always been here," the Emir observed as he watched them work. "The sands of time have chosen to reveal it to us."

It took them only a few minutes to sweep the gypsum granules away from the surface. When it was finally and fully revealed, Sarn knelt before it, looking at the designs engraved in the ancient stone.

Sarn knew that with his touch he would release the power that guarded the treasure.

"Go ahead," Malek whispered to Sarn. He almost appeared to be smiling. "Open it."

Sarn was reluctant. Dassai, Malek, and the rest of the power-mongers sickened him, but he had no choice. He was their pawn in a desperate game. But he was determined to outlast them all; and in the end he would find a way to break their stranglehold on him.

Sarn studied Marin in the fading light. Something stirred inside him, but he was unfamiliar with the feeling. He knew that she was much more than she appeared, and in a way, he was bound to her. Still, she would fall like all the others, and it pained him deeply that he did not have the inner strength to resist the compulsion. He could not allow anyone—least of all her—to divert him from his course.

It was the only way.

21

SIMPLE.

Break the seal and remove the lid. Then Malek would force Marin to deposit the books into the well, and Sarn would reseal it. If they could do it quickly enough, perhaps the ghuls would not attack.

Sarn was caught in the middle. Rather than creating the destruction, he would be merely a spectator. The Emir had orchestrated everything, from the decoy in the palace to using Marin to find the resting place of the fifth book.

Sarn wondered how he could possibly have been so blind to Malek's intentions. Usually he knew at once when someone had turned on him. He had allowed this to happen as surely as he had allowed Marin to reach parts of him he had always kept locked away. Over time, he had grown so weary of his deceptions and illusions that he had let his guard down once more. If he wasn't careful, he would pay for this lapse of attention with his life.

He had to find a way regain control of the situation. And it must end with the killing of Malek himself.

Even if it was the last thing he ever did.

22

SARN HAD one choice to make.

He had to do it. Once the seal was broken, he could not allow Marin to die with the rest of them. He closed his eyes and saw her as he had seen her that fateful night, a shadow against the setting suns. She was beautiful, but he had thought that from the first moment he'd seen her. There was more to it than that; she was compelling in a way he'd never known before. Now she was the only thing that kept him from releasing the ghuls.

Sarn had never felt this depth of emotion for anyone. He vaguely remembered having felt something like it for another woman who had also cared for him—but that was long ago.

This was different; it was far more powerful. The need to protect Marin Altaïr struck him to his very core.

Sarn would let the others die; he did not care what happened to them. In fact it would be better if they perished; it would be much easier if it were just he and Marin.

Of course, he also knew that this could never happen. Yet he had to try. He was tired of living a lie—the illusion that life had meaning, or someday might have. Other lives were guided by the hand of fate—a sense of purpose that showed them the straight path. Were they different in some way? Had they been chosen by some inexplicable game of chance long before this world even came into existence? Were those people who seemed to have perfect balance in their lives—blessed by virtues such as patience, kindness, generosity, and the capacity to love another person—simply singled out by fate? Or was it an illusion for them as well?

Sarn sighed and shook himself from his musings, and focused again on the present. *If I could only find a place where we can be together,* he thought.

Even for the briefest of moments . . . .

23

RAMMAS SHADED his eyes with his hand.

He scanned the horizon, gazing at the cloudless sky for a moment before turning to Emir Malek and Ciris Sarn. Sarn knelt before the stone seal he had just uncovered. Marin stood behind him, anxiously clutching the leather bag that contained the Books of Promise. Where the ground had been a smooth, uninterrupted layer of sand just moments ago, now there was a crater revealing an intricately inscribed capstone.

A fierce wind blasted across the landscape as Rammas made his way over to Sarn, kicking sand up into the air, forming small whirlwinds, sand-dervishes whirling across the dunes. The sand stung Rammas's exposed cheeks and lodged itself in his flesh. He pulled a long strip of cloth from his pack and wrapped it around his face and neck. Beneath the scarf, he did his best to spit out the grit. He squinted against the onslaught.

The landscape stretched out interminably, waves of gypsum that swirled into and out of one another in an ever—changing estuary of sand. In the distance he spied a rift, a small canyon of exposed limestone rock.

Sarn remained silent as Rammas approached. His attention was focused on the ground before him. The suns glinted off the lid that sealed the well. The stone was a brilliant white, and it nearly blinded Rammas.

"I want to know what is going on, and I want to know now," Rammas demanded, his face flushed with anger.

"As you can see, I am about to open the well," Sarn replied calmly. "What we seek lies within."

The Emir's met Rammas's gaze and nodded. Rammas turned

back to Sarn, who appeared to be hesitating. "I don't like this," he said.

Sarn waved away his concerns. "Don't trouble yourself. I will open the seal, and then all five books will be in their rightful place."

"This treasure has caused enough strife. It is a plague upon the world," Rammas said. The thought made his adrenaline rise.

"It has," Sarn said. "And Fajeer Dassai was behind it all. He betrayed us. He wanted the books for himself."

Rammas knew his only hope was to kill Sarn. It was himself against an unbeatable foe. Perhaps, Rammas reasoned, luck would be with him. He had to smile a little at the thought.

As Rammas reached for his dagger and Sarn's hand touched the stone, the ground beneath them began to tremble. Rammas was surprised by the sudden quake. He gathered his wits. The time had come; he must kill Sarn this very moment—or all would be lost. Rammas grasped his blade tightly as he struggled to maintain his footing, and lunged at the assassin.

"You are too late, Rammas!" Sarn shouted.

"We all are!"

SARN LASHED OUT.

The thundering pulse continued to reverberate beneath the surface as he rolled to his side and threw a handful of sand into Rammas's face. Rammas screamed and clutched at his eyes.

Malek drew his sword and aimed the point at Marin's throat. "The books," he said. "Take them out and throw them in with the others!"

Marin reached for them, but hesitated. From the other side of the dune, Maroud and Lavvann rushed to her aid, but they were too slow.

Malek clutched Marin's hair with his left hand and pressed the blade of his sword against the soft flesh of her throat with the right. His face was twisted in a mad grimace. "Do it *now!*"

Marin seized the books.

A rush of hot air burst out of the well. Malek stood against it. His attention was fixed on Marin. Behind him, Lavvann and Maroud drew nearer. Rammas moaned and wobbled on his knees, his eyes squeezed shut.

Marin dropped the books on the sand. "You want these four to join the fifth? Here they are! *You* throw them in!"

Malek drew his arm back to strike her, but Sarn struck first, and both men fell to the ground in a spray of sand.

Ghuls rode the hot wind up from the pit and rushed toward the first people they saw: the two men coming to Marin's aid, Maroud and Lavvann.

Malek lashed out at Sarn, but his swing was too high, and his blade cut nothing but air. The hilt slipped from his sweating palm. He tried retrieve it, looking around for Sarn. But the assassin had disappeared.

"It doesn't matter," Malek shouted. *"I will kill Marin first, and then I will kill you!"*

At that moment, he heard movement behind him. He turned just as Sarn thrust his sword at his face.

His scream was cut off abruptly as the point of the sword rammed through his open mouth and out the back of his head.

Sarn pulled the sword back, and Emir Malek fell dead.

SARN SNEERED.

He watched Malek tumble down the dune and come to rest in a widening pool of dark red.

The thunder of galloping hooves brought him his senses. Out

of the east in a cloud of sand and dust rode a massed company of horsemen. They wore long, flowing white garments, their heads and some of their faces completely covered. Sarn recognized them. The White Palm.

Marin and the others drew together in a defensive circle. As the riders drew nearer, the ghuls encircled the opening, pursuing anything human. Despite the danger, Sarn appreciated the irony of the invaders' timing.

The ghuls were fiendish creatures. Each had the muscular body of a strong man, with large, pointed ears and razor-sharp teeth like those of a wolf, easily capable of tearing a victim apart. Their fingers and toes ended in long, curved claws—talons so sharp that one blow could slice open a man's belly. They walked on two feet, yet with an animal-like gait, capable of covering a great distance with each stride.

The ghuls roared through the chaos in pursuit of Lavvann and Maroud. One of the demons broke off from the chase to maul Rammas, who was still on his knees, blinded. Blood and entrails splattered the ground around his body. The ghul tore his head from his neck and tossed it aside, abandoning it in search of other prey.

Sarn sidestepped Rammas' corpse, caught up in the frantic battle. The ghuls were relentless; they had no capacity for mercy.

Sarn struggled to find Marin and the others. He heard a dying man beg in a gurgling whisper, "Please . . . kill . . . me . . . "

Sarn paused and glanced back at the fallen *badawh*, who was convulsing in agony. Sarn thrust his blade through the man's eye.

Better to die quickly, he thought.

He found the others in the center of the melee, fighting off not only the White Palm and the ghuls, but Haradin as well. Sarn grabbed Marin's hand and pulled her toward him, beckoning Maroud and Lavvann to follow. They fought their way out of the skirmish and sprinted toward Sarn and Marin.

The three of them followed the assassin with the battle raging all around them. They would not be safe until every single one of their enemies had been slain. With weapons and cunning, they launched a counterattack.

"This way!" Sarn said.

Marin stumbled, spun to her right, and almost fell. She regained her balance quickly and managed to get her feet moving again, but when she looked up, Sarn was nowhere to be seen.

He was gone.

26

MARIN RAN.

She strained to reach the top of a sand dune. There was a sound like an eruption from beneath the desert. Suddenly a ghul was there, slavering, its mouth a wicked maw of razor-sharp teeth. It lunged toward her.

"The ghuls are bound to us!" Marin realized this even as Sarn yelled the words.

Marin did not see Sarn nock the arrow, but she saw the bolt sink into the ghul's face—piercing it just below the nose. Just as the demon fell, a second ghul grabbed Sarn from behind and tossed him high in the air. He landed hard, his leg bent awkwardly behind him.

Marin realized she was about to die, and wondered briefly if her life had meant anything. She took a step back as yet another ghul advanced on her. Out of the corner of her eye, where Sarn had landed, she saw movement; Sarn was still alive. Had she failed to avenge the life of her husband? Would she see him in paradise? She closed her eyes and waited for the worst.

It never came.

She opened her eyes to see the demon sprawled on the sand, its eyes wide open, mouth dripping blood, lifeless.

Marin went over to where Sarn lay broken. His breathing was labored and shallow. "When I realized you were no longer behind me . . . I came . . . to find you," he rasped.

Sarn had saved her life. She had not expected that she would be indebted to him. It would have been better if the ghul had killed her, or killed them both. At least then she could be reunited in death with Hiril—and she would no longer be tortured by the dilemma of whether Sarn deserved life or death.

"Forgive . . . me," Sarn whispered.

"You ask too much," Marin said, tears welling in her eyes. She knelt beside him. "Are you blind to all that you have done?"

Sarn said nothing, but the look on his face told her everything.

Marin was sobbing. "You took from me my life . . . my future . . . my love."

She looked for a reply, but did not really expect one. Tears that she had repressed for a long time began to flow.

"Hiril was my love, my reason for living. You murdered him in cold blood and left me to pick up the pieces of my life. I vowed that I would find and kill you."

He remained silent.

"My intentions have always been to kill you . . . not to offer forgiveness."

Sarn gasped for breath.

Marin sighed through her tears. "And now," she went on, "you have been betrayed by your own failings rather than by my designs. This may sound strange, but you have relieved me of a terrible burden. You see, while it is no longer in my heart to kill you, neither is it there to forgive you." She paused. "So I will simply walk away, and I will *let* you die." He would soon come to know just how his victims had suffered before they died, she thought.

Marin stood, turned, and left him there.

27

MARIN RETURNED to the capstone.

She scavenged the battleground, filling a discarded pack with rations. She also grabbed several waterskins that had fallen during the fight. A lone horse remained, bloodied, but alive and uninjured. Marin looked up at the suns. *Could she make back to the oasis?*

Next she tore strips of bloodied cloth from the hem of her garment and tied them around two swords. On a dried palm frond she wrote a brief message and buried it under a few inches of sand next to the swords. If Maroud or Lavvann had survived, either or both would surely return. In any event, she hoped someone she knew would find her message sign and retrieve the note:

Rammas has fallen, so too Malek. Sarn I left to die.

Marin then found her comrade and, exhausted and sore as she was, did her best to bury him. It might not have been proper, but it was respectful under the circumstances. She placed some of his belongings in the saddlebag with the food and remounted.

Ciris Sarn was nowhere to be seen. She looked out across the endless expanse of desert and suddenly felt overwhelmed. Self-doubt and pity pierced her heart. Somewhere out there in the sea of sand lay the assassin, his body broken, dying. He might already be dead. And Marin had left him.

Her thoughts turned to the Books of Promise. Where were they now? And if Sarn died, would the *sha'ir* suddenly appear?

She had no idea how long she waited there, pondering these questions. It didn't really matter, she concluded. Time had stopped once she'd made the decision to abandon Sarn. And, she realized, she was a different person now.

Yes, she had undertaken the task for the sole purpose of killing him; in fact, the elation she had expected to feel from the revenge was second only to the satisfaction she would derive from the justice meted out. Or perhaps, she wondered . . . was it the reverse?

But she had not known that she could feel such sorrow—the sorrow that weighed on her heart now—for a murderer. Least of all the murderer who had crushed her heart by taking away her reason for living: Hiril. She brushed tears off her cheeks with the back of her hand and took a deep drink of water before spurring her horse on.

As she rode, her thoughts became more turbulent. How could she simply walk away from a man who had professed his guilt and then atoned for it by saving her life? Was she no better than he?

No, she could not accept that about herself. Whatever kindness Sarn had shown at the end of his life was completely overshadowed by his many misdeeds. Regardless of his actions just before death, his actions in the past proved that he deserved to die. Such a belief was the equivalent of pardoning a condemned murderer moments before he was scheduled to be hanged—because he now shed tears of contrition. No, by then it was not only too late but meaningless as well.

Ciris Sarn had made a career of killing people. He had done so relentlessly and without remorse. And sometimes those people were innocent. No, Sarn was not a decent man. Once she considered all these things, Marin knew she had made the right—and just—decision.

I should not have walked away, she thought. *It would have been more honorable to thrust my blade through his heart and end his suffering. Yet how many did Sarn cause to suffer before they died by his hand?*

Marin was certain he had not always given his victims that luxury. She was right to walk away.

Besides, she thought, *now the books will forever remain here, hidden, lost. They've caused too much violence and bloodshed already.*

As for Sarn—

25

TORRE LAVVANN knew he was fortunate to be alive.

If Maroud had not been by his side during the battle, he would not have been so blessed. Maroud had saved them by proving he was well versed in the ways of the Haradin and the White Palm.

The young man had indeed been well trained. Once they escaped the fighting, Maroud instructed Lavvann to follow him to the top of the highest dune they could find. There they stripped and knelt upon the crest, heads bowed and arms crossed. They placed their weapons on the left side and all other possessions on the right.

Maroud told Lavvann to remain silent in that position of penitence. According to customs held sacred by both sects, those who were about to be killed could plead for mercy. Maroud hoped that when the *badawh* saw this, their lives would be spared. It was strange lore, to be sure, but Maroud was convinced it would work.

Two men of the White Palm were the first to spy the men kneeling on the dune. They gave each other a quizzical look before heading up to see why they'd suddenly and so easily acquired two prisoners. Brigands did not usually surrender.

Maroud spoke to them. Lavvann did as instructed and said nothing. Lavvann did not understand the language, but as he listened and watched the body language of the White Palm *badawh*, it became evident that they were going to let them live.

Maroud confirmed this with a whisper. "We will be safe. Don't worry, Torre. I convinced them that we were here in disguise on behalf of the Rassan Majalis to follow, capture, or kill Ciris Sarn and any others involved with the books."

One of the *badawh* laughed and spoke to Maroud, who joined him in laughter. The *badawh* spoke to his companion in a tone that indicated to Lavvann that all was well.

Maroud turned to Lavvann. "This man and his partner are White Palm. He told me he is glad that he found us before any of the Haradin did, as we probably would have been sold as slaves—even if they had believed our story."

"We are fortunate indeed," Lavvann murmured.

Lavvann and Maroud were permitted to find mounts and gather provisions so that they could return to the oasis. In the process of collecting what they needed, Lavvann found the message Marin had left. It reminded him of that other note he had discovered when they were seeking the kayal in Aeíx.

He thought of how their fate had been altered and wondered if Marin still lived. She had been like a daughter to him. He wished he could have been there when Sarn fell. Did Marin feel as if her loss had been avenged? Lavvann wanted to know the details of what had happened in the desert while he and Maroud were with the White Palm.

"We need to move," Lavvann said. "Hopefully Marin will be there. Then we make for Riyyal. I am eager to leave this place behind."

Maroud turned to the *badawh* and spoke again, then turned back to Lavvann. "I asked them if they would be joining us, but they will go their own way. They wish us a safe return."

The White Palm riders raced off into the desert. Lavvann stood by his horse and watched them fade into the distance. He drew a deep sigh of relief and absently patted the beast's neck.

"I hope I never live to see this again," he said to Maroud.

"Most definitely," Maroud agreed. "I am also glad they left us the camels."

Lavvann smiled. "To Waha al-Ribat!"

29

THE AIR was cool and alive.

Marin stood outside the caravanserai. A light breeze caught her robe as she looked outward past the smooth, white stone balustrade that surrounded the building. Tears dried on her cheeks. When she thought of Hiril, she cried again. Sobbing had come all too naturally to her these past two nights.

"Life is not easy, Marin," Lavvann said, approaching from behind.

Startled, she brushed the tears from her face and turned. "Torre! You're here! Where is . . . "

"It was easy enough to find you," Lavvann said. "Sallah is well."

Marin sniffled.

Lavvann gave her a warm smile. "You do not need to be ashamed because you are weeping."

"I know. I weep for Hiril . . . for not being stronger."

"You did what was in your heart. Hiril would not have been ashamed."

"Can you tell me what you would have done, Torre?" Marin looked at him earnestly.

"No, I cannot. But I am a man, and men are different. You did what you believed was right, and it does not make you weak. You are a woman . . . and I am very proud of you."

"I wish now that I had not come. I wish that someone else could have killed Sarn. I will always have doubts, a pain that will forever have a hold on my heart."

"It will pass in time." Lavvann put his hand on her shoulder.

"Oh, Torre, already the memory of my husband fades. When I close my eyes I can no longer see him. When I try to recall his voice, I can't."

"You will see him again, Marin. Keep that with you always.

He is near, and will come to you in your dreams. You will not forget him."

Marin wept again.

30

THE CALL to morning prayer broke the silence of the dawn. Marin rubbed her right thumb across her left palm as she had done many times since that fateful battle in the desert where the Books of Promise were lost. She felt no lingering effect of the 'Evil Eye' curse laid upon her by the *sha'ir* in Aeíx. The relics must have come to the hag, as well as the soul of Ciris Sarn. Marin shuddered, her thoughts drifting back into the past once again. *What have I done?* She drove it away from her mind, trying to forget, and hoping someday she would not have to remember.

She looked out toward the northeast, beyond the clustered roofs and soaring minarets of Janeirah.

She hoped it was for the last time.

Marin breathed deeply as the chains of sorrow that had kept her bound to the past finally crumbled away.

Lavvann had joined her again after returning to the city. "Where will you go now?" he asked.

"I will follow the coast up to Tanith, and then sail across to Ruinart," she replied. "There is still good work to be done, and I wish to be a part of it."

"Yes, of course. Only you can make that decision." He paused. "Always remember that a door remains open for you, should you wish to ride with the Four Banners again."

"Thank you, Torre. I mean that. You have been like a father to me in many ways, and I will forever remain grateful for all that you have done. And Sallah, too. Please remember this."

"There is no need to worry, Marin. For many years I have seen you as a daughter, one of whom I am very proud." He smiled at her in a way that made her heart swell. It was a smile of sincere joy. Of pride.

"Go to Ruinart," he encouraged her. "There is much there for you still—and I am certain you will do great work. Naturally, I will expect a few moments of your time when you are able." He gave her a broad smile.

Later that day, Marin, Sallah Maroud, and Torre Lavvann gathered again. Tall trees lined the banks of the emerald waters, bathed in the warmth of the suns. The midday air was mild, welcome relief from the desert heat.

Marin took stock of herself. On this particular day, she wore a white-fringed shawl about her shoulders. Her skin, kissed golden by the suns, perfectly complemented the long golden locks that had escaped from the haphazard knot at the top of her head.

It's nice to feel clean again, she thought.

TWO DAYS later, the three companions left Janeirah.

The great city had long been bound to the river and the sea. Fertile farmlands stretched for miles on either side of the river. To the northwest was a large harbor, one of the most important in all of Nahkeel, second only to Tivisis in size and number of ships.

Steep streets ran straight down to the harbor. From the summits of these streets could be seen ships of all nations. Along the main thoroughfare, ancient villas and palaces still stood proudly. Marin thought Janeirah was one of the most beautiful cities in the world.

She had rested here long enough. It was time to leave for Tanith, and then on to Ruinart. She longed to explore the lands she had never seen, and reexamine those she had visited in passing. Then she would secure passage across the Ras Mansour back to Cievv.

Part of her wanted to get back to her duties, to feel productive again. She needed, in a small way, to feel that she'd contributed not only to her own salvation, but to that of countless others as well. The days of solace by the sea in Janeirah were the cure she needed to make Sarn a permanent part of her past.

She would go to the marketplace and purchase fine fabrics for a new dress. How long had it been since she had allowed herself that luxury? She could not recall. She had seen beautiful dresses in the cities she'd visited, but now, as she studied the women in the streets, she realized the fashions had changed during the time she'd spent pursuing Sarn; and she had missed it all.

She would acquire new spices for her pantry, too. She loved to cook, and she looked forward to making a real meal again.

She caught a glimpse of herself reflected in the water and thought, *Why am I suddenly interested in all these domestic details?*

Of course she knew why these things suddenly mattered. She was ready to move on, and part of doing so meant nurturing a new relationship. Her love for Hiril would never die—but he would want her to remarry. He had always said she should never stop living simply for him.

Well, that was easier said than done, but with some help from her friends—Torre, Sallah, and of course, Ilss Cencova—she would eventually break through the wall of tears and try living again. For now, she was mostly content. Perhaps, one day, love would come again. There would be a man who would treat her with all the love and respect she could wish for.

Marin gazed at the many ships in the port. Right here, right now, she was at peace with herself—and ready, she hoped, for whatever should come next.

The past was gone, and the future loomed before her.

She chuckled as she pondered this, remembering the words spoken by a close friend at her wedding: "Marin . . . Hiril . . . listen to me," he'd said, waving his finger at them to underscore the seriousness of his tone. "The past never returns, and the future never arrives."

She'd found that amusing and, to a certain extent, profound. Although she'd never forgotten the words, neither had she ever really given them much thought. Until now. She reflected on the point he'd been trying to make, and suddenly, it became crystal clear.

All we ever really have is the present.

Epilogue

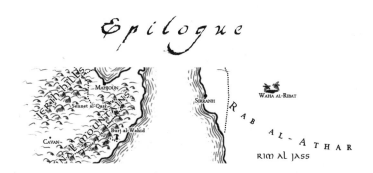

A SHELTERING SKY

26.4.793 SC

7

THIS WAS the seventh time he had been in the cave.

The ink was nearly dry as he finished the last stroke. He slipped the vial of russet ink into a pouch that fit perfectly in an inside pocket.

He was not the only one who had been here. The rough walls were covered with signs that others had come here and, therefore, knew of its existence. Amber light poured in from the opening above, washing over the painted wall. He studied each of the signs briefly before returning outside.

Rain had not fallen for many days, and it would be some months before it came again. He looked up and saw not even the slightest smudge of white in the cobalt sky. Somewhere above, he heard the call of a *kiyeh* falcon chasing away two burial kites. At his feet he saw the indentation of scales in the rough soil. It had been a black-hooded asp—aggressive and lethal—but it had passed some time ago. The valley floor just outside the cave opening was littered with many prints. He could make out tracks from small game as well as those of a nimhr and a haloc. Both of these sets had been made recently.

He was not alone. Others had come here with him, but they were gone. The battle was over, the last sounds fading away in the early hours of the morning. At first light they had carefully searched for anything of value that might have been left behind. But An'sut remained in the Valley of the Cave as he had always done.

His kind had, for as long as anyone could remember, trailed behind the wanderings of the White Palm and, at times, the Haradin hunters as well. There was an ancient, unwritten understanding between them; they were not to interfere, and in doing so were free to claim what they could find. It was the way of the desert.

Intuition had brought him here—more than just the memory

of the cave and the ritual of painting his mark. An'sut had felt this once before when he'd found a man still drawing breath as the hot, dry wind drained the last traces of life from his broken body.

He remembered taking his staff of rosewood and prodding the man just under his ribcage. He'd watched as the man quivered and then writhed weakly. An'sut made a tracing in the sand around the man—his claiming pattern. He'd thought that perhaps the man could be saved. An'sut was not a strong healer, but there was some hope. He understood that what mattered most of all when it came to healing was the strength of the wounded one's spirit.

An'sut had soaked long strips of soft linen in a balm made from citrus honey and healing oils. Then he wrapped the cloth around the man, binding his wounds. He'd covered him with palm fronds and laid him in a canvas hammock. Later, with the help of others, he'd carried the wounded man southward into the deep desert.

Therefore he would walk through the valley before seeking oasis of Waha al-Ribat once more. Noon shadows followed the contours of the cliffs, forming layers of myriad colors that clothed the rock walls from the base to the crest. An'sut tracked the feeling through the wash of gravel and sand that curved away from the cave. The heat here was not unbearable, as the suns' radiation could not penetrate completely into the basin. He passed through a narrow opening between two boulders, noticing the tracks of predators that had come here before him.

The breeze carried the stench of a dead camel. An'sut heard the patter of small feet as something darted into cover. Small rocks and pebbles tumbled from above as the unknown creature scrambled higher into the cliffs. *So this is what I was to find*, An'sut thought.

It was then that he saw the man.

2

CIRIS SARN looked up at a sky the color of sapphire.

A sound in the distance roused him, and his vision blurred as he turned his eyes from the suns. Their heat engulfed him, though they had not yet reached the meridian. He tried to move his arms but could not. He felt something firm and warm make contact with his head as he turned it.

He lay beneath the carcass of a dead camel.

His memory returned slowly. He was in pain.

He was somewhere amid an ocean of sand. The last thing he remembered was digging a hole along the back of the camel in an effort to use it as cover against the blazing heat.

Marin had left after the ghuls had been slain, taking the horses northward, back toward the oasis. After she was gone, Sarn realized that some of his strength had returned, and attempted to find shelter. He had been hoping to make it to a ridge of low, broken hills a half day's journey to the east. If fortune was with him, there would be caves in which to shield himself from the suns until their setting brought the cool evening air.

However, the distance had proved too great and the dunes unforgiving. Falling into a basin, he'd rolled up against a wounded camel that had crawled off to die. Sarn knew of the water sack deep within the beast's hump, yet he could do nothing, as he had no blade in which to cut it out.

He'd sensed a presence nearby and smelled the musky scent of an animal, but saw nothing, although he heard a low, guttural growl and soft pads hitting the sand. Whatever it was, it was nearby.

Sarn had little doubt that it was a *nimhr*, a fierce, solitary desert cat that patrolled the dunes in search of prey. It was very close: it had caught the scent of death. It had come for him.

From the opposite direction came a different sound—short,

erratic, and high-pitched. Another predator had come to claim the kill. Yet as suddenly as he had heard them, both were gone again.

There was nothing Sarn could do, and he had no will to care. His body was broken, but worse were the deep, suffocating waves of loss and pity that had wrapped his spirit in a shroud of remorse.

Marin had left him. And she was right to do so. He would die here without the peace he had longed for, the world fading out of time and memory. Yet he was not sad. Sarn welcomed death— and the final release it would bring—with open arms.

Still he remained quiet and did not attempt to move. There had been no further sounds. Sarn was vulnerable, lying on his side with his weak legs folded awkwardly beneath him. He was wounded, in pain, and had no weapons or protection—not even the strength to stand, let alone run. Barely able to focus, he looked up and saw two black canine legs just a few steps away. A haloc or dire? Maybe it had killed the cat.

Sarn rolled onto his back. His head began to swim. He saw something else in the dimming light: a flutter of indigo cloth, the color of a deep ocean. "I'm hallucinating," he gasped. He could not tell if his eyes were open or shut. But he could see nonetheless.

The air was full of chants whispered in an unknown language. Was it real? Or had he fallen into a mirage of dreams brought about by exposure and thirst? Against the contrast of a bright, washed-out sky, Sarn looked up at the shadowed face of a jackal.

He closed his eyes again.

About the Author

VAL GUNN, as his wife enjoys saying, is a jock-nerd. Both sports and prose seemed to come natural for him–though he wrote off the writing for a time to pursue a playing and coaching career. He has been fortunate to travel and live in many exotic places around the globe. As an on-again, off-again expat; Val is cursed with a perpetual case of wanderlust. This was tempered a bit in 2003 with the birth of their triplets. For the moment he and his family live in northwest Florida–*but don't hold your breath.*